WITHDRAWN

WHERE TWO HEARTS MEET

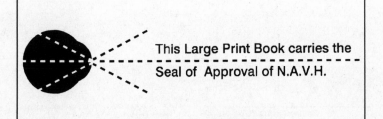

PRINCE EDWARD ISLAND DREAMS,
BOOK 2

WHERE TWO HEARTS MEET

LIZ JOHNSON

THORNDIKE PRESS
A part of Gale, Cengage Learning

GALE
CENGAGE Learning·

Farmington Hills, Mich • San Francisco • New York • Waterville, Maine
Meriden, Conn • Mason, Ohio • Chicago

GALE
CENGAGE Learning®

LIBRARY OF CONGRESS CATALOGING-IN-PUBLICATION DATA

Names: Johnson, Liz, 1981– author.
Title: Where two hearts meet / by Liz Johnson.
Description: Large print edition. | Waterville, Maine : Thorndike Press, 2016. | Series: Prince Edward Island dreams ; book 2 | Series: Thorndike Press large print Christian romance
Identifiers: LCCN 2016039878| ISBN 9781410494320 (hardcover) | ISBN 1410494322 (hardcover)
Subjects: LCSH: Bed and breakfast accommodations—Fiction. | Large type books. | GSAFD: Love stories. | Christian fiction.
Classification: LCC PS3610.O3633 W48 2016b | DDC 813/.6—dc23
LC record available at https://lccn.loc.gov/2016039878

Published in 2016 by arrangement with Revell Books, a division of Baker Publishing Group

For Hannah
on your *mumble, mumble* birthday.
Thank you for always making the
trek with me
to find three o'clock snacks
on the buffet.
Thank you for being my sister,
traveling companion, and friend.
And most of all, thank you
for not making me
eat more than three bites
of that lobster.

And for you, the reader.
Thank you for traveling
to PEI with me.
May you find peace and hope and
enough grace for every situation.

1

There was only one thing better than the smell of freshly baked cinnamon rolls in the morning: The *taste* of freshly baked cinnamon rolls in the morning.

Caden Holt pulled a pan of piping hot sweet rolls from the bottom of her double oven, breathing in the intoxicating aroma and patting the golden-crisp top of a roll to the rhythm of her favorite Broadway soundtrack. Her mouth watered and her toe tapped as she slathered a bun with her signature cream cheese icing. The white glaze oozed down the side of the treat, and she caught the errant drip with her knuckle. Closing her eyes, she licked her finger clean before tearing off a corner and popping it in her mouth.

A tremor swirled down her back as sweet, sweet sugar exploded in her mouth, everything good and right with the world.

It only took three more bites to finish off

her usual morning treat — after all, she had to make sure breakfast for the guests was up to par — and she immediately regretted devouring it. All that was left was a drop of icing on the scalding pan. But a chef didn't fear heat. She'd gotten second-degree burns from less worthy causes.

After peeking over her shoulder to make sure she was still alone in her sanctuary, only the morning sun for company, she touched her finger to the tip of her tongue, scooped up the dribble, and licked it clean.

The sweets this morning would certainly pass muster, but she hadn't even started on the main dish. While breakfast desserts were her favorite part of a meal, she didn't work at a bed-and-bakery. As the executive chef of Rose's Red Door Inn, she made a full meal to start every guest's day off right.

Muted footfalls and hushed voices trickled from the floor above, promising that said guests would soon be poking their noses into the dining room, looking to fill their empty stomachs.

But for the next thirty minutes, she had the kitchen all to herself. Utterly, entirely, blissfully to herself. And the original London cast of *Mamma Mia!*

Lisa Stokke belted out her solo through the speakers tucked into the corner of the counter between a fully equipped stand mixer and canisters of the essentials. As Lisa's voice swelled, Caden turned a wild pirouette that would have had her forever banned from the Great White Way — not that she'd ever been there, or on any stage, for that matter. She slammed into the kitchen island and bounced off the refrigerator, grabbing the edge of the counter to keep from tumbling all the way to the floor.

Her foot caught on the corner of a cabinet, and she laughed out loud as Lisa reached her high note and Caden hit her low point. Arms flailing as she fell, Caden scrambled for anything that would help her stay upright. She managed to grab hold of a single sheet of white printer paper hanging from the silver clip on the refrigerator. As soon as she tugged it free, her rear end hit the floor and she lost her grip on the page, which — aided by the fan in the far corner — slithered between the fridge and the nearest cabinet.

"No. No. No." She shifted to her knees and crawled toward the black hole that had swallowed that morning's instructions.

Caden's boss, Marie Sloane, always left a list of special guest instructions on that clip. Food allergies. Gluten sensitivities. Young guests with picky palates. It all seemed innocent enough until one guest the previous summer had failed to mention his peanut allergy upon registration. Caden's famous peanut butter and jelly French toast had nearly sent him into anaphylactic shock. He was one forkful of deliciousness away from a serious emergency when his wife noticed his hives, and Marie called for an ambulance to rush him to the hospital in Charlottetown. He'd made a full recovery and joked later that he'd married his wife for her observational skills.

But the memory still made Caden's insides squirm.

Food had such a strange and wonderful power. Wielding it made her feel simultaneously significant and vulnerable, fearsome and fragile.

To do her job well she needed the piece of paper glaring at her from the depths of the crack between wooden cabinet and stainless steel appliance. The unmoving refrigerator stood like a sentinel, refusing to budge from its guard. She tried to reach the page anyway, poking her chubby fingers into the crevice, but they didn't make it much beyond her second knuckle. If she could just slide the fridge over.

She leaned her shoulder into its side, but it only groaned, taunting her to try again.

She did and got the same result.

Kneeling between the cabinets and island, she put her hands on her hips and huffed a sigh that stirred a wisp of hair that had escaped her French braid. And sent it right back into her face.

She needed something long and narrow. With pinchers.

Tongs.

She pulled herself up on the edge of the alternating black-and-white counter tiles before rifling through the middle drawer next to the dishwasher. Spatulas and spoons tumbled about as she dug for the tongs she usually used to flip bacon. The tangled utensils scraped together, nearly falling onto the floor as she stretched her fingers to find what she was looking for.

Finally she hooked a handle with the crook of her finger and yanked it — and a deformed whisk — free.

Caden arched her wrist and sent the whisk toward the trash can, its wire loops swishing down the plastic liner.

Just as the cast of *Mamma Mia* burst into the rousing show closer, she lowered herself back to the floor. The tip of her tongs clicked to the rhythm of the song as she hunched over her prey, eyeing it for the right angle. She moved in slowly, deliberately, try-

11

ing not to disturb the sheet until it was safely in her grasp.

She just . . . had . . . to . . .

"Rats!"

Even as she bumped the corner of the paper, she recognized her mistake.

The paper fluttered, loosened by her miscalculation, and slid beneath the fridge, completely out of reach.

Perfect.

She scrubbed her hand down her cheek and scratched behind her ear. Maybe if she glared at the spot where the paper had vanished, it would miraculously reappear. That was about as likely as a lobster crawling into her boiling pot.

Two loud footfalls right above her head made Caden jump, and she spun in the direction of the clock on the microwave. Thirty minutes until breakfast time. Fifteen until Marie came to check in and began serving the first course, a fresh fruit salad Caden had prepared the night before.

She'd run out of time to whip up the seafood quiche she'd written on the large calendar hanging by the door to the dining room. At this point, scrambled eggs and roasted potatoes would have to do.

But first — the allergy list.

Marie sometimes left a copy of the manifest in her office, so Caden hurried down the hallway from the kitchen to the little room between the living quarters and the rest of the inn. Seth, Marie's husband, had built the nook into the restored home so his wife would have a place to manage the inn's daily goings-on.

Caden tried to step lightly — no easy feat on the seventy-five-year-old wooden floors. They seemed to creak and moan even when she hadn't taken a step. It wasn't until she had almost reached the door that she realized it was partly open, and soft voices echoed within.

"It can't be as bad as that." The deep voice belonged to Seth Sloane, but it didn't sound much like the contractor turned innkeeper who had swept Marie off her feet. It was as thick as the red clay that gave Prince Edward Island its famous color. He cleared his throat, but that didn't help much. "There has to be something left. We had a good season last year. And you've put together a great marketing strategy."

"But most of what is left is going to the lawyer." Marie sighed, her voice as strained as her husband's. "And we're only half booked for this summer. After this week, we have at least two empty rooms all season."

"Maybe they'll fill. Maybe we'll get another guest for all of June and July. Maybe that princess bride will decide to uncancel her wedding and the whole party will rebook and stay an extra week . . ."

"That's a lot of maybes."

Caden held her breath, wishing she could somehow sneak back to the kitchen and ignore the tremor in Marie's tone or the way her voice hitched when she mentioned a lawyer. Marie hadn't said anything about a legal situation. Was she facing an immigration issue? Or worse, carryover from her case against the man who'd assaulted her? Marie had said that his conviction was final. Could it have resurfaced?

Marie said something else, too low for Caden to hear, and her stomach twisted. This clearly wasn't a conversation she was meant to hear. But she couldn't leave until she had her instructions. She raised her hand to knock right as Seth spoke.

"Maybe if we talk to your —"

"No." Marie lost all hint of uncertainty, her tone sharper than Caden had ever heard before. "We're not —"

Caden spun toward the kitchen at Marie's outburst, the floor shrieking like a never-ending fireworks display.

"Morning, Caden." Seth sounded both

14

surprised and relieved at her sudden presence.

She turned back, an apologetic smile slipping into place as she pushed the door open a few inches more. "I'm sorry to interrupt. It's just that the instructions fell under the refrigerator, and I need to get breakfast going."

The tightness in Marie's jaw didn't release, even as she shot a glare at her husband, who managed an unrepentant shrug. Then she turned to the computer and printed out another page with the guests' details. Her motions were sharp and controlled, her frown fixed in place.

"Here you go." Marie's voice held none of the strain that seemed to permeate the room, but there was a sadness in her eyes that turned Caden's mind into a battlefield. She wanted to ask, but Marie clearly didn't want to share. So she backpedaled as fast as she could.

Marie and Seth remained silent as she hurried down the hall, and when the door swung shut behind her, Caden let out a whoosh of air.

Whatever was going on in there was intense. And it didn't involve her.

Except that Marie was her best friend.

And what she'd heard sounded like the

Red Door might be in trouble.

Which meant they were all in trouble.

A slamming door on the second floor jolted her into action. Scanning the page in her hand, she made note of two lactose sensitivities and one pineapple allergy. No cheese on the eggs for some of those guests. And the fruit salad was a simple peach and berry concoction. No problem there.

As she whisked a dozen eggs in a glass mixing bowl, she glanced out the kitchen window, enjoying the view of her herb garden and a corner of the bay beyond their neighbor's back porch and a narrow field of wildflowers.

She'd spent her whole life staring at that same patch of rippling blue. And though the kitchen had changed, the window over the sink was always the same. The morning sun caught the tip of a wave, and it sparkled like a diamond.

Forcing herself away from the view she'd always loved, she sprayed the bottom of the pan and poured the beaten eggs into it, bubbles immediately forming in the yellow mixture.

As she stirred the eggs, she risked another glance out the window.

A man stood between the inn and the water. He was far enough away that she couldn't make out his features or even tell if she recognized him. He certainly wasn't one of their neighbors, all of whom had a distinct stoop and slow stroll. But there was an appealing easiness to his gait, and she watched him walk the shoreline. As he bent to pick up a small duffel bag, his shoulders pushed at the fabric of his leather jacket. A gust of wind fluttered his dark hair, and he ran his fingers through the loose strands in an infinitely male move.

Nope. She didn't know him.

She'd have noticed a guy like that walking around town. North Rustico wasn't big enough to hide in.

After all, she'd been trying to hide here for years.

It never worked.

She stirred the fluffy eggs, giving them another dash of salt and pepper. And just a hint of garlic for good measure.

The door between the kitchen and dining room swung in, sweeping Marie's chipper greeting to the waiting guests with it. "Breakfast will be right out."

Caden turned and raised her eyebrows in question.

"Breakfast will be right out. Won't it?" Marie's brown curls had crossed the line from fun to frazzled, and the apron she looped over her head didn't help the situation. Whatever she and Seth had been talking about that morning had left her in a knot, so Caden squelched the urge to tease her boss.

"Fruit is in serving dishes in the fridge."

Marie already had half of them loaded on the silver tray, so she scooped them up and whisked back through the swinging door.

Oohs and aahs over the crystal goblets of mixed fruit carried from the dining room, and Caden couldn't help the rush of pride through her middle as she plated scrambled eggs and roasted red potatoes, adding a cinnamon roll platter for each table.

With each swish of the door, Marie scooped up more plates, the lines around her mouth easing until an actual smile fell into place.

"This is so good," one guest mumbled around a mouthful of food. "What's in these eggs?"

Marie giggled, and Caden's heart gave a little leap of joy. She could easily imagine her boss sidling up to a table and giving everyone there a saucy wink. *Our chef only makes the best.*

Except Marie didn't say that. She didn't say anything about how Caden hunted out fresh eggs three times a week from the hens at Kane Dairy. She didn't say that Caden started her day at five each morning to make sure every guest was full and happy before leaving to explore the island. And she didn't say that Caden had a knack for serving up the best sweet rolls in town.

In fact, Marie didn't say a word about Caden at all.

"That's our little secret." And she left it at that.

A fist in her stomach sent Caden bending over the sink, head hanging low and heart even lower.

She loved this job. She loved this kitchen. She loved Marie.

But lately it felt like they might not love her back.

"Excuse me."

Caden's head snapped up at the unfamiliar voice, but she had to duck into the laundry room to find the source.

Face-to-face with the man from the beach, she yanked on the strings of her apron as she stared unblinking into his gray eyes. But the bow at her waist caught in a knot. Her fingers suddenly forgetful, she fumbled with the fabric.

He poked his head through the back door, holding the screen with one hand and his leather jacket in the other, one foot on the ground and the other on the outside step.

The planes of his face didn't shift, and the muscles at his throat stood in sharp relief to his otherwise relaxed pose. Which she only just realized blocked the bag she'd seen him carrying earlier. His deep brown hair was disheveled, standing on end above his right temple like he'd fallen asleep with his fingers combed through it and his head resting in his hand. His jaw boasted at least a day's worth of beard.

"Are you Marie Carrington Sloane?"

Caden glanced over her shoulder, half expecting to see Marie materialize, but she remained alone. Alone with a man who knew Marie's maiden name. No one used Marie's maiden name.

Especially not Marie.

"No." She dragged the word out, still jerking at the knot at the back of her waist, desperate to be free of her apron. "Can I help you with something?"

"This is Rose's Red Door Inn." And then, like he wasn't quite sure, "Isn't it? They said it was the big blue house between the boardwalk and the water."

She nodded slowly. "The one with the red front door. And a sign out front."

That earned a quarter smile as he let go of the door, holding it in place with his shoulder — a rather broad shoulder at that — and grabbed a brown leather journal from the back pocket of his jeans. It wasn't much bigger than his palm, but as he thumbed through several pages, she could see that tiny scribbles filled every crevice and corner. Folding the notebook at its spine, his finger ran the lines until he nodded and looked up. "Rose's Red Door Inn. North Rustico, Prince Edward Island. Marie Carrington Sloane, proprietor."

He offered only the facts and no commentary. Who talked like that?

"And Seth too." The words popped out before she'd really considered them, but something about the way he kept saying Marie's full name made her insides churn and the hair on the back of her neck jump to attention.

He wouldn't be a guest. They only arrived between three and seven. They never used the back door. And they most certainly never invaded her territory.

His forehead wrinkled as he gave his book another once-over, so she expounded. "Seth Sloane. Marie's husband. Co-owner."

Squinting harder at the page in his hand, he shook his head.

Well, he could shake it all he wanted. That didn't make Seth's presence any less real.

Or Caden any more inclined to let this guy loiter on her back stoop. She pressed her hands to her waist and pulled herself up to her full height. Which wasn't considerable. But what she lacked in height, she made up for in breadth. And she used all the generous width of her hips as she marched toward him, praying that he would just back away.

Then she could go tell Marie about this strange visitor.

But he didn't budge. He just closed one eye in an almost wink and stared up at her. "Sorry. I didn't get that note. My editor — Garrett de Root — he made the arrangements."

"What arrangements?"

His gaze suddenly jumped over her shoulder, and she followed it.

"Caden? Is everything all right?" Marie's hands were full of empty breakfast dishes, which she carried like she'd spent her college years in the service industry. Although that was far from the truth.

"This guy . . ." She flung a hand at the mystery man, who promptly stepped inside and reached out his hand.

"Adam Jacobs."

Marie looked at the stacks in her arms and managed only a shrug. "Adam?"

"Yes, ma'am. I believe Garrett de Root contacted you about reserving a room for me."

Marie's half smile turned into a frown. "I wasn't expecting you until tomorrow. I don't have an open room tonight."

2

Adam Jacobs was homeless.

Brilliant.

Just brilliant.

He jabbed his fingers through his hair and squeezed his eyes shut against the stabbing pain in his right temple. This was supposed to be a relaxing sabbatical.

A forced vacation. But still relaxing.

"Come in. Let me look at my paperwork." Marie waved him in and then marched into the kitchen. "There must be some mistake."

Sure there was. He'd let Garrett book his travel.

Arranging for transport to Afghanistan was no problem. Running the news desk at *America Today* was a breeze. Keeping up with seven grandkids didn't make him break a sweat.

But getting the details right on a required sabbatical? Well, that was out of Garrett's purview.

Adam picked up his bag and stepped into what looked like a mudroom, walking past the frowning blonde, who was still fighting with the loud apron circling her waist. Her brows formed a perfect V, and despite the fire shooting from her ice-blue eyes, he gave her a half grin. "Sorry to interrupt your morning, ma'am."

Her jaw dropped, but she clamped it shut just as quick. As he slipped into the kitchen, she followed right behind him, the smell of cinnamon wrapping around him like a physical hug. Its arms were strong, supported by a subtle waft of pepper, and as he made it to the kitchen island, he saw the true source of the heavenly scent. Four golden cinnamon rolls decked in white sat in a perfect line on the cooling rack.

Suddenly his stomach rumbled, and he laughed as he put his hand over it. "Those smell incredible."

"They taste even better." The elusive lilt of her voice suggested she was on the verge of singing, only she found him unworthy. Her accent carried a hint of laughter in it, a note of happiness despite the wariness in her gaze. As if she could read his mind, she continued. "But they're for guests."

"Mr. Jacobs is going to be our guest, Caden." Marie returned, spreading several white pages across the clear space on the island. Her forehead wrinkled with apology, quite the opposite of her cook, who crossed her arms, backing into the corner between the fridge and sink.

Marie let out a half laugh and gave Caden a knowing nod. "Would you get him a cinnamon roll, please?"

Caden didn't say a word, but she spun and pulled a pristine white plate out of a tall cupboard. She had to stretch to her tiptoes to reach the top of the stack on the second shelf, and he almost offered her a hand. But she struck him as the type who would refuse anyone's offer.

And whatever he'd done when they first met still had her nose wrinkled like he smelled of sour socks.

He didn't.

He was pretty sure, anyway. When he'd made it back stateside, his duffle and everything in it had been scoured and scrubbed. No T-shirt or sock had escaped the heavy wash cycle. Plenty of soap. And even more fabric softener.

Funny how three months in the mountains of the Middle East had made him forget just how amazing a soft cotton T-shirt fresh from the dryer could feel. He checked the one he was wearing to make sure it was clean, running his hand over the front.

Yep. He was good.

Caden scooped a sticky bun onto the plate and slid it across the black-and-white tile. He caught the dish with one hand and scooped up the roll with the other. Tearing into it, he had to physically hold back the moan of pleasure as it melted on his tongue.

Three bites later, he looked up to find two sets of slowly blinking eyes on him. Caden's pinched features had vanished, replaced by a satisfied smirk as she waved a fork in front of her face.

Marie's stunned expression was no less comical. "Enjoying that?"

Maybe he hadn't been successful keeping his groans of appreciation to himself.

"Very good." He swallowed the large bite still in his mouth. "Just like you said. Tastes better than it smells." And somehow that was true. So light, yet filling. The cinnamon roll triggered every one of his taste buds, then circled back around and hit them again just because it could.

"You make these?"

She looked mildly affronted. "I sure didn't buy them at the grocery store."

He nodded. "I was afraid so."

Caden's smirk turned into a full-blown smile. Oh, she knew what she'd done. Now

27

that he'd had one of her cinnamon rolls, he was hooked. There'd be no settling for store-bought. And the chances of him making one himself? No one in their right mind would take those odds.

All white teeth and captivating dimples, she held out the fork. He shook his head, gesturing with his already sticky fingers. "No use now."

The roll disappeared in two more bites, just as Marie looked up from the pages before her. "Mr. de Root was very clear in his email that you'd be arriving tomorrow." Her voice softened, and her eyes followed that lead.

That sounded about right. Garrett probably saw the *island* in Prince Edward Island and thought he was sending Adam to Fiji. Where it was already tomorrow.

"And I don't have any open rooms until then." Marie sighed out the last word.

He shrugged, his gaze falling on the three remaining rolls. "What would it take for you to send the leftovers with me?"

A pop of air, which sounded suspiciously like a laugh, escaped from Caden, and she quickly clamped her lips together as her eyes opened wide.

With a wink and a grin that had always gotten him extra brownies at the mess hall, he tried again. "I mean, if I have to find another room in town for the night, maybe you'd take pity on a poor traveler who's been on the road for too long."

"That's just it," Marie said.

His grin faltered. This did not sound like the start of an easy acquiescence.

"There are no other rooms in North Rustico."

"What do you mean? They're all booked?"

Caden shook her head. "There are no other hotels in North Rustico."

Well, slap him silly and call him a fool. He thought he'd given up backwater towns when he left rural Tennessee. But somehow he'd landed in a one-horse town on an island that thrived on tourism.

"There are some cabins for rent down the road." Caden slipped his plate away as he licked the icing off his finger.

He perked up. "That'll work. Could you point me in that direction?"

Marie's frown made the cinnamon roll he'd just inhaled churn. "It's July first. Canada Day. And the Crick — I mean, North Rustico — has one of the biggest celebrations in the country."

"Canada Day?"

"It's like the Fourth of July in the States." Marie shuffled her papers together, her fingers nimble. "You know. Fireworks. National pride. Barbecues."

"And vacationers." He didn't even have to form it as a question. Between the Americans dashing north for their own holiday week and the Canadians celebrating on the island, the place was full.

"There's nothing available for miles. Probably nothing between here and halfway to Charlottetown."

His stomach sank, and he massaged the spot above his ear that was ripe to burst.

Brilliant. Perfectly brilliant.

He'd hopped a cab that morning from the Charlottetown airport to the Rustico boardwalk, the one that the driver hadn't been able to shut up about. And he'd been right to rave. The morning sun reflecting on the blue harbor sparkled brighter than any sapphire on earth, and the easy clap of the waves set his pace at half his usual. Green trees and lush grass lined each side. And then there was the sand along the shore. It wasn't desert sand, but neither was it the Georgia beaches he'd visited in his childhood. Soft and welcoming, it stretched toward the water as much as the waves reached for the land.

The beach had spanned before him, beautiful and blissfully empty.

He'd claimed those quiet moments for himself, trying to figure out why Garrett had sent him to this specific spot to get his mind off what had happened.

This seaside village barely qualified as quaint. A couple shops, a few fishing boats, and an ice cream shop made up most of what he'd seen so far. That simply wasn't going to get the job done. Adam needed distracting. He needed a challenge. He needed anything but what kept him tossing and turning late into every night and dragged him out of bed early every morning.

If he'd stayed in Charlottetown, maybe he'd have a bed for the night and enough entertainment to keep him from dwelling on the past.

And the uncertain future.

At least Caden's cinnamon rolls served as a temporary distraction.

Pressing his hands to his hips and eyeing said diversion, he sighed. "Looks like I'm in trouble then. If I'm going to have to sleep under the stars tonight —"

"Don't be silly." Marie waved her hand like she could build an extra wing onto the house in an afternoon. "You can have Taco Bed."

Caden's eyes went wider and, if possible,

bluer. "No. Where would it go?"

But Adam was still caught up on the unfamiliar phrase. "I'm sorry. The taco bed?"

Blonde hair flying as she shook her head, Caden waved her hands back and forth in front of her. "He's not a kid."

He let his gaze fall down his own body, trying to see what she did. He wasn't particularly tall — not quite six feet — or broad. But he had seen enough of the world to wear a hole in the tread of his favorite Chuck Taylor sneakers. The farmer's tan had grown so thick it wasn't likely to ever disappear, and a day and night of travel had left him wrinkled and ready for a hot shower.

But he was still stumped by her odd comment. "Thanks, I guess."

"No, it's not that." A faint pink tinged the fair skin at her neck, and she pressed one hand to it, not quite covering the pretty blush. "Taco Bed is a rollaway. It's for kids when a family needs an extra mattress. It's awful."

Marie's wary smile echoed Caden's concern. "Taco Bed is functional, but it's not exactly designed for adults."

"I've probably slept on worse."

Caden mumbled something that sounded

a lot like, "I doubt it." But Marie's sharp glance silenced any more comments.

"I'm homeless without your generosity, so it's the beach or the rollaway."

"I'm pretty sure someone would call a Mountie if you tried to sleep on the beach," Marie said.

"A red-jacket-and-brown-hat Mountie?" The picture tickled him, and he tried not to let his amusement show as Caden gave a solemn nod.

Now that would be a story he could write. Arrested for loitering by the Royal Canadian Mounted Police. Jailed because he had nowhere else to go. Running with Prince Edward Island's toughest gang — two grandmas on the lam for stealing knitting yarn.

He laughed at the very thought.

He'd guess PEI had about as much crime as a deserted paradise.

Garrett wouldn't be clamoring for that story. But writing it might be enough to keep Adam occupied for the next two months. Two months of waiting. Two months of wondering. Two months of forced sabbatical.

"This bed must be something else to have such a unique name."

Caden groaned. Marie laughed. Adam

grinned.

He'd find that granny gang another day. Today he needed a place to set down his bag, wash up, and get some sleep, maybe a place where the nightmares weren't quite so loud.

Taco Bed had earned its name.

When Adam rolled over on the thin mattress the next morning, the edges curled around him, sheets and blankets pooling in the middle. The yellow linens were unmistakably a taco shell, and he'd never felt more like ground beef in his life.

His feet hung off the end of the metal cot frame, and as he tried to hold the mattress down with one knee and the opposite shoulder, it still wrapped around him. He shifted again, and the accompanying screech filled the entire storage room he'd called home for the last twenty-four hours. The short leg wobbled, and the springs dug into his ribs.

It had been like that all night.

Still not the worst sleeping arrangements he'd ever had.

As he swung his legs over the edge to a metal cry that made his ears bleed, he scrubbed his face with both hands. His beard was longer than usual, and his hair stood straight up.

Coffee.

A hot shower.

And a cinnamon roll.

Then all would be right with the world.

Or at least what he could fix of it.

The coils groaned as he stood, the hardwood floor sighing as he walked to his pack and pulled out his cleanup kit. Marie and Seth had found him a little corner in a small room off their basement apartment. It even had a small bathroom. And when he emerged, he was a little less ground beef and a lot more porterhouse. With some coffee he'd reach T-bone level.

And a leftover cinnamon roll? Well, that just might get him to filet mignon.

He strolled up the wooden steps, trying to remember which of them had squeaked when he'd followed Seth down the afternoon before. He skipped the one he thought he remembered and landed hard on the offender, a loud groan ricocheting off the walls in both directions.

He cringed and risked a peek over his shoulder. Holding his breath, he waited for a sign of life behind the apartment door. After a long moment of utter silence, he sighed and crept the rest of the way to the landing.

The dining room was empty, its mis-matched tables set with lace placemats and small white reservation cards on pedestals. He glanced around and did a double take when he saw his own name at a four-seater.

His name alongside a couple.

The Eisenbergs.

He jerked back and looked around for whoever had assigned him to this spot. He hadn't seen it the night before. Not that he'd been looking. He'd been wiped out after walking half a dozen miles down the road and back. But at least he had a lay of the land. A lay of the very small town in which he'd be spending his summer.

A subtle pounding behind his eyes pro-pelled him toward the kitchen.

Questions about the name card could wait. Caffeine could not.

He swung the door open to an empty room, a dark room. He hadn't even noticed the gentle lights in the rest of the house. Probably left on for the safety of wandering guests like himself. The kitchen wasn't set up with the same, and the ethereal glow on the horizon on the far side of the window promised the sun was on its way, but not yet awake.

He dragged his fingers over the wall until he found a switch and turned on the overheads, immediately searing his retinas. He clamped a hand over his closed eyes and let them adjust to the brilliance by removing one finger at a time.

Several long minutes without coffee passed before he could sort out the kitchen, but when he did, his stomach dropped.

There was no coffeemaker.

He spun in a slow circle, checking every crevice on the tile counter. A rope in his chest began to tighten into a knot, and he rubbed at it through his T-shirt.

Garrett had made him promise he wouldn't pick up a bottle again. Adam hadn't been so sure he wanted to remember everything that had happened the last month. Or that he'd want to be aware of what was to come. But Garrett had stopped him on his way out of the office just the same.

"You can get lost in the bottom of a bottle of Jack if you think it'll help. Go old-school moonshine if you really want," Garrett had said, taking a shot at Adam's redneck roots. "But know this. It's not going to change the past. And it can only ruin your future."

"I won't pick it up again."

Garrett's red mustache twitched like he wasn't quite sure he believed Adam.

"I'm serious. We've been through this. I

was young. I was reckless. I didn't have — I didn't know — I was lost." Adam had heaved a painful sigh, one that carried every longing for a changed past.

If he was honest with himself, he'd admit that he was as lost now as he had been his senior year of college.

The deaths were different.

The fault was still his.

But he no longer drank anything stronger than coffee.

As long as he could find it.

His longtime editor wouldn't be so cruel as to send him to a place that only served tea. Would he?

Of course not. That was just too heartless. Even for Garrett.

Swinging open cabinet doors, he found the most meticulously organized cupboards he'd ever seen. Every plate sat in its perfect stack. Every canister boasted its contents on a white label. Even the spices were organized alphabetically.

But no coffee.

Adam stuck his head into the cabinet below the sink and froze at a sharp cry.

"What are you doing in here?"

He jerked to stand up, cracking the back of his head against the underside of the cabinet. Spots danced before his eyes, which flooded with tears as he cradled the knot. One eye half closed against the throbbing pain, he eyed Caden in all her morning glory. Arms full of open egg crates, she stood frozen at the entry to the mudroom, forehead wrinkled and mouth hanging open.

After a long pause, during which Adam's skull began to piece itself back together, he tried for a smile. He settled for a grimace. "Coff-ee?" His voice cracked, and he cleared his throat. "I was just looking for coffee."

Apparently she decided his injury had rendered him innocuous enough. Shuffling to the island, she set down her bags and the load of white eggs and put her hands on her hips. "You're not supposed to be in here. Guests don't come into the kitchen."

"With a welcome like that, I'm not surprised."

Fire shot from her eyes, and he found his first true smile of the day and an urge to chuckle.

"Well, I'm not technically a guest yet, am I?"

Caden's blonde hair swung as she opened the refrigerator and began putting her haul away. "It doesn't matter. The kitchen is only for Red Door employees."

"Uh-huh. And yesterday I was . . . ?"

"Lost." Her nose swung in his direction,

her glare following it past the pert little tip. "I'm not joking, Mr. Jacobs. I have to begin breakfast, and you need to leave."

"If you'll share the coffee, I'll give you a hand."

"No, you will not."

He grabbed a copper pot hanging from the rack above his head and held it out to her, hoping she wouldn't notice the way the light bounced off the shaking metal. "I'll boil my own in this. I'll even wash it when I'm done. No extra work for you. Please, just take pity on a man in need."

That last pathetic plea finally broke her, and a smile tickled the corner of her mouth, even as she tried to force it into a no-nonsense frown. Her dimples won.

"I knew you were far too kind to trifle with a desperate man."

"You know no such thing."

"But I had a hunch." He leaned his fore-arms onto her counter but jumped back as she swatted him with the corner of her paper bag.

"I suppose anyone who suffered an entire night on Taco Bed has earned a good cup of coffee." Caden grabbed a teapot from the corner of the stove, filled it with water, and set it to boil. Then she pulled out a pristine French press.

His senses kicked in, fabricating the familiar aroma and bracing richness.

"But I'm telling you now. Starting tomorrow you'll have to use the single-cup coffeemaker in the dining room." The words carried a hint of humor, and maybe a touch of pity too.

He spun toward the other room, then back, staring hard at the ceiling as though he could reimagine the entire room and find that coffeemaker he'd walked directly past. But it wasn't there. And she must have been able to read his mind.

"It's on the antique buffet. Along the far wall." She collected her fixings — flour, oil, and salt — before catching his eye again. "I put sweets out there every afternoon at three."

"Like leftover cinnamon rolls?" His stomach did a barrel roll of glee at the thought.

"You probably think your night on Taco Bed earned you the last one."

He lifted a shoulder. "I've slept on worse, but I'll say whatever you want me to for that roll."

Both of her eyebrows disappeared behind a fringe of golden hair hanging over her forehead. "Worse than Taco Bed? I didn't even think that was possible."

"When you've been around the world as

many times as I have . . . well, it's part of the job, I guess."

Her eyebrows reappeared, crushed together in confusion.

But he didn't want to answer her unspoken questions. He didn't want to rehash the Middle East or relive the sound of mortar shells exploding. Or feel the crushing regret when he'd realized the picture had made page four.

Instead, he pasted on a desperate smile. Fitting, as he was a little desperate. "So if I stay out of your kitchen, I can have the last?"

Dumping two cups of flour and a couple pinches of salt into a large mixing bowl with one hand, she pointed to a rubber container tucked beside an old-fashioned silver bread box with the other. "Promise."

He held up three fingers in a mock Boy Scout salute before flipping open the plastic lid. He nearly climbed inside with the sweet goodness.

The teapot let off a sharp whistle.

Coffee.

The two together? Perfect.

3

Adam eyed his breakfast tablemates again. They'd introduced themselves as Levi and Esther Eisenberg of Brooklyn. Four children. Thirteen grandchildren. And seven great-grandchildren. "So far," Esther was quick to add.

Probably both in their early eighties but not enough wrinkles between them to outline a map. Only the silver hair and knowing eyes gave them away.

Levi stretched to pick up a butter dish on Adam's side of the table. As he did, his shirtsleeve crept up his arm, and Adam's stomach dropped. He blinked hard, trying to convince himself that he hadn't seen what he knew he had. But the evidence was there in a faded blue tattoo. A tag on Levi's upper left forearm.

Adam caught the older man's eye and held his breath.

Could it be?

Could Levi be a Holocaust survivor?

Adam had interviewed thousands of people for hundreds of articles. But never once someone who had survived a concentration camp. Never someone who had witnessed it, lived it, thrived after it.

His own grandfather had served in the war, but he'd never wanted to talk about it. Even when Adam was studying the great wars in his college history courses and had asked for stories or memories, Grandpa Wyatt hadn't had more than a word to say on the subject.

Perhaps Levi would be different.

Adam automatically leaned in. It wasn't a conscious action, but neither was he unaware. He just knew that he'd waited years to hear the kind of stories Levi had to tell.

"Are you going to eat that?" Levi frowned at his wife's berry muffin as he slathered butter on his toast. "You never eat sweets."

Esther poked her fork into the blueberry dessert, which wore a golden halo of rich frosting. Sighing as she chewed and swallowed the first bite, she nodded. "Well, it looked good. Besides, he seemed to enjoy his first."

Adam jerked his head up from his second muffin, a rueful grin seeping across this face. "Guilty."

Esther ate another bite, gave another little sigh of contentment. "So, Adam is it? Tell us about yourself."

Not exactly what he had in mind. He was hoping to hear their stories. But Esther seemed eager.

"Where are you from?" she asked as she gave her muffin — of course, it was still her first — another good stab.

"All over, I guess. I grew up in Tennessee, but I've been in Washington, DC, and abroad for the last few years."

"Abroad?" Esther latched onto that one little word, her eyes lighting. And Adam couldn't help the corresponding lightness in his own chest. She quickly swallowed another bite before continuing. "Where have you been? We went back to Hungary — well, I went for the first time — almost twenty years ago now. It was amazing. So beautiful. And then we went to Germany . . ."

Adam's eyes grew wide as Esther continued, his heartbeat picking up speed.

Levi jumped in before she could go on. "Where'd you say you've been?"

The same caution that Adam lived by flickered across Levi's features. He had secrets too. A past he wasn't eager to unveil.

And that made Levi infinitely more interesting. And more likeable.

"Lately?" Adam poked at his muffin, pursing his lips to the side and drumming his fingers on the table in front of his plate. "Here and there. The Middle East."

"Israel?" Esther sounded like a child meeting her hero for the first time.

"Yes, ma'am. I've been to Jerusalem a few times. Even swam in the Dead Sea once. It's a beautiful area."

Esther grabbed Levi's arm and tilted her head as if to say that if a young man got to go to the Holy Land, she should too. But he shook his head.

"Have you been?" Adam asked, wondering at the exchange between the two. Levi looked a little bit sad, but his mouth was set in a firm line.

"Not yet," Esther said.

Levi shot her a squinted glare.

She rolled her eyes and crossed her arms.

Adam's gaze darted between them, and he could practically feel the tension coming in waves across the table. He wished he could slide beneath the table, but he wasn't about to give up the last of his quiche or the half of a muffin left. He filled his mouth with another bite and chewed on in diligent silence.

Levi patted his wife's arm, and when she

didn't respond, he turned back to Adam. "What brings you all the way to Prince Edward Island from the Middle East?"

He swallowed, the muscles in his neck and shoulders growing tense as he glanced toward the family sitting next to them. A young mom wiped her toddler's face, and the towheaded girl bestowed them with a gap-toothed grin. Levi smiled in return, and Adam let out a quick breath. Good men gave genuine smiles. He'd learned that as a child.

Turning his attention back to their table, Adam scratched behind his ear. "I'm taking a short sabbatical."

"From?" Esther seemed to have given up her grudge as she laid her hand on her husband's.

"Well, I'm a writer. So I suppose I'm taking a break from writing. Two months without a deadline. Two months of not much of anything, I guess."

"It's a shame you feel that way," Levi said.

Adam's eyebrows shot up. "What do you mean?"

"Only that every writer wishes he had an uninterrupted month to write. Imagine the great American novel you could come up with in two entire months off."

"Huh." Adam looked toward the ceiling,

then back into Levi's steady eyes. "A novel?"

"Sure. Every reporter's got one they've been dying to write. Don't you?"

He scrubbed the stubble across his chin, searching his mind for a fictional idea. There hadn't been time to think about that when the nonfiction kept him so busy. "Not really."

"Levi was a star reporter," Esther said. Levi shrugged as though to brush off Esther's note of praise. "Oh, don't be so modest, dear." With a pointed nod to Adam, she said, "He was a Pulitzer finalist."

"The boy doesn't care about some silly award I didn't even win thirty-five years ago."

Adam leaned forward, elbows on the table and hands clutched in front of his plate. "Wow. A Pulitzer?"

"Finalist. Everyone gets caught up on the first word and misses the second."

Adam dismissed the qualifier with a wave of his hand. "Still. That's impressive. Do you still write?"

"No." He held up his hands, palms down and fingers curled in permanent arches. "Too many years on an old typewriter. The doctor says if I don't do my exercises, I'll lose most of my dexterity soon."

Adam nodded in understanding but

cringed on the inside. Losing the ability to write was like losing a limb.

He should know. He hadn't been able to string three words together in more than a month.

"You ever think about voice transcription?" he asked.

Levi shook his head. "Without the rhythm of the keys, I don't think I could get from page one to page two."

Adam immediately understood.

Right then Marie joined them from the kitchen. Her smile was full and extra pink this morning. "Good morning, Mr. and Mrs. Eisenberg. Mr. Jacobs. Did you get enough to eat?"

All eyes zeroed in on the three muffin shells on Adam's otherwise empty plate. He leaned back and patted his stomach. "My compliments to Caden. Are there any leftover muffins?"

She rested her hand on the back of Adam's chair. "Three o'clock on the buffet."

"I'll be there. Tell Caden not to be late."

Marie's laugh trickled out as she picked up their plates.

Esther wiggled against her wooden seat until she sat a little taller, her eyes shining with questions. "Who's Caden?"

Caden dropped her skillet into the sudsy sink water at the shriek that carried down the hall two hours after breakfast. The guests who were leaving had already checked out, and the rest had taken off to explore the island. That meant the yell had come from either Marie or Seth. Or Adam, who had reclaimed his storage room.

It was hard to tell if the cry came from pain or joy. Either way, she whipped a dish towel from its hook and tore across the kitchen.

At the swinging door, she collided with Marie, nearly sending the tiny woman to the ground. Caden grabbed Marie's elbow to keep her upright, but the wild-eyed look on her face didn't abate.

"They're sending someone." She waved her phone between them. "They're going to feature Rose's Red Door." Her voice rose until it filled the whole room and the adjoining one, nearly drowning out the original Broadway cast of *Aida,* who had been keeping Caden company.

"Who's coming?"

"That's just it. I don't know. It could be anyone. Anytime."

"What's going on? Are you —"

Marie cut her off before she could finish her question. "We have to get ready. There's so much to do. We have to do a thorough cleaning and get our best room ready, and then there's the activities. We have to sell the whole island, all of it."

Try as she might, Caden couldn't seem to catch up to Marie's train of thought as it careened off the tracks. Leading Marie to the kitchen island, she set a glass of orange juice in front of her and patted her back. "Take a deep breath."

The bright pink spots in her cheeks glowed as Marie guzzled the juice before clunking the glass back on the tile. Eyes wide and shoulders rising and falling in rapid succession, she looked like she'd won the lottery. Or lost everything.

It was still hard to tell.

With nerves firing and heart hammering, Caden tried for a gentle tone. "Is someone hurt?"

"No, of course not. It's just that there's —"

Caden waved a hand to silence her boss. They'd had a few of these conversations during their friendship. The ones where Marie was going at Boston speed and Caden was rolling along at the pace of the tide.

"Let's try this again. From the beginning. A little bit slower this time."

Marie nodded, holding out her phone, her breathing still too rapid, hands shaking.

Caden finished wiping her still damp hands on the towel before reading the screen.

Marie,

I just heard from the editor at *Rest & Retreats* magazine. She wanted me to do a mystery visit to Rose's Red Door Inn because she's considering featuring your inn in the spring issue!

Of course, I had to tell her that we'd met and kept in touch, so she said she'd find someone else.

Do you know what this means? Spring is *R&R*'s biggest issue, and it always features the six best bed-and-breakfasts in North America. The editor said they'd narrowed their list down to the top fifteen, and they're sending writers to visit each one over the next two months.

Don't let me down! I know I'll see the Red Door on the cover!

Ciao,
Rosalinda

As she handed the phone back to Marie,

Caden's fingers trembled, her stomach already in a knot. "I'm not sure I understand."

"Rosalinda is the woman I met on my trip to Boston two years ago, the travel writer who was writing a piece on Dalvay-by-the-Sea after William and Kate visited there." Marie stared at her phone for a long second. "*Rest & Retreats* magazine is interested in the Red Door."

Caden bit back the question she really wanted to ask. *Why?* They weren't particularly special, were they? Other inns on PEI had more rooms, more local amenities, and a more experienced chef.

And they were still trying to get off the ground. They'd struggled to lure guests from the more established inns in Charlottetown to tiny North Rustico.

Rose's Red Door was familiar. It was safe. It was home.

But she wasn't naive enough to think one of the biggest travel magazines in North America would feel the same.

Marie nodded, her gaze devouring the email once again. "We have to impress them."

Caden gave her boss her best smile and dunked her hands back into the dishwater, retrieving her forgotten skillet. But there was no denying that this news didn't come without an extra load of pressure. "I suppose that means we'll have to impress every guest we have this summer."

"Don't be silly. We'll do that anyway," Marie said, an extra sparkle in her voice. Grabbing a clean dish towel, she dried the pan after Caden rinsed it off.

"For sure." She'd try her best.

Suddenly Marie's smile faltered. "We need this coverage."

Caden's heart skipped a beat, but she wasn't quite sure why. Maybe it was the sudden stiffness in Marie's shoulders or the memory of what she'd heard the morning before.

She replayed Seth and Marie's urgent whispers, and again they made her stomach swoop and her skin break out in goose bumps. Something was most definitely wrong at the inn. Slowing the motion of her scrub brush, she stared hard into Marie's face, a crank in her stomach tightening. "Are we in trouble?"

Marie lifted a shoulder but didn't respond.

Another wrench in her stomach. "How bad is it?"

Bay-blue eyes filled with sadness even as she squared her shoulders and raised her pointed chin. "We're half empty this summer."

"Isn't there some marketing we could do or specials we could offer? Even if we fill up the rooms at a discounted rate, at least that's some income. Right?" The thread of hope in her tone wavered on the last word.

Marie was the one with the MBA from Wharton, but Caden could read the lines on her face. Discounted rooms might get them through the rest of the season. But just because the tourists went home didn't mean that the bill collectors stopped asking to be paid. Mortgage payments were due even in the winter.

"We're doing everything we can. I've run as many ads as we can afford, and your pictures of the island are a huge hit on social media. But the cabins down the road are undercutting our prices. And without an infusion of cash or a full summer next year . . ." Marie turned her back and reached to hang the copper skillet on the rack above the island, her voice dropping so that Caden had to lean in to catch the last devastating blow. "I just don't see how we'll be able to do the repairs we'll need to keep our doors open."

"What about the money from your mom? Isn't there any —" Caden clamped her mouth shut. Pain flashed across Marie's features, and it felt like a blow to Caden's chest.

"There's no money right now."

Her words were clipped, sharper than a paring knife, and Caden shrunk away from them. The truth hurt, and the idea of losing the inn she held so dear stung. Especially when it had just opened two summers before.

"I'm sorry." Marie put a hand over her eyes, pressing her fingers into the headache that was almost certainly taking root. "It's gone." She sighed and ran both hands through her dark curls. "My dad is suing me for what's left of my trust fund, and in the meantime, the court has blocked any access to it."

Caden gasped. She hadn't met Marie's father on his only trip to the island, but what she knew of him wasn't flattering. The man had tried to use his own daughter's pain to leverage some kind of real estate deal two years ago. So she shouldn't be surprised that he'd take her to court.

But still . . . parents didn't do things like that.

Or maybe some did.

Marie dragged in another raspy breath. "The lawyers are so expensive. And now we're in so deep that we can't stop, but the case could drag on for years. Without the money in the trust fund, I won't be able to pay attorney fees, and we certainly won't be able to fix the inn's roof."

The Red Door's roof needed to be fixed? That was news to Caden, but there wasn't time to dwell on it.

The misery in Marie's words poked at Caden's heart, and she pulled her friend into her arms. "I'm so sorry. What can I do?"

Marie's shoulders trembled as she sniffled against the tears that were breaking free and running down her cheeks. Stiff as a pine tree, she seemed to be doing everything she could to keep from falling apart.

"It's sweet of you to offer." A shaky breath broke her words. "But I don't know what to do except fill up the inn next summer. If we aren't at least 90 percent full, I'm afraid . . ."

Marie paused, and Caden pulled away enough to look into her friend's red-rimmed eyes. "What? What's going to happen?"

As soon as she asked, she realized she didn't want to know the truth. Because it was written in Marie's downtrodden gaze and quivering chin. And it made her insides twist into a knot that her seafaring grand-dad would have been proud of. The pain in her heart was palpable, and she pressed a fist to the center of her chest, trying to alleviate the sharp ache.

With a fortifying breath, Marie shook her head. "We'll have to close the inn."

4

Caden wished with all her might that she hadn't asked what would happen to the inn.

It couldn't close.

It just couldn't.

She couldn't fathom her little world without the Red Door. Without her kitchen. Without Seth and Marie. She couldn't go back to working in her dad's bakery every day. She couldn't give up her students.

Letting go of Marie, Caden stepped back. "There has to be something we can do."

"I don't know what else to do except keep the rooms full and the guests happy." Marie straightened her back into perfect posture. "And make sure we get picked for that magazine feature."

"Good. How long do we have to get ready?"

Marie consulted her phone. "Rosalinda said sometime in the next two months the editor is going to . . ." Her voice disappeared, her gaze focused on one of the four chains attaching the rack of pans to the ceiling. Her jaw worked back and forth, the muscle jumping like she was chewing a large wad of bubble gum.

"Marie?"

"Could it be?"

The knot in her stomach pulled a fraction tighter. "What?"

Tongue poking out the side of her mouth, Marie rubbed her hands together. She blinked twice and pressed her lips together. "Rosalinda said writers are being sent 'to visit each one over the next two months.'"

When she failed to continue, Caden nudged her for an explanation. "And?"

"Maybe that means our mystery guest will be here for two months. What if he's already here?"

Caden tried to bring up every table place card she'd prepared the afternoon before. The Wilkersons had just checked out. And the Abbotts and Stryers would follow quickly after. Levi and Esther Eisenberg had only recently arrived for an extended stay. But they were both retired. That only left . . .

"Adam Jacobs."

Her stomach dropped faster than a falling soufflé.

The Adam Jacobs. The one who had

shown up unannounced at the back door. The one who had in two days already spent more time in her kitchen than any other guest had ever dared. The one with the dazzling gray eyes and slightly crooked nose.

The one who was far too handsome for his own good.

Or hers.

"No. It can't be him." Caden attempted to keep her voice from revealing the very real fear that she might be wrong. "He showed up a day early —"

"Because his *editor* sent him." Marie leaned heavily on the key word. "Maybe it was a test. Maybe it was part of the evaluation. To see if we'd find a place for him to stay. And we provided him with . . ." Her eyes bulged until they eclipsed her face.

When it was clear that Marie couldn't bear to finish the thought, Caden filled in. "Taco Bed."

With trembling hands, Marie covered her cheeks and the blush that rose there. "I gave a magazine reviewer a rollaway bed in a storage room."

"At least it had a roof and an attached bath."

Marie rolled her eyes as if to say Caden was not helping.

Caden scrambled to find something encouraging to say. "And besides, you don't know that Adam is the reviewer. It could be someone else."

"He was sent here by his editor." Marie ticked off her argument on her fingers. "I heard him telling the Eisenbergs that he's a writer and that he's here for rest. And he's the only guest we have staying for two months." The way she waved her hand around the kitchen, she looked like she'd won an argument in court. "Who else could it be?"

It couldn't be him. It just wasn't possible. "Two months seems like an awfully long time. How long does it take to review an inn?"

Marie shrugged. "No idea. I've never been reviewed before." She picked up the towel she'd set down and made lazy passes over another pan, but her face reflected the speed of her thoughts. "It makes perfect sense. They said two months. He's here for two months. He has to be the one."

"Why don't we ask him?" Caden said.

"Would he tell us the truth? I don't think so. It's a mystery visit. We're not supposed to know he's the travel writer."

That was the most logical argument Marie had made all morning.

"Besides, we don't want him to know that

we're onto him, that we know he's the reviewer. He might think we'd give him special treatment."

Caden gave a couple sweeps of her scrubber to a serving platter under the water. She followed the motion of the morning waves in the bay, hoping they'd give her the rebuttal she needed. But all she could come up with was how familiar it all seemed. She could almost see the movie playing out before her.

She'd seen this same trope in dozens of films. Guy, clearly hiding a secret, shows up out of nowhere. Girl falls for guy. Guy's secret is just what he needs to rescue the girl. Guy and girl live happily ever after.

Except Caden was most certainly not the girl in that screenplay.

Her odds of a happily ever after were as good as the inn selling out for the next ten summers by the end of the day.

This was not a movie, and Adam Jacobs was not going to rescue anyone.

Still, she couldn't shred the hope that Marie had wrapped around herself. "Maybe we shouldn't put all of our eggs in Adam's basket."

Marie's eyebrows jumped, a wicked grin spreading across her lips, despite the remaining tear tracks still marring her cheeks.

Heat pooled at Caden's throat, and she flung a finger of water at her boss. "Oh, you know what I meant." Marie gave a half laugh, half cough that sounded like assent, and Caden charged on. "It just seems strange to me that Rosalinda would send a letter telling you about the reviewer *after* the reviewer had already arrived. It doesn't make any sense that she'd wait so long to tell you — so long that the magazine had time to find *and* send another reviewer."

Marie's hand stilled in mid-swipe, leaving two drops of water on her cheek. "Maybe she's been too busy. Or on assignment. Or trying to meet a deadline. Maybe she just forgot until today. Who knows. But what I do know is that Adam is here right now."

"Don't we have other guests booked in August? Couldn't it be one of them?"

With a slow, considering nod, Marie agreed. Her gaze hung on the cabinets on the far wall, but it was clear she saw only her calendar of bookings. "A few."

"Don't you think it could be one of them?"

After a long pause, Marie shook her head. "Maybe, but are you willing to risk it? Because I'm sure not." She wasn't going to give up on Adam the hero, and if Caden knew her best friend, Marie would do everything she could to make him happy.

"We have to make the rest of his stay so fantastic that he'll forget about Taco Bed." Marie covered her face again. "I can't believe we put him in the storage room."

Caden cringed too, but stretched for a silver lining. "It was better than a night on the beach."

"Barely." Marie turned back to her phone, which she'd left on the kitchen island, and typed in several notes on her to-do list. "He doesn't have a car or any plans, at least that's what he told the Eisenbergs. We'll have to get him out on the island, let him experience some of the natural beauty, amazing people, and great food."

At least Caden could do her part from the kitchen.

"We'll make Adam fall in love with Rose's, just you wait." Marie squeezed Caden's arm, the light that had nearly been extinguished from her eyes beginning to flicker once again. "And you'll show him around."

The morning's berry crumble muffin turned to a stone in her stomach. "Wait. What?" Caden swallowed the bitter taste in the back of her throat. Marie had to be joking. Caden couldn't show him around. She wasn't a tour guide. She didn't even greet guests. Strictly back-of-the-house jobs for her.

"You're kidding, right?" Caden chased after Marie, who'd set down the pan she'd been drying and disappeared down the hallway. "What do you mean, *I'll* show him around? There's no way. I can't."

Marie, dish towel still in hand, spun it before flopping it over her shoulder, never bothering to turn around. "Of course you can. You're the perfect person to show off the island."

"No. I'm the perfect person to stay in the kitchen and whip up breakfast." Caden pressed her hands to her hips, hoping that even though Marie couldn't see her, maybe she'd feel the firm stance. "There must be someone better. What about Seth?"

That warranted a quick glance over her shoulder as Marie swung into her office. "Have you met my husband?"

Caden bit back a groan.

"I love him to death, and he's an amazing man. But he's not a tour guide. He can get across PEI, no problem. But explore off the beaten path? Not so much." The corners of Marie's eyes crinkled with joy as she spoke about the man she'd married only nine months ago. "Besides, he's booked solid this summer between upkeep at the inn and doing some renovations at the church."

Okay, she'd picked the wrong candidate. There had to be others.

"Well then, what about Jack and Aretha? The antique store practically runs itself." That was a bit of a stretch, but at least the other newlywed couple had a vested interest in seeing Rose's Red Door succeed. Jack Sloane had opened the inn to honor his late wife's dream. But after falling in love with Aretha, he'd handed the reins over to his nephew, Seth, and Marie. Of course, he still kept an eye on the inn that carried his first wife's legacy.

"No one knows this area of PEI like Aretha," Caden tried again. "She's been in the Crick forever."

"True, but no one loves this island more than you do."

Caden's lips pursed, and she wrinkled her nose. Marie might be right.

The first time she'd seen it on a map, she'd wondered how the island's inhabitants managed not to step right off. This oft overlooked birthplace of the Canadian Confederation seemed to fit in the country's back pocket. Most tourists were drawn here to see Anne's Land, the famous red shoreline and Green Gables of the island's fictional redheaded orphan. But there was

67

so much more to these shores she loved. Even Maud — as L. M. Montgomery's friends called her — knew that the best, truest beauty of the land was found in the flowers, trees, and burbling brooks. It was in the whisper of the wind through pine trees that hugged the sky. It was in the glimmer of the sun reflecting off the bluest water she'd ever seen.

The island's murmurs had a way of settling every nerve and making her forget every heartache.

Granted, Caden didn't have much to compare it to. She'd only ever ventured as far as Halifax, barely a three and a half hour drive over the bridge. And that one trip to visit a friend in Toronto. But the city had been big and loud and too fast, and she'd sprinted for the safety of home.

Yes, she loved this island.

But that didn't qualify her to help someone else fall in love with it.

"What about you? You're from the States, and you love it here. Why don't you show Adam why he has to write about it?"

Marie shook her head hard. "I have to do everything I can to get us booked up next summer. And maybe round up a few more guests for this summer. We could use the money to get us through the winter."

"But what about breakfasts and my classes?" The word *classes* promised too much structure for the twice-weekly afternoon gathering of five teenagers in her kitchen. But she was teaching them some culinary basics — or at least trying to. And it had become one of her favorite parts of the summer.

"Can you work it around them?" Marie stretched her slender neck to look back at Caden, her eyes wide and filled with hopeful appeal. "He seems to like spending time in the kitchen. Maybe you can take him to the farmer's market or to the dairy. Invite him on a walk. It doesn't have to take all your free time. It's just that . . ." Sadness rushed through Marie's voice, and she swallowed, trying again. "With everything with my dad . . ."

No, it wasn't sadness. It was much deeper. It was heartache pouncing on betrayal's back, scrimmaging like two tomcats.

The tone of Marie's words wrung Caden's heart like a dishrag, and she barreled toward her friend, sweeping her into a hug. "Anything you need. I'll do it."

Marie blinked her tear-filled eyes. "Will you make sure Adam gets out of the inn and experiences the island? Don't let him get bored."

She didn't have a choice now. Even if she was in over her head.

Adam picked up the French press and poured the last dregs of coffee into his mug. He took a sip with a grimace before downing the cold brew in one swallow.

Caffeine. Just what the editor ordered.

Or something kind of like that.

As he rinsed the cup out, a voice on the far side of the door caught his attention.

"But what about breakfasts and my classes?" It was clearly Caden. And she sounded about as happy as a mouse in a snake pit.

He tiptoed to the door as Marie responded, her words firm but too quiet for him to distinguish. Pressing his ear against the crack, he made out a line. "He seems to like spending time in the kitchen."

Snapping back, he bumped into the corner of the island.

They were talking about him. He was sure of it.

Almost.

A thread of uncertainty sewed its way through him, and he leaned into the door again. Why in all creation would they be talking about him? He hadn't done anything but beg coffee and sweets off Caden, complimenting her exceptional culinary skills with every bite. And he'd suffered Taco Bed without complaint. They had no reason to bring him up.

Maybe he'd lost more than his ability to write. Maybe he'd lost his reporter's instincts too.

Fear, or something like it, made Marie's unclear words tremble, and suddenly there was a soft cry.

Then Caden cut in. "Anything you need. I'll do it."

There was a long pause, and he almost felt guilty for listening from the kitchen, especially after he'd promised Caden he'd stay out when she'd given him the last cinnamon roll. But not guilty enough to step back.

"Will you make sure Adam gets out of the inn?"

He jumped from his post and stopped breathing, but he missed the rest of Marie's request. Her words were too soft to distinguish.

And then an almost indecipherable sigh from down the hall. "Yes."

Adam jerked away, his ears still ringing with the words he shouldn't have heard. But he couldn't unhear them now, and he sure wasn't going to pretend there wasn't a reason they wanted him to get out of the inn. It was clear they weren't trying to get him to leave completely. After all, Marie could have simply refused to let Garrett reserve a room.

But there was something in the inn they didn't want him to see. Something they wanted to keep him away from.

He tugged at the back of his neck, matching the pull in his gut. Its familiar lurch called him to dig, to uncover the secrets behind the Red Door and its inhabitants. Its voice was deep, clear, and full of promise.

If he could find a story, he could find the words that had escaped him every day since the explosion. If there were secrets to uncover, there was a story to write and a column to fill. If he could pinpoint a scandal on this tiny island, he just might be able to turn in the article that was due.

The article that might save his job.

Was there a secret at Rose's Red Door Inn that could really be so powerful? Was that why Garrett had sent him here?

Adam shook off the questions, refusing to look for answers.

He was out of the newspaper game, and he wasn't going to look for a story where there wasn't one. He needed to get back to Washington. Busy, boisterous, exciting

Washington. Restaurants and plays, art and history. It was enough to keep a man's mind occupied. Enough to make him forget Connor's parents' faces at the memorial service.

Suddenly Caden's footsteps clipped down the hall, and Adam scrambled for cover. He wasn't supposed to be in the kitchen. And he sure didn't want her knowing he'd overheard her conversation. He couldn't make it out of the swinging door into the dining room before she arrived. But maybe . . .

He sprinted for the far wall, nudging the entrance open.

Caden's eyes went wide when she saw him, her gaze flitting to the swaying door behind him and then back to his face. "I thought we had an agreement."

"Huh?" He schooled his breathing, trying not to give away the thundering of his heart. But his confusion wasn't a front.

"I gave you the cinnamon roll. You promised not to invade my kitchen again." She crossed her arms over her ample chest, no sign of her dimple in her severity, although her lips twitched like she was trying to find a smile that refused to stay put.

Right. He'd said he'd stay out. And he would have, but for the coffee. His gaze dropped to the mug in his hands, and he held it out in a terrible Oliver impersonation. "Please, ma'am, may I have some more?"

Her lips pursed, eyes flashing with the verbal beating he probably deserved.

But then — despite lips locked in a tight line — she snorted.

And he did too.

The tension in the room disappeared like an ocean storm, first thick and gray and an instant later clear sky for miles.

"You can have whatever's left." She waved a towel at the French press. "But you might want to nuke it for a few seconds."

It probably would have been better warm, but she didn't need to know that he'd already pilfered the last of it. Picking up the glass carafe, he jiggled it around and stared into the bottom. "Looks like we're out."

Caden gave only a shrug and a shake of her head. Maybe she didn't think him worth another pot this morning. But she took the press, emptied the grounds, and dunked the glass into her dishwater. "Let me wash it. I'll make you another one."

"Really?"

Her hands moved in efficient, fluid motions, and he was so busy watching her fingers that he almost missed her half smile.

It wasn't fully engaged, far from reaching her eyes, but it was much warmer than the glare she'd given him when he'd arrived the day before. So he responded in kind, leaning in and whispering, "Thank you."

She bit her lip, apparently unsure what to say. After one stop and start, she settled on, "You're welcome." The words were soft, but there was a gentle lilt to her tone, a Maritime accent, that swirled a warmth in his chest, and he drew even closer to her, wishing for a little more of whatever infused her voice.

As he drew near, she jumped away, scooping up the teapot and setting it on the stove. She moved through the motions, measuring the coffee grounds, preparing the press, and checking the water in silence. Always with an eye on him. Watching. Waiting for something. He didn't know what.

Several times she opened her mouth and looked like she had something to say, but then she shut it, returning to the task at hand.

He squinted at her, trying to decode her strange actions. It had to be because of what she and Marie had been talking about in the back hallway. About getting him out of the inn. But why?

When the coffee was ready, she held up

the carafe and he mimicked her move with his mug. Steam swirled over the rich liquid. He backed slowly toward the dining room, simultaneously hoping for an easy escape and dying to know what had been on the tip of her tongue for the silent minutes.

As his hand flattened against the swinging door, she pinched her eyes closed, sucked in a loud breath, and let out a deluge. "I was thinking about going to the East Point Lighthouse today. Doyouwanttogowithme?"

She spoke the question so fast that her words made no sense, and he had to lean forward, trying to distinguish them. "Excuse me?"

Another sigh and an exaggerated eye roll — pointed at him or herself, he couldn't tell — followed. Staring hard at her hands, she slowed down. "Lighthouses. The island has a bunch of them. And the North Coastal Drive over to the East Point Lighthouse is very pretty. Would you like to gowithme?"

To let her off her clear and towering ledge of nerves, he tried for an easy grin, despite the questions tumbling cartwheels through his mind. "Does anyone actually still use lighthouses?"

Finally she looked at him, her pale eyes bright enough to challenge the lighthouses in question. "For sure." The light in her eyes flickered. "I mean, not as much as they used to. New technology is important, but there's nothing like seeing a light in the middle of a storm to warn you away from danger."

Or call you to safety.

"Besides, they have the best views of the island and the ocean." As she spoke, a gentle smile fell into place, her bottom lip plump and pink, her dimple in fine form. "Sometimes I go up there just to find a bit of quiet."

"You mean the rest of the island isn't quiet enough? Or are your show tunes too loud?"

Her perfect white teeth flashed in the light coming through the window, and she hurried to turn down the soundtrack that still thrummed through the kitchen. "When I lived with my parents, so did my brother, his wife, and their five kids. I had to share a room with two of my nieces. One never stopped talking during the day. The other talked in her sleep."

Adam couldn't hold back the laugh that escaped. "I can imagine." He squinted to the ceiling, trying to conjure a house that full, that loud. "Actually, no. I can't even imagine."

"Not from a big family?"

"Nope." He didn't mean to clip the word

so hard, but he sure didn't want to spend his summer thinking about his family. Not the one member who was still alive. And especially not the ones who weren't.

Her gaze swept over him, and she nodded as though she understood he didn't want to continue in that vein. "It's still a pretty place. I thought you might like to see some of the island while you're here."

Or her boss had talked her into getting him out of the inn.

"And you don't really seem like the type looking to explore Anne's Land," she said.

He narrowed his gaze, studying her. "Oh, I've read *Anne of Green Gables.*" At her arched eyebrows, he quickly amended his white lie. "Well, I saw the movie."

That earned him a cheeky smirk, and he was chuckling before he even realized it, telling her the rest of the story, which he'd never before admitted. "I was trying to impress the pretty girl in my college English class."

Caden's chin dipped, her smile taking a quick hit before jumping back into place. It happened so fast he almost missed it, but the flicker felt more like a punch to his gut.

"Did it work?" she asked.

"No, she didn't give me a second glance.

But I liked the movie enough to watch the sequel."

"Well, the second movie isn't much like the books." Her laughter sounded like rain falling on the National Mall, quiet pings of humor. "But maybe we should make our way over to Cavendish."

"Cavendish?"

"Green Gables, the national historic site where Maud's aunt and uncle lived, is just down the road, and she modeled Avonlea after the Cavendish of her time."

"But now it's . . ." He let his words skip off his tongue, hoping she'd fill in all the terrible havoc the land had suffered in the last century.

"Oh, it's still a stunning shoreline. The water sneaks into the land, filling every crevice and washing everything clean. Pine trees grow right up to the shore, and wild-flowers line every path." She closed her eyes and inhaled as though she could smell those blossoms even now. "The beaches are a little more crowded, but you have to know where to go to disappear."

For someone so eager to return to the hustle of the big city, Adam found a strange appeal in Caden's words. Maybe it was the way she so tenderly described the land she clearly loved, cradling each syllable like a newborn kitten. Maybe it was the little smile that played across her lips, the one he openly stared at. And how he'd already told her something he'd never told anyone else.

Or maybe it was the hope of disappearing altogether.

Either way, he fought the tug in his chest that wanted to accept her invitation by taking another sip of his steaming cup. He had work to do. He didn't know what it was yet, but he'd find it. Or . . .

Well, there was no *or* about it. His options were to find something to keep his mind occupied or dwell on the article, the explosion, and the face of Connor's mom. It wasn't just an easy choice, it was the only choice.

Because at night, he didn't have any say in the matter.

He'd dig up whatever story Garrett had sent him to uncover. And until he talked with Garrett and knew what that was, he wouldn't go anywhere with Caden Holt.

Caden glanced over her shoulder, her feet picking up speed as she scurried down the road. The Red Door stood tall and proud, guarding the harbor, concealing the scene of her rejection.

Her stomach rolled as she replayed the

embarrassing memory. Adam had been perfectly polite, but his answer had been firm. He wasn't interested in sightseeing with her. He wasn't interested in spending time with her. He wasn't interested in her. Period.

She'd heard the same thing from Mitch Baker in grade eleven. Long before Jack and Seth refurbished the old Red Door, she'd stood on the harbor boardwalk in its shadow, hoping for a chance with the boy she'd known since primary school.

She didn't have one.

Instead he'd told Bethany Burke — the prettiest girl in school — that he'd rather muck out the barn at Kane Dairy than go to the annual lobster dinner with Caden.

Even now, ten years later, the memory twisted her stomach, and she wished she hadn't so heavily sampled the raspberry brownies she'd made that morning, which now seemed to be playing a game of tag in her middle.

She'd been a fool to think that Adam would respond any differently than Mitch had all those summers ago.

Even if her motives were different this time, Caden hadn't changed all that much.

She glanced down, hating the way her shirt stretched around her hips and the sound of her jeans rubbing together with each step.

Too many curves. Too many inches.

This was what Adam saw. And it wasn't what men looked for.

Cute, maybe.

Cute, at best.

One of the women from the ladies' auxiliary had patted five-year-old Caden on the head and said to her mother, "She's rather adorable, Glenda. Look at all this lovely blonde hair and those sweet little dimples." And then the ever-present zinger. "If you can only keep her out of the cookie jar."

She'd known — even back then — that her mother and the church ladies whispered about her weight, how she was round and her older brother was "a twig of a thing." It seemed the only meterstick they knew to use to judge her. And no matter how many times they measured, she always came up short.

Tears stung her eyes, unexpected and unwelcome. And she rubbed them away with the heel of her hand.

Her mother loved her.

Glenda had given up a trip with the ladies' auxiliary to care for Caden when her appendix had to be removed. She'd held Caden so close when her best friend had moved away. She'd stayed up countless nights helping Caden perfect new recipes. She'd listened as Caden struggled with the decision to take the job at the inn two years before.

Glenda's words of praise, listening ear, and giving heart left no doubt about her love.

Whether Caden was worthy of it . . . well, that wasn't quite as clear.

Her feet ate up the road, and Caden flew through the back door of the bakery — her father's bakery — hidden by the darkness of the storage room. Pressing her forehead against a bag of flour sitting on a wooden shelf, she wiped away the remaining tears, swallowing a sigh.

"That you, Pumpkin?" Her father's voice carried from the kitchen, which was tucked between her hiding spot and the one-room store.

No. She didn't want to be Pumpkin, round and useful for only a season — today. But she had to be useful for this summer, or she wouldn't have a job beyond August. Marie was counting on her. Caden had promised. She had to get Adam to fall in love.

But she'd never gotten anyone to fall in love before.

Certainly not with her. And she'd never tried to get anyone to fall for the island.

She rocked her back against the orange shelves and covered her face, praying for some kind of supernatural escape from the promise she couldn't possibly keep. Perhaps a hurricane would sweep her off the island. Or an urgent call from Adam's editor would have him winging his way to Bali or Timbuktu. Anything that would save her from having to invite him on another outing, from embarrassing herself again.

She held her breath.

And waited.

Nothing happened.

Except another call from her dad. "Come in here and help me roll out pie crusts."

Just as she'd feared. She was going to have to do it all again.

5

Adam flew forward, the force of the explosion in his dream propelling him upright in real life.

He blinked against the midnight black of his room, pressing a hand to his chest as it rose and fell fast and loud. The orange blast had been printed against the backs of his eyelids, so he stared hard at the far wall as he swung his hand to the antique nightstand. He thumped against it with an open palm, the wood's groan echoing in the otherwise silent house.

Empty.

He pinched his eyes closed but snapped them open the minute he saw the small mud home. Its russet walls, crisp square windows, and inviting door were sharp and strong. But then, in an instant, it was all a fireball so bright it blistered his skin.

His arm swung through the nightstand's airspace while he stared at the ceiling, praying he'd connect with a bottle.

Any bottle would do.

But there wasn't one.

That figured. He'd spent the last eight years praying God would help him stay away from alcohol. Adam didn't think he was going to miraculously start dropping Jack Daniel's onto bedside tables now.

No matter how much he needed the absolution brought by the bitter burn.

"It's not going to change the past. And it can only ruin your future." Garrett's words rang through his mind, and Adam scrubbed a hand over his face. Flipping back the bedcovers, he stumbled to his feet, glaring at the clock. Barely two in the morning. Back in Washington he would only have been in bed for an hour after a long day in the newsroom, a trip to the gym, and a late dinner with friends. Maybe they'd catch a show or a concert. There was a new jazz club three blocks from his apartment. And his favorite coffee shop always had good live music on the weekends.

Back in Washington . . . well, he wouldn't be here. With too much time on his hands, looking for a story that probably didn't exist.

This was all Garrett's fault.

Growling at the phone, he snatched it up

and punched the button to call his editor. Washington was an hour earlier than PEI, and Garrett wasn't in the habit of going to bed until his section did. If there were reporters still hunched over their keyboards punching a story to life, Garrett would be there watching.

And reporters were always there.

"I figured you'd call after ten minutes," Garrett growled before the first ring had even finished.

"To do what?"

"Beg me for a better assignment."

"I'm not . . ." Well, actually he *was* looking for a better assignment. Or really a better location. "I thought this wasn't an assignment."

Garrett grumbled under his breath. "It's not. Officially. But you owe me an article eventually. You signed on to write a four-part series, and I've only published three."

"I can't." The words tasted sour, and Adam tried to swallow them down, tried to get rid of the defeat that weighed on his shoulders. He'd gone freelance barely six months before, and his second agreement had been with Garrett. Adam hated letting him down. But the words just weren't there anymore.

"Thought so. That's why you're in the

frozen tundra."

The old man sounded so smug, so sure he knew exactly what Adam needed. But how could he when Adam didn't even know what he needed? He just knew he couldn't write anymore. He couldn't piece an article together. Not when there were real consequences to the words he wrote.

"It's not the tundra. It was eighty degrees today. People were swimming in the ocean."

"That sounds nice." Garrett's voice dropped half an octave. "Why people, not you? You like to swim."

Because he'd been holed up in his room wondering why Marie and Caden had been conspiring to keep him out of the inn. Because he'd desperately needed rest after another almost sleepless night. Because hiding out in a tiny room seemed easier than facing whatever memories this tiny island might conjure.

"I do like to swim. In a pool. With lane lines and goggles and no tides."

"Excuses."

As he rounded the corner of his bed, Adam tripped on the frame, his toe stinging nearly as much as Garrett's accusation. Of course Garrett was right, but that didn't mean he wanted to admit it.

"Listen, kid. You owe me a story."

"I know I do."

"And not just any story." Garrett kept going like Adam hadn't said anything at all. "The editor-in-chief expects a front page–worthy story. Above the fold."

Adam stomped a path from wall to window — and the view of the moonlit harbor — and back before remembering that the rest of the house was asleep and wanted to stay that way for another five hours or more. Flopping onto the foot of the bed, he hung his head and stared at the grain of the hardwood.

"Above the fold" meant a shocking, sensational story.

If it bleeds, it leads.

Every newsman knew the old adage. And many editors still lived and breathed by it. Including Gloria Lennon, the editor-in-chief of *America Today.* If an article didn't feature death, injury — physical or emotional — or mayhem, she told her reporters to find a new angle or a new story. Even when Adam had been unable to write a follow-up after the explosion, Gloria had found another reporter to write it.

The problem was, sometimes the lead caused the bleeding.

And he couldn't be responsible for that. Not again. Not for a third time.

"I think I'm going to come back to Washington. I'll have better luck finding a story there." But writing the story he found . . . well, that would be the hard part.

"If you were on assignment, could you leave just because you were unhappy?" Garrett slowed his words, as though speaking to a freshman reporter.

"I'm not on assignment." He tried to keep the misery out of his voice by massaging the back of his neck. But the truth was he didn't want to find a real story in this little inn on the rolling shoreline. He wanted to curl up and become invisible. He wanted to disappear. Just like Caden had said she sometimes did. "There's no story here." Maybe saying the words aloud would make them true.

Garrett paused for so long that Adam jumped to his feet and paced the length of the room, keeping his footfalls silent this time. Finally Garrett said, "You sure about that?"

Adam's head snapped up. "What do you mean, am I sure? Of course I'm sure." He sniffed in a loud breath through his nose, closed his eyes, and immediately flinched them back open. "What's your game, de Root? Why did you send me here?"

"Well, your soon-to-be sister-in-law is

from PEI. And even though she got out as fast as she could, she says it's beautiful."

The unfamiliar phrase felt like a kick to his gut. *Sister-in-law?* "Russell's getting married?"

"Do you ever talk to your brother?" Garrett sounded too much like Adam's mom. She had hated that the brothers — only two years apart in age — were light-years apart in every other arena of life.

Adam scooted around the straightforward response to the question and asked one of his own. "When's the wedding?"

"Next summer. In Nashville."

That made sense. Russell had become some sort of bigwig in the music industry since graduating from Berklee College of Music. He'd produced a Grammy-winning country album right out of college, eventually starting a label of his own. If Garrett was to be believed, Russell had signed some of the biggest names in country and crossover music in the previous five years.

But that was all hearsay and thirdhand information.

Adam hadn't had a face-to-face with his brother in a little over eight years.

Not since the funeral.

Not since Russell had gone off on Adam for showing up sloshed out of his mind, stumbling down the aisle between the pews, and nearly sitting on Great-Aunt Muriel's lap.

The memory sent a knife through his temple, and Adam leaned his forehead against the cool wall. It did nothing to ease the ache or the embarrassment that still roiled deep in his chest.

"Why am I here, Garrett?"

"I told you. You owe me a story. And if you don't produce one, Lennon is never going to hire you again. And she'll get you blacklisted by every other editor in town."

Right. His job was on the line. "You know I can't produce the article she wants."

"The one she sent you to the Middle East to write, the story she hired you to cover?"

"The one that might put more lives on the line."

Garrett sucked in an audible breath, the phone crackling with the effort it took. "Is that what this is about? You think that whole fiasco was your fault?"

Yes.

Because it was.

"Adam, listen to me. You didn't set off that bomb. You didn't plot that explosion. You didn't kill those boys."

Maybe. But that didn't make him innocent.

"You've got to keep writing, or they'll win."

"Oh." Adam's laugh was soft and humorless. "Manipulation by patriotism. That's low even for you."

"Well, a guy has to try."

"And a guy isn't going to get a story out of me that way."

"Fair enough." Garrett managed a soft chortle. "Stay where you are. Find the story that's there."

"On the island or at the inn?"

"Maybe both."

Adam ground his teeth and pinched the tip of his nose, waiting for something more to go on. Anything would be better than what he currently had. Which was an innkeeper who wanted him out of her inn — at least during the days — and not much else.

When it was clear that Garrett wasn't going to go on, he nudged him. "Are you going to give me any lead?"

"You already have everything you need to figure it out. Think of it like a jigsaw. You just have to put the pieces together. You used to like doing that. Remember?"

Sure. But that was before.

"Get some sleep. Start fresh in the morning."

Easier said than done. Adam flipped his

phone onto the nightstand, eyeing the red numbers of the alarm clock. They'd been on the phone for almost half an hour, and even though his eyes burned and the skin on his arms crawled under the tug of sleep, he wasn't going to find any rest in that bed.

And if he wanted to keep his job as a freelance journalist, he was going to have to find whatever was at the end of this wild goose chase. Garrett wanted him to find his rhythm again, get back into the swing of writing. And the sooner he found it, the sooner he could go home.

Propping a pillow against the headboard, he picked up his Moleskine notebook and flipped through his notes from Garrett until the words doubled, stacking on top of themselves, unreadable.

And then there was only darkness, pierced by an orange fireball.

Caden flew through the back door, arms brimming with bags of goodies from the farmer's market. But she dropped everything the instant she saw the dark outline of a man in her kitchen.

"It's me."

She flipped the light switch, illuminating her ever-present visitor. He'd come for coffee every day since his arrival, swearing each time was his last.

"You said you weren't going to be in here again." She tried to sound stern over the wobble in her voice and the wild pounding of her heart as she stooped to pick up her groceries.

Adam was there before she could even reach the first bag, scooping them into his arms, his usual mug dangling from his pinky finger. "Where do you want them?"

Pointing toward the corner of the counter, she ducked in the opposite direction. As she pulled the French press from its cupboard, his grin widened to a full-on smile, crinkling the corners of his eyes. Only then did she give him a second look, a long survey. His eyes were bloodshot and the tip of his nose was pink, like he'd spent too much time basking in the summer sun. Except he hadn't. He'd barely left the inn for the last few days, as far as she could tell.

Adam's plain gray T-shirt was wrinkled, half tucked into equally crumpled blue jeans. His dark hair stood up above his left ear, and she had to wrap her hand into the hem of her shirt to keep from flattening the wayward locks.

He seemed to sense the direction of her gaze, and he ran his fingers over his scalp, succeeding only in making the rest of his hair pop up in odd intervals. Then he grinned like a ten-year-old asking if he'd gotten the mud off his face.

Except he wasn't a child. Which was never more evident than when he stepped into her personal bubble, all broad shoulders, square jaw, and long fingers grasping his empty cup.

Apparently she had a job to do. Several of them.

Forcing herself to back away slowly, she took a shaky breath, her heart still thundering from the fright of finding him here.

Sure. That seemed like a reasonable excuse for her runaway pulse.

"What are we making today?"

"*We?*" Her ears twitched at the word. "I didn't realize you were here to help."

He shrugged one shoulder and pursed his lips as his gaze settled on the teapot she placed on the stove. An un-answer if ever she'd seen one.

"I'm making donuts."

His head ticked to the side, eyes wide. "Homemade donuts? For me?"

"Well, they're not all for you." Setting her top oven to preheat for a bacon and egg casserole, she shot him a sharp glance over her shoulder. "But if you ever manage to make it to the dining room, Marie will be serving them."

He laughed as he slid his mug across the tile counter and back again while she set up the deep fryer.

"Would you grab those bowls out of my bags?"

His forehead wrinkled, and he pointed to his chest as though asking if she was actually speaking to him.

Her stomach lurched. Had she crossed a line? If Adam really was the travel reporter, he might not appreciate being put to work. And Marie would probably have a word or five to say about it. But he'd nearly volunteered.

Besides, he kept showing up in her kitchen. And everything in here did its job, or it got tossed. Adam was no exception. "If you insist on taking up floor space, you might as well be useful. No one and nothing gets a free ride in this kitchen."

"Useful?" He rolled the word around on his tongue like he was chewing a handful of burnt popcorn.

"You could start by making the coffee." She pushed the French press in his direction.

He frowned, and the muscles in her shoulders squeezed tight.

Now she'd done it.

He hummed low in the back of his throat until it reached the tips of her toes. "I'll make you a deal."

"Deal?" She managed a half breath, pretty sure she wasn't going to like what he was about to say.

"You let me come for coffee every morning —"

She opened her mouth to say that he already did, but he shook his finger and silenced her with a quick "Uh-uh."

"All right. You get coffee, and . . ."

"And you get an assistant."

Caden couldn't hold back the snort that leapt out.

Adam clearly got the absurdity of his offer — after all, sous chefs studied for years — and he quickly amended his offer. "I mean, I can carry things, reach the top shelves" — he stretched to show off his vertical range — "and taste things."

"For sure." But he had a point. If he was helping her out around the kitchen, maybe she could get him to join her outside the kitchen. Around some of the island's best haunts. Seeing and experiencing her favorite parts of her homeland.

She sucked in her bottom lip and narrowed her gaze onto his too innocent expression.

"Really," he said. "I'll do nearly anything for a guarantee of good coffee. Every morning."

Uncrossing arms she hadn't even realized she'd crossed, Caden gave a slow nod, even though it made her stomach squirm. This was probably a terrible idea. She shouldn't be putting the travel writer to work — but how else could she do what Marie had asked? "And if I need help carrying donuts to church after breakfast?"

"For a donut, I'm your guy." He reached to shake her outstretched hand, but she snapped it back before his warmth became tangible.

"That wasn't our deal. We said for a cup of French press joe every morning, you'd do whatever I asked."

His raised brows and bugging eyes were almost comical as he huffed an incredulous chuckle. "I don't think I mentioned anything about doing whatever you said. I said I would give you a hand in the kitchen in exchange for *cups* — plural — of coffee. But if you throw in an extra muffin, donut, or cinnamon roll every day, I could probably make myself available for *most* situations."

"That's an awful lot of qualifiers."

He nodded. "But it's a fair deal." The sparkle in his eye said that even *he* didn't believe that was true.

Pursing her lips to the side, she eyed his hand, which he held at the ready to seal their agreement. Maybe this wasn't such a great idea. Adam was clearly getting the better half of the bargain.

After all, she'd run this kitchen by herself for almost two and a half seasons. She didn't actually need him.

Still, this might be the only way to talk him out of the inn and under clear blue skies and dancing pine trees.

"One carafe of French press every morning, and you have to share with me. And an extra sweet roll to go. After breakfast." Her gaze darted to the dining room door to make sure that no one overheard. "And you can't tell the other guests."

"Deal." He pumped her hand before she'd even lifted it from her side, his skin warm and rough, callused. Strange. She'd assumed that the plush life of a travel writer didn't involve much heavy lifting. Maybe his baggage was heavier than she'd guessed.

When the kettle whistled, he dropped her hand and flew into action, measuring coffee grounds and setting them to percolate. That was the extent of his help until she found a decidedly less rumpled Adam on the front porch five hours later.

He sat in one of the wooden Adirondack chairs, his shoulders hunched as he poured over that little leather notebook he'd pulled out of his pocket during their first meeting. With the stub of a dull pencil, he underlined and circled a word, but she couldn't read the tiny script from over his shoulder.

"You ready to help me carry donuts over to the church?"

He jumped to his feet, slamming his book closed and stuffing it in his back pocket. His face twisted with something unrecognizable, but he wiped it clear before she could study it, leaving her to wonder what he was hiding in that little book. "Absolutely."

In the kitchen she stacked three pink boxes in his arms and took two of her own.

Inhaling the cinnamon and sugar goodness, he let a slow smile creep into place. "These belong in a church because they smell like heaven."

Caden let out a belly laugh as she held open the back door. But he nodded for her to go out first. "I bet you use that line on all the donuts."

"Just the ones that are holy."

She nearly tripped down the steps, her groan mixing with his laughter. "That was terrible."

"I know." But his deep chuckle didn't sound at all apologetic.

She led the way between the bakery and the Lions Club, and as they passed Aretha's Antiques and a slew of familiar cars, she nodded. "That's Aretha and Jack's store. Jack opened the Red Door a little over two years ago."

"That's not very long ago. Why'd he sell it to Marie and Seth?"

"He didn't. He gave it to them."

Questions flashed in his eyes, his forehead wrinkling, but they'd already reached their destination.

The green lawn of the white-steepled First Community Church beckoned to them, large, leafy trees practically begging for someone to take advantage of their cool shadows. Caden slipped into a shady patch, dancing away from Adam for three steps, but he didn't seem to notice. Those questions that had been in his eyes had settled into the corners of his mouth, screwing it up in thought.

Just as she opened her mouth to ask what he was thinking, she spied a sports car in the parking lot. Everything ostentatious and sparkling in the midmorning sun, the bright blue car stood out like a horse in a chicken coop.

People in Rustico didn't drive zippy little cars like that. They weren't practical in the winter, even less so during the working season.

But it was somehow familiar. She'd seen it before. Or heard about it, maybe.

A strange rock settled in the bottom of her stomach, and Caden hugged her donut boxes even tighter. It wasn't dread exactly. More like a liberal dose of caution wrapped around uncertainty.

"Nice car."

She couldn't tell if he was talking about the make, model, or V8 engine certainly under the hood. Swallowing the lump that was looking for purchase in the back of her throat, she nodded. "Then again, anything beats being carless for the summer."

He stepped right into her jab. "I've been carless for a lot longer than the summer."

"You don't have a car?"

"Nope." He balanced his boxes, reached for the front door, and held it open, nodding for her to go first. "I've spent more nights on the road on assignment than I have in my own apartment the last three years."

"Really?" Except . . . actually, it made

sense. Travel writers had to travel, right?

She'd had her doubts about his identity, but maybe Marie had been right.

"When I came home a couple years ago, my car had completely given up. It wasn't worth it to pay for repairs, so I scrapped the old junker and make do with the subway."

They stepped into the church foyer, the dimness nearly blinding by comparison. She blinked quickly to get her bearings, but before she could take even a step toward the office, Father Chuck called out to her.

"Caden!" His voice carried from the stairs that led to the basement, joy lifting his words like a seagull on a stiff breeze. "And you've brought a friend."

"Father Chuck, this is Adam Jacobs. He's staying at the Red Door and offered to —"

Her voice cut off as a second set of footfalls climbed the stairs. Around Father Chuck's shoulder, a mass of perfectly coiffed honey-blonde hair peeked out. Wide violet eyes — which hadn't been that color when they were ten — blinked, and glossy rose lips twisted into the perfect facsimile of a smile.

The rock in Caden's stomach tripled in size, crushing everything inside her except the blood that rushed to her face and buzzed in her ears.

Father Chuck turned to his shadow with a wide grin. "Of course, you know Bethany Burke."

6

Adam reached for Caden's back as her face went ashen. His response was entirely reflex, and he dropped his hand before actually touching her, stopping where he could feel her warmth but not her body. She seemed stable enough on her feet. Giving her a little breathing room, he watched her face and plastered on a matching fake smile.

"Hello, Bethany." Caden's voice was hollow.

"Well, well. If it isn't Caden Holt." The willowy blonde eclipsed the stairs and reached for Caden's shoulders, tugging her into an awkward embrace around donut boxes and giving her a peck on each cheek. Her voice was pleasant but not too sweet. "I haven't seen you in ages."

The whole scene reeked of a performance. And as Bethany's huge eyes batted up at him over Caden's shoulder, Adam didn't know if the play was for his benefit or Father

Chuck's.

Caden stood stock-still, the muscles in her face taut, eyes wide and filled with something that looked an awful lot like fear. It tugged at his insides, and he wished he could whisk her to safety. But he was the newbie in this situation, and if he'd learned anything as a reporter, it was better to wait and observe than dive in headfirst.

"I didn't know you were still on the island. Of course, I should have guessed. You're still working at your dad's bakery, I see."

"Actually —"

"And who's your friend?" Bethany cut her off, dropping Caden like a limp fish, and turned to Adam, her full lips pursed, cheekbones pronounced. Long, full lashes beat an uneven tattoo, and he almost asked if she had something in her eye.

He hugged his boxes with one arm and held out his other hand. "Adam Jacobs."

She clasped his hand in both of hers. "Bethany Burke." Her gaze danced between him and Caden. "Caden and I are old friends. How do you know each other?"

If Caden's pinched features told the true tale, Bethany hadn't been much of a friend. Probably more of an arch nemesis. He'd had one of those in high school too.

Still, he couldn't seem to look away from

Bethany's glowing eyes, which met and held his with a boldness he hadn't seen yet on this island.

"I'm staying at Rose's Red Door Inn for the summer."

"Oh." Bethany's smile turned oddly knowing. "Of course." But he didn't know what she thought was so obvious. And he didn't have time to ask before Father Chuck stepped in, clapping him on the shoulder and steering the group toward the kitchen.

"Those donuts smell divine, Caden. Thank you again for volunteering to provide them for the morning fellowship time."

A touch of color returned to Caden's face, and she nodded with a genuine smile — warm and serene and the complete opposite of what she'd bestowed on Bethany. "Adam deserves credit for carrying the heavy boxes over."

He chuckled at the overstretched truth. "Hardly." With a shrug, he added, "And Caden gave me an extra one at breakfast this morning."

"Then you like sweets?" Bethany put her hand on his arm, too warm, too familiar, and he shrugged it off.

"I suppose. As much as the next guy."

Caden let out a soft snort — a sound he'd come to know in just a few days as uniquely hers, uniquely in response to him. It stirred in his chest, and he shot her a secret smile, which she returned with interest.

Bethany, completely oblivious, rattled on. "Oh, then you'll have to try my honey-glazed sticky buns next week. All the church families take turns bringing pastries. You *will* be here next week, won't you?"

"At church?" The last time he'd slipped inside a church had been for a meeting in the basement. It had been more than eight years since he'd been to church for anything other than AA.

"Of course, silly." Bethany's purr rubbed at his nerves.

And it had been at least twenty years since anyone had called him silly.

He didn't particularly like the moniker. But he kept his mouth closed, giving a halting nod in response.

Father Chuck ruffled his salt-and-pepper hair, shooting Adam a half smile and pointing into the narrow confines of the kitchen. "We're sure looking forward to these donuts tomorrow."

"I wish they could be fresh," Caden said. "But I don't have time in the morning to make breakfast at the inn and get the extras over here."

"No one ever complains about your offering." Father Chuck unloaded the boxes, stacking them next to the old white refrigerator that whirred its protest at being plugged in. With a conspiratorial wink, he added, "I think the attendance goes up when people know the breakfast is from you."

Pink swelled at Caden's throat, and she ducked her head with a quick shake.

Adam followed the rising line of her blush, but stopped at the small frown that pinched her lips. She seemed to doubt the pastor's words, even though there was no evidence to contradict him. In fact, Adam was thinking about visiting the church if only for another donut. Father Chuck's rationale wasn't far-fetched at all.

Bethany, apparently uneasy in the lingering silence, bubbled over to fill it. "Father Chuck and I were just discussing the annual lobster cook-off and fund-raiser. I'm helping my mom organize it this year."

"Oh?" Caden's head tilted up. "Did you move back to the Crick?"

Bethany's eyes turned genuinely sad, but somehow that emotion didn't match the words the followed. "Well, Mom and Dad are getting a little older, you know. There have been a few scares."

"I'm sorry to hear that." Caden looked truly apologetic.

Adam wasn't quite convinced by Bethany's story. He had a few more questions he wanted to ask. After all, Bethany hadn't actually said that her parents needed her help or that she'd returned to help them. Implications didn't cut it in his profession.

He'd had a few sources who spoke like that when he was working the metro news desk. He'd ask a direct question, and they'd give a response that didn't quite answer said question but still expected a return favor.

The problem with half-answers and side-stepping conversations was he couldn't write a story based on those. They only served to make him more curious.

But this was neither the time nor the place to grill Bethany Burke about whatever she was hiding. Instead, he retraced the conversation until he found something worth digging into.

"Lobster cook-off and fund-raiser?"

"Of course!" Bethany's hands jumped to her hips, and she turned a pointed stare on him. "Don't tell me you haven't heard of the famous North Shore Lobster Cook-Off."

"Afraid not."

Bethany shook her head and tsked Caden as though the queen of England was coming for a visit and Caden had forgotten to

111

wash the china. "It's only the best event on the island."

"Now, that might be stretching the truth a bit too far." Father Chuck leaned against the worn tiles on the counter, his feet stretched out to reach the opposite row of cabinet doors. "But it is a service to the community. Last year we raised enough to reroof a widow's house, help a family adopt an orphan, and start a scholarship program for local students."

"All with lobster?"

"Well, it's not just lobster." Bethany waved her arm as though encompassing the entire church and its grounds. "We have a lobster and mussel dinner, and everyone brings a side dish to share. We have a carnival and a ceilidh."

"A what? A kay-lee?"

Caden finally spoke up. "It's a traditional Irish community dance."

Adam's eyebrows must have reached his hairline for the laugh that Caden gave him. "We do it a little differently here. It's more of a show than an actual dance. There's a local family that plays traditional Irish jigs and step dances."

"And it's a kay-lee — like k-a—"

"Like c-e-i-l-i-d-h." Caden pointed to a flyer on the bulletin board across the hall from the kitchen, and he squinted at the announcement, which featured a picture of a fiddle and some colorful ribbons.

"How does that spell kay-lee?"

"It's Gaelic," Bethany tried to explain.

But Caden knew the best response. "We just go with it."

"Fair enough." He shrugged. "And when does this lobster extravaganza happen?"

"The second-to-last weekend in August. You'll still be here, won't you?"

It wasn't just Bethany's hopeful eyes staring up at him this time. His stomach rolled at the expectant look in Caden's baby blues. He was supposed to be here. Garrett expected him to be here.

Except he'd been plotting a way off of this island as soon as possible.

Find a story, write the article, and get back to real life. It was a simple plan, and if it actually worked, he'd be back to Washington long before anyone made a lobster quiche or presented him with a plate of the succulent meat.

Saying those words out loud proved harder than he expected as he glanced into the faces surrounding him. They wanted him here.

That was new.

The platoon he'd been assigned to wasn't

exactly thrilled to have him around. A civilian to keep an eye on, an extra mouth to feed, an extra cot in an already packed barracks.

Connor was the first guy in two assignments to befriend him.

And Adam had repaid him by sending him into a fireball.

Shaking his head to get his thoughts back into a safer zone, he managed one of the half-answers he so despised. "I do love lobster."

Bethany squealed and squeezed his bicep. "The cook-off is the best part, and this year, we're bringing in a celebrity chef from the mainland as one of the three judges. The two local judges are skilled in the kitchen too. All the local cooks bring their best lobster recipes, and the competition gets fierce. I've won it the last three years."

"And what does the winner win?"

"Bragging rights, of course. And a gift certificate from a local business. In fact, my mom — she's the president of the ladies' auxiliary — is organizing the event this year, and she asked me to help collect donations and plan the setup here at the church."

"So you'll give someone else a chance to win this year?" Father Chuck asked.

With furrowed brows, Bethany shook her

head. "Of course not. I'm already perfecting my recipe. It'll be my best yet."

Adam glanced at Caden, whose arms were crossed over her chest, her features pinched and impossible to read. "That doesn't seem fair."

Bethany snapped back as if he'd slapped her.

He scrambled to explain without sounding like a jerk. "I only mean, if your mom is in charge of the event, won't you have an advantage?"

She waved off his argument with long fingers and perfectly manicured fingernails sparkling in the overhead fluorescents. "It's a blind judging." Her gaze settled heavily on Caden. "So my only advantage is that I'm a better chef than everyone else in town."

Father Chuck's eyes bulged, and he raised a fist to his mouth to cover an airy cough.

Adam, too, had to conceal the smirk that insisted on showing up.

But Caden seemed stung by Bethany's careless words. Her cheeks paled and her mouth drew tight.

"Well then, perhaps Bethany and I should get back to juggling the details." Father Chuck ushered them out of the kitchen, Bethany leading the way and rattling on like an old Humvee.

"You're right. We have so much to put together." With a laser focus on her competition, she added, "And I still need to get some runner-up prizes. Do you think Rose's Red Door Inn would like to donate a free night's stay? It would be great marketing for them."

"I don't know," Caden said. "Maybe. You should ask Seth or Marie."

"Perfect. I'll stop by soon. I hope to see you there, Adam."

His skin crawling like he'd stepped in an anthill, he tried for a smile, but from the grin on Caden's face, he was afraid it came out as more of a grimace. "Maybe."

With an arm around Caden's waist, he swooped her out of there. When they reached the shade of the oak on the far side of the lawn, he let out a long sigh. "Is she always like that?"

"Bethany? Afraid so." Her lips remained tight, and he caught a glimmer of sadness in her eyes just before she said, "She's always gotten whatever she wants, and she doesn't know how not to." She remained silent for several steps before her wistful whisper carried on the wind. "Must be nice."

Adam nodded, not quite sure how to

respond to the flash of insecurity. But it didn't matter, as she caught his eye and gave a playful shrug. "And now you've invited her to the inn."

"That wasn't me. You're the one who told her to talk to Marie or Seth."

"But she could do that tomorrow at church. She's coming to the inn to see you."

She had a point, and no amount of his mock indignation was going to change that.

They fell into an easy rhythm, their steps matching the steady clapping of the waves on the far shore. They'd covered almost the entire distance back to the inn when she finally spoke again.

"So, you'll be at the lobster cook-off?"

He shrugged. "Apparently it's the only place to be that night. Are you going to enter?"

Forehead and nose wrinkling, she squinted at a distant mussel boat winding its way through the underwater farms. "I don't really have a choice."

She wasn't half-bad at half-answers, taunting his reporter's urge to dig deeper. But before he could ask his first question, she shot him an impish grin. "Now I have to get to work."

The following Monday Caden thought

about what Bethany had said the whole time she cleaned up the kitchen and set out the ingredients and utensils for her afternoon class.

But she was no closer to deciding on a recipe for the lobster cook-off than she had been at the beginning of the summer.

She'd been putting off making the decision, but if Bethany, a trained chef who — until her recent return to the island — had owned her own restaurant in Toronto, was working on her submission already, then Caden was a step or fourteen behind.

Even if the cook-off was seven weeks away.

She'd steadily earned second prize since grade ten. The first years, she'd lost to her grandmother, then her own father. Three years ago, she'd been primed to win. She had the most creative recipe, which her grandmother had helped her perfect, and her dad had decided not to enter.

It was going to be her year.

Until Bethany, fresh from a yearlong program at the Culinary Institute of Canada in Charlottetown, whipped back into town, stealing the blue ribbon and all the glory.

Caden hadn't managed to claim first place in the years since, always in Bethany's shadow.

The problem was, second place wouldn't

suffice this year. *This* summer the inn needed better. She had to do better.

A stomp on the back steps, followed by urgent voices almost too low to hear, signaled the arrival of five teenagers. One of the girls whispered, "You have to ask her."

Caden frowned. They weren't usually an inquisitive group. At least not about something that required hushed tones.

"No. Ford should do it."

"Why me? I'm a guy."

"Obviously."

Caden could picture any of the girls rolling her eyes in exasperation to go along with that snarky comment.

One of them managed a quick knock that sounded more like the screen door had caught the wind than a solid announcement. It was quickly followed by more frantic whispers that she couldn't distinguish.

What had these kids in such a spat? She'd been teaching them to cook some basic meals in the Red Door's kitchen twice a week for more than a month, and they'd never been quite so stirred up.

Caden wiped the furrow from her face. There was only one way to find out. "Come on in, guys. Close the door behind you."

Gretchen and Iris ducked into the kitchen,

followed quickly by sisters Whitney and Jeanie and the lone male attendee, Ford. He'd told his mom he wanted to learn how to cook, but Caden had a sneaking suspicion that he really wanted to stir up something sweet with Whitney.

"Hey, hey, Caden!" Ford bellowed his greeting, and Caden cringed, hoping the inn was empty save for the housekeeper, Judith. Though his voice carried, his eyes held a nudge of uncertainty. "What're we cooking up today?"

The five faces surrounding the kitchen island varied in age and appearance, but all held a distinct pinch of tension. "Everything all right?" Caden asked.

They nodded a little too enthusiastically, making her stomach twist. But when she started to ask again, Iris grabbed the recipe card in front of her. "Pumpkin spice pancakes?" she said, her dainty nose turning up.

"But we made waffles a couple weeks ago." This from Whitney, followed quickly by Ford's adamant grunt of agreement.

Caden nodded. "Then it's a good thing that you have to eat breakfast more than once a month."

Jeanie elbowed her older sister, who took the jabs — verbal and physical — with a smile. "I suppose."

When it was clear they didn't have the courage to ask her whatever it was they'd been squawking about on the back stoop, she set her pupils to work mixing the batter. Leaning over their shoulders, she corrected a mismeasurement by Ford — who was too busy watching his pretty redheaded neighbor to notice that he'd grabbed a three-quarter cup instead of a half cup — and pointed out a tiny eggshell in Gretchen's mixing bowl.

"Get your finger wet and stick it in near the shell." Caden demonstrated, removing the splinter on her fingertip to several open-mouthed expressions.

"That's like magic." All the girls giggled at Ford's words, but his eyebrows remained at full mast. "How'd you learn to do that, Caden?"

Without a pause, she said, "Like you said. It's magic, and a magician never reveals her secrets."

Again, laughter filled the room, over-whelming the obnoxious hum of the stand mixer that Caden had moved to the kitchen island so everyone could help.

When the mixture in the bowl was a bright orange color and smelled of cinnamon and ginger and all things autumn, Whitney and

Gretchen took turns scooping it into pancake form. The others worked up a cranberry compote topping in the saucepan over the open burner.

As Iris reached for the sugar, Jeanie poked her, following it up with a knowing glare. Iris shook her head, eyes darting at Caden.

There was definitely something going on, and it was making Caden feel like she'd taken a ride on a beater. But she wasn't sure if she wanted to know what had her kids wrapped up so tight.

Despite the ever-unspoken questions, the class went smoothly. In fact, they hadn't had such a drama-free class since she'd started them off with a simple grilled cheese and tomato soup more than a month before. It had been so simple that not even the most insecure cook could ruin it. Better to start off easy and build their confidence, she'd hoped. Now they moved around the kitchen with an ease that some of their moms couldn't even claim.

Her heart swelled as she patted Iris on the back.

"Good work. That smells amazing. Be sure to keep stirring so that it heats thoroughly but doesn't burn to the pan."

Iris nodded, but instead of turning back to the compote at hand, she cocked her head to the left and asked, "Is it true that Bethany Burke is back in town and going to beat you at the lobster cook-off?"

Caden grasped her apron, wiping her suddenly sweaty palms over the blue gingham fabric. Forcing what she hoped was a grin, she cleared her throat. "What makes you ask that?"

"Well, Ford's mom —" Iris tried to explain.

Whitney quickly cut in. "She's in the ladies' auxiliary with my mom and Mrs. Burke."

"And I saw Bethany at her dad's store," Gretchen chimed in.

Jeanie, the youngest of the lot, nodded silently, suddenly looking more ten than her fifteen. All of them fidgeted, shoving hands into pockets and rubbing the backs of their necks, eyes trained on the ground at their feet.

When the silence had hung in the air too long, Ford spoke in the softest voice she'd ever heard him use. "Is she going to beat you again?"

Caden's stomach churned as she looked into five concerned faces. They were genuinely worried about her chances. She was too, but that didn't mean she'd own up to it.

Sometimes she felt far removed from these young faces filled with hope and encouragement and no fear for the future. It felt like a generation since she'd been in their shoes.

But they were at most twelve years younger than her. She'd gone to school with many of their older siblings, sat in church pews next to their families, and cheered for them at holiday pageants. She'd babysat two of them and passed her paper route off to Ford's brother.

It was easy to feel far removed, but there was no such thing in North Rustico.

Caden couldn't tell if it was their concern or her own worry that made the backs of her eyes sting. She had to force herself to point to the gentle bubbles indicating the pancakes were ready for a flip. "Those'll get too crisp if you're not careful."

Whitney spun, flipped her pancakes, and turned back before spouting, "Ford's mom said that if Bethany wins the cook-off, the Sloanes —"

Gretchen interrupted, grabbing her friend's arm. "Don't!"

But that was like trying to unspill a cup of oil.

Caden swallowed against a sudden thickness in her throat, shuffling toward the door. She needed some fresh air and wasn't sure she wanted to know how Whitney was going to finish her thought. But nothing the teen said could be worse than the words that echoed through her own mind.

If Bethany wins the cook-off, the Sloanes will replace me.

She couldn't afford to come in second this year.

7

Adam scoured the inn for the third time before finally finding something of interest. And it had absolutely nothing to do with his story.

In the little notch of the front porch, where it wrapped around the side of the house and looked over the northern coast of the island, he discovered Esther and Levi, hand-in-hand in matching Adirondack chairs. Esther, her back to Adam, hovered over a number puzzle in a book spread across her lap, a pencil in her free hand tapping an easy tempo. Levi reclined, eyes closed, his breathing matching the rhythm of Esther's tap-tapping.

"Want to join us?"

Adam jumped at the low words. He'd been sure the old man had been lulled to sleep in the shade of the towering pine trees. Moreover, Adam hadn't made a sound as he approached the couple.

"Downright eerie, isn't it?" Esther joined the conversation without ever looking away from her game. "He used to do that to the kids too. Calling out to them when they tried to sneak in after curfew."

"A little something I picked up during the war." Finally Levi swiveled in his chair, looking over the rounded back with a pointed glance that dared Adam to ask the questions at the front of his mind.

But some reporter's instinct deep in his gut told him to wait. He hadn't earned the right to ask Levi anything at all. Especially not about his war experiences, which clearly hadn't been part of D-Day, the Battle of the Bulge, or the Siege of Dunkirk. Levi had purposefully phrased his response to sound like he'd fought during World War II, probably trying to see if Adam was paying attention.

He was.

Levi waited to see if Adam would take his bait and then asked, "How's your novel coming?"

"My novel?"

Esther gave up her puzzle for a moment, turning to face him as well. But her fingers never left those of her husband. "The one you finally have time to write."

Adam patted the journal tucked into his

back pocket. It was supposed to be filled with notes on Garrett's article. Except in the last few days he'd only found about half a page worth of information worth noting. The other new scribbles in there were mostly about the rolling tide, whispers in the pines, and one seagull frantic to unearth a discarded sugar cone. He'd stood completely transfixed for nearly fifteen minutes watching that ridiculous bird, rooting for it.

"I'm still not sure I have a novel to write." How could he write a hundred thousand words when he couldn't even manage to find fifteen hundred for a feature?

"Are you reading anything then?" Esther's pale brown eyes were nearly swallowed by the shadows surrounding them, but it couldn't dim their enthusiasm. "Levi loves those Clive Cussler books. The military thrillers."

"Those are good," Adam agreed.

Levi looked away but didn't disengage. "You spend some time in the service?"

"Not exactly." He shook his head. "More like with the service."

Esther's painted eyebrows peaked. "With?"

But her husband cut her off. "Embedded?"

Levi pounced on that much faster than

Adam intended, but he couldn't deny it now, so he gave a quick nod before realizing that the other man was still looking over the sea. "Yes."

"Where?"

There were a couple different answers to that one, and none of them were what Adam wanted to say. So he fell back on a half-answer. "Where the Marines are fighting."

Levi squinted back in his direction, his eyes so sharp that Adam worried the old man could see the truth written all over his face.

Clearing his throat and staring hard at the ground, he took a quick step back. "Good to see you both. I have to find Caden."

"How is your little friend?"

Adam didn't like the way Esther emphasized the word *your,* as though he was her only friend. Or more accurately, *she* was *his* only friend. He didn't want people talking about her, especially not the way Bethany had spoken about her, as though Caden wasn't even in the room. But then he thought he heard Esther follow up with something under her breath that sounded an awful lot like, "She's just about the sweetest thing I've ever seen."

He shrugged off the question with a mumbled, "Good. Fine. I guess. I promised

129

I'd help her with something." Which wasn't entirely untrue. He was her assistant now, so if she was around the inn, then he was required to pitch in. He just didn't know if she was around.

Levi didn't let him get more than two steps away. "Let me know if you want someone to bounce around ideas for your story."

"My story?" Adam paused, heat rushing to his neck, heart hammering. Levi was sharp, but had he already latched on to the story Adam was digging for?

"Your book."

"Right."

He sped off down the porch, sailed through the inn's moniker, and poked his head into the empty parlor. At the dining room entrance, he stopped short, letting the scent of pumpkin pie settle over him like a warm coat on a chilly fall evening. It didn't take much guessing to figure out that the smell was coming from the kitchen and his favorite little friend.

Flinging the door open, he said, "It smells like you're pumping Thanksgiving through the air ducts —"

His nose had been up in the air, thrilling at the tantalizing scents of mingling cranberries and spicy pumpkins, so when he noticed that not only was Caden nowhere in the kitchen but it was filled with five kids he'd never met, he froze in mid-stride.

Ten eyes blinked at him, five jaws hanging loose. They stared at him as though expecting him to make an introduction. But for the first time in his memory, he didn't have a word to say.

"Who are you?" It was the boy who spoke first. He wasn't rude exactly. It was more like his words dripped with suspicion, protection. But he wasn't a regular in the kitchen or around the inn. Adam would have noticed his gangly form loping around the grounds or down the harbor boardwalk.

"You're not supposed to be in here," the littlest one piped up. She was a full head of red hair shorter than her cohorts, but her stance said he'd regret it if he pressed her. "The kitchen is off-limits."

"What are *you* doing in here? This is Caden's kitchen."

"Right." The other redhead, who looked like a slightly older version of the feisty one, stepped forward. "And I don't think Caden would appreciate you being here. You should go before she comes back."

Something pricked at the back of his neck and he rubbed it absently, all the while glaring at the guardian teenagers, who seemed to think he was the one out of place. But he'd made a deal to have access to this room. These kids — whoever they were — didn't belong in the house, let alone the room that had become his post-nightmare sanctuary.

Finally he said, "I think I'll wait for her to get back."

Suddenly an acrid odor filled the room, and all six of them cringed at the same moment. The girl closest to the stove shrieked, "See what you made me do! The cranberries are ruined!"

"And the pancakes!"

The kids had one volume — loud — as they scurried around the stove top. The boy flipped what looked like a Cajun pancake, which added to the assault on his nose.

Adam was tempted to run, but Caden still hadn't reappeared, and he wasn't going to leave these hooligans to their own devices. With his luck, they'd burn down the whole house and eighty percent of his earthly possessions with it.

"Someone turn all the burners off."

The voice rang clear and steady from the side door, and every head in the room snapped toward Caden, who, head high, marched across the room and took control of the smoking pan. "Get me a glass bowl right now."

The little one seemed to pull a bowl out of thin air.

Caden made quick work of salvaging the tangy sauce, separating what she could from the cremated remains on the bottom. Setting the pan in the sink, she held up a hand when one of the girls moved to turn on the faucet. "It needs to cool a little bit first."

The girl nodded and backed away with quick steps.

Then Caden stacked the blackened pancakes on her flipper, tossing them in the trash with an economical motion.

"I thought I told you to keep stirring the compote" — her tone was sharp but not angry — "and to flip the pancakes before they burned."

"We were —"

"But he came in."

"He's not supposed to be here."

"Who is he?"

All the kids spoke at the same time, their arguments jumbling together as Caden's gaze swung to him, as though only then realizing Adam was there. Her eyes were wide and liquid and rimmed with red. Even her cheeks and the tip of her nose were flushed. It was more than just the burned breakfast, and he had the urge to slug whoever had made her look so unhappy.

"Are you okay?" He mouthed the words, and she seemed to understand, giving him a gentle nod. The tilt at the corner of her mouth suggested that she was happy he was there, so he took a firm step forward. All of the kids made a mirrored move back.

"Is he supposed to be here?" The little redhead wrinkled her nose, making the freckles disappear in her distaste.

Caden swung an arm wide to include him, her hand resting lightly on his forearm. It was maybe the first time she'd touched him for no particular reason, and it filled him with warmth. He stepped closer at her gentle tug.

"This is my friend Adam. He's helping me out in the kitchen this summer."

"Ohhhhh." The kids spoke as one, contrition sweeping across all of their faces.

"And he's a guest here."

Caden's simple statement seemed to suck all the air out of the room. Two of the girls hung their heads while another stared at the ceiling like it had received Michelangelo's brush.

But Adam understood. "They were only protecting your kitchen from an unknown intruder."

The boy nodded like it was the obvious

conclusion.

Shooting an unbelieving glance from Adam to the boy and back again, Caden pursed her lips and crossed her arms. "That was all?"

From the back of the pack: "And then the cranberries nearly caught on fire."

Everyone chuckled, and Caden relaxed, pointing to a cupboard above the sink. "Grab another plate. Adam can join us for what wasn't ruined."

No one had to ask him twice. Sliding into a spot next to Caden, he bumped her elbow with his, giving her a silent nod to make sure she was all right. Her smile was compensating for the pain in her eyes, but her dimple had yet to make an appearance, and like a kick to the shin, he realized he missed it.

With a wobbling grin, she waved him off, sawed into a pancake, and took a bite.

Sure. This wasn't the time or place to talk, so he followed her lead, devouring the slice of pumpkin heaven and asking for seconds and thirds.

Between mouthfuls, he asked the question that had never been answered. "So why are these guys here?"

"Caden's our teacher."

"She's teaching us to cook."

"Twice a week —"

"Summer school."

"My mom can't cook." This, of course, from the boy.

Again, it sounded more like a jumble of words thrown like spaghetti at the wall, but what stuck made a little bit of sense. Caden had opened her kitchen during the school break to pass her love of cooking to kids who might not have learned otherwise.

Sweet. And not just the rich berry sauce he kept shoveling in his mouth.

"Caden's the best cook on the island."

Her cheeks flushed again at the praise until one of the others chimed in.

"Until Bethany —"

The older redhead elbowed the one who had to be her sister into a silence so heavy it felt like breathing through wet cement.

Color drained from the girl's face, and Caden cleared her throat. "That'll be all for today. I'll see you on Thursday."

"But what about cleanup?"

"I'll take care of it this time."

The little one waved, and Caden nodded as they filed through the mudroom and out the back door. She stacked up the dirty dishes.

"Let me give you a hand," Adam offered.

"No."

He wanted to argue. After all, what good was an assistant who didn't do dishes? And there was definitely something deeper going on. Especially if it had to do with Bethany Burke.

But the immovable line of Caden's neck compelled him to agree. With a quick farewell, he slipped into the dining room and beyond.

Whatever Caden's story, it wasn't going to help him keep his job, but it was infinitely more interesting than the one that might.

"Have you talked to him today?" Marie's cheekbones stuck out as she pursed her lips, her hands stilling over a tray of yogurt parfaits.

"Of course I have." Caden had talked with Adam every morning of the nearly two weeks he'd been at the inn. But that wasn't exactly what Marie was asking about.

"You know what I mean. Have you talked with him about the inn and the article?"

Caden flinched. She'd known this was coming. After all this time, she had nothing but leftovers to show of her friendship with Adam. Marie thought Caden needed to press him harder.

Which meant she had to invite him out. Again.

The knots in her stomach joined her thudding heart, threatening to make her sick.

Marie didn't understand. She couldn't understand the memories, the reminders that Caden hadn't been part of the popular crowd. She hadn't been part of any crowd, actually.

In her small school, she'd been the painfully shy, awkward girl who'd rather spend the day with her mom's best friend, Aretha, than meet up with the other kids for a swim at the beach.

It wasn't until she'd reached high school that she'd even begun to come out of her shell, to begin to make friends. But then there had been Bethany. Bethany, who always had her life together. Bethany, who had thrived on pointing out Caden's faults.

And even though she knew that was all in the past, Bethany's return to the island and the pressure from Marie to win over Adam's pen made her feel eighteen again — uncertain and alone.

"Please, Caden. I need your help." Marie was pleading again, fear etching her words until some of them were barely louder than a breath. "You'll take him out. You'll talk us up."

She'd already agreed to. Now she just had to find the courage to ask. Again.

The morning meal prepped, Marie disappeared into her office, closing the door so she and Seth could talk. Until a couple weeks ago, Marie never closed the door to her office so she and Seth could be alone. If Marie's prodding wasn't enough, the hushed hallway reminded Caden that the situation was serious.

Running a hand through her hair after she pulled off her apron and hung it on the hook by the back door, she took a deep breath and tried to pray for courage. It amounted to little more than an appeal that Adam had left the inn.

As she stepped onto the front porch, she found the answer to her a prayer was a resounding no. Adam sat across from Levi, a game of checkers in play between them.

"Caden, dear." Esther greeted her with a hug, a hand on each shoulder, and a quick kiss to her cheek. Her lips were cool and soft. "Breakfast this morning — mmmmmm! So good!"

"I'm glad you liked it."

"Liked it?" Levi muttered from his rocking chair. "She hasn't stopped talking about it since she started eating it. Yammered the whole way through breakfast and practically swooned over that egg thingy."

"The salmon and goat cheese frittata?"

The Eisenbergs ignored her question as Esther swatted at her husband. "I did not talk the whole meal. Tell her, Adam."

Adam's gaze lifted from where he'd been studying his next move and shifted back and forth between the couple. Clearly deciding there was no right answer, he said simply, "Yes, ma'am."

Esther looked as though she might ruffle Adam's hair, which she'd probably done to a dozen grandkids. And Caden had a strange urge to run her fingers through his disheveled mane herself. It couldn't possibly be as soft as it looked.

Adam caught her gaze, and she felt her stomach drop, afraid he could read exactly what she was thinking.

"Are you going home now? Do you need someone to walk you?" Esther was nudging Adam out of his chair before she'd even finished asking the question.

"We're playing a game here," Levi grumbled. But his grumble for his wife was filled with amusement.

Caden quickly shook her head. "I'm all right. I don't need — I'm not going —" The lump in her throat settled on her voice box, and the words that she tried to say never made it past her lips.

Adam made it to his feet, his shoulders so

broad and his smile warm.

Her breaths came in shorter spurts, and the air was suddenly far too sparse.

Ask him. Just ask him.

She opened her mouth, but he beat her to it. "I've been beaten at checkers three times already today. I could stretch my legs. Anyone want to join me for a walk along the boardwalk?"

Levi made a move to stand, but Esther plopped a hand on his shoulder, holding him in place, her gaze squarely on Caden. "You go with him, bubbala."

She didn't know exactly what the word meant, but it was said with such endearment that Caden couldn't help but smile in response, which loosened the knot in her stomach a fraction.

Adam tipped his head as if to ask if she really wanted to go, and Caden shrugged like she hadn't been trying to ask him for the same thing.

"Sure you don't want to join us, Levi?"

He stared up at his wife and shook his head. "Apparently *I* don't want to go."

"All right, but I want a rematch tomorrow." Adam laughed as he led the way down the front steps. Caden trailed close behind him with a quick wave to the other guests.

Across the street and down another set of

steps, they reached the old wooden walkway, turning toward the small fishing village where the boards ended and the red clay met the rolling waves.

Caden tipped her head back, breathing in the warmth that caressed her face and inhaling the scent of grass and water and a hint of boat fuel. It smelled like home.

"You really like this place, don't you?"

"It was my favorite place in the world when I was a kid."

"You ever think about living somewhere else?" he said.

"Why?" He laughed out loud, but she was serious. "Have you ever been somewhere so beautiful, so peaceful, so soothing?"

He frowned. "I don't —"

She brushed his arm, which slowed him down. "Close your eyes and listen. Do you hear that?"

He gave her a sidelong look but did what she said. "Uh-huh."

"I've heard those waves my whole life. Every day. The same rhythm. It never changes." She paused to revel in the familiar. "When I was young, I tried to run away from home, but I only got as far as the beach right over there. I just sat on the shore, staring at the waves. I couldn't be somewhere without it."

"So what happened to your great escape?"

"Oh." She clucked at the memory. "My dad found me about thirty minutes later and made me go home and clean my room."

"Which was the reason you'd run away in the first place?"

"Yep."

They meandered in companionable silence for several minutes until he asked, "How did you end up at the Red Door?"

"Marie hired me. Before she owned it, actually. She talked Jack into taking a chance on me."

Adam squinted at her, his mind clearly trying to put the pieces together. "Jack . . . and Aretha? From the antique store?"

"Right. Jack and Seth were renovating the inn, and Marie came along to help put the finishing touches on it. She picked out all the antiques and created themes around them. She did a great job, don't you think?"

He shrugged. "Hadn't really noticed."

He hadn't? That seemed strange for a travel writer. What was he looking at if not the details? Maybe he was looking for a deeper story, one filled with human interest pieces. Well, the Red Door was dripping with those too.

"I mean, the old Underwood typewriter in my room is a nice touch."

"Marie and Seth used to write each other notes on it." Her voice dropped to a whisper. "I think that's how they fell in love."

Adam stopped at the end of the boardwalk and stretched out his arm to indicate she should cross the street first. "Really? So there's a piece of a love story in my room?"

"Who knows? That's an old typewriter. There could be a piece of a lot of love stories in your room."

He chuckled at that. "Does it still work?"

"Sometimes. The ribbon is wearing out, but you could get enough for a message in a bottle."

"So Marie and Seth fell in love while working on the inn?"

She nodded.

"Then how did they end up owning it?"

Caden stopped on the sand, staring across the water and following the path of a freighter gliding along the distant horizon. "There was an accident . . . well, a pipe burst, and the kitchen was destroyed. Jack couldn't afford to fix it, and he couldn't afford not to open. Marie saved the inn."

"So she was a partner."

"She was a friend."

His eyebrows pinched together, confusion filling his gray eyes, but he leaned in, definitely interested in the story. "She *gave*

144

Jack money to redo the kitchen?"
"And he gave her the inn."

8

After three days of internet searching, Adam had gained exactly one new piece of information. Marie Sloane was a common name.

There had to be a connection between Marie and the story he was supposed to find here. People didn't just give money away. Even to their friends. Even to family. Not the tens of thousands it would take to fix a destroyed kitchen.

But Caden had been sure that Marie saved the inn when it was at risk of never getting to open.

If she had that kind of money to pour into an untested inn far from the airport and PEI's biggest cities, then there was probably more of it. A lot more.

He just needed to follow the money.

A cop friend had told him that when leads started going dry, detectives followed the trail of cash. It always led to the perp.

Adam had found out early in his newspaper career that the same was true when hunting for a story. He just had to figure out where Marie's money was coming from. Then maybe he'd know why she had set out her shingle as an innkeeper on this tiny island.

He'd spent his spare time that week on the web, searching for a Marie Sloane with that kind of dough. But every one of the results he'd clicked through had been a dead end.

Even the website for Rose's Red Door Inn was a bust.

Seth and Marie Sloane welcome guests from around the world to Rose's Red Door Inn on Prince Edward Island's fabled north shore. Enjoy a break from the hustle and bustle of life on the Gentle Island.

We're a short drive away from exciting Maritime history and more than fifty active lighthouses, the inspiration for L. M. Montgomery's classic book, *Anne of Green Gables,* lush golf courses, and the rocky red cliffs that give this island a distinctive charm.

Every morning our executive chef prepares a three-course meal featuring local products, so you'll be ready to explore all

that Prince Edward Island has to offer.
    Won't you come for a visit?

Nothing useful there.

At least nothing that related to Marie.
Those rocky red cliffs sounded interesting,
but he didn't have time for that. Even if the
island never ceased to amaze him.

His gaze shot to his journal, where he'd
jotted a few more notes about his last walk
with Caden. The warmth of the summer
sun. The easy chug of the fishing boats. The
simple greeting she gave to every person
they passed.

The sum of these parts was more than
small-town living. There was a gentleness to
it. A peacefulness about it. Here, it wasn't
about forgetting. It was more about enjoying every moment. But in order to do that,
he couldn't think about the past, which had
become the only thing he did really well.

Of course, none of that was going to help
him keep his job.

Marie's money was his lead. Even if it was
a dry one.

The web search of her name had
drummed up a fistful of social media accounts, a hundred personal address listings,
and at least one natural healing clinic in

Australia. Clearly he needed to narrow his search.

Adding Prince Edward Island only gave him more Canada Page listings, which looked an awful lot like the white pages of his childhood. Strangely, even those people weren't actually on the island. Most were from Ontario or Nova Scotia.

Marie Sloane United States gave him nothing better.

He needed a city, a company, or at the very least a state. He needed a tip.

Pounding the delete button on his keyboard, he covered his face with his other hand. There had to be something out there. Pretty, rich girls didn't just appear.

Maybe he was going about this from the wrong angle. Maybe Seth held some answers. The tall man was relatively quiet, popping up around the house, always a hammer or wrench in his hand, an easy grin in place.

Seth Sloane brought an endless stream of doctors, lawyers, and one contractor. Opening up the image search, he scanned the page for a familiar face. But none of them seemed to match.

Scrubbing his chin with an open palm, Adam slammed his laptop closed and stored it back in his bag. He had to get more info from Caden.

It had been another restless night, another early morning. But with a glance at the clock, he decided it wasn't too early to make his trek to the kitchen.

"You outdid yourself today."

Caden finished wiping off the counter before turning toward Adam's voice. "You liked it?"

"I ate mine and half of Esther's."

She put her hands on her hips in mock indignation. "That woman spoils you, and you take advantage of it. I swear, she's going to offer to adopt you one of these days, and you're going to take her up on it."

He shrugged and kept his shoulder almost to his ear as he leaned his right arm against the doorjamb. "I probably would."

She laughed at that and pointed at her stand mixer. "Would you put that away for me?"

"No class today?"

"That's tomorrow. And we're making lemon chicken and wild rice. No need for a mixer for that."

After he transferred the equipment to the bottom shelf, he stood and caught her eye. There was a twinkle there that made her stomach twist in an all-too-familiar but not at all unwelcome motion. "Got any plans today?"

"What did you —"

Three solid thwaps on the back door cut her off, but she hadn't even taken a step toward the mudroom when a buttery voice rang out. "Hello!"

Pain stabbed through her temples. She knew that voice all too well.

Bethany's blonde head popped around the corner, her ponytail precisely messy and makeup and jewelry perfectly in place.

Caden rubbed below her eye, dislodging what was almost certainly the very last of her mascara. And the lip gloss she'd put on six hours earlier before leaving her house had been gone before she'd picked up fresh eggs from Justin's dairy. Her shirt clung to her back — and to all of the lumps she wished weren't there — from the sweat she'd worked up in the kitchen.

At her worst, Always Perfect Bethany put every other woman in town to shame.

Caden just made her look that much better.

"Oh, Adam! It's so good to see you again." Without an invitation to enter, Bethany strolled into the room and straight to Adam's side, resting her hand on his arm like they'd known each other forever.

Caden tasted copper, and she squeezed her hands harder at her waist. "We weren't expecting you today."

Bethany looked at Adam and rolled her eyes as though they shared a private joke. About Caden.

Her stomach pitched and her hands shook. Grabbing her hand towel, she wrung it until it couldn't take another twist.

Bethany's smile couldn't be any more fake. Still, she flashed it like a professional beauty queen, which she was — if they counted the Little Miss Lobster contest when they were eight. Bethany had worn a frilly white dress adorned with a lobster-shaped apron. Caden had worn a full-fledged lobster costume.

"I said I'd stop by." Her voice was so sweet it made Caden's teeth hurt.

But Adam liked sweets. A lot.

She held her breath, waiting for him to lean into the woman at his side. Instead he wriggled out from under Bethany's touch, putting an extra foot or two between them and keeping his hand up as a bit of a shield.

Caden's insides did a little dance of joy.

Bethany kept talking so she didn't have to address the minor slight. "I came by to talk with Marie and Seth. About the donation for the fund-raiser." She didn't bother giving anyone else a chance to interject. "I need to talk to them about a job too."

"A job?" Lights flashed in front of Caden's eyes as Whitney's words bounced around her brain like a broken video game, shooting off sparks wherever they landed.

"Sure." Bethany had the gall to act like her words were innocent. "I'm a chef without a kitchen. And just because I'm back in town to care for my parents doesn't mean I don't want to work. I'm looking for an executive chef position. I thought Seth might know of an opening."

Caden wanted to scream for Bethany to stay away from Seth and Marie, to stay away from the Red Door, *her* Red Door. This was her home, her kitchen, her safe place. And Bethany couldn't have it.

Except that wasn't entirely her decision.

A better-known chef might be a boon for the inn. Bethany could have contacts in Toronto that would help fill rooms.

But Marie wouldn't toss Caden out in favor of Bethany's connections. Would she?

A strange rock formed in her stomach. It wasn't entirely implausible. Marie was desperate to save the inn. They all were.

Despite a bubbling anger, Caden managed, "I think Marie is in the office."

Bethany wasn't paying any attention, her

eyes firmly on Adam. "Well, I didn't *just* stop by to see them."

Caden's anger changed form, turning to a searing jealousy.

"I have to go to a winery near the East Point, and I thought you might like to go with me, Adam," Bethany said. "It's a gorgeous area, and they have a lovely tasting room."

His eyes grew wide then nearly closed, filled with something that Caden could only call longing. It made her chest ache, and the towel in her hands gave a groan of agony. She quickly looked down, released the embroidered linen, and folded it onto the counter, preparing for the words she knew were coming.

Except they didn't.

The air was thick with unspoken words, and Caden looked up. Bethany leaned in and batted those ridiculously long lashes. Adam stood his ground, a war flickering from his knotted brow to his rapidly working jaw.

After thirty of the most painfully quiet seconds she'd ever witnessed, he squeezed his eyes closed, took a breath that stretched his chest, and shook his head. "I don't drink."

There was more to it than that, but Bethany didn't seem to know to be curious. She was too busy preening her hair to cover the rejection.

Caden almost laughed out loud. Bethany may have had everything else a girl could want, but she'd never learned how to take a rejection.

"Besides, I have plans with Caden."

"You do?"

"We do?"

The women's words overlapped, Caden's filled with confusion and Bethany's with displeasure.

Adam nodded. "We were just deciding where we're going when you came in." Bethany's look of disbelief couldn't derail him. "The north shore, right? Where the red cliffs and rocky shoreline are."

Apparently Adam had done his homework. That was one of the most striking beaches on the island. It didn't sing like the sand at Basin Head or ripple like the shorelines near Summerside. But its monstrous sandstone cliffs bled traditional PEI to Caden.

"Right. The beach. I forgot."

Adam gave her a silent thank-you, while Bethany just looked confused.

"I guess I could go to the beach today," she said.

No one invited you.

Caden chomped into her tongue to keep the words in her mind from finding voice.

"We wouldn't dream of keeping you from the winery. And you haven't talked with Marie about the donation yet." Adam extended his arm behind Bethany and, without ever touching her, ushered her out the door and down the hall to the office. "We'll see you later."

"At the lobster dinner."

"Sure."

"And sooner?"

Adam swung the hall door closed, Bethany's voice disappearing on the other side of it. Her steps echoed on the hardwood until two raps on the door at the end of the hall were followed by the squeak of hinges and hushed voices.

"So, ready to go?" he asked.

"You were serious?"

His teeth shone, perfect and straight, and sent a pang she couldn't explain to the center of her chest. "Absolutely."

"All right. But I have to make a quick stop first. Well, two, actually."

Caden ducked into her house, quickly changed from her everyday work uniform — a black T-shirt and dark jeans — into

156

hiking shorts and sneakers, and grabbed a bag from the fridge as she hurried back out the door to meet Adam. He stood on her step, peeking through the window like he was curious about what was inside, but she closed the door behind her with a solid thud. She didn't have very many guests, especially not men. And she didn't particularly want to know what he thought of her tiny one-bedroom cottage.

Well, that wasn't quite right. She just didn't want to see his frown in response to her meager abode.

Holding up her bag, she stepped past him. "I need to drop this off for Aretha."

"Of the antique shop. And Jack."

"That's right." She shot him a congratulatory smile. "She's been sick, so I made her some soup and biscuits."

"Biscuits? What kind of biscuits?"

"The kind that aren't for you."

He laughed, falling into step beside her as they reached her garage, a separate structure with an old padlock door. Except she never locked it. "It's a few minutes over to the beach, so hop in."

It was barely a two-minute drive to Aretha's house, but as she pulled onto the street, she recognized four of the cars parked out front. Aretha had company.

Including Caden's mother.

"I'll just pop in. I'll be right back," she said, eager not to have to introduce him to a houseful of curious women. Adam moved to unbuckle his seatbelt, but she waved him off. "Really. It'll take me less than a minute. Stay put."

But when she got to the door, Adam was by her side with a wide smile that made her stomach sink. "I want to meet the famous Aretha and Jack."

There was no time to push him back to the car as the inside door opened, leaving only a thin screen barrier. Aretha's white hair flashed in the sun, her ever-present curls in perfect form. "Caden, honey. We weren't expecting you."

Holding the bag out in front of her, she said, "I didn't realize you'd be busy. Mom said you weren't feeling well, so I brought you and Jack some seafood chowder."

"How sweet." The woman, whom she'd called Aunt Aretha as a child, pushed open the screen. "Come in. It's just the auxiliary. And bring your friend."

"No, that's okay. We're just dropping this off. We have to go."

Aretha gave her a don't-argue-with-me frown, and there was nothing to be done but follow.

Caden mouthed "Sorry" over her shoulder as she ducked into Aretha's dim living room. Every seat in the room — including three kitchen chairs that had been brought in for the occasion — was taken by a woman, most of them gray-haired and well retired. Caden caught her mom's eye and smiled as the room fell quiet.

Aretha took the lead, reaching to take Adam's hand. "Aretha Franklin. No relation to the singer."

Adam's deep laugh filled the lingering silence, his eyes sparkling with the humor that everyone knew when the pale, petite woman introduced herself that way. "Adam Jacobs. It's very nice to finally meet you." His grip nearly swallowed the frail bones and thin skin of the woman's hand, but he never flexed his forearm, letting her go with a gentle release.

"Oh, don't tell me Caden's been talking about me."

"I'm afraid so, ma'am."

Pale eyes settled on Caden, and she squirmed like she'd been caught skipping school. But there was humor in Aretha's gaze and a touch of a smile falling into place.

"Only good things," Caden quickly added. "I promise."

"That's true," he said.

No one spoke for several long seconds, and the weight of eight sets of eyes on her — clearly wondering exactly who Adam Jacobs was — turned suffocating. She swallowed the lump in her throat, wishing for all she was worth that she could put her hands in her pockets and stand in front of a roomful of women with the same poise Adam had. His grin charmed all the ladies of the auxiliary. Mrs. Fieldstone even patted her bouffant and gave him a wink.

Finally the woman next to her mom leaned over. "Is that your nephew from Halifax, Glenda?"

"No." Her mom's frown seemed a mixture of confusion and astonishment with a pinch of hope. "We haven't met."

Every eye in the room opened wider, every mouth hung slack, and Caden could see the wheels turning, trying to identify the handsome island visitor. The too-handsome-for-Caden visitor.

Her mom jumped up, suddenly remembering the etiquette she'd hammered into Caden all those years. "I'm Glenda Holt."

Adam shook her hand, his smile growing even wider. "Of course. Caden's mom. I should have known. You both have the most vivid blue eyes."

Glenda's neck turned pink, and she ducked her head.

"Adam Jacobs."

The very house seemed to hold its breath, waiting for a reveal of his identity.

"Adam is staying at the inn for the summer," Caden said.

Everyone exhaled at the same moment, and a community giggle released the last touch of tension. "Of course." They didn't say it, but it was spoken on every face. *That makes more sense.*

Amid the tittering, Caden thought she heard, "He looks more like my Bethany's type anyway."

It was true. But it didn't stop the sting of the words, which settled on her like a wicked sunburn.

Only Aretha's knowing eyes seemed to see beyond the unexpected duo. Her gaze shifted from Adam to Caden and back, each volley assessing and measuring. Finally she gave a decided nod. "Welcome to the island."

"Thank you, ma'am."

"Oh, it's Aretha or nothing."

"Yes — Aretha."

Glenda reached for Caden's hand, which still held the paper bag. "Will you stay for tea and scones?"

Adam's entire posture changed, his shoulders snapping and neck alert.

"No." She cut off his next question, entirely certain it would be about the type of scones. "We have to go." Caden pushed the bag into Aretha's embrace. "Here. You should refrigerate it."

"Thank you, dear." Aretha kissed her cheek.

Caden reached for Adam's arm and towed him out of the room and away from the wagging tongues that suddenly had enough fodder to keep them going for the rest of the afternoon.

When they were back in the car and on the way to the national park, Adam finally spoke. "They're . . ."

"I know." She plastered a smile in place, hoping it would cover any bitterness that tried to sneak out. All of those women, save her mom and Aretha, thought no one but her cousin would want to spend time with her. They thought she was a lost cause destined to end up an old maid in her hometown.

But that wasn't true.

Well, she might end up the spinster aunt, but she was far from lost, and she was certainly no one's charity case. After all, Adam had asked her to go to the beach.

Not the other way around.

Even if it had been to get away from Bethany.

They entered the park, driving along the two-lane road that felt like someone had paved it and promptly forgotten about it. Even the Confederation Trail, a trans-provincial bike path, was deserted. A few cabins tucked in the tall grass on the land side of the road were the only indication of civilization.

Caden pulled into a small alcove, parked, and led the way down a sandy incline. At the bottom she looked to the left. In that direction the beach was beautiful but unre-markable save for a wall of red sandstone.

"That's pretty amazing."

"You haven't seen anything." She spun him around, and his jaw dropped.

A red carpet of rocks spread as far as they could see, blue waves rolling into the ones that had dared to fall in the water's terri-tory. Some rocks were small, others larger than her car. Beyond them a red finger plunged into the sea, its sheer cliffs drop-ping thirty meters straight down.

"Whoa."

She couldn't have said it better herself, and she took off for the outlet, jumping a trickle of water fighting its way through red sand to the ocean.

Behind her, Adam called out, "That's freezing!"

He'd stooped to put his hand in the stream and was frantically flinging it around to dry it off.

"The gulf water is warmer."

"How do you know?"

"I grew up swimming on this beach."

He splashed a wave as it rolled out, then ran as another tide chased him inland. "You're right. The water's nice."

"It's shallow here. All around the island, actually, so the water is much warmer than most of the Atlantic."

He marched on, stopping every ten steps to pick up an unusual shell or poke at a beached jellyfish. The wind whipped his shirt around his waist, and when he jumped onto a giant rock, he made a pirate's pose, turning his face into the wind and drinking in the salty air.

"A guy could get used to this."

She stopped at the base of his conquest and put her hands on her hips. "Don't you have beaches where you're from?"

"Tennessee? No. We have ponds and lakes and rivers. And the beaches in Maryland . . . well, they're crowded and touristy and completely the opposite of this place."

"What about when you travel? Haven't you seen deserted shores like this?"

His gaze stayed on the horizon, and his voice took on a faraway wonder. "Caden, there's nothing like this in the world."

She didn't have anything to add, so she let him soak it in, sending up a simple prayer that he'd write about it, that he'd find a way to do it justice in his article.

At length, he reached down to her. "Come on up. This is an amazing view."

She stared at his hand, his fingers solid and welcoming. Rubbing her hands together, she paused. She didn't have to go up there. And even if she chose to, she could make it up by herself. The rock had three natural steps, worn smooth from hundreds of years of wind and salt spray.

"Come on."

Eyes trained on his face, she slipped her hand into his, and he wrapped it in a firm but gentle grip. It was protective yet confident in her ability as she climbed the rock.

When she was finally by his side, he smiled. "Are you going to tell me what was going on earlier at the inn?"

"Which part?" She immediately knew what he was asking about, but she didn't have a ready answer.

"The part where Bethany was blatantly

fishing for your job."

"Oh, you noticed that?"

His laugh spurted, tickling her like gentle fingers even though he'd let go of her hand. "I would have had to be on another planet to miss that."

"Right." She let out a long breath. He wanted to know the truth. She wanted to know his too. "Maybe first you'll tell me why you don't drink."

9

Adam dropped his gaze to Caden's feet — anything to keep from watching her eyes.

"You noticed that?"

"It wasn't exactly other-planet obvious, but yeah, I noticed."

He rubbed the back of his bent neck, trying to massage away the knot that had settled right between his shoulders. But it only twisted tighter as the silence dragged on.

This was his own fault. He'd opened the door for her. He shouldn't be surprised that she'd walked through it. But it didn't mean he was eager to divulge all of his secrets.

Still, she wasn't going to give him answers unless he gave her a few of his own. It was the same with Levi, who held his left arm and the numbers tattooed there close to the vest. But with every shared meal, game of checkers, and walk around the inn, Adam got closer to those secrets, to that story.

A slice of his history might coax Caden into sharing a slice of her own — something beyond the glimpse of insecurity she'd shown him in the past.

And he was interested in a slice of just about anything Caden wanted to offer.

"Did you want to go to the winery with Bethany?"

"Yes." She frowned, so he pressed on. "Well, I wanted to go to the winery anyway." His clarification earned him a half smile.

"I could see it on your face when she asked."

"And you thought I wanted to spend time with Bethany?"

"A little bit, but I hoped not."

Her blatant honesty was like the sun shining on his soul, warm, comforting. "It had nothing to do with her, and everything to do with —"

"Having a drink."

He nodded. "You know the feeling?"

"No. I've never liked the taste. Not beer or wine or the hard stuff. None of it. But when I was growing up, one of the girls in my class, her dad liked it. Too much."

He bit the inside of his cheek and crossed his arms over his stomach, hoping that someone who had never known the wrenching pull of alcohol wouldn't think less of someone who did. "I can relate."

"But you're so . . ."

"Sober? Handsome? Addicted to coffee?"

Her chuckle was a pity laugh at best. "I was going to say young."

"Oh, alcohol is an equal-opportunity thug. It sucked me in at twenty-one."

Her forehead wrinkled, and she pulled on her left ear. Squinting eyes seemed to be trying to picture him that young, that stupid, but she was clearly coming up short.

"I was in a fraternity at the University of Tennessee. We were supposed to be about community service and civic responsibility. We were actually about seeing who could drink more than the other brothers and then laughing when he fell down the stairs, too wasted to walk."

She cringed, and he felt it at his very core.

And he hadn't even told her the worst of it. That was a bigger slice than she needed. Or wanted.

"Not my finest moments. In fact, ninety percent of my regrets are from my last two years at school. I went to a lot of parties, woke up with a lot of hangovers, and skipped a lot of class."

"How did you ever graduate?"

"I was always a pretty good writer, and that last year was mostly journalism classes and articles for the student paper. Somehow I managed to get to class enough to pass, but I'm pretty sure I was drunk the whole time I wrote my senior thesis."

He'd intended to shock her, but instead of surprise her face was filled with compassion. She clearly didn't understand.

"I was a fairly high-functioning drunk, but there was always a can in my hand and a bottle on my nightstand."

"Why?"

He looked away, following the outlet that jutted into the ocean, and tried to find the words to explain. "I thought it would help me get through the stress of school and work and finding a job in the real world. And then it was just easy. It felt good." And it would make him feel good again.

He wiped a hand down his face. He hadn't been searching the table by his bed in the hazy space between awake and asleep as often this week. But right now, as he spoke about why he'd been persistently drunk, he craved the relief burning down his throat, its fingers slipping through his chest until every part of him relaxed. Until his brain numbed and eventually forgot.

He needed to get to a meeting.

"But you don't drink anymore?"

"No." *Please don't ask me why.*

"Why?" A gust of wind picked up her hair, whipping it around her head, and she wrestled the short locks back into place, tucked behind her ears. "How bad did it get?"

There was no half-answer to that question. The truth was too terrible to speak aloud. He'd give anything to be able to forget the day of the funeral. But of all the memories that alcohol had stolen, that wasn't one of them.

"Bad."

She waited for him to go on, and he met her gaze, silently begging her to change the subject. But she held him rapt with those blue sapphires, nodding at him as though she could get him to keep going through her own force of will.

Finally she whispered, "The kids I'm teaching think Seth and Marie are going to replace me with Bethany."

"What?" Adam sputtered for air, trying to keep up with the hairpin turn. "They wouldn't. They love you. You're an amazing chef."

"That's sweet. But I'm not professionally trained, and I've never run my own restaurant. I have a stable of breakfast recipes, but Bethany could open an all-day restaurant out of the Red Door's kitchen. It wouldn't have to be just for guests, and . . ." She definitely had more to say, but she seemed to struggle to find the right words. Opening and closing her mouth twice, she crossed her arms and hunched against the breeze kicking up from the water. Finally she sighed. "I'm afraid I might not be the chef the inn needs."

Sadness rang through her voice, twisting his heart with it.

He could relate. He'd spent his whole career certain of one thing — his ability to write the story. And a little more than a month ago, that had been stolen in one explosion. Caden worried that she couldn't produce what the Sloanes needed from her. He knew he couldn't produce what his editor demanded.

"I'm pretty sure Bethany is going to suggest that Seth hire her instead. And it makes sense. From a business perspective, it could be good revenue."

"But those kids in your class, they seem to love you." It was hard to tell if the glow on her face came from thoughts of her students or the perfect angle of the sun. "Why would they think you'd be replaced?"

"Because their parents do."

"Does everyone know everything about each other in this town?"

"Pretty much." She flashed a sad smile at him. "It's not so bad until you're the one everyone wants to get rid of and you can literally feel the weight of every gaze on your back as you're singing in church."

"That's why I usually prefer being drunk in a church."

He'd meant it as a bad joke, but she latched on to something in his tone, cocking her head to the side and studying his face. She could see right into his heart, and he desperately needed shutters to keep her at a safer distance.

Slowly, thoughtfully, she nodded. "You were drunk in church? Is that why you stopped drinking?"

Such an honest question deserved an equally honest answer. But getting the word out was harder than he'd thought it would be. "Yes."

At a light touch on his forearm, he glanced down. She pressed her hand there, willing some sort of strength into him, a spark traveling right to his heart. Squeezing his eyes shut, he opened his mouth and tried not to think about the words that flowed out so quickly.

"It was my parents' funeral. Eight years ago. I'd won — well, they were coming to visit me at school. There was an accident. It was raining and a truck swerved into their lane." He wrinkled his nose and rubbed at his forehead as the scene played out in his mind again. "I couldn't face their funeral without a six-pack. I just couldn't.

"I was late getting there, and the minister had already started the eulogy. So I stumbled down the aisle and tripped over my Great-Aunt Muriel into the family pew. My brother sat next to me, practically steaming. He was so mad at me. Before the wake, he pulled me aside and got right in my face and told me to get sober or get out."

Her hand squeezed his arm, but she didn't look away. And she didn't say anything.

"I deserved much worse. He should have disowned me — well, he sort of did."

"But you were . . . what? Twenty-two?"

He nodded. "I was stupid and immature, but I disrespected my parents and every person who showed up to honor their memory. That isn't an easy thing to forgive."

"Have you talked to your brother about it?"

"We haven't spoken since."

She looked uncertain for a moment and then threaded her arms around his waist, yanking him into a hug both unexpected and healing. Frozen for a moment, he reveled in the simple joy of being held. As a man in an inflexible career, he didn't get hugged very often, except by women who wanted more, offered more.

But there was no doubt about Caden. She offered only comfort and a friendship that he hadn't even known he needed.

Wrapping his arms around her shoulders, he rested a cheek on the top of her head and inhaled the fresh scent of the surf that clung to her, underpinned with the ever-present cinnamon and nutmeg.

A strand of hair escaped from behind her ear, dancing on the wind, and he reached for it, tucking it back into place. As he dragged his thumb along the edge of her ear, her body grew tense. Suddenly she jerked away and clambered over the edge of the rock, dropping five feet to the sand below.

"We should probably go."

She practically ran to the car.

The next week Caden set out the ingredients for a highly unusual Monday afternoon class.

Gone were the typical recipe cards outlining one meal. Instead there was a pile of cards — every recipe different, every one featuring lobster.

Marie knocked on the door frame like she

needed permission to enter her own kitchen. "What's on the menu today?"

"Nothing exactly." Caden unpacked another bag of groceries.

"That's a lot of food for nothing."

Caden looked at the counter heavy with packages and chuckled. Pasta and rice. Cheese and Kane Dairy eggs. Bread and flour. Sugar and spices. A hundred staples filled every available surface of the tile counter from sink to fridge.

"Mark Crowder offered me a couple lobsters from his last catch, so I thought we'd do a little experimenting today. See what the kids might want to enter in the lobster cook-off."

"They're all entering?"

Caden nodded. "It was part of the deal when we started. It's a final exam of sorts."

Marie's lips twisted, like she was fighting hard to keep a smile at bay. "You ever worry they might beat you?"

Her pulse skittered, a strange weight settling on her chest. "Not until right now."

"I was kidding. You've got this in the bag."

"You think so?"

"This is your year, Caden. You know it, and the whole town knows it. You're going to put the inn on the map." Marie crossed her arms over her chest. "What are you going to make?"

She ducked her head, shifting a box of elbow pasta to the back of the counter and pulling three red potatoes to the forefront. "I'm not sure. I haven't thought about it too much."

That wasn't exactly the truth. Actually, it was more of a bald-faced lie.

She'd spent every night of the last week wide awake, staring at the ceiling and trying to figure out what would beat Bethany. She could go traditional with a straight-up lobster tail and butter, but the judges — especially the guest celebrity chef — would expect something more exciting. Menu items like lobster macaroni and cheese were overdone. She'd seen a recipe for a lobster paella recently. That was unusual and exotic. But it seemed to miss the heart of the island, and the guest judge would certainly be looking for that.

Caden's lobster corn chowder had been a hit with Aretha and Jack, if the usually quiet man's profuse praise was to be believed. He'd sought her out at the grocery store a few days before, his footsteps following hers up and down the aisles until he finally tapped her shoulder. "That soup."

For a long moment she thought that was all he would say, his gaze falling to the basket in his hand and staying there. So she gave him a little nudge. "Which soup?"

"The chowder."

"Oh, did you like it?"

He nodded quickly. "Had two bowls myself. I was so full Aretha nearly had to roll me to bed, but it was worth every bite. So creamy, so rich. And those biscuits. Never had anything like those cheesy garlic biscuits before."

She didn't have the heart to tell him that they were a knock-off of the biscuits served at a large seafood chain. Of course, she'd tweaked the recipe over the years, adding a dash of paprika and replacing the garlic powder with fresh garlic.

"I'm glad you liked them, Jack."

"I almost asked Aretha if she'd ask you to teach her how to make them. But it would hurt her feelings."

Caden's cheeks blazed. "Aretha is a lovely cook. I learned a lot in her kitchen."

"Of course. I know I'm a lucky man." He winked at her, the love for his wife clear in his eyes.

"Next time I make a batch, I'll be sure to save a few for you."

"You're a sweetheart." He winked again and then disappeared around the end of an aisle.

Her lobster corn chowder and biscuits never disappointed. But Bethany had won with a seafood chowder two years before. If the judges remembered — and Bethany was sure to remind them — she'd lose points on originality.

"Well, you should start." Marie's voice made Caden jump, dragging her mind back to the present. "Thinking about what you're going to make, that is. When Bethany was here the other day, she sounded like she'd already decided."

"Oh?" Caden tried to sound nonchalant despite the rapid and immediate increase in her heart rate. She failed miserably. The real question of the hour bounced around her mind like a fly trying to escape through a closed window.

Did she try to talk you into dumping me and hiring her?

"She said she's been practicing with her recipe, mixing it up. And she's looking forward to impressing the guest judge."

"Any idea who it is?" Again she tried for nonchalance, a casual question. Again she failed. Her face felt too tight, like she'd fallen asleep on a sunny beach. Her palms grew damp as her fists tightened to match the clamp around her lungs.

Marie shook her head. "She only said they

were going after a chef from Toronto. Apparently he owns a handful of restaurants that cater to the upper crust. It sounds like he might be working on a TV show too."

"So what you're saying is, he's way out of my league." And her chances of impressing him were less than none.

"Our league." Marie walked across the room and purposefully bumped into Caden's side.

Except they weren't exactly from the same small town. Marie's life in Boston had been defined by the elite. Before she escaped to PEI, she'd dined at the best restaurants and picked out her wardrobe at Fashion Week. Her summer home had been bigger than the Red Door, and her future had been guaranteed.

"You forget that I know where you came from."

Marie conceded the point with a simple nod. "But this is my league now."

"What else did Bethany say?" The question popped out before it was fully formed in her mind, and she immediately wanted to pluck it from where it hung over them.

"Not much."

Marie didn't seem to think anything of the question, and Caden clamped her mouth closed to keep from asking what she really wanted to know. Had Bethany asked for her job?

"She asked for a donation for the fund-raiser."

"Oh?" That was old news.

"We're going to give away a two-night stay." She nudged Caden with her elbow. "The bids will be flocking in if only for the food."

Caden gave an obligatory laugh just as footsteps pounded up the stairs and the screen door squeaked.

"Ready for us?" Ford asked before he made it out of the mudroom.

"Always."

The kids filed in like troops for inspection, backs straight and chins high. At least there were no pointed elbows and urgent whispers today. They all greeted Marie with a quiet, "Hi, Mrs. Sloane."

Marie wasn't much older than Caden — only a few years — which prompted the question, why didn't they call her Miss Holt?

Then again, Marie was from away. Caden had known this group too long for formality.

"Looks like you're going to have a fun class today," Marie said. "I'll leave you to it."

"What're we making?"

Caden waved to Marie before giving the group a pointed look. "That, Whitney, is entirely up to you."

Five matching frowns appeared, clearly for different reasons.

"Why does Whitney get to pick?" Jeanie shot her sister a hard glare.

Whitney quickly agreed. "I don't want to pick."

"Where's Adam? Will he be here this afternoon?"

"I think we should make waffles again," Ford mumbled. In response to several curious stares, he rolled his eyes and heaved a great sigh. "I tried to make them for my parents on Sunday. They tasted like socks."

Caden couldn't hold back her laughter and waved her arms to silence all the chatter. "Calm down." Pointing a finger and a direct gaze at Whitney, she said, "You are choosing what *you* are making." Then she turned to Ford and repeated the phrase. And again and again until she completed the circle.

Her pronouncement was met with narrowed eyes and one tiny voice. "So we're all making something different?"

"Exactly. You've got to start thinking about what you're going to make for the lobster cook-off."

"Do we really have to enter?"

"Yes."

Ford shrugged. "It's not like we're gonna win."

"If entering was about winning . . . well, you all know I've never won. Does that mean I shouldn't enter?"

"But at least you have a chance." Gretchen twirled one of her chestnut curls around a finger. "You're good."

"And you will be too. It takes practice. And experience. And when I'm too blind to read my recipe cards anymore or too weak to lift a lobster quiche out of the oven, I expect you all will still be winning the cook-off."

"Ditto."

They all spun toward the deep voice coming from the dining room. Adam stepped in, his grin easy and making every girl in the room titter as much as their mothers and grandmothers had at Aretha's.

"Do you mind if I steal your teacher for a minute?"

Caden's stomach dropped straight to her shoes, and her heart hiccupped as he pointed into the other room.

This was no big deal. He just needed to talk with her.

Her throat went dry, clearly disagreeing.

Really. This was nothing unusual. They talked all the time. In fact, they had talked a dozen times since the beach. Just the two of them. Alone in the kitchen. Before the rest of the inn woke up. That morning they'd even made plans to visit the East Point Lighthouse the next afternoon.

But this was different. This time he had singled her out while she was busy. He was pulling her from her responsibilities to talk with him. This was important.

Like maybe he was going to put his arms around her. Again. And she'd be able to hear the quickening of his heart beneath her ear. The smooth cotton of his simple gray T-shirt against her cheek.

Except, he wasn't going to hug her. Definitely not. Or touch her hair. Or stare at her mouth with that crooked little grin on his own.

Or make her want him to be her first kiss more than she wanted to save her job.

Oh, Lord. She needed some help and a good reality check.

Even if he did try — which he definitely wasn't going to — she'd probably take off at a dead sprint.

Again.

She'd been doing such a good job of not

thinking about him or their walk on the beach. Or the way he smelled like sunshine and aftershave. It was so much easier to focus on Bethany and the inn and helping Marie. But suddenly, as she came face-to-face with an intentional moment alone, her nerves packed up their bags and took off for parts unknown.

Beating her head against the kitchen counter sounded less painful than walking into the dining room with him, but with five pairs of eyes trained on her every move, she could do nothing but point at the stack of recipe cards. "Look through those, and when I get back, we'll start cooking."

Adam swung the door closed behind her, leaning in until her heart stopped. His wide shoulders blocked her view of anything else, and she stumbled back into the slate-blue wall, catching herself on flat hands at her sides.

"Are you okay? You look really pale."

Terrific. She was dreaming about kissing him. He thought she looked like a wilted carnation. "I'm good. It was just warm in there."

"Good." He stabbed a hand through his hair and looked over his shoulder. "Listen, I know we made plans for tomorrow. But I can't make it."

"Sure. Of course. Yeah. You have plans and stuff." Her right arm flapped in front of her, and his eyes followed it in confusion.

"No. I . . ." He sighed and rubbed his middle knuckle beneath the tip of his chin. The clench of his jaw made a muscle jump, and suddenly he wasn't the only one concerned.

"Adam, what's going on? Are you okay?" She reached for him but yanked her hand back at the first sign of warmth.

He clamped his lips closed until they nearly disappeared, then squeezed his eyes closed in a matching move. "I'm fine. I hate breaking plans with you, but there's a meeting tomorrow, and I need to be there."

"A meeting?"

"An AA meeting."

"Oh." It popped out before she had time to figure out how she was supposed to respond. "I mean . . . um . . ." She tried to name whatever she was feeling and compare it to the feelings she was supposed to have. But it was all new. She'd never been ditched for AA. Cuter girls and bigger parties? Sure. But after what he'd confided to her on the rock, she knew this wasn't a brush-off. He needed some encouragement from people who understood the struggle. In the end, she only offered another "Oh."

The muscle in his jaw relaxed a fraction. "Don't have a lot of friends going to meetings?"

"Actually, you're definitely the first." She pressed her palm harder against the wall at her back. "But it's no big deal. We'll make it to the lighthouse another time."

"Are you sure?"

"For sure."

He nodded a quick thanks. "I'll see you in the morning anyway."

She watched him walk away before returning to the kitchen, wishing she had something that could help him. Wishing she knew how to tell him how much she needed him to write about the Red Door. But she didn't. For now, she only had a kitchen full of expectant students.

"All right. Everyone have your recipes picked out?"

They waved white cards.

"What are you going to make for the cook-off?" Whitney asked.

"That's a secret." One she was going to have to figure out. Soon.

10

After breakfast the next morning, Adam bounded down the inn's front steps, rubbing damp palms down his cargo shorts. Just as he reached the walkway, he heard a familiar voice.

"Where you going in such a hurry?" Levi asked.

Adam tipped his head down the road, beyond the three-way stop. "Going for a walk."

"Mind if I join you?"

"Not at all."

The older man's knees creaked as he eased down the steps, clinging to the white rail and finally meeting Adam on the grass. Adam had to consciously slow his pace to stay even with Levi's ambling gate, but he was quickly glad he did.

Levi took careful steps, watching his path as though expecting a vine to reach out and wrap around his ankle. "I took a little spill getting off the subway a couple years ago."

Adam had a sneaking suspicion that *little spill* was code for a nasty tumble, but he didn't interrupt the slow words filling in the gaps.

"Esther got all riled up and made me see my doctor."

Adam conjured a very clear, very amusing mental picture of Esther up in arms over her husband's health, and it made him smile. Her hands had probably fluttered furiously, her face pulled tight as she waggled a finger in a poor doctor's face. "You fix him. You hear me? You fix my husband."

He kept his humor in check, instead giving Levi a nod of encouragement.

"Some little girl who was younger than my granddaughter said I'd chipped a bone in my hip. Ha!" His step over an uneven patch of concrete was a little more cautious than his I'll-show-them speech suggested, and Adam reached out, ready to catch Levi if he stumbled. "Doc told me I had to stay off it for a month, and then if it hadn't healed, she was going to do surgery."

"So did you? Stay off it?"

"For about a week."

That sounded about right. It would seem this man wouldn't be kept down.

"Did you have to have the surgery?"

189

"Nah." His Brooklyn accent hung a little heavier on his single syllables. "She thought I was a pushover, but there's more to me than meets the eye."

It was true. Levi wasn't particularly tall or broad. If Adam had to wager a guess, he'd bet that Levi had spent a few of his formative years literally starving in a Nazi work camp. Maybe he would have been a bigger man if he'd grown when he was supposed to.

But he had a spirit that made Adam forget his stature.

"Esther has me watching every step, threatening to put me in a home if I break a hip for real." She would do it, and they both knew it.

When they reached the intersection at the end of the harbor road, Adam pointed to the left. "I'm headed to the church."

"Figured." Levi's eyes flickered with a knowing that made Adam want to bolt. "Me too."

"You're going to the meeting?" He hadn't meant to sound so shocked, but he couldn't keep his tone in line. The man had survived a maniac who tried to eliminate his entire race. But he'd succumbed to the siren song of a bottle?

"Don't look so surprised, boy." Levi hiked

up his trousers, a throwback to the sixties and a time when men wore suits to the office, despite the bright sun and low breeze. "We've all got a few secrets, don't you know?"

"Sure. I know. I just didn't think that someone like . . ."

"Like me? What do you think I am?" His pale brown eyes glowed amber as his wide mouth pulled into a tight line.

Adam searched for the right words. "I think you probably have a pretty incredible story, and I wouldn't pretend to know it."

Levi nodded. "Good." Pursing his lips like he'd sucked a bad lemon, he squinted toward the white steeple in the distance. "I left Hungary in 1946, an angry, angry orphan. Barely eleven, I was sent to live with my uncle's family in Brooklyn. And when there's that much anger in a boy, he has but three options. Forgiveness, the bottle, or death. I chose the bottle."

Adam let out a long breath. He had a hunch what the meeting leaders would say. *What's in the bottom of a bottle can't change the past, and it can only ruin the future.*

But what he really wanted to know was how long it took to drink that pain away.

Maybe, if he knew the pain would ebb, it might be worth it to go back, to give up eight years sober for the hope of relief.

"Problem was, no matter how much I drank, I still remembered."

The problem was, Adam hadn't started drinking to forget. It had started as a social activity, but it had numbed his ability to deal with reality. When he quit, he discovered he didn't know how to handle the tough stuff. He didn't want to handle it.

As they reached the church lawn, its green grass rolled out like a red carpet, Adam stopped. "What exactly did you remember?"

Levi clapped him on the back, his hand surprisingly firm. "All of it."

With that he swung open the front door of the church and stepped into the cool interior.

Adam followed him in, craving the reminder that the booze wouldn't heal the pain or turn off the nightmares. He was going to have to figure out another way to deal with that.

His career was counting on it.

That Sunday Adam found himself back inside the First Community Church of Rustico. This time sitting in the last pew on the right as women in bright floral dresses swept down the aisle, herding children both big and small into the right rows.

It had occurred to him early that morning — between the orange fireball and a double cup of coffee — that the entire community congregated at the church every week. What better place to fill in some holes?

Not to mention Father Chuck had said something at the meeting on Tuesday that had been poking him like a cactus in his shorts. "When you have trouble believing, surround yourself with people who don't."

Adam wasn't so sure what he believed anymore. It had been easy when he was a kid. His mother's faith had been enough to sweep him along, carrying him to safety in her current. She never doubted, never faltered. Her every step had been true and right in his young eyes. She'd believed in grace and faith and most of all love.

But without her, he wasn't so sure he could believe in those things.

He wanted to.

Who didn't want to believe that forgiveness could be given, even to the undeserving? That no one was beyond grace?

But the steps he'd learned in meetings said he had to make amends for his actions. Except there was nothing he could do to make his mistakes right. He couldn't bring Connor back or ease a family's grief.

Adam had sat in another pew not unlike

the one beneath him now. In a small Boston chapel overflowing with active and retired men in uniform, he'd watched Connor's mom hug a folded American flag as tears poured down her cheeks. His little sister had held onto her dad's hand until her knuckles were white and her arms shook.

There were no amends for that kind of pain.

So there was no forgiveness.

But he wanted to believe that there could be.

So he'd followed the ones who did.

As though his thoughts had conjured her, Caden stepped into the sanctuary. Her gaze landed on him immediately, a warmth filling her face as she wove her way to him.

"Adam? I didn't expect to see you here."

It felt strange to stay seated while she stood, so he joined her. "You know how it is. This town is downright lonely on Sunday mornings if you're not at church."

She looked around his shoulder at the otherwise empty pew. "Are you sitting with someone?"

Before he could respond, Aretha Franklin joined them, slipping an arm around Caden's waist and hugging her side. Only then did he realize Caden too was wearing the unofficial church uniform, a flowing dress covered in pink and yellow daisies. It stopped at her sweetly dimpled knees, and he couldn't help but sneak a look at the rest of her legs, which were gently tanned, probably from their walk on the beach and a hundred others. He liked that she liked being outdoors.

But he quickly glanced away. He had no right to be looking at her legs.

Especially under Aretha's watchful eye.

In a church.

Instead he focused on the dimple in Caden's cheek that was equal parts surprise and pleasure.

"It's good to see you again, Adam." Aretha held out her hand, her skin nearly translucent.

He accepted it in a gentle shake, wondering if he should bow and kiss it instead.

"You can't sit all the way back here."

He looked over his shoulder, half expecting to see a reserved sign on the seats. "I can't?"

"You can sit with Caden and her family."

"I can?"

Caden let out a little snort — *his* snort. "Come on." She led the way to the third pew from the front on the left and pointed out the members of her family in quick succession. Mrs. Holt he'd met at the ladies' thing at Aretha's house. Mr. Holt was a burly man with a fair beard and intense eyes. Adam caught Dillon's name but missed his wife's and lost track of the kids after the second of five.

He'd never been so happy to hear piano music, his cue to sit down without having to remember any names. Caden slid into the pew, and he slipped in beside her. She held the hymnal but didn't seem to need it, closing her eyes and lifting her face toward the wooden cross at the front of the sanctuary as she sang every word in a clear alto.

He didn't try to sing along, simply enjoying Caden's voice as it harmonized with the others.

After four verses of three different hymns, Father Chuck took the podium and read from the book of Ecclesiastes. "Two are better than one, because they have a good return for their labor: If either of them falls down, one can help the other up. But pity anyone who falls and has no one to help them up."

Father Chuck ran a hand through his salt-and-pepper hair before launching into a passionate sermon about the importance of friendship. While the pastor's eyes roamed the room, Adam couldn't help but feel a surge when they landed on him, like this message was meant for him, like the minister knew that his words at the meeting would propel Adam to this service, this pew, this seat.

Pity anyone who falls and has no one to help them up.

It wasn't the fall to be pitied but the isolation.

Adam hadn't been exactly alone since his fall. There had been a million interviews with his military handlers. Then, of course, Garrett had given him a shove to get back in the game. But they weren't his friends. They were business associates who needed to solve his fall so that it didn't reflect poorly on them.

None of them wanted to help him up.

Except maybe . . .

Hoping Father Chuck wasn't looking right then, Adam risked a glance toward his elbow and discovered not only Caden but also the youngest Holt, snuggled onto her lap. Caden rubbed a hand absently down her niece's arm, both of their faces focused at the pulpit.

Caden.

She'd become his friend.

Somewhere in the last four weeks, he'd failed to notice how much he'd come to look forward to their mornings and sometimes afternoons. She'd listened when he unloaded a story he didn't even know he needed to share. And then she'd done the only thing she knew to. She'd held him. And she'd encouraged him to go to a meeting, no judgment or censure in her voice.

Adam smiled back at Father Chuck. If this sermon was intended to help him realize the unexpected friendship of this trip, then it had succeeded.

He was still contemplating that as he listened to the rest of the church sing a final hymn. When they filed out at the benediction, he felt a tiny hand slip into his. Jerking his head down so fast that his neck popped, he discovered the little Holt ambling at his side. She couldn't be more than three or four, and her giant blue eyes stared back up at him. "Mom says I can't leave without my big person."

"And I'm your big person?"

"Uh-huh." She tugged on his hand, winding her way through the crowd and dragging him along behind.

His eyes darted around, searching out someone who was actually responsible for her. As they burst into the sunlight, he caught sight of Caden two steps behind them.

The girl tugged for freedom. "Can I go

play? Please!"

"Stay under the tree." Caden grabbed the sweater that the girl shrugged off as she bolted for a group of kids about her own age. "Violet likes you."

"Really? She doesn't even know me."

"Like that's important." Caden sniffed. "Violet has a very defined set of criteria for her big person, and when we were singing the last song she said she thought you'd do."

"I'm . . . honored?" Adam chuckled. "And what are my responsibilities as Violet's big person?"

But there was no time to find out as Mr. and Mrs. Holt joined them, followed shortly by Mrs. Burke, her grin ear to ear. "Have you heard all the talk about Bethany's cakes for fellowship time this morning?"

Actually, no.

But she wasn't looking for a response.

"She got up at five thirty this morning to make *fresh* mini cherry Bundt cakes. They were gone almost as soon as she delivered them. People have been talking about them all morning."

"I'm sure they were delicious." Mr. Holt crossed his arms over his chest, but he didn't look entirely convinced. And the man had taught Caden much of what he knew, so Adam was inclined to agree with him.

Still, Adam couldn't take his eyes off Caden, who looked like she'd taken a foul ball to the stomach. Shoulders drooping, arms wrapped around her middle, she stared hard at her sandals.

The weight of Mrs. Burke's gaze fell heavy on him. Her words from the week before echoed somewhere deep inside him, stinging his chest and making his stomach roll. *He looks more like my Bethany's type anyway.*

Well, he didn't know what Bethany's type was.

But he did know that she wasn't *his* type. He'd always preferred women with warm smiles, and a dimple or two never hurt. He liked them kind and thoughtful, the type who would drop off chicken soup to a sick neighbor or drive all the way across town to help a friend move. That wasn't Bethany's shtick. No matter how her mom tried to play her up.

"We'll be sure to try one next time." Aretha's arrival to their little group seemed to be Mrs. Burke's signal to leave, and she swept away with a curt nod and flippant wave to her fellow auxiliary ladies.

Aretha slipped an arm around Caden's shoulders and gave her the squeeze Adam wished he could. It wasn't easy to show concern in this element. Everyone treated

Caden like she was some sort of tour guide for the poor reporter from the States. He couldn't tell if they pitied her — for what, he had no idea — or him for being stuck with her. But they didn't get it. He'd had more fun with Caden than he had since college.

He really wanted to pull each of those old biddies aside and remind them what common courtesy looked like. They spoke about Caden like she wasn't even present, like she wasn't part of their community. How quickly they'd forgotten that a few weeks before she'd cooked for an inn full of guests and then made seven dozen donuts for their church.

Not a single donut had come home. He knew. He'd asked.

They were quick to accept her gifts.

And just as quick to forget who gave them.

Caden wasn't going to remind them. That would just get the tongues wagging and make her the center of attention, something she clearly didn't want. He didn't really want it either. But he was like a new toy. Curiosity had them buzzing around him for the moment. It wouldn't last.

With a wink and another squeeze, Aretha said, "I heard those little cakes went so fast because Bethany only made two dozen of them."

Mr. Holt grunted.

"And Josie said they tasted like the cherries came from the Boston States."

Adam's ears were piqued at the unfamiliar phrase, especially after his recent stop there. "Boston States?"

"Oh, hon, my granddad and his friends all used to call the United States the Boston States. And some of us old-timers still haven't kicked the habit. I forget that Marie is the only one around here actually from Boston."

The hair on the back of his neck jumped to attention, and he shoved his hands in his pockets to keep from rubbing them together. "Marie is from Boston?"

"Sure is. But we love her anyway."

His stomach flipped and his mind began to race. Was it just a coincidence that he'd been sent to an inn run by a woman from Boston, Connor's hometown?

Garrett didn't do coincidences.

Neither did Adam.

Connor was somehow connected to Marie Sloane. He would bet his career on it.

11

Adam politely declined Aretha's lunch invitation, offering an excuse about meeting work deadlines and rushing to the inn.

As soon as he returned to his room at the Red Door, he closed the door and flipped open his laptop. His fingers were stiff and awkward as he typed *Marie Sloane Boston* into the search engine. He held completely still for the two-thirds of a second that it took to return pages and pages of absolutely useless drivel.

Releasing a sigh, he stared at line after line of social media accounts, an article from the *Los Angeles Times* about a Ruth Marie Sloane, and too many obituaries to count.

He covered his face with his hands and pinched his eyes closed against a tiny drum beating inside his temple.

It stung his brain, like a sword piercing the lobe behind his right eye.

He'd found Marie's city, but the information wasn't falling into place like he'd expected it to. He was missing something.

Or forgetting it.

He gasped at the sudden realization. Garrett had given him Marie's full name. Adam had called her by it that first day on the back stoop. But he'd been so jet-lagged that he hadn't thought about why no one else called her that.

What was it? What was it?

Biting the end of his tongue, he flipped through his journal, the pages blurring and words all running together. There. Stabbing a finger against a page, he wrenched the book open and skimmed the contents.

Marie Carrington Sloane.

He hadn't heard that name since his first day in North Rustico, and then only because he'd used it.

He quickly typed in Marie's maiden name plus Boston and hit the search button.

And then he fell back on the pile of pillows cushioning the headboard, a long, slow breath finally finding its release.

Eight of the ten results on the first page couldn't have been more obvious if they had a blinking neon sign around them. All of them pointed to a page on the Carrington Commercial Real Estate site, so he clicked through to the first. A press release about the newest addition to the Carrington team.

MARIE CARRINGTON TO JOIN CARRINGTON COMMERCIAL

Boston commercial land developer and philanthropist Elliot Carrington is proud to announce that his daughter, Marie Carrington, is joining the Carrington Commercial Real Estate team. A recent MBA graduate of the Wharton School at the University of Pennsylvania, she is tasked with expanding the growing company's public outreach and community service.

"We're a family-owned, family-oriented business, and I could not be more pleased to have my daughter in the new role of director of marketing and development," says Mr. Carrington. "Her youth and energy will add a fresh perspective to our ever-evolving industry."

Adam's skin crawled at the condescending words. Elliot Carrington wasn't the kind to give a hoot about family-owned, family-oriented anything. Real estate magnates rarely did. But the press release served to remind readers of his philanthropy and made him appear a loving and devoted dad.

If that was the case, why had Marie left

her dad's company to run an inn? And Caden had said Marie arrived in North Rustico when Jack still owned the inn. It couldn't have all been rainbows and chocolate cake.

Adam moved on to the second search result, this one a quote from Marie in a *Boston Herald* story about a Carrington condo unit that had been slated for construction in an area that had quite recently held a low-income housing development.

"We're pleased to announce the development of Harbor Sights Condominiums, which will undoubtedly add prestige, revenue, and appeal to the community."

She sounded a little bit too much like Elliot Carrington for Adam's taste. In fact, he'd bet good money that the elder Carrington had fed Marie that line for their sales and marketing packet. Money and pride. That's what the community leaders wanted. And that's what Elliot had given them.

He'd also bet that no one had asked the low-income housing tenants what they wanted.

The article was almost four years old. The low-rent homes had long since been demolished, replaced by too-rich condos filled with residents who endlessly touted their "urban" living arrangements.

This wasn't the story Garrett wanted. The one he'd almost certainly sent Adam to find.

So he kept digging, every link sending him deeper into Elliot Carrington's business dealings. Every press release reeked of smarm. Every announced agreement set a clear pattern of stomping on the little guy, each a twist to the vise on his insides.

The Carrington name had plenty of money, and it wasn't a far stretch to think Marie had used some of it to open the Red Door.

But then what?

The trail and his story ran dry after that.

Besides, Marie had been removed from the Carrington Commercial website, her former position now filled by a guy whose picture showed him with too much grease in his hair and not enough teeth in his smile.

Marie hadn't been active in the company in well over two years. But that didn't guarantee the connection had been severed. After all, Elliot was still her father. Maybe she was still a part of it.

Garrett knew.

He'd known about all of it.

Which meant this island exercise was both a trial and a test.

Pass it and keep his job. Fail and . . .

Well, that wasn't even an option.

He set his laptop aside, leaned his elbows on his knees, and perched on the edge of his bed. Resting his face in his hands, he closed his eyes and tried not to remember how it used to be.

The old Adam never failed to find the story.

The Adam before the explosion kept digging. He wasn't afraid of hurting someone. He didn't even know he wielded that kind of power.

But now he knew. And he wasn't sure he could hold life and death in his words again.

He hadn't known when he turned in his last article what would come of it. It hadn't been anything unusual. Two months into a three-month stint with his Marine unit, he had finally found his rhythm and his steady sources. They were unofficial, of course. The grunts couldn't speak for the unit or the military, but Connor O'Dwyer and his translator, Aamir, had made Adam feel as welcome as a man with no military training could be.

Adam wasn't part of the brotherhood. How could he be, an outsider with an agenda and a deadline?

Still, on a stifling spring day in a mountain range whose name Adam could never spell right on the first try, Connor had tossed him a tub of Nutella and a spoon. "Help yourself."

"Seriously?"

"Sure. Just try to save some of it for the guys on their way back in."

It was just a bud of friendship, but it was enough to lead to a shared meal and then another. Once, Adam asked Connor what it was really like out there — beyond the makeshift walls. Strapping on his flak jacket, Connor had smirked, his Boston Irish freckles crinkling together. "You'd never make it out there. You're too soft."

Aamir was the only native Adam had met in person, a gentle soul in a Shaquille O'Neal body. His shoulders didn't look like they'd fit in the Humvee as it barreled out of the compound, but he'd squeezed in beside his handler, refusing to be cowed by the terrorist leaders, who threatened all translators.

It was Adam's third article from the field, and he had a special feeling about it. Certainly nothing as big as a Pulitzer. But it was a good piece. A sharp commentary on the translators who served alongside the American military, the risks they took from their own countrymen.

It wasn't a celebrated job. Or a safe one.

When local terrorist leaders suspected that

one of Aamir's friends had helped the Americans, the man's dad had been assaulted, his sisters threatened.

So when the article was done, Adam had kept Aamir's name as far from the piece as he could.

The world wasn't as big as it used to be, and he'd been hyperaware that an online article in *America Today* could make it to the Middle East as fast as it could to the White House.

Garrett had confirmed receipt of the article and an accompanying picture from another independent photojournalist. The article ran. Nothing happened, except for a few pats on the back from superior officers who had read it. "Good stuff," the captain who looked like George Patton growled.

And then just a week later, Adam had been cleared to accompany Connor's squad on a harmless patrol. They weren't hunting out insurgents or searching for IEDs. They were going to visit a cooperative informant.

They had said it would be safe.

The orange fireball flashed on the back of Adam's eyelids.

Always the image of Connor and Aamir walking into that mud home. Then the explosion.

Adam pressed his fists against his cheeks,

fighting the burning at the back of his eyes and sniffing against the itch in his nose at the memory.

In an instant Connor had been gone, and Mrs. O'Dwyer had had nothing to bury, no marker to remember her youngest boy.

"He loved this old church," she had said at the memorial service, the tip of her nose red and her pale eyes hollow. "When he was a boy, he'd run away from home when I told him to do his chores." The stained glass windows of St. Cassian's Chapel echoed a roomful of polite chuckles. "But I always knew where to find him. Daydreaming on the back pew in this very room. I think he'd like to know some other kid had a safe place to run to now."

She'd donated a memorial bench to the hundred-year-old church for other runaways. But when Adam had sat on the smooth wooden pew, he'd felt more lost than ever.

He was supposed to make amends for his sins. But nothing could atone for robbing Mrs. O'Dwyer of seeing her son fulfill his dreams.

Adam pinched his nose and sniffed hard against the emotion clogging his throat and pounding at his temples.

Either Garrett was a master puppeteer or

211

he knew Adam better than he knew his own kids. If Garrett had known of Marie's connection to Boston, had he also known that Adam's only connection to the city was Connor O'Dwyer? And that that tenuous link was more than enough to pique Adam's interest in Carrington's business?

Likely.

And he probably knew a lot more.

Picking up his phone, Adam called his editor's desk. It was a Sunday afternoon, but there was still a paper to put out. Garrett would be there.

His fingers drummed against his knee, and he cleared his throat twice before the third ring.

"De Root."

"Jacobs." He matched Garrett's harried clip, only a note of irony in his voice.

"Well, well, if it isn't the prodigal reporter."

Adam could almost see the old editor leaning back in his chair, hands stacked behind his head, one ankle crossed over the other knee. The posture always an open invitation to chat.

"I don't think I qualify as a prodigal if I didn't want to leave."

"Point taken, kid." Garrett chuckled. "What's on your mind?"

"Boston."

There was a long pause, and Adam imagined a slow smile working its way across the usually sullen face. "Anything in particular about Boston?"

"You know what about Boston." He ran a hand over his chin before digging his fingers into his hair. "Carrington Commercial."

"So you figured out the connection." Garrett sounded more grouchy editor than satisfied uncle, but the words still filled Adam with a hint of pride.

"That is why you sent me here, isn't it?"

"Perhaps."

Adam tugged on his hair, wishing he could see the other man's face and gauge just how much information he might be able to get out of him.

"Why Boston? Why Carrington's daughter?"

"Why not?"

Wrinkling his nose, he sighed. "Have you always been this cryptic?"

"Probably. Can't remember. Old age and all that."

Adam's laugh burst out like gunfire. The man was at least twice Adam's thirty years, but he didn't know the meaning of *slow down.* His body and brain were always running, always firing on all cylinders.

"Nice try. But if you want me to write this article, I'm going to need a few more details."

"You used to do your own investigating. Did you forget how to dig up your own leads?"

"I am digging up my own leads. I'm interviewing an informant. Who also happens to be my editor."

That earned a chuckle on the other end of the line, and Adam let go of his hair long enough to drum his fingers on his knee.

"Why point me to a story about Boston now?"

"You know why. You have a vested interest in a piece of property there."

"St. Cassian's Chapel. And . . ." He let the word linger, praying that Garrett would fill in the rest.

"And, keep digging."

Adam let out a long breath. This was a test. Or maybe practice. Maybe it was only to serve as a reminder that he still knew how to put a story together. Either way, he wasn't going to drop St. Cassian's Chapel or Carrington Commercial.

Somehow he didn't think that an investigation would uncover a significant donation from the developer to help restore the old church building. But he felt sick at the very thought of Carrington laying a hand on Connor's favorite place.

"You written much lately?"

He glanced at his journal. It was filled with single lines about the sharp smell of sea air and the cool embrace of the ocean breeze.

"Not much."

"Hop to it, Jacobs. You owe me an article."

"For sure." He chuckled at himself. Apparently Caden's mannerisms were rubbing off on him.

Well, he could think of worse things.

As he ended the call, he glanced at the clock. Two in the afternoon was a little early to call it a day, although he couldn't think of anything he'd rather do than crawl under the black-and-white quilt and ignore the rest of the world.

He needed to talk with someone at St. Cassian's, but they would be busy with services today. He'd have to wait until tomorrow.

Maybe he could press Marie or Caden for more than the scraps he was trying to pull into an eight-course story. But getting more out of them would take a bit of finesse — something he'd grown a little out of practice with.

At least he and Caden had become

215

friends. Maybe she'd open up to him. But he'd have to pick the right time. It had to be a natural conversation. If he came on too strong, she'd know he had more than a casual interest. And she'd probably clam up.

In the meantime, he should start putting his notes into some sort of order. With a sigh, he propped his pillows against the antique wooden headboard and leaned against it. He flipped open his laptop and reached for his notebook.

Instead of the ordered outline he should be writing, his fingers tapped out words entirely of their own.

There's a strange magic in the cinnamon-scented air of Prince Edward Island. The locals don't seem to notice it. Maybe it's become so wholly ingrained in their daily lives that they take it for granted. Maybe it takes an outsider like me to recognize the enchantment that lingers somewhere between towering pines and red sand shores. And I almost missed it.

The words flowed until his chin bobbed against his chest and his eyes refused to remain open.

Caden bent to put another plate in Aretha's dishwasher as the older woman covered a small plastic container of lunch leftovers. Jack moved the roast pan from the stove top to the counter by the sink, a smile wider than their cozy kitchen stretching his mouth.

"You okay, Jack?" Caden asked.

"Oh, ignore him." But Aretha's matching grin said she did anything but. "He's just glad he didn't have to do the dishes today."

Jack gave an affirmative shrug, his eyes sparkling.

"How could I not help clean up after you made such a great lunch?"

Aretha picked up a dish towel but didn't reach for a damp plate. Instead she leaned back against the oven handle. "Why didn't your handsome friend join us?"

Caden's gaze shot to Jack, who seemed wholly oblivious. "Aretha." Her voice sing-songed into a scold.

"What?"

Caden nodded toward Jack.

"Oh, honey. I'm old and married, but I'm not dead."

Jack let out a throaty laugh and kissed his wife on the cheek. "You most certainly aren't." The deep wrinkles on his weathered face stretched into a smile once again. "You have good taste. You married me, didn't you?"

Aretha swatted her towel at her husband of only two years, but the mirth in her eyes couldn't be denied.

"I'll be in my workshop if anyone needs me," he said as he ducked out the back door. Aretha's gaze followed him, her smile growing when he shot a wave meant just for her over his shoulder.

Caden suddenly jerked her head down and focused on the swirling dishrag in her hand. The scene seemed too personal, too intimate, and she was an intruder. She'd known Aretha for all of her twenty-seven years, and Aretha had been alone for every one of those.

Until Jack came along.

Aretha had been married once before. Before Caden was even born. Her husband had walked right out of Aretha's life, leaving her on her own without an income and without a direction. Somehow she'd found her way. She'd opened her antique shop. She'd sung in the church choir and hosted the monthly ladies' auxiliary meetings. She'd become a staple in the community, shining bright even among the lighthouses.

Caden had assumed Aretha was happy and whole and that she'd grow up to be very much like her someday — funny, friendly, and forever alone.

Until Jack came along.

Strange how it wasn't the weddings of her twentysomething friends that made Caden wish for one of her own. It was the marriage of a woman forty years her senior that made her wonder what it might be like to share her life and love with a man.

"So, where is our dear Adam today?"

Her cheeks flamed and she choked on absolutely nothing. Aretha couldn't possibly have known what she was thinking at that exact moment, but putting Adam anywhere near thoughts about her love life wasn't safe or helpful.

Her interest in him was entirely related to *Rest & Retreats* magazine.

It had to be.

"I don't know where he is." That was only a half-truth. She'd watched him scurry back to the inn after declining Aretha's lunch invitation. His forehead had been wrinkled and his nose flared. Something was on his mind, but he'd kept his mouth shut.

"Uh-huh. And just how much time have the two of you been spending together?"

She shot a sour expression at the older woman. "What's that supposed to mean? We're friends. Marie asked me to show him

219

around the island. That's all."

"Marie asked you to show him around?"

"Didn't she tell you?"

Aretha shook her head. "I thought the two of you were . . ." Her voice drifted off into an unspoken question.

Caden clutched a damp hand against her stomach, wishing with her whole heart that she didn't have to shatter Aretha's imaginings. Maybe if Aretha had thought there was a natural friendship between her and Adam, it wasn't so terrible for Caden to imagine the same. If Aretha thought he might like her for more than her coffee and pastries, Caden could let herself begin to believe it too.

Even though she knew the truth.

"He's a travel writer. For a magazine."

"Rest & Retreats?"

She locked eyes with Aretha, her mouth hanging slack. "How did you know?"

The laugh lines in the corners of Aretha's pale eyes deepened, and she pressed an age-spotted hand to her cheek. "I wrote to them months ago. About the Red Door."

"Why?"

"I heard they were looking for unique summer vacation spots, and I knew Marie could use the press. Besides, I figured there was no way they'd ever pick our little corner of the world."

"Well, they did."

Aretha's mouth gaped open, then closed, as she scratched at her neck and surveyed the ceiling. "I never expected . . . But how do you know?"

"A friend of Marie's emailed to say we're finalists."

"Are you sure Adam's the reporter?"

Caden ran a hand over her hair and tucked it behind her ear. She'd been the one asking all of these questions only weeks before. But Marie had been so sure of Adam's identity. And somewhere along the way, she'd begun believing it too. Maybe it was the way he talked about writing or the notebook he carried around or the time he spent staring at the old house.

He was the reporter they were expecting. And he was the one who was going to rescue the next summer.

"For sure. He's the one."

"Then you're . . ."

She tried to hitch the corner of her mouth into an actual smile, but settled for something akin to a grimace. "Showing off the island."

"I thought you loved PE Island. You look like it's the most painful job you've ever had, and I know for a fact that scrubbing the equipment at your dad's bakery when you were twelve was worse."

Finally she found a genuine smile. "I do love this place. It's just not how I thought I'd be spending my summer — trying to impress an American reporter who's used to big-city life. I mean, he's from Washington, DC." She flung her arm as far as she could reach from the left to the right, mostly because she had no idea where his hometown was.

Aretha leaned forward, dangerously close to the arc of Caden's arm. "So what are you doing to impress him?"

She shrugged, suddenly uncertain about her plan so far. "I took him into the national park."

"To your beach?"

"For sure."

"Uh-huh." Aretha pinched her chin between her thumb and forefinger. "And?"

"And what? And I showed him the boardwalk. And I was going to take him to a lighthouse."

"And?" The single question was so filled with expectation that Caden's stomach took a small leap.

"Mostly he spends every morning in my kitchen, and I give him coffee and an extra pastry." Because that was the foundation of their friendship. Dark roast and cinnamon streusel.

He'd never given her a hint that he wanted anything more.

Except . . .

There had been that moment on the rocks. He'd told her something he clearly didn't share widely, and then he'd looked at her like he'd looked at that blueberry muffin his first morning at the inn.

She didn't have any idea what that meant. She could read a recipe card splattered in oil and covered in jelly. But she couldn't read a man's expression.

So she'd run.

Only now she wondered what might have happened if she'd stayed.

"So he likes to eat."

"Everything."

"Then if you want to impress him" — Aretha put a firm hand on her shoulder and squeezed, and Caden immediately knew what she was going to say — "you're going to have to win the cook-off. That's the best way to stand out in this community. Show him how special you and the Red Door are."

She clasped her hands in front of her. Aretha was right. Caden had figured that she'd have to win the lobster cook-off to cement a spot in Adam's magazine. But winning the cook-off could mean landing in an even more intriguing — yet troubling — spot.

The spotlight.

Her throat closed, and she managed only a wheeze. "I know."

With a curt nod and a crisp clap of her hands, Aretha reached for her recipe box. "So what are you going to make?"

Her insides were already a mess, and that one simple question made them feel like they were going to explode.

"I have no idea."

12

"St. Cassian's Chapel, this is Megan speaking."

Adam cleared his throat, took a deep breath, and tried to remember how many times he'd done this before. Remembering how good he used to be at this job didn't calm the tumult in his gut. Somehow this was different. This was personal.

"Hello?" The girl on the other end sounded polite but concerned. Maybe he'd left her hanging for longer than he thought.

But as he opened his mouth to answer, his tongue felt thick and untrained. And he owed Connor more than tripping over his lines. Squeezing his eyes shut, he did something he hadn't done in years. He prayed.

God, give me the words.

"My name is Adam Jacobs. I'm with *America Today.*"

"America Today?"

"The newspaper."

"The newspaper?"

They weren't going to get anywhere at this rate. "Do you have a manager I could speak with?"

"Um . . . not really."

Right. Because it was a church, not a Walmart. "Is there someone who oversees your office?"

"Regina."

Time seemed to stand still as he waited for Megan to pass the call along to Regina. But there was no movement on the other end. Only a never-ending silence. Finally he checked his phone to make sure they hadn't been disconnected. They hadn't.

"May I speak with Regina?"

"Oh, sure. Just a sec."

He covered his guffaw with one hand, suddenly feeling more like the experienced journalist he was and less like a rookie reporter.

"This is Regina Holmes." Her voice was firm, confident, and at least four decades older than Megan's. "How may I help you?"

He figured it was better to start from the very beginning. He wasn't going to assume Megan had made any of the introductions. "My name is Adam Jacobs. I'm with *America Today,* and I'm writing a story about St. Cassian's Chapel."

"What kind of story?"

He went with his steady fallback, half-answers and new directions. "I attended a memorial service there back in June."

"For Connor?" He was about to ask how she'd read his mind, but she seemed to know his question before he could voice it. "We don't do too many memorial services since we don't have a cemetery on the grounds. But the O'Dwyers have been good friends since Connor was a boy." There was a quake in her voice, and it ripped at Adam's chest as though it had found its way inside and was clawing for release. "Were you a friend of his?"

He wasn't sure he could get a word through the fist around his windpipe, but he managed a strangled, "Yes, ma'am."

He was also responsible for Connor's death. But she hadn't asked that.

"What can I do for you, Mr. Jacobs?"

He framed his response four ways in his mind, trying to find the least offensive, least shocking, but all of them felt like they'd land as soft as a brick on glass. Maybe there was no helping it. "What can you tell me about Carrington Commercial?"

Regina didn't gasp or sputter, but there was a tiny intake of air on the other end of

227

the line that indicated he'd nudged a sore spot.

"Nothing."

"You're not familiar with Carrington Commercial at all?"

"I didn't say that." Her Boston drawl turned pointy, each syllable clipped. But it didn't sound like anger, so he poked again.

"Do you know the nature of Carrington Commercial's interest in St. Cassian's?"

"I do."

"Can you share?"

"No."

Adam ran his hand over his hair, hoping it would clear his mind. He knew how to bounce back from a straight-up shutdown. At least he used to.

Clearly she knew something. If she couldn't answer his questions, which questions could she answer? The ones she wanted to.

"Ms. Holmes, how long have you worked for St. Cassian's?"

"Nearly thirty years." Her tone hitched like she wasn't sure where he was going with this line of questioning, but the prickles in her voice had eased.

"Wow. Thirty years in the same job?"

"Oh, not all in the same position. I started off answering phones and putting together the bulletin. Then I went back to school so I could handle the books. Now I'm the office manager." The last words held a note of pride.

She'd worked her way up, and he'd bet that she was managing more than the office. She probably knew the pulse of everything and everyone within the church walls.

"You must love it there."

"Oh, yes."

"What makes St. Cassian's so special?"

She hemmed and hawed for only a moment, not like she was trying to figure out her answer but rather was trying to find the right phrase. "The people here — they're my family."

Her words were like a fist to his ribs.

Connor's mom had said the same. The people there had cared for Connor the child and cheered for Connor the young man. And when his life was cut short, they grieved for the man they loved.

A searing flash at his temple shot straight through his head from ear to ear, and he cleared his suddenly dry throat. Remorse — regret — pummeled him like a prizefighter.

Sucking in a painful breath, he reached for the right question to keep her talking. He wanted to pry, to prod. But pushing Regina Holmes to tell him more than she wanted to felt too much like strong-arming Connor's favorite aunt.

And he refused to sink to that level.

"The O'Dwyer kids were my favorites in Sunday school." Her voice took on a faraway tone, and he could picture her staring off toward the narrow row of stained glass windows just below the ceiling. "Little Connor always brought a dime for the offering and a weed for me."

"A weed?"

"Oh, he thought they were wildflowers, and he said his dad always brought his mom flowers on Sundays, so he should bring me some."

Little freckle-faced, redheaded Connor O'Dwyer had had a crush on his Sunday school teacher.

He shoved his fist against a fierce ache in his chest. Tilting his head back, he stared at the ceiling and prayed that the scratchiness at the back of his throat wouldn't choke off his words. "I'm sorry for your . . . well, I'm sorry he's gone."

"We all are."

Why did she have to say it like that? Like every one of the hundred families at St. Cassian's blamed him for stealing one of their own. His vision blurred, so he jabbed the heel of his hand into his eye. He couldn't take much more of this, especially when she wasn't giving him anything more to go on.

"Thank you for your time, Ms. Holmes."

"You're welcome. Mr. Jacobs, is it?"

"Yes, ma'am."

She made a noncommittal sound, and he almost hung up.

But *she* didn't.

So he leaned forward and held his breath as though the silence could somehow reveal the answers he needed. It hummed with an electric charge, but still she said nothing.

He opened his mouth to ask her if there was something he could do for her. But with a reporter's muscle memory, he snapped it closed. Garrett had taught him early on that informants wouldn't talk over him. If he wanted to hear what they had to say, he'd have to shut up long enough to let them say it.

After what felt like an hour, Regina gave a small cough. "You were a friend of Connor's?"

He was so eager, he began almost before her question ended. "Yes, ma'am."

"You know about his bench?"

"Yes, ma'am."

She swallowed, thick and audible. "I officially have no comment about Carrington

Commercial. And that is all I can say about that."

Silence reigned again, and after a long beat, he realized she wanted him to confirm. "I understand."

"I'm glad we understand each other." Her voice dropped until he was leaning forward in a vain attempt to hear her better. "But they're going to get our land and tear down our building."

"What do you mean?"

"Just what I said. The bank is about to foreclose on our mortgage, and Elliot Carrington is chomping at the bit to level this land and replace us with high-end condos that no one in this neighborhood could afford in a hundred years."

His stomach lurched like he was on a plane flying through a hurricane.

That couldn't be right. Carrington couldn't just tear the chapel down.

"But your building is from the early 1900s. Wasn't it paid off years ago?"

"Oh, the original building was." She paused, and he could faintly make out the sound of footsteps on her side of the call. He wanted to scream at them to hurry up. St. Cassian's — and Connor's bench — was on the line. Didn't they care?

Regina took a quick breath, and he could

practically see her looking around her work space to make sure she was alone. "There was a contractor, Jordan something or another. See, the church was doing well. Growing. And we needed more space. But we don't have any more land. So he was supposed to build a basement beneath the Sunday school rooms, on the back of the building."

Adam didn't even need her to finish her story before he jumped to his feet and marched the confines of his room. It had never felt so small, his strides eating up every foot back and forth. His fist shook at his side, and he searched for something — anything — to throw.

"He lifted the building, ruined our foundation, and took off with our deposit. We had no choice but to take out a loan."

"When was that?"

"Four years ago."

"And Jordan? Was he prosecuted?"

Regina sighed. "No. He took our money — and others' too — closed up shop, and left the country."

He snatched the pillow from the head of his bed and chucked it at the wall as hard as he could.

The impotent flop to the hardwood floor was less satisfying than he'd hoped.

"So why can't you make the loan payments? If you were growing . . ."

Another sigh, this one pain-filled. "We're a church of blue-collar workers. Like Connor and his family. His dad worked at the same factory as his grandpa for twenty years. Until it closed two years ago."

And when the people were broke, the church was broke.

It didn't make sense that God would let something like that happen. Why would he allow a church to crumble under that kind of economic pressure?

Adam covered his eyes and tried to picture the old building, the kind faces at Connor's memorial.

"Is there any hope of getting it declared a landmark?"

Regina sighed once again. "We talked with the Boston Preservation Society, and there's not much they can do."

She didn't need to explain. In the city of Paul Revere, the Old North Church, and a hundred other Revolutionary War treasures, an unremarkable turn-of-the-century brick chapel — especially one with a newly renovated foundation — wasn't particularly compelling to the Boston Landmarks Commission or the community at large. Except for those who found family there.

"What are you going to do?"

"We're going to pray, Mr. Jacobs."

Adam hung up the phone not entirely sure that prayer would be enough to stop Carrington Commercial from tearing down the church and the only memorial to a man who'd died because of him. Adam couldn't sit by and let that happen.

Which, of course, was why Garrett had sent him here in the first place. He could have gone anywhere to relax, but Garrett had known that Adam couldn't — wouldn't — give up on a story for Connor. And revealing the underhanded dealings of a corporation willing to demolish a church for a profit — well, that was a bonus. One *America Today*'s readers would eat up.

And if Marie Carrington Sloane knew what was going on, he had a solid source.

13

Friday morning Adam arrived in the kitchen before Caden. Thinking he might have missed her, he poked his head into the long dining room, but it was empty as well. He ducked out the back door and looked for her form in the garden. But she wasn't there either.

Strange. She was always in before six, finishing up the food prep.

He should call and check up on her. Except he didn't have her number.

Back in Washington, he'd barely been introduced to someone before he had their phone number and email saved in his contact list. And at least half the time he never saw or spoke to them again. Now he woke up every morning excited to share a cup of coffee with Caden, and he didn't have a clue how to get in touch with her.

He turned twice in the kitchen, stared at the oddly silent radio, and put his hands on his hips.

Surely if there had been an emergency, Marie or Seth would be here, making sure that breakfast was served. But what if no one had contacted them? What if she had been injured on her walk to the inn? Most of the side streets didn't have lights, and it was dark. What if someone hadn't seen her until it was too late? What if . . .

No, it was a small town, and everyone here knew Caden and her family. They would know she was expected. If someone found her, they would contact the inn. Surely.

Caden had to be on her way.

His only option was to make coffee and try to silence the what-ifs while he waited. Rattling around in the kitchen, he set out the French press, filled the teapot with water, and watched while it didn't boil. With a morning harrumph, he put the coffee grounds in place and turned back to the stove top. Still no boiling water.

He tapped his toe, crossed his arms, and paced for three minutes.

Still no telltale whistle.

And still no Caden.

He peered out the window, craning his neck for any sign of her. Only the morning light on the eastern horizon greeted him, the sun just breaking over the water and turning it a shade of orange he'd never seen before.

Suddenly the whistle on the teapot shrieked, and he jumped to pull it from the stove. He'd just finished preparing the French press when the back door rattled, slammed, and a grumbling woman stumbled inside.

Relief washed over him, a clean rain rinsing away the worry that had had him dancing around the kitchen. He didn't have time to get too close to people, between jetting off for three-month assignments at the drop of a hat and spending too many nights in the newsroom following up on just one more lead. It wasn't exactly conducive to building lasting friendships. In fact, Garrett, his pseudo uncle, was the closest thing he had to a best friend.

Until now.

Until Caden.

And when she hadn't been where she always was, his mind had immediately conjured the worst, his life without her friendship.

He sucked in a deep breath, drinking in the sight of her before bursting out laughing.

A scowl firmly in place, she threw her bags on the counter. Half her hair had fallen out of its ponytail, the blonde strands wind-blown and ratty like something had tried to build a nest in there. The sleeves of her dark gray top had been shoved to her elbows, but one was trying hard to fall back to her wrist. Her cheeks were red, and she squinted ice-blue eyes at him. Hard.

"Just exactly what's so funny?"

"Nothing." He tried to keep his grin under wraps, but when she shoved her uncooperative sleeve back up her elbow — and it fell back down — a chuckle fought its way out his nose. That just made him laugh harder.

She scowled harder. "Easy for you to laugh. Did a hen try to eat your hair this morning?" Whipping a tray of fresh eggs out of her bag, she shook her head. "I don't think so."

"What happened?" He reached for the eggs and put them in their designated spot in the refrigerator. When he turned back, Caden was as shell-shocked as ever.

Heaving a tired sigh, she leaned her forearms against the top of the kitchen island but offered no explanation.

He poured a cup of coffee and held it out to her. She took it with a nod of thanks and nothing more. But she didn't take a sip for several extended seconds.

"Do you want to talk about it?"

She eyed him like she wasn't quite sure how honest she could be. "I have to get breakfast ready."

"Put me to work, boss."

That made her chuckle, just as he'd hoped it would. She pointed to the fridge. "Grab me the bowl of pie crust dough and the ham." She quickly washed her hands and set to work rolling out half of the dough into an even quiche crust. "Will you dice the ham into cubes about this big?" Her fingers were a quarter-inch apart, give or take. "Oh, and turn on the oven for me — 350."

"Sure."

As he worked on his tasks, she began lining a glass pie pan, grumbling something under her breath.

"What was that?"

Her pink cheeks turned three shades darker. "I got attacked by a chicken this morning."

He tried so hard to keep a straight face, forcing his eyes to focus on the hunk of meat in his hands and not at the pretty blush creeping across her face. But when she continued, he couldn't keep a snort from escaping.

"She thought I was trying to push her out of her nest." Then, like she needed to clarify for his sake, "I wasn't. But she didn't know that. And she went after my head like her life depended on it."

"What were you doing?"

"I was at Justin's picking up fresh eggs." She said the other man's name like Adam should know who he was, but he couldn't place the reference. "He has a coop out back, and I pick up eggs at least three times a week. None of the birds have ever given me a second look." Justin must be her contact at Kane Dairy. She'd mentioned getting her eggs there before.

"Until today."

"Yes." The word came out on a groan, and she shook her head as she collected said eggs, broke them into her mixing bowl, and whisked them into a froth. "It hurt like getting your finger slammed in a door. Over and over again."

He winced, his own hand burning at the very thought. "I'm sorry. Are you all right?"

"I'll live. But fending off the hen got me off schedule, and I dropped an egg in the battle, so I had to clean it up. And then I was even later." She scooped the ham that he had cut into her bowl, added a pinch of salt and several dashes of pepper, and kept mixing.

"Grab the cheese and shred it, please.

241

Both kinds. And hand me those scallions on the second shelf."

He complied, and she chopped the green onions like they'd been conspiring with the hen in question. When she reached the tip of the scallion, she pointed her knife directly at him. "And then someone tried to run me over."

He held up both hands, one with a block of pepper jack cheese. "It wasn't me."

"I know it wasn't you." She looked between him and her knife — twice — before lowering her weapon. "I was off my morning rhythm, and I thought I'd save some time walking down the street instead of along the boardwalk. And they probably just didn't see me, but I literally had to jump out of the way."

He stopped shredding as a tightness in his chest stole his full attention. "Were you hurt?"

Caden frowned, but it looked like it was more from annoyance than pain. "I stubbed my toe and ran into a parked car, but I'll live."

"Whew." He feigned wiping sweat off his brow, but if he was completely honest with himself, her words released that strange band around his lungs so he could finally take a full breath again. "I'm sure it was hit-or-miss there for a minute."

She gave him a sarcastic eye roll as she scooped his shredded cheese into her mixture. After giving it a handful of solid whippings, she poured it into two pie plates and slid them into the oven.

"So what should we do today to make up for your traumatic morning? What should we explore?"

Her eyes went wide, her grin spreading. "I'd love to, but . . ."

His stomach clenched as a wrinkle settled in right between her eyebrows.

"I have plans today. I have to do a trial run of my dish for the cook-off."

"But that's weeks away."

"I know, but I'm trying a new recipe. One that Aretha lent me, and I have to make sure I work out any kinks before the competition." She ran a hand down her floral apron, twisting her finger into the edge. "I might have to make it three or four times before I get it perfect."

She didn't say the words aloud, but he could hear them ringing through the room.

And it has to be perfect.

"I suppose this has something to do with Bethany."

"Yes . . ." Again, an unspoken word. *And.*

"And what else?"

She shrugged and turned away. "You know."

But he didn't. He knew about Bethany, who was apparently after Caden's job. He knew about Caden losing to the perky blonde too many times. He knew about wanting to represent the inn.

He also knew — somewhere deep in his gut — that there was more. Something he most definitely did not know.

"All right then. Let me help you with your trial run. What are we making?"

"It's an individual contest. Chefs can't have any help preparing their entries."

He shrugged. "But what about help shopping for ingredients and official taste testers? There can't be a rule about a taste tester test tasting the trial run."

She laughed as he tripped over his repeated t's but nodded. "I suppose you're right. After breakfast, I'm going to the farmer's market to pick up supplies."

"Perfect. I've never been to a farmer's market before. I'm sure I'll be loads of help." He chugged his cooling coffee. "You never answered my question. What are we making?"

"Asian lobster cakes with a tarragon aioli."

His smile started to dim, but he forced it to stay in place. That didn't sound like

Caden at all. It sounded like some over-priced menu item in a swanky New York bar. Where was the influence of the island she loved, the comfort food she excelled at?

Well, if she thought an Asian lobster cake was her best chance to win, he'd support her. And he'd eat every last bite.

Because he was a good friend like that.

And because he loved lobster.

When Caden finally checked her hair in the bathroom mirror after breakfast, she shrieked. Adam had conveniently failed to tell her that the chicken's painful attack had left more than a few bruises. It had left a rat's nest in her hair.

And she'd worn it all morning.

Frantically running her fingers through the mess, she tried to turn it back into something resembling order. But even her ponytail seemed intent on ruining her morning. With a flick of the elastic band keeping her hair in place, she patted her head and turned from the mirror. Some things couldn't be rescued.

Adam and Seth were chatting in the kitchen when she returned. Adam immediately caught her eye. "Ready to go?"

"Almost. Let me just get my list together."

Seth shot her a secret grin. "Where you

two off to today? Hiking the Homestead Trail? Swimming at Basin Head? Walking the floating boardwalk?"

Adam shook his head. "No, but that last one sounds fantastic. What is that?"

"At Greenwich Beach there's a trail that leads to a boardwalk that floats over the marshlands and up to white sand dunes," Seth said. "And just beyond those is a great beach that goes on forever. Marie loves it, and we get out there at least a few times every year. You should definitely check it out."

Adam nodded. "Definitely. But not today. Today we're going to the farmer's market."

The look of confusion on Seth's face almost made Caden laugh. She shrugged. "I have to practice my cook-off entry, and he offered to help."

Puffing out his chest in mock dignity, Adam tucked his thumbs into fake suspenders. "I'm the official taste tester."

"It's a good job if you can get it." Seth grinned and clapped Adam on the shoulder. "Caden, Marie wants to talk with you later if you have a minute. She's checking out a guest and returning a few phone calls, but if you're around this afternoon . . ."

Her stomach sank an inch. That didn't sound good. "Should I wait around?"

"Oh no." Seth smiled, but it never reached his eyes. "Whenever you get back from your errands, just stop by the office. Have a good time."

And they did.

Caden loved showing off the colorful produce and local goods in each stall of the long, narrow market. Nearly every vendor asked about Adam, and he took to introducing himself as a professional taster. Caden just rolled her eyes and kept moving. They picked up fresh ginger and cilantro from her friend Wendy. And scallions from Ted in the far corner.

She saved their visit with Mark for last. As they approached Mark's booth, Adam stared at the newspaper-wrapped packages. "What is that?"

"The main dish."

"Lobster?"

"For sure."

Mark's booming voice carried his greeting. "Caden Holt! What a treat. Wasn't expecting to see you today."

"Hi, Mark." She grabbed his outstretched hand and shook it.

"I saw your dad last night. He said you had a new friend. This must be him."

Oh, perfect. Did everyone in this town know about Adam? And did they have to call him her "new friend" in front of him?

But Adam didn't seem to mind a bit. He just took his turn shaking Mark's hand. "Adam Jacobs of Washington, DC. Good to meet you."

"Adam's been helping out in the kitchen at the inn."

"Oh, really?" Mark seemed impressed, his smile turning into a thoughtful frown. "Caden doesn't let anyone into her kitchen. You must be very skilled."

"Absolutely. The best." For a long moment Adam gazed toward the rough-hewn beams holding up the roof on the old barn, but he couldn't keep the joke going any longer. His laughter rang out loud and clear. "Honestly, she takes pity on me and gives me a cup of good coffee and an extra pastry every morning."

Mark's eyes widened. "Like that mocha chocolate cake thing?"

Adam held up three fingers — one for each of the cupcakes he'd eaten — and Mark's eyes opened as far as they could under his bushy eyebrows. He stared at Caden in all seriousness. "When this guy takes off, let me know. I'll fill his spot."

The warmth that had been swirling in her chest suddenly froze, forming instant icicles.

Adam would leave.

And it would hurt a lot more than she wanted to admit.

Swallowing the daggers in her throat, she forced a smile into place. "We need a lobster. About a pound and a quarter."

"How funny. I need lobster too."

The high-pitched voice sent a shiver all the way down her back, but Caden forced a kind greeting. "Hello, Bethany."

"Caden." She bobbed a quick nod, then immediately turned her attention to Adam. She was far too comfortable running her hand along his arm, and it made Caden cringe.

She had spent every morning with him for a month, shown him her favorite places on the island, and talked with him about his past. And she still didn't feel free to touch his arm for no reason.

Then again, Bethany had always been good at flirting with the boys.

If only Caden could be free with Adam like she wanted to. In her kitchen, they teased and laughed, joked and smiled. But outside that safe zone, she wasn't the same. She wasn't as strong. She wasn't as confident.

Bethany was chattering on about the upcoming lobster dinner. "We're expecting at least two hundred people, and Mark is providing our lobsters at cost."

Mark tipped his head in a mock salute. "Yes, ma'am. My family's been getting the church lobsters for the dinner for almost ten years. Happy to help out again."

"So why are you picking up a lobster today, Caden? Working on your entry dish?"

Caden managed a stiff jerk of her chin, which she hoped passed for agreement.

Peeking into the sacks Adam carried, Bethany wrinkled her nose. "Ginger and tarragon. Going for some Asian flavors? That could be interesting."

Adam piped up. "It will be."

"Oh, are you helping?" The arch to Bethany's perfect eyebrow seemed to say she was just waiting to pounce on a rule breaker.

"Only tasting it. Quality control and all that."

Bethany chirped like she'd never heard a funnier joke, but the sound made Caden's ears ring.

"Well, I hope it does better than the macaroni and cheese you made last year. What did it place? Fourth, was it?"

Caden swallowed the urge to correct Bethany. Her mac and cheese had come in second. But making an issue out of it wasn't going to make her look any better in front of Adam and Mark. "Something like that."

"Well, I'm working on a super-secret recipe. I was perfecting it before I had to leave Toronto, and I think the world is just about ready."

Adam, everything polite, asked, "Why did you leave Toronto?" His face showed no hint of cynicism, but there was a tiny inflection in his voice that Caden knew and loved. She caught his eye and gave him a little smile.

Bethany's hands flapped about. "Oh, you know how it is. When your parents need help, you rush home no matter what."

Adam looked like he'd just dropped a skillet on his foot, pain searing the lines of his face.

Because he didn't know. His parents hadn't been around for eight years. And if she had to guess, she'd say he'd give just about anything to have them back.

Completely oblivious to Adam's expression, Bethany rambled on. "So, did you hear about the guest judge we've secured for the cook-off?"

Caden shook her head, already something stirring in her stomach.

Bethany tossed her too-perfect hair over her shoulder with a flick of her wrist. "My Toronto restaurant was a smashing success, and I met lots of other chefs while I was there. Including Jerome Gale."

Mark let out a low whistle. Caden's jaw went slack. She couldn't find a single sound in response.

"Who's Jerome Gale?"

Thank God for Adam. Educated, smart, talented, and completely unfamiliar with the Canadian food scene. His innocent question stole the wind from Bethany's announcement and gave Caden a moment to collect herself.

Bethany laughed and tapped a finger on Adam's shoulder. "You're so funny. Jerome Gale. He owns Broad Bistro, Seven Twenty-four, and Tudor. You must have heard of him."

Adam pursed his lips to the side and shook his head slowly.

"He has his own show on the Cooking Network. *Just Jerome?*"

Another head shake from Adam, and Bethany seemed to take this one personally.

"Well, trust me. He's a great chef, and he's coming to judge our cook-off. And Mom is calling Marie today to reserve his room at the Red Door."

Caden's hands suddenly went numb.

Jerome would be staying in her B and B. Eating her food. Every day.

If she lost this competition, she wasn't only going to embarrass herself and the inn.

She was going to do it in front of Adam and all of North Rustico. And one of Canada's premier chefs.

It would be a disaster.

14

"Are you up for one more stop today?"

Adam switched his bags from one hand to the other, surprised how much a one-pound lobster could add to his load on the way back to the inn. "Sure. What'd you have in mind?"

"Justin —"

"From the dairy."

"Right. Justin Kane, who owns Kane Dairy."

He frowned at the too-easy way Justin's name rolled off her tongue.

This was new information. He'd pictured Justin as a kid working a summer job shoveling out cow stalls. He'd imagined the kid wasn't much older than the ones in Caden's cooking class.

But now he didn't know how to picture the other man. He could be a young guy working a start-up, maybe someone Caden knew from grade school. Or he could be a grandfather type who'd worked the farm for a hundred years.

He much preferred the latter option.

"He said he has a block of cheese that I ordered a couple days ago. I'd like to try it on the asparagus side dish tomorrow." She looked up at him, her eyes as blue as the cloudless sky and twice as pretty. She blinked into the sun, whose light turned her hair a rich honey color and left a halo on the crown of her head. The little dimple in her left cheek made a quick appearance as her lips paused in a smile. "Mind if we stop to pick it up?"

In that moment he couldn't have denied her the moon had she asked for it.

He choked on nothing but the air he was breathing.

"Are you okay?"

"Sure. No." He let her thump his back several times as he wheezed out the words. Her hand was smaller than his but firm and strong, and when she wrapped her other hand around his arm, he leaned into her contact. "I'm good."

"You sure?"

"Just a . . . nothing. I'm fine."

He regretted saying that as soon as she let go. He could still feel the warmth of her touch where her hand had been.

"Good. The dairy is right down the road."

In true North Rustico fashion, they passed a small field with four brown cows loudly lamenting the warm weather. They went one more street down and turned a corner. A large white barn loomed before them, a two-story white farmhouse sat on the next lot over, and a giant white and blue wooden sign between the buildings said "Kane Dairy, Est. 1964."

If the sign was to be believed, then Justin could be at least seventy years old.

That worked for Adam.

That worked really well.

Caden led the way into a small side structure built right into the barn, and Adam was surprised that it didn't smell more like cows. But the little room had good insulation, and apparently its own air supply. The scents of fresh-baked bread and strong cheese made his mouth water.

"Morning, Carol."

The kind-eyed octogenarian sitting behind a display of cheese rounds looked up from the mass-market paperback in her hands. "Caden, dear. Justin said you'd probably stop by today. Your cheese is ready. I'll box it up."

"Thank you." Caden glanced at the door opposite the one they'd entered. "Are they around?"

"The boys? 'Course they are. Probably causing trouble somewhere." Just as she finished her words on a chuckle, the door Caden had indicated flew open and two arguing, muddy men marched in.

"I told you to turn off the hose," the shorter of the two complained. He was wet from the top of his head to the tip of his black ponytail, and he ran a hand over his face, sending water flying.

"No, you told me to turn the spigot," the other countered.

Adam had met Caden's brother before — at church. At least, he thought the lanky redhead was Dillon Holt. It was hard to tell for sure under the stripes of mud across his cheeks.

"And you turned the hose," the first groused.

"Well, I got confused."

The wet man was just about to launch into another verbal volley when he spotted Caden. Ignoring her brother, he crossed the small room in three steps, put his hands on her shoulders, and leaned in to kiss her cheek.

Something inside Adam exploded.

It flung shrapnel into every major organ, leaving a fireball in its wake, and he could feel the steam coming out of his ears.

He hadn't exactly spoken for her, but in that moment he knew as sure as fire that she didn't belong with this long-haired farmhand.

Caden laughed and wiped off the man's wet kiss. "You're filthy. What are you doing?"

"Showing you what a jerk your brother is."

"Oh, I've known that since I was seven."

"Hey!" Dillon stepped forward and hugged his little sister, leaving a brown trail along her pale gray sleeve. "I was just giving Justin what he asked for."

Whatever monster had survived Adam's internal blast gnawed on his insides like it hadn't eaten in weeks.

This. This was Justin Kane. Broad and stocky like he wrestled cows for a living. Which he did. He didn't have a quick smile, but he clearly possessed a charm that had Caden leaning into him and put a twinkle in her eye.

Justin Kane. Decidedly not seventy.

Just as he'd feared. Justin was about his age, and he and Caden had almost certainly gone to school together, known each other for years. There was a history there Adam couldn't compete with.

And — God knew — he did want to compete.

Adam cleared his throat and stepped forward.

Caden looked up, her eyes dimming for a split second. "Oh, guys. I want you to meet Adam."

"We've met." Dillon stepped forward and shook his hand with a firm grip. "Good to see you, man."

"And this is Justin Kane," she said.

Yes. He'd put that unpleasant bit of the puzzle together on his own. Still, he stepped toward the other man, who eyed him cautiously.

"Good to meet you, Adam. Welcome to Kane Dairy." Justin's handshake had a little extra mustard on it, his forearm muscles bunching under the effort. Adam had never been more thankful that Connor had gotten him lifting weights while he was on assignment. He gave as good as he got, supremely satisfied with the flicker in Justin's eyes.

When Justin finally pulled his hand back, he asked, "So how do you know our Caden?"

"Not yours," she quickly amended. "Adam is a guest at the inn. And he's been helping me out in the kitchen."

"You're a chef?" Justin looked doubtful.

"No. But I'm good at reaching tall shelves." Adam probably only had an inch or two on Justin, but he stretched to his full height.

"He's my official taste tester for the cook-off."

"Ah, a quality-control guy." Dillon thumped Justin on the shoulder with the back of his hand. "Maybe we should hire him."

Justin's scowl made Adam smile. "Speaking of the cook-off" — Adam held up the cooler with the lobster — "this guy won't stay alive forever. Should we head back to the inn?"

"Yes."

Carol held out a brown cardboard box. "Here's your cheese, honey. Stop by anytime."

Caden fished two twenties out of her pocket, but Justin waved her off. "Keep it. I owe you for the bread anyway."

Caden had baked the bread that smelled like heaven? He shouldn't be surprised. Everything she did in the kitchen was perfect.

"Then we're even?"

Justin nodded, his ponytail flopping.

Adam would have traded the lobster in his bag for a pair of scissors to give Justin a good trim.

"See you on Sunday." She waved and led the way outside and back toward the Red Door.

As soon as Caden tossed the lobster into a pot of boiling water, Adam's phone rang, the screen lighting up with Garrett's name.

"I need to grab this."

"Sure, take your time." She didn't even look up from poking the poor shellfish, whose dark shell immediately began to turn orange. "The cakes won't be ready for an hour or so."

He scooted out of the kitchen, answering his phone just as he reached the empty porch. "Hello, Garrett."

"You don't sound happy to hear from me, Jacobs."

He wasn't. But he wasn't about to tell his editor that either. "What can I do for you this fine day?"

"Fine? Ha!" He sounded anything but amused. "It's ninety-five degrees outside and 300 percent humidity. I'm pretty sure I saw a squirrel sweating on Pennsylvania Avenue."

Adam took a deep breath of fresh air. It smelled of grass and ocean and peace. He smiled as he took another one. "It's about seventy-five degrees here. The sun is shining, and the air is rich with the scent of earth and sky. And I'm going to eat lobster cakes in about an hour. This is definitely a fine day."

Garrett harrumphed his annoyance.

"But you probably didn't call to hear about how relaxing and peaceful Prince Edward Island is."

"Those are some finely tuned reporter instincts." Garrett was laying the sarcasm on thick, and Adam had a gut feeling he wasn't going to like where this conversation was headed. "How's my article coming along?"

Whenever Garrett claimed ownership of an article, it meant one of two things: either it was late or he wanted it ahead of schedule. Since Adam had a full four weeks left on the island — presumably to write whatever story he discovered — Garrett was going to ask for it early. As in, now.

Adam gave him a half-answer. "I've been doing some writing." He conveniently left out the part about what exactly he was writing.

"Good. Send me your story."

Well, that was abrupt. Apparently Garrett had decided to forego the niceties.

"It's not exactly . . ."

"I don't care. Send me whatever you have. We'll whip it into shape."

"Why the rush? Don't I have another month?" Except even if Garrett did have the time, Adam might not. The church was about to go into foreclosure, and the article couldn't help if it didn't run before the bank stopped waiting.

Garrett's feet clomped hard on the tile floor of his office. "The editor-in-chief wants you back on the job."

"I am on the job." *Sort of.*

He sighed. "No. You're on sabbatical. Time off to recuperate from a rough assignment. Time to complete the article you owe me. But Gloria wants you back to work."

"But the article's not done." *Or started, for that matter.*

"Like I said. Send me whatever you have."

"Well, it's actually not really . . . I don't have much . . ." Brilliant. He sounded like a twelve-year-old trying to explain his missing homework. Next he'd be blaming it on the dog.

"Spit it out, Jacobs."

Taking a steadying breath, he focused on a row of kayaks taking a tour of the bay. "I've been writing mostly travel pieces."

"Travel?"

"About the island. It's gorgeous here. Un-

263

like anything I've ever seen. It's lush and tranquil and full of these people who genuinely care about each other and strangers too."

"Sounds like a great place but a terrible feature."

"Do you think maybe the weekend magazine could use them?"

"Sure. Maybe. Send them along with the article. I'll take a look. But send me the Carrington article."

Adam scrubbed his face with an open palm. "I don't have it yet."

"I hope that means you're trying to figure out the perfect lead or waiting on a quote from your source."

He sucked in a breath, held it for a short second, and then spit out the truth. "I haven't started it."

Silence was worse than screaming. His heart thumped painfully, filling the void, as he waited for Garrett to say something. Anything.

"I handed it to you on a silver platter." Garrett spoke like each word was its own complete thought. Then he swore under his breath. "I know you've had a rough go of it, and I want to help you get back on your horse. But mostly I want to see my article. You're supposed to be a professional writer."

"I *am* a professional writer." Perfect. Just perfect. Now he was arguing with Garrett, who had helped him get this time off.

But the article they were talking about, the one Garrett had served up, was too big to do poorly.

The trouble was, Adam didn't know if he could do it any other way.

"No. Professional writers write. Even when they don't feel like it."

Garrett's words felt like a backhand to his face.

He was right. He was absolutely right.

But that didn't take the fear away, the fear that made his hands freeze every time he tried to write a story with so much at stake.

"I know."

"Then quit using the O'Dwyer kid as an excuse. It wasn't your fault."

Adam closed his eyes against that orange fireball, but it still burned his eyes as though he was looking at the sun. It stole his breath, and he forced his sweating palms down the legs of his jeans. "That's easy for you to say."

"Yes it is. And I'm the one who ran the picture next to the article."

"But I should have warned you." Adam felt like a petulant kid. Worse, he sounded like one.

"Maybe. But you didn't." Garrett grumbled something under his breath that Adam was pretty sure he didn't want to hear. "Listen, here's the truth of it. That translator knew what he was risking when he signed up to help the US military. They all do. They know it's considered treason by the terrorist groups. They know it puts their whole families at risk. But they do it anyway."

Adam leaned his elbows on his knees and put his face in his hand. "Maybe they didn't know it was him. Maybe they didn't realize Aamir was helping us out. Maybe they didn't know where he lived."

"They would have figured it out."

They would have too. The terrorist cells in the area had had little eyes and ears all over the town. They knew the military moves before Adam did. But he'd served them the identity and location of the unit's translator on a platter. Alone, his article had been vague about the man's identity. Run with the photo there could be no mistake about the native man taking the terrorists out at the knees.

"But maybe they would have figured it out after Connor went to his house. After he was safely in and out. And then he'd still be alive."

Connor hadn't been the target of the

266

explosion. Aamir had been. The good guy from Boston had been collateral damage.

"That's a whole lot of maybes and might-have-beens," Garrett said. "And that's about the worst way to live."

"I know it."

And he did. But forgiving himself for a crime that hadn't been entirely his fault was a lot harder than hanging on to it. No matter how heavy, the pain reminded him that he wasn't innocent. That blood was on his hands, and like the steps said, he should make amends wherever he could, however he could.

He owed Connor that article. He owed Connor a great article.

"I'll get the piece done. Just give me a few more weeks. I need to interview some more sources."

"All right. I'll hold Gloria off for a little while longer. In the meantime, send me those travel articles."

"Will do."

15

Caden slid her lobster cakes into the fridge. They had to cool for at least thirty minutes before she could put them in the pan. Anyway, Adam had disappeared, and she'd promised to let him taste them.

After closing the refrigerator door, she strolled down the hall in search of Marie. Seth had said she wanted to see her.

The office door was open about an inch, and a light inside barely broke into the hallway. She risked a quick knock, and the door immediately swung open. Marie smiled from her tall office chair, rolling away from the entrance and into the back corner of the cubbyhole.

"Come on in. Shut the door."

Caden's heart gave an extra skip. This couldn't be good news if it required a closed door.

"What's going on?"

Marie's grin flickered, and when she got it

back into place it was a mere shadow of her real smile. "We're going to need a new roof in a year or two."

Caden blinked, trying to put the information into place. "Do you want me to help reshingle?"

That drew a full laugh. "No. I don't want you on the roof. Seth can do most of it. But there are still costs for the materials and tools."

"For sure."

"And you know that capital is low." Marie tried to put on a brave face, but concern made her eyes glassy. "I've got to go fight my dad for the rest of my trust fund. We just need enough to get us through another two summers, then the inn will be a viable business."

"What about Adam and the magazine article on the inn?"

"It'll help. But honestly, I've been crunching the numbers. Selling out all of the guest rooms for the summer will keep us afloat. It won't cover the new roof. We need both."

Caden leaned against the closed door and stared at the ceiling. There had to be a solution other than the trust fund that Marie's mother had left behind. But there wasn't another source of income. When Jack had opened the inn, he'd maxed out the business loans restoring the old house. And Caden sure didn't have more than a few dollars to rub together.

"What can I do?"

"I need you to cover the inn while I'm gone."

She felt a little seasick. "Cover, how?"

"Well, Seth is going to go with me."

An anchor hit the bottom of her stomach, and she sagged against the door.

"We'll be gone at least two weeks. And I need someone to check guests in and out, make sure Judith knows which rooms need to be cleaned and which ones are vacant. And, of course, greeting the guests at breakfast and providing any tourism information they might need. You know this area better than anyone. And I'll show you where all of my information is."

A tremor deep inside her tried to force its way out. It seemed to scream its objection.

She was better in the kitchen. Knowledgeable in the kitchen. Comfortable in the kitchen. It was where she was at her best.

And Marie wanted to take her out of it?

"But what about breakfasts and . . . shopping and . . . and Adam?" With each addition, her stomach twisted tighter. "There's so much to be done. And . . . two weeks? In the middle of our busy season? And the cook-off. And my classes."

Marie jumped out of her seat and crossed the room. It wasn't until Marie grabbed her hands that Caden realized they were shaking.

"We need your help."

"Of course. I'll help. But . . ." A low voice in her heart whispered four little words she hadn't heard there before.

You can do this.

This wasn't a disaster. It wasn't on par with forgetting her coat during a PEI winter or Taco Bed.

But this had repercussions.

"Aretha and Jack will be around. They'll help out. And if you need some help in the kitchen, Bethany Burke offered to lend a hand."

The seasick feeling in her middle turned to stone, and she swallowed the snide comment in the back of her throat. Of course. Bethany, who was after her job, had volunteered. Out of the goodness of her heart, certainly.

Bethany, who smiled too hard at Adam. Bethany, who got whatever she wanted.

Well, she couldn't have Caden's job. Not without a fight, anyway.

Caden crossed her arms and squared her shoulders. "I'll do whatever you need. I'm sure Aretha and I can handle it."

Marie's pinched features instantly relaxed, and she clasped her hands below her chin. "Thank you, friend. I know you'll be busy, but it's only a couple weeks. And I knew we could count on you."

"Need anything else?"

Marie shook her head, so Caden excused herself and marched back to the kitchen. She wrenched a sauté pan from the rack hanging from the ceiling. Pans clanged together, and she quieted them with a gentler hand.

With a sigh, she leaned against the counter and hung her head until her chin rested on her chest.

"Want to talk about it?"

Adam's voice made her insides leap, but she gave him only a noncommittal shrug. "Not really."

She couldn't tell him about the inn's crisis, how much they needed the *Rest & Retreats* article, or how Bethany's return to town made her feel like she was fifteen again. Fifteen and terrified of the great big world. While her classmates had been busy planning their escapes from North Rustico — at least to the University of PEI in Charlottetown — she'd wanted nothing more than to stay where it was familiar.

Where it was safe.

"I just got a tongue-lashing from my editor for holding up an article." He was so matter-of-fact about it that she had to look at his face to see if he was being honest. The intensity in his gaze never wavered, and she scrambled for something to do to get out from under it.

After pouring a touch of oil into the pan, she turned on the burner and pulled the lobster cakes from the fridge.

"Ready for an afternoon snack?"

He nodded and rested a hip against the island, his eyes following her around the room. She could feel their embrace like a physical touch, sending tremors up and down every inch of her exposed skin.

She pressed a hand to her chest, then dropped it to her side. But that wasn't enough. She ran her hands down her arms and finally landed on her hips. Her full and curvy hips. And a bloom of regret filled her. If she was prettier . . .

What?

If she was prettier, he'd pull her into his arms? If she was thinner, he'd never want to look away from her? If she looked like the girls in the magazines, he'd want to show her off on his arm?

She didn't spend a lot of time dreaming

of looking a specific way or hoping for the pounds to miraculously fall off her hips and thighs. But for just a moment, she wished she could be the kind of woman Adam Jacobs might want. An outgoing beauty with a quick smile and a brave heart. The kind who whipped up a mean French toast but never ate it.

But she was never going to be that woman.

And even if she was, Adam was writing about her inn. There had to be ethical lines about reporters and the inns they wrote about. And Adam would never cross one of those lines.

Oil popped and sizzled as she set four lobster cakes in the hot pan. She kept her gaze trained on them, afraid to find that Adam was still watching her.

Equally afraid he wasn't.

The woman he wanted probably wasn't afraid of anything.

"So, my boss is ticked at me. How about you? What did Marie say?"

"That she and Seth need to make a trip to Boston."

Out of the corner of her eye, she saw his neck stiffen, his facial features tighten. But when he spoke there wasn't even a hint of tension in his voice. "When is that?"

"Next week, I guess. They'll be gone for a

couple weeks, and she asked me to take care of things in the meantime."

"You don't exactly sound thrilled about that."

She flipped the cakes and watched the oil bubble around them while she considered her response. It would be so easy to tell him the truth, to tell him how miserably unprepared she felt to run the front of the house. But she couldn't admit that to the person who was judging everything about the inn. Marie said they still needed this article. And they needed it to be great.

"It's just a lot, you know? Between prepping, cooking, and teaching in the afternoons, I already have a full schedule."

"Sure. I get it." She didn't know what to say and prayed he'd fill in the hole. Like always, he came through. "Speaking of your class, how are the kids doing on their cookoff recipes?"

As she scooped one of the cakes onto a paper towel, it cracked down the middle. She frowned and transferred it to a plate. The crack turned into a ravine, then another. The flaky insides tried to hold together, then seemed to just give up. Her insides did the same, and she let out a tired wheeze.

Finally she held up a crumbling lobster

cake. "Better than I am."

He covered his mouth, but his chuckle still made it through a gap in his fingers. "Maybe it's only aesthetics."

She frowned and poked at the cake with a fork. Another chunk fell off.

With a shrug, he said, "Maybe not."

Holding the plate and fork out to him, she wrinkled her nose. "Try it?"

Adam made an expression that reminded her of a knight going off to battle, picked up the fork like a weapon, and scooped up one of the chunks. With a glance to heaven — and probably a prayer that it wouldn't kill him — he popped it in his mouth.

He chewed with thoughtful motions, like he had to tell his body exactly what to do to eat the lobster cake. His jaw worked one way and then the other.

Not a good sign for a recipe that had promised melt-in-your-mouth results.

After what felt like a full minute, he swallowed. Then he grimaced.

She squeezed her eyes closed, fighting the burning sensation behind her eyelids. This wasn't the end of the world. It wasn't even the end of the competition. This was why she told her students to do practice runs. Recipes that promised big results sometimes required tweaking.

But all those rational thoughts just made the weight on her chest heavier, and she held her breath against a sudden hiccup that threatened to break free.

Her eyes were still closed, but she instantly knew something around her had changed. The air was charged with an emotion — a pressure — she couldn't name, had never known before. A plate clattered against the tile counter at her side, and she clasped her tingling fingers in front of her. Squinting into the unknown, she prayed for courage.

Adam stood right before her, close enough to touch, close enough to touch her.

And the compassion in his eyes told her she didn't need to be brave with him. He wouldn't demand anything of her.

Instead, he rubbed his thumbs across the apples of her cheeks, cupping her face and angling her head so she had to look right into his face. It was everything serious and grave. But when he opened his mouth his words were soft, lilting, funny. "Maybe it's better with the aioli."

Caden sniffled and laughed at the same time, which released a single tear. He quickly swiped it away, the pad of his thumb setting her skin on fire, and his eyes followed the motion. Which promptly set the rest of her on fire.

The air between them vanished, but she couldn't care. Air was overrated and completely unnecessary when he was three — no, two — feet away. She could only stare at his mouth, his lips, the two-day-old stubble that somehow seemed ever-present.

"You should try it."

It took a long second to shake the fog from her brain.

The lobster cakes. He was talking about the disaster on her kitchen counter.

She didn't risk looking toward the ruins, every one falling to pieces on the paper towel. No need to be reminded of her unmitigated failure. Instead, she confessed the truth she'd never told another soul. "I don't like lobster."

His head twitched to attention, and the corner of his mouth eased its way up. "Excuse me?"

"I don't care for it." Her voice came out quiet, but about half an octave too high, and she forced it back into a normal range. "It's . . . sweet and . . . chewy."

"And you're entering a lobster cook-off. And you grew up on this island, where lobster fishing is a huge industry. And you have it on your menu." He looked just about ready to release a full belly laugh. "But you don't actually *like* it?"

She wrinkled her nose. "Not even a little bit."

He chuckled, rich and pure, his whole face breaking with joy. She joined him, her giggle lighter but hampered by a swelling swarm of butterflies in her stomach.

He didn't seem to be suffering the same nervousness, but she couldn't calm the rush inside. Tugging on her ear, she forced herself to stay put. Pacing wasn't going to help. That would only get her farther away from him.

And God knew she didn't want to be any farther from his laughter than she had to be.

Suddenly the humor on his face disappeared, and his thumb ambled its way from her cheek toward her chin, catching on the corner of her mouth for a long moment.

Everything inside her melted, and she had to put her hands on the counter at her back to keep from turning into a puddle on the floor.

Is this what it felt like to be kissed? Or almost kissed?

She wouldn't know. No one had ever tried before.

But if it always felt like this — at once terrifying and electrifying — she wasn't sure she could survive a second go-round.

She gave herself a mental shake. She had to quit running ahead of the moment.

He wasn't going to kiss her. Those lines were surely in place. He was being friendly.

Only, none of her friends had ever been this close to her. None had ever stared at her with such an intense gaze that it made her fingers and toes curl.

Just enjoy the minute. Just enjoy him.

Adam.

"Hmm?"

Oh dear. She'd said his name aloud.

Nope. The little voice in her head confessed the whole, ugly truth.

She'd full-on *sighed* it. Like an actress in those cheesy movies her mother loved so much. Like a lovesick teenager. Like Adam when he saw her cinnamon rolls.

Lord, just take me now. She couldn't possibly survive this much embarrassment anyway.

But her prayer went unanswered, except by the deepening dimples in his cheeks. And then his mouth shaped her name on a barely there whisper. "Caden."

This — whatever *this* was — couldn't be happening. Things like this didn't happen in her kitchen. Especially not to girls like her.

She just wanted it to go on forever.

The thumb that had left her lips found her chin and settled into the small cleft there. It trailed back and forth, sending her swaying to the rhythm of the shivers running down her arms.

"I like lobster."

"Uh-huh."

"I like lobster a lot."

She had a feeling he wasn't talking about lobster anymore.

Suddenly the counter wasn't enough, and she needed a stronger anchor. Grasping for the only thing she could, she twisted her hands into his impossibly soft, black T-shirt and held on for all she was worth.

He leaned in a fraction, and she had to release her breath to make room for the hummingbirds suddenly filling her chest. They flitted from one side to the other. And nearly popped when he slid his hand around her back.

With a gentle tug, he pulled her from the security of the counter. Into his embrace. He was her only stability now, and he knew it. His hand was warm and tender, and somehow it began to put together the scrambled pieces of her insides, just to whisk them apart again.

He was an inch from her, and she could

see every freckle on his face, count every one of his eyelashes, feel every breath against her lips.

This moment, this feeling, was everything she'd ever dreamed it could be. And so much more. And she had never —

"Caden, can we talk about — whoa."

Adam stepped away so quickly that she swayed with him, nearly tripping over her own feet. The loss was like being doused in a bucket of cold water, and a shiver raced down her spine as she grasped at the slippery counter tile to stay upright.

Before she could even take account of the situation, Seth's deep laugh filled the entire kitchen, and her face burned from her ears to her neck.

"I didn't mean to interrupt you two." His voice held a symphony of humor, and he pressed his hand over his mouth. "I can come back."

Caden couldn't manage to get her gaze past the knees of his jeans — let alone up to his eyes — so she clasped her hands in front of her and pretended that her boss hadn't just interrupted her first kiss.

Oh dear. She'd had more than her share of embarrassing moments, but this was the very worst.

And it didn't help that she could feel

Adam's presence. Two feet to her left. Warm and solid. His breaths were quiet and steady. He stood like a bodyguard, reminding her she wasn't alone.

But he didn't say a word. No apology. No excuse. No explanation.

Why didn't he *say* something?

Seth cleared his throat and put his hands on his waist. "I'll, uh, just come back later."

She swallowed the desire to run. She'd never wanted to bolt from her own kitchen before. But she was pretty sure the urgency in her legs was prompting her to duck through the mudroom, sail through the back door, and disappear forever.

Instead she took a deep breath and pretended her face wasn't aflame and her insides weren't dying a slow death. "Need something?" Forcing herself to look up, she met Seth's gaze.

His grin was warm and friendly. There was no hint of ridicule or judgment. Only a deliberate look in his eyes that said he understood. Because she'd had to stomp down the hall before so she didn't walk in on him kissing Marie in this very kitchen.

Her stomach flopped like a fish out of water.

Seth loved Marie.

Was she beginning to feel the same for Adam?

With one quick sentence, Seth swooped in to save her from having to analyze her feelings. "We confirmed Jerome Gale's upcoming visit."

Of course, the celebrity chef. "When does he arrive?"

Seth wrinkled his whole face like he couldn't apologize enough. "While we're in Boston."

Her insides had no more room for nerves or butterflies or flopping fish, so she nodded and plastered a grin in place. "What do you need me to do?"

"I was hoping to talk through the room and menu for his stay."

"For sure."

That seemed to be Adam's cue to leave. He reached for her hand and gave it a gentle squeeze. "I'll see you later. Definitely in the morning."

"Uh-huh." But she couldn't look him in the face. She couldn't look past his long, tan fingers against her pale skin.

He squeezed again, and her insides declared mutiny.

Adam needed to go. He needed to leave, or she'd never make it through a conversation with Seth, let alone another second on earth. There were too many feelings for her to unpack, too many emotions to name while he stood beside her, and she couldn't possibly do it while Seth was in the room.

Please, just let him leave.

Adam let go of her hand and strolled toward the door.

Thank heaven for answered prayers.

16

The next days ticked by faster than dragon-fly wings. Every minute of the week had been filled with learning the reservation system, credit card processing, and cleaning schedule.

More went into the day-to-day running of the inn than she'd ever thought. And Caden had to learn it all. Perfect it all. In a week.

On top of her own duties in and out of the kitchen.

She hadn't had a moment to breathe, let alone work on her failed cook-off recipe. Which was why she was back in the inn late Sunday evening, giving it another try. The clouds covered the moon, and the only exterior light came from the intermittent lightning. And the occasional sweep of the lighthouse's beam across the water.

The day had been cool, the only warm spot a moment when Adam had sidled up beside her on the church lawn. Hugging her sweater beneath her chin, she had watched her nieces and nephews play beneath the big oak tree.

Adam brushed her elbow with his. "What are you staring at?"

"Oh, just . . ." She waved a hand toward the children as Bethany swooped in to pick up one of the kids who had taken a spill. The little girl with brown ringlets smiled up at Bethany, and Caden frowned. There was some compassion in Bethany. Some kindness.

But if that was the case, why was she always so unpleasant to Caden?

Adam's gaze followed her motion, and he grinned in Bethany's direction.

Suddenly a terrible question popped into her mind, and she blurted it out before she could stop herself. "Why haven't you asked Bethany out? She's clearly interested in you."

He blinked fast, his forehead a map of confusion. "What?"

Oh no. If she could take that back . . .

Her stomach rocked and her head swam, and she scrambled for anything to cover her gaffe. "I mean . . . I didn't mean that . . . not like it . . ." She slapped a hand over her mouth but couldn't look away, her eyes unblinking, her teeth clenched.

Adam's confusion softened until a crooked grin lifted the corner of his mouth. Then he dropped his voice until they were the only two who could hear it. "It's been my experience that people who act like they have it all together rarely do. I'm not interested in stepping into whatever mess is going on in her life."

His words, which she thought were meant to encourage her, only made her insides squirm more. She most certainly didn't have it all together, and if he didn't like messy, he couldn't like her.

Maybe her fear showed across her face. Maybe he could read her mind. Maybe he just knew what she needed to hear. It didn't matter because his next words were perfect.

"I'm not afraid of messy. I've got plenty of my own. I just like to know that the girl I'm interested in isn't afraid of it either."

She'd practically walked on clouds the whole way home. He'd confided in her, and somehow that was almost as special as their almost kiss.

Now she was snug and warm inside, daydreaming about the timbre of Adam's voice and lining up the ingredients for lobster cakes. Adam was up in his room, and Levi and Esther had gone to the city to watch a show.

It was almost like being all alone in the big house, so she turned up her cooking music — the *Newsies* soundtrack — and set to work.

She had just slid the cakes into a skillet when a loud crash shook the ceiling. She ducked down and looked out the window. Maybe lightning had hit a tree. But all she saw was the steady rain streaming down the glass pane.

Then a loud groan followed. This time she was sure it had come from the second floor.

Adam was the only one up there.

Racing for the back stairs, she sent up a prayer. Her legs couldn't have taken the stairs two at a time even if she'd been skinny, but she pumped them as fast as she could, winded by the time she reached the landing. But she couldn't stop.

She slid on the wooden floors, nearly missing Adam's door, and caught herself on the jamb. "Adam! Adam!" She rapped on his door with staccato strikes, but he didn't answer.

A lump formed in her throat, blocking her breaths and adding to the rapid tattoo of her heart.

Be okay. Be okay. Be okay.

"Adam! Can you hear me?"

Another groan sounded on the far side of

the door, and she forgot that she was the innkeeper and he was a guest. In that moment she only cared about her friend. She twisted the knob and shoved her shoulder against the door.

It flew inward, and she nearly stumbled to the floor.

Which was already occupied by Adam.

Dropping to her knees at his side, she pressed her hands to his face. A band squeezed her lungs, and she could only gasp. "Adam? Are you all right? What happened?"

Only then did she realize she was kneeling in a puddle, her jeans soaking up the water and turning cumbersome.

Frantically she looked for the source of the spill but didn't see anything until Adam groaned again. When he reached to touch the back of his head, a stream of water leaked from the ceiling. It hit him square in the stomach, turning his T-shirt into a sponge — a very poor one.

He must have slipped on the water and hit his head.

His eyes turned grayer than usual as he blinked twice. "I'm okay."

"I think you hit your head."

He grimaced, touching his fingers to the

underside of his skull. "I'm pretty sure of it."

Somehow his joke broke the fear that had been clutching her chest, and she caught a full breath, releasing it on a half-laugh.

With a moan of pain, he cupped his wound and began to sit up. She wanted to push him back down, but the rain was still streaming onto him. Maybe they could get him to the bed.

Except there was another leak spitting onto the quilt.

She had to get Seth and Marie.

Except they were hundreds of miles away.

And she couldn't call them home for a leak in the roof.

She was on her own for the moment. And the sudden realization made her mouth go dry.

"I'm all right." He squinted again and held out his hand. "Just need some help."

Wrapping her fingers around his wrist, she pulled Adam upright, then helped him get to his feet. He groaned and grumbled with every move, and she couldn't help but doubt his assurance.

"Do you want me to call an ambulance to take you to the hospital?"

With hunched shoulders and a hollow laugh, he shook his head. "I'm fine." Rubbing at the small of his back, he sighed. "Just feeling older than I thought I was and more than a little embarrassed."

Caden tried to chuckle, but there was nothing to do but hold on to his elbow and help him into the hall, which hadn't turned into a swimming pool yet.

"Let's get an ice pack for your head and let you sit down for a while."

He grunted what she assumed was an affirmative response and draped his arm across her shoulder, hers around his waist. There was no space between them, no air to breathe. It was not the time to think about how well she fit there or how good he smelled. It wasn't the minute for analyzing the line of his jaw or the stubble that always seemed to grow there. It wasn't the moment for daydreaming about what might have happened if Seth hadn't walked into the kitchen a week before.

But it took everything inside her not to.

They swayed and stumbled down the stairs, but as they approached the kitchen, she straightened up. A foul smell permeated the back hall, and her stomach flipped.

She cried out as she helped him to a stool and raced for the stove, where her lobster cakes had been ruined. Again. They were black and crispy and soaked in oil that had splashed across the stove top.

At least she hadn't set the whole place on fire.

She turned off the stove, set her pan to the side, and turned back to Adam.

There were too many things that needed her attention to be upset over ruined lobster cakes. Especially when she didn't even like them. Instead, she dug out a bag of frozen blueberries and held it out to Adam.

He shrugged, gingerly pressing it against his injury. "That'll work."

"Don't move. I'll be right back." She picked up two giant pots, hurried back up the stairs, and placed one under each leak. Then she raced to find towels to mop up the mess. Shuffling around on her knees, she soaked up as much water as she could and hugged the wet rags all the way to the laundry room.

By the time the leak in Adam's room had been contained and she was back in the kitchen, she was out of breath and sweating. Wiping her hand across her forehead, she sighed. "I am so sorry about all this."

The color was returning to Adam's cheeks. "It was my fault. I jumped out of bed too fast when I realized I was being dripped on and then slipped."

"And our roof shouldn't have been leaking."

He lifted a shoulder, leaning the same elbow on the counter. "No harm done. I'll be fine."

"Are you sure?"

He nodded, pulling the blueberries away as he ran a hand over his hair. "It's just a knot. I've had worse."

She sighed with relief, resting her hands on top of the island and giving him a wavering smile. "Maybe you could leave this part out of your article, anyway."

Adam frowned, and not only from the pain throbbing down the back of his neck. "Out of my article?"

Her grin turned guilty. "I know we're not supposed to know."

"Know what?" Had his fall knocked something loose? He honestly had no idea what she was talking about. And he didn't like the way her eyebrows played in the shadow of her bangs, innocent but knowing.

"About the article for *Rest & Retreats*. I don't think their readers want to hear about an inn with a leaky roof, but I promise we'll get it fixed before the spring issue."

"*Rest & Retreats?* The spring issue?" He sounded like a confused parrot. He felt like one too, but no matter how hard he searched his shaken brain, none of what she said made sense.

She nodded slowly, the highlights in her fair hair dancing under the kitchen lights. "The travel article. Six inns are being featured. And mystery writers are being sent. One of Marie's friends sent her a letter about it." She paused to catch her breath after a long run-on. "And your editor sent you here. Right?"

"Yes . . ." He dragged the word out, not at all sure how the two thoughts were connected or where this conversation was going. Not quite sure he *wanted* to know where it was going.

"Your editor at *Rest & Retreats.*"

He shook his head, ignoring the pain because somehow finding a way to the same page as Caden was much more important. "No. My editor is at *America Today.*"

Caden's forehead wrinkled, and she pressed one finger to her lips. "But you write for *Rest & Retreats.*"

He had the distinct feeling they were having two very different conversations, so he paused and put a little distance between them, walking to the far side of the room. She stared into his eyes, but the confusion didn't dissipate.

"Why do you think I write for a travel magazine?"

"Well . . ." Her gaze dropped, then shifted side to side as she seemed to search for answers to questions he didn't even know to ask. He wanted to help her, to fill in whatever she didn't understand. He just didn't have any idea what that was. "You're a travel writer."

"I'm *not* a travel writer." The short sentence burst out on a rush of breath and bewilderment. "Why would you think that?"

"What?" If her features had been covered with confusion before, it doubled now. Her nose wrinkled like she'd caught another whiff of the burnt lobster cakes, and her lips pursed to the side. "You're not a travel writer?"

He shrugged. She could repeat his words over and over. It wouldn't change them. "Not until recently. Not even officially. I sent a few travel articles to my editor, but I haven't heard anything back."

Finally she looked back into his eyes, her face wiped of any expression. Hands clenched in front of her, she whispered, "You're not doing a feature on Rose's Red Door Inn?"

"No — wait, what?" The throbbing in his head tripled, and he pressed a hand to his temple in a vain attempt to relieve a bit of the pressure. He'd lost any sign of the tracks for this conversation. She'd thought he wrote travel articles. But how . . .

He scrubbed through every memory of the last six weeks, hunting out any foundation he might have given for her mix-up. He'd mentioned his writing, talked about his editor, and always had his notebook in reach. But he'd never talked about what he wrote. Had he?

Of course not. Because then he'd have to tell her about Connor and the explosion. And he'd rather sleep on Taco Bed again than watch her face crumple when she realized just what he'd done.

Caden still looked stunned, like her entire world had been thrown off its axis. "But you're supposed to do an article about the inn and make everyone love it and come stay at it. We need the money to keep the doors open." She snorted, but it wasn't with humor. "To fix the roof. We have to fill up the Red Door next season, and we need you." Her eyes grew wider with every word, and by the end of her verbal explosion, they eclipsed her face. "We were counting on you." Even though her voice dropped to a whisper, it hit him with the force of a sledgehammer.

They'd been counting on him to save them.

And he'd had no idea.

The world shifted. His stomach rolled. And he sank against the counter, leaving Caden five feet away and overflowing with confusion.

Caden rubbed her forehead and then chewed on her fingernail. She must have misunderstood. He couldn't be saying what she thought he was saying.

They'd all assumed.

They'd all *known*.

He was the one who was going to save the inn. He was going to put them on the map. He was going to fill their pockets again.

Except, he wasn't.

"Why does the inn need to be saved? Isn't it doing well?"

Caden hemmed and hawed for a moment. It wasn't her business, and she had no right to reveal what was going on with Marie's dad. Still, Adam looked genuinely concerned. "Capital is low. If we don't sell out for the whole season next year, we might not be able to make the repairs we need and keep things going. We needed your article . . ."

"To drum up business." He scrubbed his

face with both hands. "I get it."

Suddenly, her stomach somersaulted. "If you're not a travel writer, why are you here?"

"I'm on sabbatical. Kind of a forced vacation."

Perfect. He was an actual guest.

Which meant in the first day of Marie's absence, the inn had sprung a leak, Caden had made the kitchen smell like musty feet, and they'd lost their only hope for the magazine feature. Maybe it would get better. Because it certainly couldn't get worse.

17

After soundly whipping Adam at not just one but three games of checkers, Levi sat back and crossed his arms. "It's like you aren't even trying today."

Adam nodded, then shook his head, then shrugged. He didn't know how to respond because he hadn't really been paying attention. Not to the board set up between them and not to Levi's comment. And it didn't have anything to do with the knot on the back of his head.

Since the night before he'd only been able to see Caden's strained face and the slump in her shoulders when she'd fully realized that he wasn't who she thought he was. He wasn't who she needed him to be.

The truth pinched like an angry crab. And the checkers game couldn't take his mind off of it.

Not even his ever-evolving plan to get Levi to talk about his tattoo could make him forget the stiffness in her neck as they'd made up a fresh bed in a dry room. He couldn't unsee the shimmer of tears in her eyes or the tremor in her bottom lip.

He'd tossed and turned most of the night, wishing he could help, praying there was something he could do.

"I could write something for you," he had offered. "I could definitely write a piece about the Red Door. I'd love to."

Caden perked up for an instant before reality set back in. "It's not just an article. It's the magazine. It has a huge readership, and when it recommends a B and B, people make reservations."

That made sense. It also felt like a kick in his gut. The only things he'd ever been really good at were writing and drinking. And neither could help the inn now.

Levi stood and stretched his left arm across his body. "I think I'm going to take a nap."

Adam frowned, a nugget of disappointment forming in his chest despite his distractions. "Are you feeling all right?" He pushed himself out of his chair so he could look the older man in the eye.

"Better than matzah ball soup." Levi's gnarled hand patted Adam's shoulder. "But I could use some rest. And then I'm going to work on my book."

"Your book?" Adam lifted his eyebrows. "I thought you said you didn't have any more words in you."

Levi shrugged a stooped shoulder. "I guess maybe I do. Turns out there might be something in the air making me want to write. And now I've got the time."

Caden's music chirped from deep inside the house, and Levi perked up to listen to the Broadway actor's rich tenor. "And a little inspiration."

"Good music?"

"Good cooking." Levi gave him an elbow nudge to the stomach. "And a good girl. I figured I'd write some legal or political thriller, but this sweet little blonde with a perfect dimple keeps showing up in my scenes. And she's way too sharp and funny to ignore."

Adam's head took a quick — and entirely too enjoyable — spin as his brain conjured said dimple. Just the memory of her smile and her hands wrapped into his shirt when he'd come so close to kissing her was all his stomach needed to take flight. But last night's revelation was all it took to sink it like a stone. "I know what you mean."

Levi chuckled. "Figured you might."

Of course. The old man missed nothing.

"What are you boys talking about?" Esther looked up from the book she was reading in a chair at the end of the porch.

"I'm going to lie down for a bit, my dear. Why don't you go on a walk with Adam."

Esther pushed herself up against the Adirondack's wide armrests and tucked her book into her bag. Her pale brown eyes settled on Adam. "What do you say? Will you take me on a stroll along the harbor?"

"It would be my honor." He gave her a quick bow, which produced exactly the chuckle he'd been hoping for.

After handing off her bag to Levi, she accepted Adam's arm. They ambled across the street and down the stairs to the boardwalk.

"Did you go to a meeting with Levi?"

Adam's head whipped toward Esther. This woman didn't do small talk. If she wasn't distracted by breakfast foods, it was apparently all or nothing.

"Don't look so surprised."

"I'm not really, I guess. I just thought the meetings were supposed to be anonymous."

She nodded. "They are. And Levi would never betray that." She squeezed the inside of his elbow, holding him to a slower pace. "But I saw you walking with him toward the church. And you came back at the same time."

"You're very astute, Mrs. Eisenberg. That's one of the traits of a good reporter, you know."

Her brown eyes nearly glowed, the creases of her face lighting from within. "Now you're just flattering me."

"No, ma'am. I would never do such a thing." Well, he might. But not to Esther Eisenberg. She commanded a certain respect. She deserved that respect. And not just because she was fifty years older than him.

He couldn't really put his finger on it, but even if he'd met her in Washington, he'd have wanted to sit by her side, hear her stories, and learn from her experience.

"Such a respectful young man." She turned away, and he wondered if she'd meant for that to stay in her mind, so he didn't comment until she went on. "Most young people these days are talking too loud, moving so fast, that they forget their 'ma'ams' and 'sirs.' Your mother must have taught you well."

The reminder still stung. Eight years and countless regrets since, a mention of his mother still made his chest burn and his hands tremble. "Yes, ma'am."

Esther rubbed the back of his hand where he had laid it over hers at his elbow. "Where is your momma now?"

"She passed away. My dad too. Eight years ago."

"I'm guessing about the time you gave up drinking."

Could this woman read his mind? The only other person on the island with a clue about his background was Caden. And she wouldn't break his confidence. He had no doubt about that.

"When a young man suffers a traumatic loss, he generally either drops a vice or takes up a new one."

There she went again, reading his mind, answering the questions he hadn't asked. And it made his stomach churn with an unsettled feeling. He didn't particularly want anyone to be able to read him so well. And he sure didn't want to rehash any of it.

Even if she was right. He'd given up alcohol after his parents' death. And he'd longed to take it up again after Connor's. He'd searched for it nearly every morning those first few weeks on the island.

But he hadn't picked up the old vice. He'd picked up a new one. Coffee and cinnamon rolls.

And Caden.

Caden. He'd been so close to getting that kiss. He'd bet good money that her lips were as sweet as the icing on her cupcakes, and just the memory of their kitchen escapade was enough to put his whole body on high alert. Muscles tense, his mind played out the memory over and over. The scent of her hair — ginger and the ocean — had consumed him. Her smile had been shy but unafraid, and her dimple had beckoned him to pull her close and never let her go.

Because he'd rather spend his day with her than with anyone else.

His ribs took another shot, and he flinched into the realization. When it was time to leave the island, he wasn't sure he'd be able to leave Caden behind.

He had to get his mind on another topic. A safer one.

"How old was Levi when he quit drinking?"

Esther looked toward a white cloud rolling lazily across the sky, her eyes shifting back and forth as though doing long division in her head. "Just over forty, I suppose. He'd been at it since he was fifteen."

"If he was a drunk, why'd you marry him?" Had he just blurted out the first thing that came to mind? Reporters couldn't afford to do that. *He* never did that.

But Esther only laughed and patted his arm. "Well, he was just about the most

306

handsome man I'd ever seen. We met in Hebrew school, you know."

"I did not know that."

"Oh yes. He was so charismatic and smart, and every girl wanted to study with him. Every girl except me."

Adam had a gut feeling he knew where this was going, but he had to ask. "Why didn't you want to?"

She giggled like she must have as a schoolgirl. "Because every other girl did. My only chance to stand out was to be different."

"So why did everyone want to be near him?"

"Because he survived."

Adam stopped walking, a weight on his chest holding him in place. It hurt to breathe. Just thinking about the soft-spoken man as a child, suffering the atrocities of the Holocaust, made his eyes water.

"How did . . . how did he survive?"

"Oh, that's his story to tell. My part of our tale didn't start until 1953 on the corner outside the Hebrew school."

Adam weighed his next words carefully, wondering just how much he could ask without being rude. "Who does he tell his story to?"

She pulled her hand free, and her smile disappeared. For a moment he thought he'd

307

crossed the line. He would give up breakfasts with them to keep from saying anything
to push the couple away. He couldn't afford
for Esther to think he only wanted to know
about Levi's past. And Levi to wonder at
his motivation.

Then her teeth flashed, and genuine
compassion glowed in her eyes. "My dear
boy. He'll tell anyone willing to share their
past with him. First." She pressed her hand
to his chest, right over his heart. "Those
memories aren't easy for him. But we all
have ones we'd rather forget, pain we've
caused we wish we could take back. Am I
right?"

"Yes, but how could it be an even trade?"

In no universe could Adam's memories
play on the same field as Levi's. Adam's
shames were of his own making. Levi's history was a massacre of a people group —
his people.

"Oh, it's not an equal exchange, but it
doesn't have to be." The corners of her eyes
crinkled.

"It doesn't?"

"Of course not. It just has to mean that
you're willing to share your stuff too."

He ruffled his hair with his palm, then
scratched his ear. It was a lot easier to hope
Levi would share his story than it was to lay

open his own.

"They're hard memories. Things I'm not proud of." He shrugged because she might be able to guess some of it, if not the worst of it. "Things that got me into AA."

Esther pressed her hand harder against his heart, and it thumped faster, somehow knowing that she wasn't done with him. "Strange, isn't it? The memories we most hate, the things we most regret, are often the ones that connect us with others."

Whatever nail she'd put against his chest, her words struck it on the head. It pierced his soul, and he nearly stumbled to his knees as his legs buckled and his head swam.

"Adam, dear? Are you well?"

He tried for a confident smile, but settled for a grimace. Pressing his hand to his brow, he tried to keep his head from falling off.

Somehow Esther knew that he'd kept his distance, kept from getting too close to anyone, by keeping his worst secrets to himself. He'd known deep down that if he opened up about the award he'd won, the one that put his parents on the road where they were killed, he'd either lose friends or forge an everlasting connection. And it was easier to keep the secrets to himself than build another relationship he could lose.

It was why he'd lost touch with his

brother. It was why his friendships in Washington were entirely superficial. It was why no one had complained when he was on assignment for three months.

It was easier to be alone than risk revealing his worst memories.

"What about Caden?"

Good question.

"Have you told her about your past?"

There was a question below the question, and it terrified him.

Have you forged a connection with her?

He wanted to climb down the slope, slip into the cool harbor water, and swim away. Mostly he didn't want to have to answer that question.

He knew what the answer was, and he wasn't at all sure he liked the depth of it.

Esther patted his arm as her smile turned knowing. "She's a lovely young woman."

"Yes, ma'am." No need to argue against the truth. But if he let her get going, there was no telling what else she'd get him to admit. Tossing his head toward the inn, he said, "Should we head back?"

"All right then. But don't forget what I said."

18

By Thursday afternoon, Caden wasn't sure if having Aretha and Jack pop in to the inn was a help. It was beginning to feel a little more like a distraction. She'd had to calm Aretha down when she showed them Adam's former room, where the ceiling had finally stopped dripping. And she'd had to convince them that they couldn't call Marie and Seth. The two had more important things to worry about in Boston.

And Caden had things to worry about in North Rustico.

Like somehow making up for whatever revenue might have come in from the *Rest & Retreats* reservations.

If things didn't go as they hoped with Marie's dad, Caden couldn't let her return to more bad news.

As long as Aretha hovered around the inn, there wasn't a quiet moment to think through her options. Caden hadn't even had time to ask Adam what he thought. He showed up every day for his coffee, and they shared about ten minutes of morning-fogged chitchat before Aretha arrived. After that, it wasn't easy to get a word in edge-wise. And certainly not about anything besides breakfast, the inn, or the newest antique Aretha had acquired for her store.

They hadn't had a moment for serious conversation in almost a week. But staring over her cup of coffee and not talking with him left her dwelling on only two options. What she was going to do about the inn. And if she'd missed her only chance to kiss him.

After all, it had been nearly two weeks, and Adam hadn't tried again.

Maybe he didn't want to.

Regret and sadness swirled deep inside her. It gnawed on her like a dog on his favorite bone.

Their moment in the kitchen had passed, and Adam wasn't likely to revisit it if he hadn't already.

If she was more like other girls, she wouldn't wait for him. She'd make a move on her own. Bethany certainly wouldn't wait. When she saw an opening, she charged through it, staked her claim, and set up shop.

That wasn't Caden's style.

Not even close.

Nope. Her style was to stew over Adam and daydream — about how it would feel to be wrapped in his arms and fully kissed — while washing potatoes for her afternoon class. Not exactly a glamorous way to spend her afternoon, but it sure beat putting herself out there only to be rejected.

A tiny voice in her head reminded her that Adam hadn't rejected her. Not exactly.

She muttered Seth's name — and a few words that would make her mother cringe — under her breath and wished for the hundredth time that he'd had the decency to wait until after her first kiss to interrupt them.

As she grumbled about her boss, the pile of clean spuds grew until Aretha walked into the kitchen, Esther in tow.

"What are you making with the kids today?" Esther said.

Caden looked from Esther to the mound of PEI red potatoes on the counter and back again. "Actually, I'm not sure."

Aretha's forehead wrinkled in confusion. "You have a lot of potatoes for 'not sure.' "

She shrugged. "I told the kids on Monday to bring their questions about their cook-off recipes. But if that doesn't take the whole class, we'll make garlic mashed potatoes."

Aretha pressed her hand to her stomach and sighed. "I love your mashed potatoes. Maybe you should serve your lobster cakes over them for the contest. Your comfort food is the best."

Caden cringed but tried to keep her face completely impassive. After a third failed attempt on the lobster cakes, she'd decided there wasn't enough time to perfect them. Not with only a little more than a week before the competition.

But Aretha was right. She was best at comfort foods, like mashed potatoes and donuts and hearty beef stew.

Those wouldn't compete with the gourmet, international plate that Bethany would offer. But Caden wasn't sure *she* could compete with that.

She was an islander through and through, and what she had to offer — what she did best — was local, stick-to-your-ribs food. The kind that Adam loved. The kind that she loved.

But she couldn't just plate mashed potatoes for the cook-off. There had to be something better. Something more substantial. Something with lobster.

"When is this lobster dinner? Levi and I don't want to miss it."

"Next Friday," Aretha replied. "And it's Caden's year to win."

Everyone expected a win. Her dad, Aretha, Marie, Adam, the kids in her class, and now Esther. And letting them down wasn't an option. She had to win.

For her family. For the inn.

For herself.

The truth sliced through her with surprising speed and realization.

She *wanted* to win. And not just for everyone who was counting on her. Not just to find a way into Adam's heart. Not just because she wanted to serve Bethany a dish of humble pie.

Caden craved a win because she'd worked hard and continued to improve as a chef.

She wanted to win because she'd always been the girl who everyone liked and no one thought very special.

She wanted to stand out, to leave a mark on this city, to be remembered as more than so-and-so's friend.

Funny. She hadn't even realized she felt that way until recently. Until one man's arrival forced her out of the kitchen and into the real world.

And his presence made the outside not quite as scary as it used to be.

"Caden has cooking in her genes," Aretha

continued.

Loosely translated, that meant she was made for the kitchen.

She'd known it and always believed it to be true. From the time she had to stand on a stool at her grandmother's side in order to reach the kitchen counter, she'd known. And when her dad hired her as his baking assistant while Dillon and their classmates ran off to get part-time jobs at the dairy, she'd known. She belonged in the kitchen.

But now . . . was it possible God had something beyond the kitchen in store for her?

"Well, our Adam will sure eat anything she makes." Esther spoke like a proud grandmother, and maybe she was. She'd practically adopted Adam for the summer.

Aretha shook her head. "You two act like you're stuck in a lobster trap, spending every minute together the last six weeks. Is there something going on between you?"

Flames shot up Caden's neck and across her cheeks, and embarrassment turned her stomach three times in a row. But she hunched her shoulders, kept her head down, and scrubbed at an already clean spot on the potato in her hand.

Aretha laughed, but Esther pushed. "I think you two make a fine couple. Adam is a dear. He's kind and so easy to talk to. And handsome too."

Esther didn't need to sing his praises. Caden had cataloged them all. From the tilt in his grin to the light in his gray eyes to the cute little way his hair stood up when he ran his fingers through it. From the way he'd opened up about his parents to the kindness he showed Esther and Levi to the praises he lavished on her cooking. In the way he joked with her students, opened the door for her, and found beauty in the same places she did. She knew he was a good man.

And handsome too.

But it didn't mean he felt the same about her.

With her mind on the lengthy list of Adam's finer qualities, her scrubber got away from her, leaving an angry red mark down the length of her finger. She dropped the potato and jabbed her finger in her mouth, sucking on the growing welt.

"Are you all right, hon?" Aretha's face filled with concern.

"Sure. At least I wasn't peeling them."

Esther nodded, but a little smirk began to tug at the corners of her lips. "I could call Adam in to take a look at it if you'd like."

Caden's eyes flew open wide, heat again

racing from her neck to her ears. She kept her finger in her mouth so she wouldn't have to respond, but that left the floor open for Aretha, whose gray curls bobbed and shoulders shook as she poked her friend in the arm. "Why, Esther Eisenberg, you're positively incorrigible."

"Only when I see two people who so clearly should be together."

Was it possible to die of embarrassment? Because the pain beneath Caden's sternum suggested that her insides couldn't withstand the pressure of this conversation much longer.

"She should tell him how she feels," Esther said.

"She's a little shy." Aretha put her hands on her hips and stretched to her full height, which was still about four inches shorter than Esther. "She'll get there. Besides, he should make the first move."

Caden's stomach quivered, but she couldn't look away from the tennis match, each volley more forceful than the last.

"Maybe he already has." Esther shot her a pointed look, and Caden frantically shook her head.

No, Adam hadn't made a move.

Exactly.

He'd made a few half-moves, a handful of

partial attempts.

Sort of.

Aretha fired back, "Well, if he had, they'd be together — I mean, to-geth-er. They're perfect. And it's obvious she's been pining for him for weeks."

Her breath caught about halfway from her lungs and she choked on it. Hard.

Did everyone know how she felt? Had everyone figured out that she was falling for the non–travel writer who couldn't help the inn? Maybe it hadn't been much of a riddle. Maybe she was as obvious as she'd been in high school.

Oh, God, please take me now.

But he didn't. And Caden was forced to stand there coughing while the two women dissected her love life — or lack thereof — as though she wasn't in the room.

For half a second she considered waving her hands and reminding them that she could hear everything they said. Then again . . . they might have something interesting to say. She leaned forward, holding her breath for Esther's next words.

Only, Esther looked stumped. As if her racehorse had failed to show up to the track. Pressing a finger to her lips, she shook her head. "I don't get it. Could it be the distance? Since he's leaving in a couple weeks?

But she's only a plane ride away. With technology these days, distance is a poor excuse. And they're so well suited."

"I don't know." Aretha's features shifted toward pensive until it looked like she'd stopped competing against Esther and joined her team.

"Maybe he just needs a little push." Esther pursed her lips until her eyebrows slowly rose. "Or a little time with her. She's been so busy the last few days."

Well, that wasn't entirely her fault. Caden wasn't the one who made the roof leak or took off for Boston. And if Aretha didn't insist on interrupting their coffee time every day, then maybe she'd have a minute to — her shoulders slumped — do exactly what she'd been doing.

Which was absolutely nothing.

"Of course!" Aretha clapped her hands together. "It's perfect. She needs to take him out. Show him some more of the island."

She had been doing that. In fact, she'd done it all summer. And it had culminated in exactly one *almost* kiss.

But they didn't care. They had plans.

"A picnic," Esther said. "He loves whatever she prepares."

"And a hike on the Homestead Trail,"

Aretha added. "There's the most romantic spot. Just a kilometer in, right on the beach."

Caden knew the place. She loved it, actually. Red sand shores, green fields, and crystal-blue water in every direction. On one bridge over a shining inlet along the trail, she'd pretended to be Anne Shirley pretending to be the Lady of Shalott.

And if she thought that another trip to the trail would change her relationship with Adam, she was pretending again. He enjoyed her company. That was clear. They were good friends. But he didn't want more from her.

No one ever had.

"And she'll make his favorite."

Caden couldn't help muttering under her breath, "Cinnamon rolls?"

Esther waved off the sarcastic comment. "Lobster and mussels."

Caden's stomach heaved at the thought of eating the chewy meat and slimy mussels.

She was saved by the loud chime of the doorbell. "I have to go. If my kids come in, have them peel these potatoes, and tell them I'll be right back."

She dashed out of the kitchen and out from under the weight of their conversation. By the time she reached the inn's red namesake, she felt like she'd shed fifteen pounds. With a quick straightening of her apron, she plastered a smile into place and swung the door open.

A beautiful blonde woman stood before her. A smart tote bag hung over her shoulder, and a brand-new, four-wheeled suitcase stood at her side. The clean, lean lines of her khaki pants and white button-up shirt were wrinkle free.

She offered a hesitant smile as she tugged on a green bobble earring. "I'm Danielle Delacroix."

"Hello. Welcome." Caden reached to shake her hand but changed her mind halfway there and swung her hand toward the inside of the house instead. "I'm Caden Holt. Executive chef at the Red Door. Marie said she's very sorry she couldn't meet you today."

Danielle's strangely blue eyes took a sweeping inventory of Caden's outfit, pausing only briefly on the large floral apron that covered her chest to nearly her knees. Slowly the smile that had been on her lips reached her eyes. "Delighted."

"Come on in. Let's get you checked in." After Danielle stepped inside, Caden closed the door and gave her a quick tour. "This is the parlor. There are magazines and books for you to read anytime you like, and cold water is always available in the mini fridge. And this is the dining room." She wound her way between tables and stopped by the one that Adam and the Eisenbergs shared every morning. "Would you like your own table, or would you rather sit with other guests?"

As soon as she asked the question that Marie had instructed her to, Caden's stomach flipped. If she wanted, this too-pretty woman could eat breakfast with Adam every day.

"Oh yes, I'd like to sit with other guests."

And just like that, the jealousy she'd felt whenever Bethany got too close to Adam demanded attention. She tried to ignore it, but it settled like a low burner in her chest — constant and irritating.

"Great." Okay, that was a lie, but it had sounded almost true. "You'll sit here then. I'll put your name on the place card." The rest of the details about the dining room rolled out quicker than she'd intended, but Danielle seemed to keep up. Three o'clock snacks on the antique buffet. Breakfast from eight to nine. Coffee and tea available all day.

As they made their way down the narrow hall to the office, Caden heard her students laughing as they took over the kitchen.

Either that or a pack of hyenas had moved in.

Danielle tipped her head in the direction of the hubbub. "What's in there?"

"Oh, that's the kitchen."

"Sounds like you have a lot of helpers."

Caden chuckled. "Not quite helpers. I teach a cooking class for high school students over the summer."

Danielle's eyes lit up. "That's fantastic. Are they locals?"

"All of them. And most of them work a part-time job over the summer too."

"How many days a week?"

"Just Mondays and Thursdays."

As the other woman asked more questions about the classes, Caden checked her into her room, handed her the keys, and walked her to her suite.

As Caden said, "This is your room," Danielle spoke too. "Have you ever considered offering a cooking class for guests?"

Caden slammed on her brakes. She opened her mouth to speak, but nothing came out. She closed it and blinked a few times. She'd never — not once — considered the idea of teaching a cooking class to the guests. But even Adam, who hadn't had any real interest in cooking before arriving at the Red Door, had begun chopping vegetables and whisking eggs for morning prep.

And in big cities cooking classes often sold out. Offering a simple weekly cooking class for guests could be an extra source of income and an added marketing point for the inn.

"Actually, no. But that's a fantastic idea."

She needed to flesh out the idea before she could offer it to Marie. She needed to talk with someone about it. To talk with Adam about it.

First, she needed to make sure there wasn't a fire in her kitchen or an upended bag of flour on the floor.

The scene in the kitchen was as chaotic as Caden had feared. Whitney and Iris were dutifully peeling potatoes at the island while Ford chased Jeanie toward the back door, threatening to dump a pile of peelings on her head. Gretchen was stooped into a lower cabinet, pulling every pot from the bottom shelf.

"What is going on here?" Caden used her very best teacher voice. It stopped Ford in his tracks, and he dropped his handful of potato skins on her clean floor. Crossing her arms against the irritation bubbling in her chest, she shot him a hard glare.

Ford hung his head, the pointy shoulders

under his white T-shirt deflating. "Sorry, Caden."

"Just because I stepped out doesn't mean you have free rein to ruin my kitchen."

Gretchen clanged two pots together, and Caden's gaze swooped onto her. "What are you doing?"

The girl looked up with guilty eyes. A roasting pan in one hand and a three-quart soup pot in the other, she shrugged. "You said you'd help us with our recipes. I was looking for a pot for my lobster chowder."

Caden sighed and ran her hands through her hair, nearly ready to tug it out. "You don't have to pull out every single pot and put them on the —"

The squeak of the door to the dining room had her spinning around to face the person she most wanted to see and least wanted to see her at the moment.

"Hey, Adam." Ford greeted him with the traditional teenage boy nod.

Adam's eyebrows drew together. "What'd you do?"

Glancing at his feet, Ford lifted one shoulder. "I dropped some stuff."

"Well, clean it up." Adam's words were clipped but not unkind, direct but not over-reaching.

Ford moved like he'd received an order

from the angel Gabriel himself. "Yes, sir."

The boiling in her chest disappeared with those two little words. She loved seeing how her students related to Adam. They clearly respected him, and he returned the favor with a dash of authority.

"Esther said you wanted to see me."

Caden had to shake herself from her thoughts to figure out that he was talking to her. "What?"

"You wanted to see me."

Yes. Always. But no. She hadn't asked for him.

Her confusion must have been written across her face because his frown quickly matched hers.

"Esther and Aretha said something about the homestead."

To her right, three pairs of teenage eyes locked on her. "The Homestead Trail . . ." Iris giggled in such a high, clear tone that she didn't need to finish the sentence. Caden could almost hear the words bouncing off the cabinet doors.

The Homestead Trail . . . is so romantic.

Pressing one hand to her riotous stomach, she tried to wave off his raised eyebrow with the other. "Oh, that was just an idea they had."

From the scene of her almost exit into the

mudroom, Jeanie said, "Are you going to take her? You totally should."

Caden rolled her eyes, shooting a prayer toward heaven in the process. *Please, don't make me deal with this in front of the kids. And get Esther and Aretha to mind their own business.*

But when she met Adam's calm, clear gaze, she wondered if she shouldn't be thankful for the older women's meddling.

"Do you have time for a hike this week?" The way his voice dropped low on the last words made goose bumps break out across her arms.

No, she didn't have time. But it didn't matter. She'd find it.

"On Sunday?"

"Done." With a brief wave, he tipped his chin and disappeared the way he'd come.

And she turned back to the mess in her kitchen. Somehow it didn't feel quite so severe when she had a hike and picnic with Adam to look forward to.

19

When his contact at the Better Business Bureau office in Massachusetts called him back, Adam couldn't wait to answer. After ten minutes, he wished he'd never heard of St. Cassian's Chapel and their contractor trouble.

"We've had plenty of complaints about Jordan Lovitt," Christina James said. "But when things get dicey, he packs up, gives his company a new name, and sets up shop across state lines."

Adam marched past the Adirondack chairs on the front porch, ran his fingers through his hair, and sighed. "What about a license? He must need some sort of construction license to work in Massachusetts."

"Sure. He had one." She spoke slowly, like he was a boy and she was explaining particle physics. "It was fake."

Of course it was. A construction con man like Lovitt wouldn't go into jobs unprepared. And the church decision makers weren't fools. They'd been swindled by counterfeit references and forged documents. And probably a lot of smooth words.

Men who preyed on nonprofits knew how to say just the right thing. They talked fast, showed pretty numbers, and made Adam want to punch a wall.

His fist was half-cocked to his ear before he realized he'd be punching the inn's blue exterior. And it would hurt his hand a lot more than it would hurt the old house. Or Jordan Lovitt, for that matter.

Scrubbing his face with his palm, he searched for any question that would bring him the answer he needed. But the BBB had given him exactly one quote for his article: "St. Cassian's will never see their money again, and there's nothing we can do about it."

It was awful and smelled like rotten eggs.

And it wasn't enough.

He paced in front of the red door, turned, and kicked at the white porch railing.

"Thank you for your time." He didn't sound very thankful, but Christina seemed to understand.

"I'm sorry I couldn't be more help. I hate to see a house of worship taken in and then left to pick up the pieces. We'll do everything we can to make sure that others know not to trust Lovitt."

Adam hung up, glared at his phone for a long second, and then pulled out his notebook. He scribbled Christina's quote at the bottom of a page before running his gaze over the other notes he'd collected for the story. As it currently stood, the piece was definitely not a David versus Goliath story.

Jordan Lovitt with his mysterious disappearing construction company wasn't a Goliath. He didn't shout his presence and dare the little guy to come out and fight. Lovitt snuck in under the cover of night, pretended to be a friend, and then took off. He was a wolf in sheep's clothing. Not a Goliath.

This article was David versus scumbag.

And readers didn't get up in arms about scum. They got riled up over the big guy taking down the little one. They wanted to see Robin Hood steal from the rich and give to the poor, not the other way around.

Which meant his story wasn't going to cut it without a direct connection to Carrington Commercial. He had to prove that they were after the church land.

And *they* hadn't been exactly forthcoming.

He'd called them twice already, left two voice mails, and received zero response. But it couldn't hurt to try again.

The phone rang on the other end of the line, and a perky receptionist answered — the same one who had answered his last attempts.

"Carrington Commercial Real Estate. How may I direct your call?"

"Corporate communications, please."

There was a long pause before she said, "And who may I say is calling?"

They'd played out this same storyline twice before, but he couldn't be anything less than up-front about who he was and what he wanted. That was how journalists got benched. Or worse. Moved to the lifestyle section.

"This is Adam Jacobs with *America Today.* I need to speak with someone in your communications office."

"I'll see if someone is available. Please hold."

Almost immediately the mailbox for James Herald picked up. And Adam left a third message, this one stronger than the last.

As soon as he hung up, his screen lit with Garrett's name, and he picked up. "Afternoon, boss." He tried to keep his voice light and chirpy, but the weight on his shoulders — the weight of saving St. Cassian's — made everything feel heavy.

"Don't 'afternoon, boss' me, Jacobs. I was expecting your article days ago. Where is it?"

"I need a quote from Carrington Commercial, something — anything — to tie them to the purchase of the land. It's the last piece of the puzzle, but it's right in the middle of the picture."

"You need your Goliath, eh?"

"Exactly." Adam clenched and unclenched his fist on top of his ever-bouncing knee, a slow spiral of tension building at his core and searching for escape through every tic of his body.

"Hmm." Garrett's grunt wasn't very helpful. But he also wasn't one to give up easily. "How many times have you called their office?"

"Three. No response, and I keep getting sent straight to voice mail. I've also emailed the communications director personally. He doesn't want to talk."

"Carrington doesn't want to talk."

"I know." Adam rubbed at a sore spot on his temple. The dull throb picked up in intensity with every passing second. "And the people on his payroll are going to hide him as long as they need."

"But without him — or at least a source

of some sort — your article is only a sob story."

Why did Garrett have to be right? It would be so much easier to write just the sad story. And if everyone knew about Connor and his bench, maybe they'd want to read an article about saving the church. But the only ones who knew about him were still battling the grief of his loss.

Or the guilt of his loss.

"Get down to Boston and sit outside Carrington's office until he has to talk with you."

Adam's stomach clenched. Leave the island? He wasn't ready to. He had plans with Caden, and he'd promised to be there for the cook-off. If he left now, he might never make it back.

And he was starting to think he had too much unfinished business on PEI to walk away now.

"I think I might have an in with Carrington's daughter. She might be able to help me make that connection."

"Can you crack her in a few days?"

The coldness in Garrett's words was a jab to his ribs. He wasn't trying to crack Marie. He liked her far too much. He liked the way she served his breakfast every morning with a smile. And the way she encouraged Caden to leave the inn and venture into the island with him.

But she was the only source he knew personally.

She also wasn't in North Rustico. She was in Boston — presumably with her dad.

He jabbed a hand through his hair and stared at the swaying tops of the pine trees across the street. "She's out of town, but she's supposed to be back next week, I think. I'll get her on the record then."

"What do you think she's going to say?"

"I'm not sure." His tone took on the same icy fingers that had laced Garrett's. It made him sick to say it, but he didn't have a choice. "I'll get something to make the article sing."

"Good. Send me what you have so far."

"Will do."

"And, Adam . . ." Garrett paused for effect, leaving Adam to fill in every possible conclusion to that introduction. Each more terrible than the last, until he'd filled in the blank with a pink slip and his name on a blacklist at every newspaper in the country, including the *Paducah Gazette.*

He had to swallow to keep his voice from trembling. "Yes?"

"I read your travel articles."

A breath of relief escaped his lungs, but it

didn't relieve the fear building inside. He hadn't been nervous about a story since he was seventeen and turning in his first article to his high school newspaper. But that didn't stop the rocking in his gut or the sudden catch in his throat now.

Garrett chuckled as if he knew that Adam had been holding his breath. "They're good."

"Good enough for what?"

"Well, you know it's not what we print. But I passed them along to a friend of mine at a travel magazine."

The sun peeked out over the storm inside. "You did?"

"She'd be ticked at me if I didn't send her articles like that."

Adam risked a smile. "Thank you."

He could almost hear the grin fall out of Garrett's tone. "Now get my article finished and send it to me."

"Next week. You'll have it next week."

Caden looked up when the office door opened that afternoon. Aretha poked her head in and held out a handful of white envelopes. "I picked up the mail."

"Thank you." She took the letters and flipped through them idly.

"Do you need me for anything?"

With a quick scan of the desk, she shook her head. "I think we're good. No check-ins or checkouts today. I'm going to prep for breakfast tomorrow —"

"And for your picnic with Adam?"

A swarm of dragonflies took off in her stomach, zipping from one side to the other and back so fast she could only register the mild feeling of seasickness.

The Homestead Trail was one of the more romantic strolls along the North Shore. Iris hadn't exaggerated with her high-pitched giggle. And it was quite obvious that Esther and Aretha were playing matchmaker. Adam couldn't be blind to their shenanigans.

They'd get out along the narrow red beach, and then what? He'd be swept up in the beauty and pressure of it all. He'd know that their scheming friends expected him to finally make a move. He'd see the towering pines and crystal-blue waters. He'd see the poor girl that no one had ever wanted before.

And he'd take pity on her and finally kiss her.

Forget mild seasickness.

She felt like she'd gone out in a dinghy in the middle of a hurricane.

Bending at the waist, she squeezed her eyes closed against the story that was playing out in her mind.

She'd rather never see him again than see him pity her.

She hadn't noticed it before, hadn't understood it until he arrived. But she'd seen pity in the eyes of half the people in this town for most of her life. It was ever-present and ongoing, like the tides and the hum of fishing boats.

They all felt sorry for the chubby girl who had never been better than second-best inside or outside the kitchen.

Adam had never looked at her that way, but maybe it was because he didn't know her well enough yet. Maybe she just hadn't caught him doing it.

Maybe she should cancel their hike.

Ugh.

The very thought put a bitter taste in the back of her mouth. She was going to skip a chance to spend time with him just because she'd told herself a story based on zero evidence.

"Caden, dear. Are you all right?" Aretha set a hand on her shoulder, its weight both comforting and oppressive, and she shook it off.

"Yes. Fine." She peeked into the concerned face hovering over her.

"There's a letter in there I thought you

might like to deliver."

She glanced at the mail, which was beginning to wrinkle in her clenched hand. Slowly releasing her grasp, she shuffled through the papers. There were a few bills, which Marie had warned her might arrive. But they could wait until she and Seth got back from Boston. Caden set them on the shelf Marie had indicated.

There was also a bit of junk mail addressed to the resident. She tossed that in the recycling bin.

And the final envelope was addressed in an easy, handwritten script.

To Adam Jacobs, care of Rose's Red Door Inn.

Curiosity tugged her mouth into a frown, and her gaze darted to the upper left corner.

In perfect letterhead, the return address boldly announced the sender. *Leisure Vacations* magazine, New York City.

Her frown was quickly replaced by a broad smile. Adam had said he'd written his first travel articles. Maybe this was good news.

"I'm going to drop this off." She jumped to her feet, and Aretha stepped back, an all-too-knowing grin in place.

"I thought you might want to."

But before Caden could get out the door,

Aretha asked, "When's our next check-in?"

"Not until Sunday. Jer—" Her voice gave out as nerves blossomed, and she had to swallow a lump before she could continue. "Jerome Gale is supposed to get here then. Maybe I should stick around the inn just in case he needs anything."

"And cancel your date with Adam?"

"It's not a date." At least, she didn't think it was, but her opinion counted for nothing when Aretha got going. She talked right over Caden.

"I don't think so. I can handle anything that might come up."

"But what if the roof leaks again?"

"It's not even supposed to rain." She wagged her finger in Caden's face. "You're not going to miss out on time with him on my watch. Understood?"

"Yes, ma'am." That was exactly what Adam would say, and the simple knowledge turned the sand in her stomach into something nearly enjoyable. She'd caught him saying "for sure" once or twice, and now she was picking up his mannerisms too.

"Now, go give him his mail."

Caden did as Aretha commanded, checking the front porch for him. But Danielle was the only person out there. She was curled up on a chair, her nose buried deep in a book. Tempted to sneak away before she got distracted from her mission, Caden reminded herself that she was still the inn's hostess in Marie's absence. She'd said she didn't need Bethany's help, so that meant connecting with guests no matter how much she wanted to hide in her kitchen or spend all her time with Adam.

Clearing her throat, she waited for Danielle to look up. "How're you doing today? Is there anything I can get you?"

A smile broke out across Danielle's face, her white teeth flashing even in the porch's shade. "Do you have any lemonade?" She wiped a hand across her forehead, swiping at a nonexistent drop of sweat as a breeze wafted beneath the overhang.

"Of course. I'll be right back."

Caden tucked Adam's letter into her pocket, then went to the kitchen to pour a glass of lemonade and serve up a blackberry cupcake with lemon frosting. When she delivered them, Danielle squealed. "Oh, this looks amazing! How did you know I have a sweet tooth?"

With a shrug and a smile, Caden dismissed the question. "Are you enjoying your stay?"

"Very much so."

"Let me know if there's anything I can

do." Caden turned to go, but the other woman's call stalled her.

"Can you recommend a lobster supper? I saw a flyer for one in New Glasgow. Is it worth the drive?"

Patting the letter in her pocket, she forced herself not to rush her response. "The drive to New Glasgow is lovely and only about ten minutes away. But there's a lobster supper at Fisherman's Wharf right across the street that's also very good." She pinched her nose at the white lie, praying Danielle wouldn't ask for specifics. Caden's parents had never gotten her inside the blue building across the intersection from her dad's bakery.

Danielle's eyes swung toward the open bay, and a single crease marred her otherwise perfect forehead.

"Make a right onto the street." She waved her hand to indicate the direction. "It's about a five-minute walk. Before you get to the intersection, it's the big building on your left."

The wrinkle disappeared, and Danielle nearly glowed. "That sounds perfect. Thank you."

Caden nodded before ducking back into the house, making a quick tour of the first floor, and saying hello to the Eisenbergs, who were enjoying a quiet afternoon in the parlor. She asked if they needed anything, but they both waved her off with paperback books in hand.

Still no sign of Adam.

With the first floor clear, that left only his room on the second. If he was even in the house. Maybe he'd gone for a walk along the beach or walked into the national park or gone to pick up a few things at the store.

As she lifted her hand to knock, she said a short prayer that he was doing any of those or a hundred other things. Quite honestly, they hadn't talked about the bomb he'd dropped. Not really. Between Aretha's chattering and all the things that needed to be done in Marie's stead, they hadn't had much time alone.

Which might have been a blessing in disguise. Because all of a sudden she wasn't sure how she felt about what he'd said.

She was mortified that she'd made such an egregious assumption. And she hated how stupid she'd sounded when he'd told her he wasn't the writer they'd been expecting.

But he hadn't exactly lied to her.

He simply hadn't known who she wanted — needed — him to be.

She was still in the midst of assigning

names to her feelings when he swung the door wide and leaned an arm onto the wall at shoulder level. His gray T-shirt hugged him in all the right places, loose at the neck and snug across his chest, showcasing its quick rise and fall. His legs were long and lean and covered with dark brown hair below the blue gym shorts he sported. When he crossed one ankle in front of the other, she couldn't help but focus on his sturdy feet.

He looked just like a man was supposed to. Solid and sure. Kind and capable. Shoulders broad enough to carry a heavy load and compassionate enough to comfort a crying child.

Or maybe a shaking woman.

Because she was suddenly quaking from head to toe.

Everything inside her quivered at seeing him so relaxed, so comfortable, and she couldn't seem to look away. But all this staring and surveying wasn't healthy for her trembling insides. Her gaze shot to his face, where a smirk couldn't draw attention from the ruffle of hair above his ear that insisted on standing straight up.

He'd definitely been sleeping. And he didn't look a bit embarrassed to be caught in such a casual stance.

"Morning, Holt."

She snorted. "More like afternoon."

"Morning . . . afternoon . . . it's all the same when you don't sleep much at night and just woke up." He ran a hand over the stubborn remnants of his bed head. "What's up?"

"Um . . ." Her memory had been wiped clean, and she could only stare at him blankly. "I . . . er . . ." She blinked five times in a row, straining to remember why she'd interrupted his nap when his nap had clearly interrupted her thought process. "I can't remember."

Running his fingernails across his five o'clock shadow, he chuckled. "That important, huh?"

"I'm sorry." She pointed down the stairs. "I got lemonade for Danielle, and before that I was . . ."

"In the kitchen?"

"No. The office. Aretha. Your letter." All the pieces fell into place as she dug into her pocket.

When she held out the envelope, the confusion on his face didn't clear. "What's this?"

"A letter."

He nodded, his eyes scanning the address and return label. She watched his features closely, but they didn't reveal a single emotion. He ripped open the end of the envelope, pulled out several printed pages, and quickly scanned them.

Caden thought about walking away. She'd done what she'd come to do, but a twitch in her middle made her feel like she was forgetting something. Staring at her feet for a long moment, she shuffled and swayed and tried not to invade whatever moment this was for him.

After a very long minute, she finally decided she should go. But as soon as she opened her mouth to say as much, Adam grunted. "Well, huh."

She had to twist her hands together to keep from grabbing his letter. Schooling her tone to keep it moderated, she said, "What's that?"

He held up the pages. "Looks like I'm a real travel writer now. *Leisure Vacations* is going to publish my article."

His words caused a strange combination of joy and sadness. "I'm so happy for you." But she grieved the loss of the article she'd been counting on.

Silence hung between them, maybe because he'd heard the half-truth in her words and didn't know how to respond. She didn't either. Dropping the letter to his side, he finally looked closely at her. His eyes were pale and slightly red from sleep, but they focused on her face so intently that she had to look away.

"Are you mad at me?" he said.

"What? No! Of course not. Why would you . . ."

He would think that because they hadn't talked about it. Because she was still trying to figure out exactly how she felt about it.

Adam pinched his chin between his thumb and forefinger and pursed his lips. "I think I'd be angry if I was in your shoes."

"Angry? Really?" That wasn't how she'd categorize whatever was tumbling around her stomach. "No. I think I'm . . . just . . . disappointed that I can't help Marie like she wanted."

He cocked his head to the side. "Help Marie?"

Heat gathered at her throat, and she wanted to take back her words, but Adam, the reporter, latched on to the little things. "It's nothing."

He took a step closer to her, and it stole all her air and any hope she had for a quick escape. "I think it is something." His tone turned low, and no cowlick in his hair could make him any less nerve-wracking. "What were you doing to help Marie?"

Oh no. Oh no.

She could not confess that Marie had asked her to show him around the island. That was how it had started, of course. But that wasn't what it had become.

But the words to express that weren't anywhere close to the tip of her tongue. With a subtle shuffle, she tried to step away. "I'll see you —"

His hand shot out to her elbow, holding her in place with a firm yet gentle grip. "Caden, tell me." His eyes turned soft, like he knew he wasn't going to like what was coming, but he had to know. "Please."

She bit her lip and squeezed her eyes closed, searching for a way to explain it. There had to be words to clarify, but she couldn't find them. "I was . . . Marie asked me to . . . You see, the article, we needed it — we still do."

A muscle in his jaw jumped, and his grip on her arm tightened just a fraction. "I think I understand. Marie thought I was the undercover reporter, so she asked you to befriend me. To make me feel welcome."

"No. It wasn't like that. She wanted me to show you around, to help you see the beauty of the island."

"Because she wanted a good review."

Oh, she was bungling this worse than

she'd thought. The way he spoke made it sound like their entire friendship was a sham. And it wasn't. It couldn't be.

Rubbing at her forehead, she tried to relieve the budding headache there. With a sigh through tight lips, she let out everything that had been bottled up. "I never left the kitchen before you came. I didn't think I had anything else to offer the inn. Sure, I love this island, but when Marie asked me to help you learn to love it too, I was sure I couldn't do it."

"But you did."

A warmth filled her chest as a strange smile tugged at her mouth. "You fell in love with PEI too?"

"Of course. How could I not? But that doesn't change what —"

"No, but that's the thing." She waved her hand to cut him off, her words already beating her to it. "That's how it started, yes. But then . . . I started looking forward to seeing you, to talking with you, every morning."

He frowned. "Is that why I got invited into the kitchen?"

Caden couldn't contain a pop of laughter. "You *never* got invited into my kitchen. You just showed up and wouldn't leave."

That brought out his crooked grin, which

sent her butterflies dancing.

"I'm sorry. I never meant to lie to you. I was doing what I thought was best for the inn, and I ended up with the best friend I've ever had."

"Really?" He looked genuinely surprised, and again she wished she could take back her words. "I'm your best friend?"

She cringed but nodded slowly.

Adam remained absolutely still.

There weren't etiquette rules for such circumstances. She didn't know if she was supposed to yank her arm free or stand around and wait for him to respond.

In the end Aretha took care of the decision with a holler up the back stairwell. "Caden? Are you up there? I need help with a reservation."

"I have to go," she said, wiggling her elbow to remind him of his hold.

With one tender squeeze, he released her arm. "But we're still on for the Homestead Trail on Sunday?"

"If you want to."

"I do."

20

"King me." Levi looked prodigiously proud of himself as he nodded at the black checker that had made it to the back row of Adam's side of the board.

Adam chuckled and did just that, stacking a second black piece atop the first. He rubbed his chin as he stared at the board, weighing his next move and the one after that. Finally, he slid a red piece forward. Levi grunted and frowned above the fist at his chin. His eyes narrowed, jumping from square to square as he studied the board the same way Adam had.

He lowered his arm and reached his left hand across his body to tug at his right ear. The movement shifted his rolled-up shirt sleeve, and a half-dozen blue numbers poked out from below it. They were thin and faded and barely visible beneath the white hair on his arms. But Adam couldn't miss them or the reminder of what Esther had said to him.

Levi would open up when he knew Adam would do the same.

If he wanted to hear Levi's story — and he did — he'd have to tell his own. Levi already knew about the alcohol and his parents' funeral. But he didn't know why they'd been on the road that day, why they'd been in the path of the tanker that jack-knifed.

He took a wobbly breath, not sure how to take their conversation deeper than jumps and kings. His stomach felt as unsettled as it had the first time he'd interviewed a key informant. But it hadn't stopped him then, and it wouldn't now.

There was a time for half-truths and almost-answers. This wasn't it.

"You ever write anything so bad that it got someone killed?"

Levi pinched his bottom lip between two fingers and let out a long whistle, his pale brown gaze never leaving the table between them. "Must have been some story."

"It was about a translator. He was work-ing with the Marines I was embedded with."

"Hmm." It was less of a word and more of an invitation to continue.

Only Adam wasn't quite sure how to. Garrett was the only other person on the planet who knew the truth about Aamir and Connor. And he'd never had to vocalize it before. The article, the explosion, and the memorial service. Speaking them aloud meant owning the guilt that came with them.

He blinked against the memories that thrashed to the forefront of his mind as Levi finally made his move. With his piece in place, the old man looked up. His eyes were deep pools, full of peace and understanding and something else that Adam couldn't name. It was like a warm hand on his shoulder and his mother's smile wrapped into one.

"I wrote a piece about this guy, Aamir. He was trying to get his family moved to the US. To protect them from the insurgents, who didn't have any qualms about killing his parents and his wife because he was helping us. Helping the enemy."

Suddenly his throat went dry, and he gulped at the glass of lemonade Caden had dropped off on her way to run some errands.

"You tried to hide his identity?"

"Yes, sir."

Levi nodded. "What happened? Someone give your editor a picture?"

Maybe he didn't have to tell Levi anything.

He seemed to know it all before Adam spelled it out. "How'd you know?"

With a shrug and a motion toward the board, a reminder for Adam to make his move, Levi tugged on his earlobe again. "If you were trying to protect his identity, then someone else had to reveal it."

"Yes, well . . ." It was the same argument that Garrett had made every time they'd had this conversation. And it still didn't sit well with him. It still made his chest ache and the air feel like it was made of cotton. "Aamir wasn't the only one killed that day. They blew up his home and a Marine who was with him." He shoved his piece into place, wishing he could push away the dagger at his heart just as easily.

"He was your friend and you feel responsible."

Levi was so matter-of-fact about it that tears burned in Adam's eyes. "I *am* responsible. For them. For my parents. They wouldn't have been in a car accident if they hadn't been on the road to Knoxville to see me win a stupid award. If I hadn't asked them to come to the ceremony, they wouldn't have been on that highway . . ." His voice failed him, and he had to clear his throat to try again to finish his thought. "They'd still be alive."

Oh Lord.

The words were the only prayer he could muster, the only thought he could manage on the end of that confession. But it didn't leave him any less conflicted than he'd been.

Levi let out another low whistle through pinched lips. "That's a lot of weight to carry. That's why you're craving the bottle, I guess."

It was.

Only, the pull hadn't been as strong the last few weeks. It wasn't the first thing he reached for or the first thing he thought about in the morning. Now he looked for Caden.

Not waiting for an affirmative response, Levi kept going. "Seems to me like that's too much for one man to carry. You know I was holding on to plenty of my own guilt too. It's hard not to when you see your parents giving up their food to feed you, taking your punishment to protect you. And in the end you couldn't do a thing to save them."

Adam's heart clenched, his fists right along with it. As he waited for more, he leaned forward, the game between them forgotten.

"I was always pretty big for my age, good Hungarian stock, I suppose." Levi flexed his arm, the muscles there still evident despite his advancing years. "By the time I was nine, I was big enough to do a man's work on the farm. I suppose the SS thought the same. When my family arrived at Auschwitz in 1944, I was shuttled into the men's camp. My mother and sisters were sent to the women's section. I don't know what happened to my brother. I never saw him again."

Levi's eyes focused on something over Adam's shoulder, but he couldn't look away from the taut face of the storyteller to see what might be there. Instead he leaned in even farther and nodded gently despite the low burning ache in his stomach for his friend's pain.

"Rebecca and Ruth were twins. Just six. They didn't last more than a month before . . . There was disease everywhere. They caught a cough. And where Ruth went, Rebecca always followed." His eyes filled with tears that spilled over, leaving a translucent trail. The hard edge in his jaw seemed to relax, as if the very act of crying released some of the sorrow.

When it became clear that Levi wasn't going to go on, Adam reached for his arm and gave it a gentle squeeze. The skin beneath his fingers was fragile, the opposite of the man who wore it.

"Took me more than thirty years to deal with losing them."

"But how? I mean, I know you tried drinking, but how?" His words were a rush, too eager to claim Levi's wisdom. Maybe his secret could become Adam's too.

Whatever this man had, Adam wanted it. Whatever had helped Levi give up his hate and not his strength, that was what he craved.

"Was it Esther?"

"No." The lines of sorrow that had become the focal point of his face began to give way to a thoughtful expression. "But she helped."

"What was it then?"

"Grace."

The single word, so softly spoken, felt like a kick in the gut from a steel-toed boot.

Adam doubled over and squeezed his eyes closed against the magnitude and simplicity of it all. How could it be so easy for Levi? Five little letters and he was free.

Well, five letters and thirty years of pain.

If that was the penance due, then Adam had at least twenty-two years to go.

"It wasn't easy." Levi clapped a hand on his shoulder. "It still isn't some days. But that's the thing about grace. It doesn't let you give up even when you want to. It gives you the strength to keep surrendering that guilt and regret."

Adam's lip quivered, and he chomped down on it to keep it still while he worked up his next words. "I'm not sure I can forget."

"Oh, it's not about forgetting, son."

A rush of tears filled Adam's eyes. He hadn't been called anyone's son in a very long time, and the simple moniker stole his breath and his thoughts.

"It's about recognizing that what we did or didn't do doesn't make us enough." A wry grin crossed Levi's face for a brief moment. "Take it from a Jew who loves the old ways and the traditions and every sacred ritual. Grace isn't about being good enough or strong enough. It's just about acknowledging your need for it and accepting it."

Adam offered an equally wry, if not quite stable, smile in return. "Watch it, Levi. You're talking like the Baptist preacher at the tent revivals my mom dragged me to when I was a child."

Levi shrugged. "I'm not surprised. It was a Baptist preacher who encouraged me to read the New Testament, to learn about Yeshua."

He nearly fell backward. He'd never heard

a Jewish man call Jesus by name or speak of him at all. "Did you convert to Christianity then? I just assumed you attend services at First Church because there isn't a synagogue in the area."

His assumption brought forth a hearty laugh from Levi that lifted the veil of sadness. "Yeshua was Jewish, you know. And so are we. But Esther and I have discovered that his grace frees us from our guilt. That's what I needed most."

Levi didn't continue, but the words left unspoken hung silently between them. *Maybe it's what you need too.*

But if he released his guilt, how would he make amends for Connor's death? How did forgetting his friend honor the fallen?

There were no easy answers. Only hope for a dreamless night and a lighter weight.

For now he just knew he wanted to talk it through with his best friend.

Caden.

When Jerome Gale stepped into her inn on Sunday afternoon, Caden had to step back, not because he was a particularly large man but because his presence seemed to fill the entire entry.

"Welcome to Rose's Red Door Inn." She

managed to get the words out despite a dry tongue.

He nodded, his jet-black hair falling over his forehead and his piercing green eyes surveying the small foyer. His gaze narrowed as it swept from the guest book on the credenza to the string of framed island pictures along the opposite wall. The features of his face — all the exact size and shape for classic good looks that offered no hint to his age — gave away nothing of his reaction.

A vise clamped in her stomach. What if he didn't like the house? Or her hosting? Or her breakfast?

She took a breath through her nose, which did little to quell the riot inside. Best to get him checked in and settled into his room.

"I'm Caden Holt." The words fell out of her mouth like she had no control of them.

"Do you own the inn?" His voice was deep and as perfectly suited for television as the rest of him.

"No. I'm the executive chef."

He stared at her for a long, silent minute, and she reached for her apron, which wasn't there because she'd tossed it aside when she'd heard his knock. She settled for running her damp palms down the legs of her jeans.

"Another chef?" His words were so low that she couldn't tell if he was pleased to meet her or planning to knock off the competition under the cloak of night. Until a wide grin spread across his face. "Always nice to meet another kitchen dweller."

Her breath came out in a loud whoosh, half laugh, half sigh of relief. Somehow he'd just compared what she did to his work, which included three critically acclaimed restaurants in Toronto, a regular appearance on the Cooking Network, and a monthly column in *Cuisine Canada* magazine.

Putting breakfast on the table every morning and treats on the buffet every afternoon couldn't be compared to his life, his role in the Canadian culinary scene.

Still, she felt a blush at her neck and quickly pressed her hand to it. "It's an honor to have you here, Mr. Gale."

He nodded again. "Jerome. Please. I'll be here for a week. We might as well be friendly."

She couldn't find a single word to say other than her normal, "For sure." Cringing at her own inept communication skills, she pointed toward the office and led the way through the dining room, giving him the dime tour. Three o'clock snacks. Front porch at his disposal. Breakfast between

361

eight and nine.

"I might not be here for breakfast tomorrow."

"Oh?" Did she sound too happy? She felt a sudden relief but couldn't put voice to it.

"I'm going to visit a friend in Souris tonight. If it gets too late . . ."

She filled in the scene in her mind. Two old friends, a clam bake on the East shore, a bottle of wine. And a reprieve from his judging for one more day.

"Sure." She tried not to smile. "No problem."

Jerome took his key, gave her a quick thanks, and carried a shoulder bag up the stairs to his room.

Caden sank into the leather desk chair and put her head in her hands. That had gone so much better than she'd hoped. But he was still staying at her inn, and he'd be eating her food and judging it — officially — very soon.

A solid thump against the door shook her from her thoughts, and she jerked her head up to see Adam standing in the entry. His gray eyes flashed almost blue, his grin just as bright. "Hey."

"Hey," she repeated, sounding impossibly inane. But he'd managed to sweep all thoughts from her brain except the memory of their last real conversation. The one where she'd blurted out that he was her best friend. And he'd remained utterly silent.

Why couldn't she ever say the right thing?

"Ready for our hike?"

"Uh-huh." When she stood, a completely different set of nerves sparked to life inside her, settling into an unsteady flip-flop. With Jerome, she worried that her culinary skills weren't enough. With Adam, she worried that *she* wasn't enough.

In fact, the whole time she packed their picnic bag she wondered what might happen on this hike. Would their conversation be awkward because she felt awkward? Would he feel like he'd been pressured to join her? Or could they just return to what they'd been — friends?

She packed leftover mashed potatoes and roast beef sandwiches — and, of course, a cupcake for each of them. As she scooped the backpack off the counter, he swooped in to snag it from her.

They traipsed through the inn and across the porch, where Esther called to them from the corner of the house. "Where are you two off to?"

Like she didn't know. She'd practically masterminded the whole thing.

Adam gave the older couple a small wave,

and Levi responded with a knowing nod of his head. "See you two kids later."

They were halfway down the walkway, side-by-side, Caden on the rock path and Adam on the lawn, when Levi called out to them again. "Stay off the grass."

Caden turned just enough to catch Levi's wink and Esther's appreciative pat on her husband's arm. But there was no time to analyze it as Adam practically jumped onto the path, and the back of their hands brushed.

It was like fireworks shooting up her arm, surprising and breathtaking.

They'd touched before. A hundred times. But the power in such an innocent connection amazed her, urged her closer to him.

Adam glanced down, a smile wrinkling the corners of his eyes. He didn't pull away. Instead his pinky finger hooked hers and pulled her somehow nearer, even though there couldn't have been more than a breath of space between them in the first place. His finger rubbed against hers, a constant reminder of its presence, until she tripped over her own feet.

He dropped her hand and wrapped an arm around her waist to keep her upright. "You okay?"

If the fire from his touch set her skin

aflame, she couldn't be any hotter.

Seriously? One touch and she forgot how to walk?

Adam didn't seem to mind, though. His arm stayed around her back, kept her tucked into his side, until they reached her car.

"So, tell me about this place," he said as they settled in. "Is it one of your favorite spots?"

"Not quite."

He raised his eyebrows, but she didn't jump to fill in the details. It wasn't easy to explain how the kids in high school had snuck off to Cavendish Beach and Homestead Trail for rendezvouses she'd never been invited to. Or how her cousin had once confessed to finding a dark parking spot just off the beach to spend the evening with her boyfriend.

Those memories weren't hers.

And even ten years later, she felt left out, as though life had passed her by and she didn't notice until it was too late.

She didn't want to have to explain that. So she hunted for a safer subject. But after their conversation two days before, she didn't know if there was any innocuous ground.

Adam didn't seem too eager to talk either,

so she drove on in silence. When she pulled into the parking lot at the trailhead, only one other car was there. Perhaps it was late in the day to take a nine-kilometer hike. But they didn't have to go the whole way. They were just going to enjoy an afternoon stroll.

If it was possible to enjoy anything when she was wound up like a ball of yarn.

Adam stepped out of the car, grabbed their lunch from the backseat, and slung it over his shoulder. She caught his eye, expecting his trademark grin. Instead he bowed his head and rubbed the back of his neck. The corner of his mouth tugged up, and his lips pursed to the side.

Like the last time they'd talked, he kept his mouth closed tighter than a clam.

Caden took a deep breath as she stepped under the canopy of green trees, meandering along the rutted path. Bursts of sunlight fought their way through the leaves, illuminating small patches of grass here and a spot of dirt there. Adam quickly caught up to her, forcing her to confront the myriad and nameless emotions tumbling in her chest.

His eyebrows furrowed, and his hand returned to the back of his neck, then snaked over his hair and down his face.

Her muscles grew tighter and tighter with every step, and she wrung her hands, then shoved them in the pockets of her capri pants. Then pulled them out again.

Someone was going to have to say something. And Adam looked like he couldn't find the words either.

Taking a deep breath, she let hers out in a rush. "I had an idea that I thought might help the inn next summer. But I don't know if it'll work."

Finally a smile eased into place. "Tell me about it."

21

Adam was too busy staring at the glow of Caden's face to notice the rut in the ground. His ankle twisted and he stumbled, but Caden was there. Almost immediately. Her hand soft but strong on his arm.

"Are you all right?"

"Yes. Fine." He shook his leg and gave his ankle a couple turns to make sure he hadn't really injured it, but all was fine. He'd have to pay more attention to his surroundings, which were almost as beautiful as Caden's timid smile. The green canopy above put a shadow over her face, but even that couldn't deter the hope shining out of her eyes.

He gave her a verbal nudge. "You were saying?"

"I had a thought." She waved her hand in front of her as if to erase that. "Actually, it was Danielle."

"The new guest?"

"Yes. She doesn't know, of course — that

the inn needs to make more money next year, I mean."

A band around his lungs squeezed. He hated that he couldn't help her, that there wasn't anything he could do to give back to the inn that had become his sanctuary.

The jingle of a bicycle bell made them both jump, and he took the excuse to reach for her hand, tugging her closer to him and out of the bike's path. The rider waved as he passed, and Caden stepped away.

Adam didn't let go of her hand.

Like it had every time they were together, being near her somehow made him breathe a little easier. It made the glow of the orange fireball always in his mind's eye burn a little softer. It made the urge to drink to forget nearly disappear.

Because he couldn't risk forgetting any of his time with Caden. That was for sure.

She looked down at their linked hands, her eyebrows knitting together as if she was trying to decide if she should pull away.

Probably because he'd been a dimwit before. When she told him he was her best friend, he should have told her the same right away. He should have opened up about why he'd really been sent to the island, to this specific inn.

And he would. But first he wanted to hear

all of her ideas.

When her dimple appeared in rare form, she looked back up at him, a simple peace in her eyes. He recognized it immediately.

He felt the same every time he was with her.

"Anyway, she heard my class making a racket on the day she checked in. And she asked if I'd ever taught an adult class."

"For guests?"

She chewed on her lip and nodded. "Do you think I could do it? Do you think people would pay extra to make a home-cooked meal?"

A bubble of excitement built in him, making even his steps lighter. "I think that's brilliant."

"Really? You don't think it's ridiculous?"

"Ridiculous?" He shook his head so hard that his hair flopped over his forehead. "It's perfect. Just imagine. Guests spend the morning exploring the island and come back in the afternoon. You have the whole kitchen set up, and all they have to do is follow your instructions. Then they have a home-cooked meal for dinner."

The skip in her step matched his, all hesitancy disappearing from her face. "And we could feature local favorites. Fresh fish and potatoes and —"

"Lobster." He tugged her hand, and she laughed.

"Even lobster." Her gait slowed, and she pursed her lips. "I might need some help convincing Marie."

"I don't think so. She'll love it. It's a feature that no other inn on the island offers. It's distinctive. It sets you apart, which is what every marketer wants."

She didn't look entirely convinced, and in that moment he'd give anything to make it easy for her. "Maybe I could help you. We could put together some recipe ideas and research other inns that offer exclusives like this."

Her eyes grew wide. "I'd love that. Thank you."

Nudging his shoulder against hers, he said, "Anytime."

"What about you? Can I help you with whatever you're working on?"

This was the invitation he'd been looking for. Still, he didn't quite know where to start. He cleared his throat, but all of his interactions with Levi and Esther felt so private.

And he couldn't begin with Connor. He couldn't jump in by telling her about his time in the Middle East, about Connor's bench at the chapel, about the pain he felt responsible for. He couldn't handle seeing her flinch or pull away when he confessed. He had to find a gentler way to explain the words that had tumbled through his mind since his conversation with Levi.

No words jumped to mind, so he focused on the landscape ahead, hoping it would give him a start.

The canopy gave way to open terrain, woods to their left and green grass around them until they turned a corner. There the sea had cut a swath into the land, the water swaying against the red sand shore. Far to their right he spotted a pale sand dune wearing a grassy cap. And more pine trees reached to the sky farther down the trail.

He turned as far as he could without releasing her hand and spied a dazzling blue pond between the tree coves. A wood and metal bridge crossed it at its narrowest point, but even there, where the water was so shallow that it began to turn purple — blue over the iron-infused clay below — it reflected the sun as though that were its sole purpose.

"Can we get closer to that bridge?" He pointed.

"It's on the trail. We'll be there soon enough."

True to her word, Caden led them past a

row of pink wildflowers fighting to reach over the knee-high blades of grass, beyond the copse of pines, and to the bridge. Standing on the wooden planks, he leaned his forearms against the railing and let his gaze drink in every nook in the landscape. From the distant dunes to the red boulders at the bridge's base, he sipped it all in.

And when he opened his mouth, the words that came out were exactly what he wanted to say. "The other day Esther told me that our deepest regrets are the things that connect us to other people."

Caden rested her arm next to his, almost touching and definitely not pulling back. "Do you think that's true?" she asked.

He looked at her profile for a moment, her cheeks soft and pink, her lips round and full and perfect for kissing.

The thought surprised him — only in that he couldn't believe he hadn't had it before. He should have been thinking it every minute of every day since he'd almost kissed her in the kitchen. Oh, he'd thought about kissing her plenty of times. There just hadn't been a private moment until now. A moment when he truly saw how perfectly her lips would fit against his.

But not now. When he needed to talk to her about something serious, when he needed to figure out if it was possible to make amends for his wrongs or if grace was his only recourse.

If he could only get through this conversation, he swore to himself that he'd come back to hold her hands and cup her cheeks. And kiss her lips.

Anticipation soared in his chest like a balloon without a tether, and he almost smiled. "I think I agree with her," he said.

She nodded. "Esther's a smart woman."

He'd thought the same thing. But their agreement didn't stop the sudden twist of his gut as he considered laying those deepest regrets bare. "I've made some mistakes."

He didn't know if he wanted her to ask what kind or if he wanted to fill her in, but when she remained silent, he welcomed the moment to figure out how and what to tell her.

"I told you about my parents."

She nodded.

His mouth went dry, and he swallowed against the desert there. "What I didn't tell you was that I asked them to come see me."

Her gaze narrowed on him, neither confused nor condemning. She was only interested in what he said.

"I had won the senior journalism award, and I wanted them to come to the ceremony with me. They were driving to Knoxville when they were in an accident."

She sucked in a sharp breath and grabbed his hand. Lacing her fingers through his, she squeezed until he could feel even the tiny scar on her palm she'd gotten from some hot oil earlier in the summer.

He gazed into the shallow depths of the water and shook his head. "The police officer said it was quick. They didn't suffer." With his free hand, he pressed this thumb and forefinger against his watery eyes. "But they wouldn't have been on that road if I hadn't begged them to come."

"You can't blame yourself for that."

"Maybe if I'd been sober I would have been aware of the thunderstorm warning and the flash flooding."

"Adam, it wasn't your fault."

He shook his head. "That's not all."

Her eyes seemed to ask the questions that her lips couldn't.

"I was on assignment in the Middle East, and there was an article and an explosion." She sucked in another breath, but he pressed on, suddenly needing her to help carry his burdens. The whole story seemed to pour out in one breath. Aamir and Connor. The bench at St. Cassian's. The sleepless nights. The pending mortgage foreclosure. The article that he so desperately needed to write. The amends he had to make.

As he spoke, her eyebrows rose, her grip on his hand tightened, and her eyes filled.

He told her about everything. Except Carrington Commercial and Marie's connection. That wasn't part of his load, and it didn't need to be part of hers either.

When he ran out of words, she clung to his arm and blinked a few wayward tears down her cheeks.

"You've been lugging that around for a long time. But I don't think it's yours to carry."

He'd come to expect her to snort a laugh at him and move on, but now her tone was sharp with an urgency he'd never heard in it.

And this wasn't the argument he wanted to hear. He'd spent eight years taking that blame and almost three months carrying the weight of Connor's death. Whether he was responsible wasn't up for discussion.

If he could be forgiven was.

"I talked with Levi yesterday. He's been through some hard losses too."

She nodded. "I saw his tattoo. I know what it means." The words came out in hushed reverence for the survivors, and only then did he rest his other hand on top of hers.

"I asked him how he's lived with those memories all these years." His throat clogged, and he had to swallow down a persistent lump. "He said it's simple. It's grace."

Where her wrist rested against his, her pulse fluttered, increasing the tempo of his own.

"Do you think it's that easy?"

Her eyebrows rose slowly before she chewed on her bottom lip, her teeth straight and white. "Easy? Grace?"

He held this breath, not sure what he was hoping to hear. But as she let out a slow sigh, he did the same.

"I — I don't know. I've never carried anything like that. I've never had a regret run so deep."

He could hear the "but" in her tone, so he prodded her on with a nudge to the shoulder.

"But I don't think there's anything *easy* about grace. It's a call to not carry your hard stuff — your grief, your regret — alone, right? It's a reminder to lay it down and ask someone bigger than yourself to handle it. Giving that up — that's hard. Asking for help — that's not easy. But it's worth

it, don't you think? Because once you realize you've been forgiven, you can forgive
yourself."

Everything inside him clenched. Forgive
himself? "And if I was really responsible for
someone's death —"

"It's not your fault."

"I have to make amends for what I did —
what I wrote —"

Suddenly the warmth of her touch was
too much, and he pulled his hands free. His
skin itched like he'd had a run-in with
poison ivy, and he couldn't stay where he
was. Adjusting the pack over his shoulder,
he resumed the path, wandering over the
uneven ground without seeing the beauty
all around.

Caden only made her presence known by
the sound of her steps behind him. She
seemed to know he needed a minute to
process. Except he really needed hours or
years. What she'd said had shaken something deep inside him.

Maybe what he needed most was to forgive himself.

When he reached a sun-faded picnic table,
he dropped to it like he was hiking Pikes
Peak, out of breath and weary.

"Let's take a break," Caden said. "Want
to eat?"

He nodded and set the bag on the table. It landed with a strange sloshing, and he met her gaze. Her red-rimmed eyes were wide, mouth hanging open as a strangled cry jumped from her throat.

"Oh no." She leapt on the bag and tore at the drawstring opening. "Oh no, oh no." The mantra died off as her fingers slipped into the bag and unleashed a pale yellow puddle across the wooden tabletop.

Adam could only watch as the contents of the bag slid onto the table. A plastic tub of mashed potatoes splashed out first, followed quickly by two paper-wrapped packages. The sandwich-shaped parcels were a soggy mess, the brown paper torn and the bread limp, sagging where they'd sustained the most damage. When a mushy white bag followed behind, his stomach sank. The twin brown occupants squished against the side could only be the chocolate cupcakes he'd drooled over that morning.

The perpetrator — a bottle of lemonade — followed with a crash, bouncing off the already squished cupcakes and landing with a citrus-scented splatter.

He leaned back, catching only a few drops on his elbow. Glancing down, he brushed them away with an easy swipe of his thumb.

Caden, however, didn't seem ready to

dismiss the mess so quickly. Her nostrils flared while she stared with unblinking eyes. The blue he was so used to seeing there turned uneasy, like the sky before a Tennessee thunderstorm.

It took several minutes before he realized that her hands were shaking.

"Hey." He reached for one hand, but she jerked it out of reach. "It's okay."

Without breaking her gaze from their ruined lunch, she shook her head and sighed. "I'm sorry."

"It's okay. These things happen." He gave her a shrug and tried to keep his smile from getting away from him, despite its insistent tug.

These kinds of things did happen. He'd just never seen them happen to her.

Actually, it was kind of nice not to be the only one in the midst of turmoil. Even for just a minute.

"No. I promised you lunch." She poked at the shell of a sandwich, and it fell apart, the structural damage complete.

"It's all right. Really." When he reached for her hand, he didn't let her pull away, leaning all the way in until his shoulder pressed firmly against hers. She twitched but stayed where she was.

With a shallow sigh, she shook her head,

still refusing to look him in the face. "I ruined our food."

He poked at the loose lid on the soaked bottle. "I think the lemonade took care of that. It's not your fault."

Her chin dipped, and her voice dropped to a whisper. "But you came out here for a picnic."

Something about her words wrapped around his heart, pulling at it, breaking it apart syllable by syllable. Could she really believe that he was here only for the food? That he spent every morning with her only because she'd promised him an extra muffin? Didn't she know that he felt peace when she was near, that her quiet strength was infectious? That he'd hike a hundred miles just to spend them with her?

No.

The truth hit him like a stone between the eyes.

She didn't know because he hadn't told her when he had the chance. And he sure hadn't shown her.

Because he was an *idiot*.

He had an extraordinary urge to pull her into an embrace, to wrap his arm around her shoulders and comfort her. But the stronger longing was to see her face, to look into her eyes as he told her the truth.

He twisted, sliding one leg to the outside of the bench.

She didn't immediately follow suit, so he gave her a little tug until she folded a leg in front of her before dropping it on the outside. Chin tucked into her chest, she remained silent.

"Caden." Her name came out on a breath, deeper than he'd heard himself in a while.

Her shoulders drew up near her ears. "I'm sorry."

That quiver in her voice ripped at his heart, especially when she refused to go on.

If she wouldn't respond to him, she was going to force him to get physical . . . and he wasn't going to argue with that.

"Caden." He whispered it again, half to warn her that he was going to get closer and half because he just liked the taste of her name on his tongue. It was better than her cinnamon rolls — if that was even possible. "Why are you sorry? I'm not."

She risked a glance up, and he took it for what it was. An open door.

Weaving his fingers through the hair right behind her ear, he cupped the side of her head. She responded immediately, sinking into his touch, eyes falling closed.

Her hair felt like silk — electric silk. It surged through him, drawing him across the wooden seat until his knee bumped into hers. The accidental contact made her jump, and she looked in his direction. Fear and vulnerability were written across her face from the tight lines around her mouth to the pinched skin between her eyebrows. She blinked slowly, uncertainty radiating from her.

He sucked in a sharp breath. He had to make her see, make her understand that she could trust him.

"I didn't come out here for lunch."

She licked her lips until they were pink and glistened under the full weight of the sun for an instant before a cloud cast them into shadows. Her eyes searched his, and he prayed she found what she was looking for. "You didn't?"

With a slow shake of his head, he risked a half grin. "I just wanted to talk with you."

"With me?" She croaked like a bullfrog in the nearby inlet, and it just made him love her a little more.

Love.

Whoa.

He didn't know when that had happened. But it was there. In the painful thunder of his heartbeat. In the fierce joy of being in her presence. In the way she made him feel safe enough to talk about things that he'd stuffed down for years.

There wasn't any other word for it.

And it slipped through his veins, its fingers finding the very core of him and promising that they could write a new story. Together.

"I want to be with you. To ask your opinion and hear what you're thinking. To make you laugh and let you make *me* laugh."

Another cloud swam in front of the sun, and the shadow across her face turned heavy. "You shouldn't say things like that," she said.

Fine. She didn't want him to say things? He'd *make* them happen.

Pressing a finger under her chin, he said, "Look at me."

She didn't.

Fair enough.

He cupped her elbow and gave it a gentle tug, scooting her an inch closer to him. Her lips formed a little frown, and he'd never seen anything quite so cute in his whole life. He let the sweetness of it blanket him.

"Caden Holt, you're something else." He took a deep breath and didn't bother forming the words in his mind before he let them loose. "You're sweet and kind and you make me laugh all the time. *And* you laugh at my jokes. That's no small feat."

She snorted just then, and he felt like he could fly.

"You're beautiful."

She shook her head fiercely, but he grabbed her chin to hold it still.

"Don't argue with me. You are gorgeous. And so brave."

Her eyes flashed up, wild and stormy. "I'm scared of everything."

"But it hasn't stopped you from coming up with new ways to help the Red Door or from running the whole thing on your own."

"Just for a couple weeks."

He pressed a finger to her lips. "That's a couple weeks longer than I'd have been able to do it. Or anyone else, for that matter."

She shook her head, and her gaze dropped to somewhere in the middle of his chest.

"And you've taken in a kitchen full of teenagers and taught them how to be self-sufficient young chefs."

She rubbed her hands up and down her thighs and gave him a faint shrug. "It's what my grandma did with me."

"But she had only one of you. And she didn't have Ford."

Laughter burst out of her, her eyes squinting closed with mirth. "True."

Adam took the opportunity to lean closer, his heart beating a wild tattoo in his throat.

"You may not be fearless, but you *are* brave."

"But our lunch . . ." She waved a hand toward the remnants as her frown returned.

He squinted at her, trying to make out her thought process. "You are so much more than what you serve." She began to shake her head like she was going to argue, but he held up his hand to cut her off. "I'm serious. You are amazing. You have such a kind heart and a gentle spirit. You know how to be still and calm when I feel like I'm going a hundred miles an hour and don't know how to slow down. But when I'm with you, I can breathe. I can just be. You are peace to me."

Tension pulsed off her in waves, a sure sign she was about to run, so he slipped his hand to her waist. Walking his fingers around to her back, he gave her a gentle tug. Her jerk forward was half flinch, half hiccup. But he didn't care. It cut the distance between them in half.

Now he just needed to cut another half. And another. And another. Until . . .

If he could get to the *until.*

Caden gave a breathy sigh, and Adam made good use of his free hand, skimming a bent knuckle along her velvety cheek to her perfectly rounded ear, then down her jaw to her chin. The corner of her mouth twitched, and he could see nothing but the sweep of her lips, a gentle bow, ready and waiting.

"You're amazing, really," he said.

Her tongue darted out to the corner, and a tremble seized her.

It was seizing him too. He could do nothing but hold on tighter until her hands clenched at his arms, lost in his embrace.

She fit perfectly.

He'd never felt the need to announce his intentions so blatantly before, but something about the wild look on her face prompted him. "I'm going to kiss you now."

Her eyes flashed with a mixture of anticipation and uncertainty. But she mouthed, "Okay."

It was all the invitation he needed.

With one final pull, he drew her fully into his arms and pressed his lips to hers. She froze for a split second and then melted against him.

She was at once thunder and silence, a hurricane and stillness. Behind his closed eyes he didn't see the orange fireball he'd grown so used to. He saw only Caden's gentle smile and heard only the memory of her laughter.

A spark in his chest grew until it engulfed him in a warmth he'd never known.

She tasted of cinnamon gum and smelled of sunshine, and he couldn't get close enough.

Her hands scrambled against his shirt, fisting into the knit fabric over his chest, but it was just a barrier between them. Letting go of her back, he guided her hands to his shoulders, where they quickly found their way into his hair. With gentle movements, she massaged the back of his neck, every motion leaving a trail of fire that ran straight to his heart.

As he tilted his head for a better angle, she let out a low whimper from somewhere in the back of her throat.

The sound rocketed through him, making his skin tingle and his heart sing.

He couldn't carry a tune in a bucket, but even he knew that sigh hit all the right notes.

When Adam finally pulled away, he pressed his forehead against hers, and Caden could see nothing but his coy grin. Only the sound of their panting breaths reached through the ringing in her ears, and she couldn't help but lean into the hand that cupped her right ear while his other thumb swept across her cheek.

All she could manage to focus on was

finding a breath, releasing it, and trying again.

Somewhere above, a third and fourth cloud joined the first two, the shade over the table growing thick. But Caden had never felt more alive. Her skin pricked like it was directly in the line of the sun's rays, and her pulse thrummed through her.

She'd waited twenty-seven years for her first kiss. Waited to be held like this. Waited to be cherished.

She'd been waiting for Adam.

"That was . . ." Even as the words fell out, she wasn't sure how she was going to finish.

It didn't matter. Adam cut her off. "Not done."

More? Her heart slammed against her ribs, and she didn't think she could survive another toe-curling kiss like that. But there wasn't time to consider it before he gently held her head in place and picked up right where he'd left off.

His lips were soft yet firm, gentle but urgent. And she followed his lead, leaning against him and reveling in his strength, which kept her upright even as her muscles turned to jelly.

One of his hands slipped down her neck, along her shoulder, and down to her elbow before snaking around her waist. She flinched as he found the hollow there above her hip, and it jerked her out of her daze long enough to realize the delicious little sounds he was making. Just like when he ate sweets.

Those silenced whatever fears she'd had about her body and her shape. She fit into Adam's hands perfectly. Hands that were pulling her even closer, to anchor her between his knees. It wasn't possible to close a gap that wasn't there, but he managed it.

And then she was lost again, feeling only the joy of his touch.

He consumed her every thought until she couldn't see or feel anything beyond him.

Until a drop of water landed on her arm. Then another on her head. And one on her cheek.

He pulled away and looked up just as the clouds directly overhead opened up.

"Guess we'd better go." He grabbed the remains of the picnic, swept them into the bag, and slung it over his shoulder before grabbing her hand and running back the way they'd come.

22

By the time Caden's students arrived for class the next afternoon, she was a complete mess.

Ford banged the back door, and Caden dropped her sauté pan, multiplying the racket as it echoed off the cabinets. As she stepped inside, Whitney asked if something was wrong, and Caden stumbled over her words. Gretchen brushed against her shoulder, and Caden jumped, spilling a cup of oil she'd left on the counter.

"Caden? Are you all right?" Iris said.

She nodded quickly, pointing at the recipe cards and ingredients on top of the island. But she was unable to get anything coherent past the knots in her chest. The ones that had started with a cold coffee mug and lonely morning.

"I know what it is." Jeanie's eyes glittered, and her smile was a little too smug. She looked from her sister to the others in the room, each glance another tug on Caden's knots. "Don't you remember? She went to the Homestead Trail with Mr. Jacobs yesterday."

Five sets of eyes swung on her, expectation evident in their eager stares.

"What happened?" Whitney's question was barely more than a breath, and she clasped her hands beneath her chin.

Well, if she was waiting for every juicy detail, she was going to have a long wait.

Caden took a deep breath, smoothed down her apron, and nodded toward the cocoa and flour on the counter. "We're making mini mint chocolate cupcakes."

"But you usually make those for the guests," Iris said.

"Yes, well, it's time you had more than me and your parents judging your skills."

Ford shook his head. "My dad tried to feed my lobster quiche to the dog. Buster wouldn't eat it either."

The girls all snickered, and Caden couldn't help but smile. It loosened the ropes in her chest, if only a fraction, and she managed an even breath.

"Then, Ford, you can work with me and Jeanie on the frosting."

His sad eyes immediately found Whitney, but he nodded in silent agreement.

Suddenly her eyes began to burn, and she rubbed at them with the heels of her hands. It was ridiculous to be emotional over Ford's brown puppy-dog eyes. But the slump in Whitney's shoulders did her in.

She didn't have to keep the two young lovebirds apart just because Adam hadn't bothered to show up for coffee that morning. Or breakfast. Or since.

Even when they weren't really talking, they had coffee. Always.

Which meant that clearly he didn't want to face her after what had happened on the trail.

After the way he'd held her so carefully. After the words he'd whispered to her. After the best possible kiss she could have imagined.

Her cheeks flamed at the very memory, and she slapped her hands over them, squeezed her eyes closed, and shook her head. "Fine. Ford and Whitney, you're with me at the counter. The rest of you are on the cake batter."

They set to work, following the recipes, and Caden checked on the cake team as they turned on the mixer and added the rest of the ingredients. It whipped and folded the dry goods into the wet, the pale flour disappearing into the rich brown of the cocoa. When it was finished, Iris turned it off, the sudden absence of the loud whirring leaving a heavy silence.

A visitor broke it. "I knew I recognized that sound. I have that same stand mixer in my kitchen."

Caden glanced up into Jerome Gale's smiling face. He stood with his arms crossed, shoulder leaning against the doorjamb between the dining room and kitchen.

"Mr. Gale." Smoothing down her apron and praying she didn't have powdered sugar on her face, Caden straightened.

All eyes in the room turned to the handsome man. He had to be in his early forties, but there was a vitality to him that held all of the teenagers rapt.

"Jerome," he softly corrected.

"Right. Of course. Do you need something?"

He shrugged, his eyes roaming from the tittering girls to Ford's openly curious stare and back to Caden.

Under the weight of his deep brown gaze, her stomach lurched in an entirely unpleasant way, as though he'd started judging her before the cook-off contest even began. She didn't like the way he stared at her. It wasn't unkind, but it was knowing. Like they shared something just because they shared a profession — if one considered them in the same field.

"Is this your staff?"

Caden began to respond, but Ford cut her off. "No. We're her students."

Jerome straightened. The movement was almost imperceptible, but there was a slight change in his height, a stiffening of his shoulders. "Really? You're learning how to cook in an inn's kitchen?"

Caden nodded, but Ford frowned. "Some of us are learning better than others."

When Jerome doubled over in laughter, Caden forgave him his too invasive stare. The sound was so sweet that it broke every vestige of nervousness in the room.

"Do you want to try one of our cupcakes?" Iris held up a spoonful of batter.

Caden hurried to stave off the request. "I'm sure he has other things he needs to do."

"Nothing that can't wait." He strolled into the kitchen and watched as Iris and Jeanie filled each cupcake liner.

"You can use another spoon to scoop it off if you need." Jerome demonstrated with a quick flick of the wrist, and before Caden could quite wrap her head around the fact that Jerome Gale was in her kitchen, the cupcakes had been baked, cooled, and frosted.

Everyone tried one, sighing into the sweet pleasure of the mint frosting mingled with the richness of the chocolate cake. Jerome mumbled his approval as Ford snuck another one.

By the time Jerome left — only after confirming the date and time of the next class — and the kids had helped her clean up the kitchen, Caden had all but forgotten what had made her so upset that morning.

Until Adam called to her as she set out afternoon treats for the guests.

"Hey there."

Caden nearly dropped the heavy glass plate of cupcakes onto the credenza at the sound of his oh-so-casual voice. It swooped through her, making her heart thump with an extra kick. Sucking in three quick breaths, she forced herself to look straight ahead.

Righting an overturned cupcake, she didn't turn in his direction. "Hi."

"So, listen." His tone picked up a thread of uncertainty, and she stole a peek at him, only to find his hands shoved into the pockets of his jeans, the toes of his ever-present Converse shoes pressed into the hardwood floor, and his gaze focused on the framed picture of the inn hanging above her head.

Oh, this could not be good. No good ever came out of a conversation that started with the word *listen*. That was a clear and immediate indicator that what was to come was bound to make her eyes burn and her insides twist into a painful knot.

Nope. She most certainly did not want to listen to anything he had to say after that.

Especially on the heels of their hike. Their failed picnic.

Their kiss.

Her lips tingled at the memory, and she pressed a hand over her mouth to keep from blurting out all the things his touch had made her feel.

And now he wanted her to *listen* to him talk about it.

Perfect.

Just what she needed to bring her down after Jerome's visit.

He shuffled a step closer but didn't touch her, which was good. She couldn't handle the feel of his hands on her again without reliving the way his fingers had walked around her waist and nestled into the hollow of her back, sending delicious tingles up her spine and down her arms.

Adam cleared his throat and stabbed his

fingers through his hair. "I feel terrible."

No. No. No. No.

He was *not* about to apologize for yesterday. For saying such sweet things. For holding her so tight. For turning everything she'd believed about herself on its head.

For her first kiss.

"I'm sorry . . ."

Maybe he kept talking. She couldn't tell beyond the incessant ringing in her ears. It ebbed and flowed with her breaths, each of them more painful than the last. His apology felt like a butcher knife to the chest, and all she could do was nod and mumble something that she hoped would absolve him of his self-described crimes and — most importantly — send him on his way.

All she really wanted now was to be left alone with the plate of cupcakes. No fork required.

"Caden? Did you hear me?"

His words barely made it through the drumming in her ears, but she nodded. "I got it. You're sorry. It's fine."

"I won't miss coffee again, as long as I'm here."

Her head snapped up, and she stared at him. Hard.

His eyebrows pinched together, and he squinted at her like he knew something was off, even if he didn't know what it was.

"Coffee?"

He nodded. "I missed coffee with you this morning. I didn't help out in the kitchen like I always do."

Right. Because he hadn't wanted to face her. Because he'd wanted to postpone this conversation — the one they were having — as long as he could. Right?

But he was shaking his head as though he could hear her thoughts. "I overslept. First time in . . . well, since college." He let out a little puff of air like he couldn't believe it. "I didn't have a nightmare, and I didn't wake up in a cold sweat. I was just sleeping. Until nine thirty."

"You were . . . sleeping?"

He nodded, scrubbed a hand down his face, and scratched at his day-old beard. A half smile tipped the corner of his mouth. "It was great. I didn't even know how much I'd been missing it. I just wish I hadn't missed our routine too."

Twisting trembling hands into her apron, she managed a painful swallow and a quick bob of her head.

He squinted even harder and took a step toward her. "What's going on?"

She shook her head a little too enthusiastically. But it was the only response she could manage, given what felt like a hundred frantic hummingbirds in her chest.

"Caden? What are you thinking?"

"Nothing."

His head cocked to the side, and she knew he wasn't going to buy a brush-off. But the emotions had been right there on the surface, and the stinging in her eyes wasn't abating. And maybe he was still going to apologize for the day before.

"Caden?" His tone dropped as he wrapped his hand around hers. Something too close to lightning shot up her arm from the point of contact, and she tried to tug her hand free. He held fast.

"Ye-es?"

"Did you think I was going to say something else?"

"Yes."

"Like what?"

If only lightning would come through the roof into the dining room and strike her on the spot. That would be infinitely more enjoyable than answering his question. She waited. And waited.

Nothing.

Not even a rumble of thunder.

He gave her fingers a gentle squeeze, a subtle nudge.

"I thought . . ." She took a steeling breath.

"That maybe . . ." She tried to keep eye contact, but his were too gray, too intense. They made her entire skeleton feel like banana pudding. So she dropped her gaze to the bunched gingham fabric of her apron in her hands and blinked against the tears that had finally broken loose.

Brushing a thumb across her cheek, he spread a damp track across her skin. "What?"

"That you were going to apologize for . . ." She couldn't bring herself to form the word, to let it pass over the lips that had touched his. The volume of her voice dropped to next to nothing. "For yesterday."

"For kissing you?"

She cringed at the cavalier way he tossed that word around, wishing both that he wouldn't and that she could be so free. "Yes."

He followed her single syllable with a low laugh. It wasn't funny exactly. But it rippled in her chest until she could barely breathe.

"I have no intention of apologizing for that kiss."

Her gaze flew back to his, and the corners of his eyes crinkled.

"I fully enjoyed it, and I think you did too." He pressed the pad of his thumb to the corner of her mouth before dragging it along her lower lip.

The rest of the world vanished, and there were only his eyes and his touch on her skin. And then he pressed his lips to hers. Gently. Tenderly. Fervently. Only the sweet smell of mint chocolate could add to the bliss of the moment. It swirled around her as his arm circled her waist, his free hand resting on her cheek, drawing her closer. And she was happy to oblige, sighing into his embrace.

It was so much more than she'd ever imagined a simple kiss could be.

But in all honesty there was nothing simple about kissing Adam Jacobs.

By Thursday, Adam had given up his seat at the Eisenbergs' table to Jerome so he could help Caden full-time in the kitchen.

At least that was what he told Levi when the older man gave him a nudge and a wink.

In reality, he was looking for every opportunity to sneak a private moment with Caden. A chance to wipe the flour off her face or brush her hair behind her ear. Or kiss her lips — just because he was free to.

The fact that his time with her was rapidly coming to an end hadn't escaped him. But he was determined to enjoy every minute of the few days he had left. Based on Garrett's last voice mail, Adam was running out of time, and the paper's editor-in-chief wasn't going to wait much longer.

If he didn't produce a story by Monday, he'd find himself conveniently free of the hassles of employment — even the freelance kind.

But as Caden smiled up at him, that prospect didn't sound entirely undesirable.

He pressed his lips to hers in a quick kiss, and a sweet pink shade washed over her cheeks as her dimple settled firmly into place.

What he'd give to see that every day . . .

Realization slammed into him so hard that he nearly dropped the tray of eggs Benedict and bacon, but he righted it just before it tipped past the point of no return.

Caden shot him a worried look. "Are you all right?"

He was giving it up. He was giving her up. To return to a job that he wasn't convinced he could still do.

But he had to.

Turning in his article about St. Cassian's and Carrington Commercial was his only hope for making amends to Connor's family.

He didn't have a choice.

"Yes. Good." The smile he plastered in place didn't tell half the story raging through him. But when her dimple returned, he turned away, letting the ache in his stomach turn over and over.

He had to go back to Washington. He had to go back to his job. And he had to finish the story.

But first he needed a quote from Marie — something that indicted her father for his part in tearing down a community icon and Connor's memorial bench.

Danielle and Jerome dug into their breakfasts with gusto as soon as Adam set their plates down, and he gave Levi and Esther a quick grin. Caden had confessed that she'd been afraid Jerome wouldn't like her breakfasts. But if the celebrity chef's enthusiasm was any indication, she had nothing to worry about.

"Are you going to the lobster dinner tomorrow?" Levi asked.

Adam nodded, but Esther elbowed her husband before he could respond.

"Of course he's going," she said. "Caden's going to win the cook-off contest, and then he's going to take her for a nice walk along the beach." She looked over the top of her glasses, staring at Adam so hard goose bumps broke out along his arms. "In the moonlight. Where it's romantic."

Danielle shot him a knowing look, and he

quickly glanced away.

Thank goodness Jerome was too consumed with deconstructing his breakfast, taking thoughtful bites, to take note of the matchmaking schemes skipping around the table.

But the ploys weren't necessary.

His match was made.

If only he didn't have to leave Caden behind. If only he could take her with him.

Would she leave the island? Would she make it in a cutthroat city like Washington?

Would she even want to?

As was the norm, when he wanted every moment to slow down so he could savor Caden's presence like he did her cinnamon rolls, the day sprinted along. Every hour became a minute. Every minute but a second.

Even the chore of washing dishes seemed to be finished in the blink of an eye when he was by her side, laughing at her stories, brushing against her arm.

Before Adam knew it, the back door slammed and Ford tromped into the kitchen. "I'm going to come in last place." With a dramatic sigh, he set a casserole dish on the island with a harsh clunk. "It's ruined."

He wasn't exaggerating. The top of the

dish — whatever it had been — was black and crispy, flakes of burnt topping crumbling onto the counter.

Drying his hands, Adam shook his head. "I think I'll leave this to the pros."

Caden snorted, that sweet noise she saved just for him. "All right. I'll see you tonight?"

For a stroll along the boardwalk, which enjoyed numerous secluded sections and isolated corners. His heart skipped in his chest, and his hands itched to pull her close. He couldn't wait to inhale her scent, drinking in the cinnamon and sugar always lingering in her hair.

"I wouldn't miss it."

As he slipped out of the kitchen, he passed Jerome in the dining room.

"Is the class about to get started?" the chef asked.

Adam nodded. "You hoping to learn something?"

With a more-than-polite chuckle, Jerome sauntered into the kitchen. "You bet." His words carried behind him, making Adam laugh too.

Red pen in hand, Adam spent the rest of the afternoon on the front porch hacking at the overdue article, tearing it apart and then putting the pieces back together. He reworked the lead, scratched it out, and wrote it again. He'd always preferred to type his first drafts on the computer and fix last drafts on printed paper. It was a habit that Garrett had instilled — something about reading it in the same format that the readers did.

He didn't know if that held true when so many of the paper's readers got it online.

Still, it helped him to look at his words in a new medium.

A stiff breeze off the bay ruffled the corners of the pages as he hunched over the checkers table, which he'd pulled between his knees.

As he drew an arrow from his third paragraph to the top of the page, he drummed his fingers against the glass tabletop. He just had to find his lead. What was the most important part of the story? If he had to summarize the whole piece in two sentences, what would they be?

A stained glass window at Boston's historic St. Cassian's Chapel depicts the story of David and Goliath. Now, like David, the church, brought low by an unscrupulous contractor, faces a real estate giant intent on seeing it destroyed.

That might work.

He rubbed his eyes but still saw the pen strokes in his mind's eye. Reorganizing the phrases, he whispered them to himself, reworded them out loud.

Paragraph by paragraph he worked out each section, fitting in a quote from Regina Holmes about the church's place in the community. About the people who counted on its support and outreach. About the swindler who'd left them broke and crumbling.

And about the mogul who was all too happy to snatch up the land, tear down the building, and leave a community in ruins.

Right in the middle of the article sat a gaping hole.

At this point, even Adam struggled to believe that Elliot Carrington could be as greedy and heartless as the article painted him.

He needed a source. A quote. Anything to confirm that Carrington really was at least half so heinous.

Adam was still staring at the blank spot on the page when a shriek from inside made him jump, sending his heart pounding and blood racing through his veins.

It wasn't the usual sounds of Caden's class, and he realized with a quick glance at his watch that they'd likely wrapped up more than an hour before.

Scooping up his pen and pages, he hurdled the low table, flung open the screen door, and flew through the dining room. He nearly slammed through the swinging door to the kitchen before he recognized the voices inside.

"We missed you so much." It had to be Marie, her voice high and clear, if tired.

"Here. Sit down." It sounded like one of the stools along the island scraped against the floor. "Let me get you a scone and a cup of tea."

He smiled at Caden's offer. She was always ready with a sweet and something warm to drink. So generous. So kind.

"Tell me about your trip."

He turned to go. No need to eavesdrop on this conversation.

"What happened with your dad?"

The simple question stopped him mid-stride. He leaned in toward the crack in the door, but quickly rocked back. He had no business listening to them. He didn't even need the knot in his stomach to remind him of that.

But then Marie sighed. Loudly. And his feet were stuck in place.

"Oh, Caden . . ."

That couldn't be good.

"I'm so sorry." Caden's words were thick with sympathy, and they seemed to be enough for a long moment. The women were so silent that Adam held his breath until all he could hear was the pounding of his pulse in his ears.

He should walk away. He should go.

But he needed a quote from Marie. And maybe she was just worked up enough to give him what he needed.

The faint tinkling of china against china seemed to announce Marie's tea was ready. "Mmm. That's good. Thank you."

"Sure." Caden's footfalls moved away from the door and then back toward it as she apparently paced the confines of the room. "Did you have any luck?"

"Not even a nibble." With each word, Marie's voice rose in volume until Adam didn't even have to lean into the door to clearly hear her words. "I visited every associate I knew in Boston — from people I went to school with to my mother's old lawyer — and no one will help us."

"But . . . I don't understand. How can —"

"My father." Marie seethed the words, the venom in her words practically tangible. "He blacklisted us with everyone I know."

"How could he do that? *Why* would he do that?"

"He dug up dirt on every single one of them. And those he couldn't find something on, he bribed or threatened to boycott or badmouth their business." Marie slurped her tea, and it only seemed to stoke the ire in her tone. "As for the why — well, he's just an awful human being. He's vindictive and cutthroat and he's never cared about anyone but himself."

That sounded exactly like someone who would buy a foreclosed church building and tear it down. While Marie had once been on her dad's staff, she certainly wasn't on his team now. That knowledge made the muscles in Adam's shoulders relax, and he finally took a real breath.

Caden paused too, and Adam could picture her running her hands over her apron, smoothing out the wrinkles and buying time until she knew what to say.

"I mean, I know he's been awful —"

Marie didn't let Caden get to the *but.*

"He's the worst!" She didn't bother even pretending to keep her voice down at this point.

Adam shifted his weight and hit a creak in the floor, which announced his presence better than the inn's doorbell.

411

"Hello?" Marie called, her voice suddenly cautious.

Well, he wasn't going to get a better invitation than that. Pushing open the door, he stuck his head in. "I heard a hubbub in here. Thought I'd investigate."

Caden's sad eyes crinkled at the corners, and she stopped pacing.

Marie's neck turned red and she covered her face. "I'm sorry. I hope you didn't hear that."

Adam shrugged one shoulder and tried to play it cool. If she was embarrassed, she wasn't likely to consent to his use of her name, her quote.

"A bit," he said. "Not a fan of your dad, then?"

"That's putting it lightly." She laughed it off, but then added a perfectly poetic assessment. "The man would steal the cardboard box from a homeless person and then sell it back to him for a profit. He has no heart, and I wouldn't be surprised if he's already sold his soul." She heaved a giant sigh. "As long as he got a good deal." Taking another sip of tea, she groaned. "He refused to see me while I was there, claiming he was too busy working on a new acquisition."

"An acquisition? New property?"

Marie didn't even look surprised at his eager question. "A church! Can you believe that? I guess the bank is going to foreclose on it, and he's going to put in a high-rise. I know I shouldn't be surprised. When I worked for him, he swindled tenants out of a low-income housing development. He got them to move out by telling them he was going to build them a new building. Instead, he built ridiculously expensive condos, which, of course, the former tenants couldn't afford. He'd planned the whole thing."

Adam glanced at Caden, hoping to gauge her reaction, hoping he wasn't about to cross a line. "Can I quote you on that?"

Caden's eyebrows pinched together in confusion, but she said nothing.

Marie looked over the edge of her floral teacup and rolled her eyes. "As long as you spell my name right."

23

"You have to leave now."

Adam pouted, and Caden had to steel herself against the pull toward his protruding lower lip.

Which had been pressed firmly against hers just a moment before.

Which had been stealing sweet kisses from her all week.

Did it count as stealing if she looked forward to them as much as he did? Maybe more?

Her hands twisted into the front of his shirt, and he gave her a slightly wicked grin, which only served to whip her stomach into a frenzy.

"But we have to pick out at least one more recipe for your cooking classes pitch to Marie."

She sighed. "I know, but it'll have to wait. I have to make my entry for the cook-off tonight." But she didn't release the soft knit in her fists.

"You haven't even let me try your new recipe."

That was true. After her disastrous attempts at the lobster cakes, she'd sought out a recipe that played to her strengths. Island comfort food. And even she'd liked her first attempt at it.

But there hadn't been time to cook it for Adam, who disappeared most mornings after breakfast. Especially not while Marie had been gone. And Ford's final cry for help had stolen her last afternoon as she helped him land on a dish even he couldn't mess up.

"I guess you'll just have to be surprised like everyone else."

He nodded but leaned in again, pressing his forehead against hers. "Save me some leftovers?"

"For sure." Her breath hitched as goose bumps broke out around her neck and danced down her arms. She trembled as his thumb swiped the line right below her lip, and she sighed up at him, her eyes closed and mouth waiting. He smelled of island air and the wildflowers he'd picked for her that morning, and he smelled like home.

"Are you sure you don't want my help?"

She swatted his arm with her towel. "You

mean, do I want you to distract me?"

He shrugged. "That too."

She couldn't help but laugh. It was true. She hadn't been able to focus on much that week, not when his hand had found hers as they stood in front of the sink washing dishes. Or when he'd walked her home at night and slipped his arm around her waist. Or when he'd surprised her with a kiss on the porch in front of Levi and Esther, who had shot each other knowing glances.

Or when she'd nearly burned breakfast for the third time that week because she was daydreaming about the way his hand had felt flat against her back, holding her close in a shadowy alcove along the boardwalk.

In fact, she'd dropped more dishes and cut her finger more times since they'd become an officially recognized . . .

Well, she didn't know what they were. And she refused to focus on that. Whatever was between them was sweet and tender and more than she'd ever dreamed for someone like her. He cared for her, protected her, and cherished her. Whatever this was, it was better than the fairy tales.

But like Cinderella's big night out, this had an expiration date. The summer was almost over, and he'd be leaving soon enough. He had to turn in his article — the one that would save Connor's bench.

Her stomach twisted. The backs of her eyes burned, and she pinched them closed to keep the tears at bay.

She wasn't going to — she couldn't — spend what little time she had left with him dwelling on the pain his departure would bring. Not when the here and now was enough to make Caden serve a woefully gooey pancake — which Marie had quickly returned to the kitchen for a replacement.

Nope. There was no way she was going to finish her lobster cook-off entry if Adam was anywhere in the house.

"Get out of here. Let me get to work."

With a squeeze of her hand, he stepped toward the back door. "I'll see you at the church tonight."

She turned to put on her apron but swung back around at a gentle pull on her arm. Adam caught her in a quick embrace, cupped her cheek with his hand, and leaned close. The air in the room vanished, but she'd forgotten how to breathe anyway.

"You're going to win tonight."

Apparently she'd forgotten how to speak too, so she offered only a brief nod.

"Good." He pressed his lips firmly against hers, then pulled back and disappeared through the door.

Her legs had turned into mashed potatoes, and she sagged against the counter. Pressing shaking fingers against her lips, she shook her head. That wasn't going to help her focus on her lobster.

At all.

After the lobster took a boiling bath, the potatoes were peeled and the leeks chopped. The stock was simmered and the flour and meat added. Caden had poured the base into four individual baking dishes, adding a dollop of mashed potatoes to each.

When she pulled the dishes out of the oven, their scent filled the entire kitchen, certainly finding its way into the dining room and beyond.

But the house was empty. Everyone else had gone to the lobster dinner already.

And a quick glance at the wall clock reminded Caden that she needed to get to the church too. Contest entries were due by six o'clock.

Her pulse thrummed. That left her only thirty minutes.

Covering each dish and packing them in her insulated delivery bag took away half of her time, and she glanced at her wrinkled shirt. A line of flour around the rim of her apron dusted her pants, but she didn't have time to change. And she'd have to check her hair in the car.

The kitchen cleanup would have to wait as well.

She snatched her keys and jogged down the back steps, trying not to jostle the containers inside her bag. The last thing she needed was a repeat of her picnic with Adam.

Well, that hadn't ended terribly.

But the food part — the part where she'd ruined their lunch — wasn't her finest effort.

And this had to be her best. Marie needed the best chef in town running the Red Door's kitchen. Her parents expected her to win. And Adam had said he knew she could do it.

She had to beat her only real competition this year — Bethany Burke.

Her car's tires flung gravel as she skidded into the only empty spot in sight. Of course it was in the farthest corner of the church parking lot. But every family in the community had come out for a good cause and a good dinner.

Caden snuck a peek at herself in the mirror and shrieked. Half of her French braid had come undone, the heat of the kitchen turning the wisps at her temples frizzy and wild. Her cheeks were redder than PEI's north shore, and whatever mascara she'd put on that morning had wiped off on the back of her hand.

But she had exactly seven minutes to get her entry turned in.

So she shook out her hair, grabbed her bag, and dashed around the side of the building.

She nearly ran into a long table jutting out from the corner, but managed to stop with minimal disturbance to her load.

"Bethany."

The blonde sat on the far side of a money tin and a roll of tickets, and she tipped her head to the side. "You sound surprised to see me."

" 'Course not." Caden wasn't startled. She'd just . . . well, she hadn't been expecting to see Bethany first thing upon arrival. Not when every hair in her ponytail was in pristine place, and Caden looked like she'd spent her entire afternoon working in the garden.

But tonight she refused to be intimidated by the other woman's bravado.

Holding up her bag, Caden smiled. "I have my entry for the contest. Where should I drop it off?"

"You have to pay to get in first." Bethany

nodded toward a sign that clearly read $20 for singles, $35 for couples.

Money. She patted her empty pockets as her stomach sank, and she glanced over her shoulder at her car. That wasn't going to help either. "I left my purse at the inn. Can I drop this off and then run and get it?"

Bethany scrunched up her nose, like she had to think hard. "I'm not supposed to."

The muscles in her shoulders tightened, and Caden fought the urge to glare at the girl who had always made her life harder. Why did she insist on being so sour?

"Please. It'll take me ten minutes, but I just need to turn in my dish for the judges first."

Bethany stared at the sky, her lips pursing to the side. "That's not how it's supposed to work."

Something bubbled up in her chest. It was new and bold and fearless, and it made her want to plant her feet and refuse to take Bethany's feeble excuse.

"I'm going to drop this off, then I'll bring you my money."

Bethany looked both shocked and a little bit pleased, like she'd been waiting for this Caden to show up, to spar with her. "Go ahead, it's fine this time, I g—"

"There you are!" Adam jogged over to her

side, pressing a chaste kiss to her cheek. "I got us a couple's ticket. Hope you don't mind."

Mind? Oh, she most definitely did not mind.

Bethany, on the other hand, lost all hint of pleasure in her features. Adam waved the ticket at her, and her perennially wrinkle-free face crumpled into confusion. "This is your date?"

"Caden. Yes. Caden is my date. Where should we put her cook-off entry?" Adam squeezed her waist, and she smiled up at him. She couldn't blame Bethany. Caden still couldn't believe that Adam had picked her. But she wasn't going to complain.

Squinting, Bethany pointed toward the kitchen. "Aretha is in there setting up for the judges."

Adam nodded and ushered Caden away. They greeted Aretha, and when Caden handed over the bag, the other woman asked, "What did you end up making?"

"Someone told me that I'm best at comfort food."

Aretha reached a gloved hand into the bag and pulled out a still steaming dish. She closed her eyes and inhaled until a smile played across her too pink lips. "Garlic mashed potatoes."

Caden shook her head and held her breath, hoping Aretha would approve. "Lobster shepherd's pie."

"Brilliant." They exchanged a quick hug before Aretha scooted her and Adam out to the lawn, where more than twenty picnic tables had been arranged. Every one was full. Deep brown clam shells and bright orange lobster claws littered the ground where they'd spilled over metal buckets at the end of each table, and the double table of side dishes was nearly picked clean.

Adam led her to a spot with two empty seats and motioned for her to slide into the bench next to Levi. Jerome sat across from them, the only one at the table not digging into a heaping plate.

"Get it done?" he asked, flashing his television teeth and all his good humor.

Suddenly her heart sank. This famous chef was going to be officially judging her food in about twenty minutes. Officially and publicly. He hadn't had any complaints about her breakfasts, though she'd been a little distracted anyway. But this contest was for all the marbles.

Her stomach twisted into a painful knot, and the smell of lobster meat made it take a painful loop.

Pressing her hand to the offending spot,

she tried to return Jerome's smile, but all she could manage was a curt nod.

"Hungry?" Levi held out a full lobster on a plate.

The shellfish's little antennae couldn't cover his eyes. They stared at her, judging her for cooking up his cousins that afternoon, and bile rose in her throat. She swallowed convulsively and grabbed the nearest glass of water. But gulping it didn't help her body's natural reaction.

At least Adam came to her rescue. "She's probably had enough lobster already today."

God bless him for knowing that her nerves had kicked in and her tolerance for the shellfish had been exceeded for the day.

But even without the beady eyes staring at her, her stomach refused to settle. It pitched to the rhythm of the nearby waves, only growing more restless as Bethany strolled toward their table.

When she arrived, she ignored Esther and Levi, nodded at Adam and Jack, and poured her too sweet smile all over Jerome. "Aretha says that they're ready for the judges to taste each of the entries." Her gaze traveled toward the kitchen, where two women from the ladies' auxiliary waited to add their voices to the judging opinion.

Caden's breath caught in her throat, and

she gave up trying to fill her lungs, instead grabbing for Adam's hand at her side. As he laced his fingers through hers, the frantic tilting of the world slowed. Squeezing her eyes closed against the throbbing in her head and the ringing in her ears, she waited for Jerome to move toward deciding her fate.

Only, he didn't. He stayed seated, saying simply, "I'll be right there."

Again, confusion crossed Bethany's features, and she pushed her hands into the pockets of her jean jacket. "Well, okay then." She licked her lips and looked at the rest of the faces at the table. "I hope everyone's enjoying dinner."

She left with an unceremonious spin, and Esther chuckled. "I wonder what's got her panties in a bunch."

Jack guffawed, and even Jerome threw his head back with laughter. "I never expected to see her here," the chef said.

Whatever giggle Caden had been about to let out hesitated in her throat. But it was Levi who asked the question probably everyone was thinking. "You know her?"

Jerome teetered his hand in midair. "We met once in Toronto. But everyone knows her reputation."

Forks dropped and eyes went unblinking.

The same question was written on every face.

What is Bethany's reputation?

He didn't expound, though. Instead, pressing his hands to the table, he stood and stepped over the bench. "Guess it's time to do my job." He gave Caden a quick wink. "I'm looking forward to something delicious."

Was that supposed to help her relax? Because it was not helping.

At all.

She pulled her hand free of Adam's and immediately regretted it. But she couldn't just shove it right back in there. So she rubbed her palms together below the table until another hand clamped over hers. This one was weathered and callused. Its knuckles were knotted, keeping the fingers from fully extending. But there was something soothing about the firm, gentle grasp.

"Bit nervous there?" Levi leaned into her shoulder but didn't quite look in her direction.

She nodded. "Just a little."

"For good reason."

A brick hit the bottom of her stomach. Was the good reason that she was a terrible chef, and she was guaranteed to lose? No. That was ridiculous. She caught Marie's

426

gaze at a neighboring table. Marie never would have let her run the Red Door's kitchen if she wasn't at least competent.

Thankfully she didn't have to ask Levi what he meant. He kept going. "It takes a lot of courage to put your work out there to be judged."

She shook her head quickly. "But I might lose."

"Winning, losing. That's got nothing to do with it." He squeezed her hands, a gentle reminder of his support. "The point is, you tried. You entered. Take it from an old reporter."

"You were a reporter? Like Adam?"

His slow nod still managed to jostle the loose skin at his neck. "Just the same. Only, I was more scared to write my first columns, afraid of what my editor would say. It's hard to give someone else permission to judge your work."

"I always enter." Her gaze dropped to her knee where their hands rested. "But I never win."

"Then you're even more brave." He cleared the gravel out of his voice and kept it low, his words just for her. "You know the sting of losing but you keep trying. That's the mark of a true hero."

The view of her legs suddenly became

blurry, and she had to tug a hand free to wipe away the escapees rolling down her cheeks.

Could it be? Was it possible that despite her fears and doubts, she still had the courage to follow her dreams? Dreams that might be bigger than her kitchen? Dreams that might include the man sitting on her other side?

Did God have bigger plans for her than French toast and eggs Benedict?

"Caden!" The cry came from behind her, and Levi immediately dropped her hand, leaving her feeling like a ship without an anchor.

She turned to find five teenagers barreling down on her. But it was Whitney's panicked face that sent her jumping to her feet. "What's wrong?"

"Ford forgot to add the cheese to his lobster grilled cheese sandwiches." The words gushed out as Whitney flapped her hands in front of her face.

Caden clapped a hand over her mouth to keep a giggle from popping out. It was always something with Ford. Between her fingers, she managed, "He forgot to add *cheese* to a grilled *cheese* sandwich?"

Ford hung his head and ruffled his shaggy brown hair with long fingers. "I just forgot."

"And you turned it in for judging?"

He nodded.

"And what exactly is on the sandwich?"

"Everything else. Lobster and butter and spinach. Just like the recipe you gave me."

Caden couldn't hold back the chuckle this time. "Well, not quite. The recipe we talked about had cheese in it."

He thumped his fist against an open palm. "Right."

"What are you going to do?" Iris asked.

"The only thing we can do." She looked at each of her students in turn, giving them what she hoped was a serious face. "Pray that the judges are all lactose intolerant and grateful for the cheese-less grilled cheese."

Adam must have overhead that because his laugh trickled down her spine, sending every single one of her nerve endings into high alert. And his humor sent the kids into a fit of giggles too.

"We do the same thing we do every day. Learn from our mistakes and try to do better next time."

"That's good advice." Adam stood by her side and wrapped an arm around her back. "You're pretty good at this teaching thing."

"Duh." Jeanie rolled her eyes. "We could have told you that."

Before Adam could respond, a tinny voice

came over the PA system. "Testing. Testing." Father Chuck tapped his finger against the microphone on a makeshift wooden stage that had been hastily constructed the day before. "Can you hear me?" The mostly seated crowd gave a rousing cheer, so he continued, waving a piece of white paper in his hand. "I have the results of the lobster cook-off right here."

The crowd let out another hoot, which seemed to be the signal for Caden's stomach to head south. It reached her toes before the yells died down, and she had to lean against Adam to keep her legs under her.

"But before I announce the winners, I want to say that we've had a record turnout this year, and we've raised over six thousand dollars, which will be divided between repairs on the community center and a scholarship fund for local students."

Caden joined the clapping, but her hands were numb like the rest of her.

She only had to hold herself together for a few minutes. Just until she knew if she'd won or if she'd disgraced the inn and humiliated her family.

Sweat peppered her upper lip, and she swiped at it with the back of her hand. But it returned in a moment despite the cool breeze coming off the water, which actually sent a shiver down her spine.

Or maybe that was her nerves.

She pinched her eyes closed and held her breath.

But Father Chuck didn't say anything more, so she peeked out of one eye. He had stepped away from the microphone to confer with Bethany's mom. When he returned to his spot, he pointed toward the three judges, who all stood off to the side of the stage.

Caden had to release her breath, and it came out in a loud whoosh as Father Chuck thanked each of the volunteer judges. "Our community's own Mrs. Dorthea Carpenter and Mrs. Sharon Tuttle. And, of course, a special thank-you to Jerome Gale. I never miss your show on Thursday nights."

Jerome gave a small bow. "Glad I could be here. Thanks for inviting me." His voice carried across the lawn, and the crowd clapped harder for him than their native daughters.

But the whole scene was making Caden's knees shake and her stomach roll.

Father Chuck needed to announce the winners soon.

Finally he waved the paper again. "The judges wanted me to let you know that there were many excellent entries this year. And some very unique ones too. Most notably an item labeled grilled cheese that was conspicuously absent of cheese."

The audience roared, looking around to see if the offender would identify himself. But it was Whitney who gave him away when she snaked her arm through Ford's. "You'll do better next year."

The boy's ears turned red, and a few of his friends hooted at him before Father Chuck could move on.

"As you'll recall, our judges do a blind tasting, meaning they don't know whose meal they're eating. So I'll be announcing the name of the dish. If you hear yours called, please come forward to claim your prize." Father Chuck tapped his palms against his legs. "A drumroll, please."

Get on with it!

Or better yet, maybe make this whole night wrap up without anyone ever judging her food.

But Levi had called her brave. He'd said it took courage to keep after it, courage to try again.

Maybe she had enough courage to hold on for just a minute more.

"Our third-place winner is the lobster mac and cheese."

Gretchen let out a high-pitched scream.

432

"I won!" She danced around as her class-mates hugged and congratulated her. Before she ran for the stage, she grabbed Caden in a tight embrace. "Thank you! I couldn't have done it without you."

Caden nearly buckled under the force of Gretchen's excitement, but it was contagious, and she'd never been more proud. She clapped hard and loud, cheering her young friend on.

After Gretchen received her prize — a gift certificate to Caden's dad's bakery — Father Chuck returned to the mic. "While all the entries were fantastic, there were two supremely delicious entries that stood out this year."

Caden took a cleansing breath.

"One is the lobster Cantonese, a dish filled with Asian-inspired flavors."

That had to be Bethany. No one else would cook something so snooty.

Pinching her lips and eyes closed, Caden leaned against Adam's side. His arm at her back kept her upright, and he seemed to understand the nervous energy that threatened to break free.

"The other entry is . . ."

God, please let him say shepherd's pie. Please let him say it.

". . . the lobster shepherd's pie, made from

local ingredients."

Clearly that was his polite way of saying it was familiar and common.

"The judges had some serious debate about which should win, and it was a split decision, so both chefs can be very proud of themselves."

She leaned her forehead against Adam's shoulder, unable to watch what was about to happen — whether she won or lost. Whether she finally lived up to the potential that everyone promised she had or let everyone who loved her down.

"And the winner . . ."

The crowd took a collective breath.

Please.

Please.

Please.

". . . is . . ."

24

Adam squeezed Caden's waist as they all waited for Father Chuck's prolonged announcement.

She had to win. She deserved it. She'd worked so hard, tried multiple recipes, and spent hours in the kitchen.

And selfishly he wanted to see her face alight with joy at least one more time before he had to leave. Garrett expected him and his article back in Washington by Monday, so this weekend was their last together.

At least for now.

Caden sucked in a sharp breath as Father Chuck explained a split decision. Every muscle in her body tensed, and his did the same.

Please, let her win this.

Father Chuck cleared his throat, put on his best smile, and ruffled his salt-and-pepper hair. "The winner is . . . the lobster Cantonese."

Caden's body turned ramrod straight. She pulled away from him and politely clapped her hands as Bethany feigned shock on the stage. "I'm so surprised," she cooed into the microphone, preening her long blonde ponytail.

But Adam was focused on Jerome's face, which held a polite smile but somber eyes. He hadn't voted for Bethany's dish. He obviously knew something about Bethany that the rest of the town did not, and he wasn't as impressed with her as everyone else seemed to be.

Which meant . . . he'd voted for Caden's shepherd's pie.

He turned to tell her that, but she was gone.

A blast of cold shot through him, and he rubbed the center of his chest, trying to calm the sudden gallop of his heart. It didn't help.

His gaze swung over the lawn as people began standing, milling about. But there was no sign of Caden.

Leaning into Esther, he asked, "Do you know where Caden went?"

"Caden?" She looked around quickly. "No. I haven't seen her since she was standing right beside you."

"Thank you." He took slow steps away

from their table, always looking. Always searching.

Her brother, Dillon, and Justin Kane from the dairy stood near the corner of the church, a swarm of redheaded kids weaving between them. But Caden wasn't there. Her parents were chatting with Aretha and Jack near the stage, but there was no sign of her unusually wild hair. She wasn't at the church anymore.

He had to figure out where she'd gone. Would she be on her favorite beach? At the lighthouse that she loved? Or in her kitchen?

There was no question which she'd pick.

With a quick farewell to Levi, Adam took off. By the time he got to the road, his legs refused to remain at a walk, so he ran for the big blue house along the shore. His feet pounded against the road, jarring his knees and ankles. But he didn't care. He had to find Caden. He had to show her that everything was going to be okay.

Even if he didn't know that it would be.

He crashed through the back door, out of breath and sweating. It fell back into place with a loud thwack as he turned into the kitchen.

Caden stood there, shoulders slumped and eyes red.

Without a word she stumbled toward him

and fell into his arms. She was sweet and soft and still smelled of the garlic from her mashed potatoes. Her body trembled with each repressed sob, and it tore at his insides, leaving him aching and raw. His throat burned as a pool of her tears turned his shoulder damp.

Yet he could do nothing but rub a slow circle on her back and whisper the truth as he knew it into her hair.

"It's all right. I know you wanted it."

She nodded and managed a shaky inhale.

"I think the whole town knows that she didn't deserve it."

Caden hiccupped something that sounded remotely like humor.

Whatever was tearing up his middle took a rest at the pleasant sound. "You're still the best chef I know — and I had dinner with Jerome Gale."

That made her snort just like she always did. And when she pulled away, tears still in her eyes, she shook her head at him. "That's a lie, but I appreciate it."

"I'm not lying. I've gained at least ten pounds since I came here." He patted his belly, which had definitely grown a little rounder in the last two months. "I've never had better food than yours."

Her cheeks pinked, and he took the opportunity to kiss each one, which turned them even redder.

Looking down, she watched the motion of his thumb, which was drawing a figure eight on the back of her hand. "I wanted this so badly for the inn. Marie needed me to win."

He cocked his head to the side. "Needed you to win?"

"You know. For the inn's reputation. For marketing." Her smile dimmed, and a fresh wave of tears flooded her eyes.

He pulled her close again and she sighed into his shoulder. "What am I going to do?"

Brushing her hair off her face, he cupped her cheek. "You'll do exactly what you've been doing. You'll finish the proposal for Marie and show her what an asset the cooking classes will be to the inn. You'll keep teaching those kids. You'll still be the best chef on the island."

She nodded against his hand, but it didn't seem like she was convinced. "And what will you do?"

"I have to go back to Washington and turn in my story. Now that I have the quote I need."

Her upper body stiffened in his arms. He understood. He hated it too, the thought of leaving her. But when she finally spoke, it wasn't about that.

"What quote?"

His heart hammered right beneath her ear, and his mouth turned into a desert. He hadn't told her. He hadn't explained about Marie's connection to his story. It hadn't seemed necessary before. Only now did he realize how it would look that he hadn't revealed it earlier.

"I didn't even think about it before."

She pulled away, her eyes narrowing and her lips tight. "About what?"

Stabbing his fingers through his hair, he looked at the floor, then over her shoulder. "It's just a quote I needed for the article about the church."

"Connor's church. His bench."

"Right. Exactly. But see, the church isn't just going to be foreclosed on. Someone is going to buy the land and demolish the building. It's kind of a David and Goliath thing."

"Sure." Her word said she understood, but her tone said she knew there was more. With each ticking second, he could see her fitting the pieces into place. "The Goliath — Marie's dad. She said he was going after a church. Is it Connor's?"

Squeezing his eyes closed because he was too much of a chicken to watch her face when he confessed, he said, "Yes."

Anger seethed off of her, rolling toward him in waves, and he peeked an eye open to see her pace the length of the island. "You came here to get a quote from Marie? For your article?"

"Not at first. I really was here on sabbatical. But my editor thought it would help me get past my writer's block if I had a story to write. One I really cared about."

"How long? How long have you known about the connection?"

He reached for her hand, but she snapped it away. "Listen, I'm sorry. I didn't mean —"

Fire burned in her eyes and licked at her cheeks, turning them red and blotchy and sending his stomach up in smoke. "You *lied* to me."

The weight and vehemence of the accusation was like a barbell against his throat. There was no defense for what he'd done. He'd messed up. But she had to forgive him.

Marching across the tile floor, she crossed her arms and glared at him. "You had every chance. You could have told me the night of the leak in the roof."

"I should have."

"You could have told me any morning before breakfast."

"I know."

She groaned. "You told me all about Connor and the article on the Homestead Trail. Why not just tell me that my boss's dad is the bad guy in your article?"

Rubbing his hands together, he started a march of his own. "I didn't know how to."

"So instead, you . . ." Suddenly her eyes grew larger, eclipsing the rest of her features and turning hard as ice. "You're quoting Marie."

He nodded. "She said I could quote her. You heard me ask. She confirmed that her dad is going after the church."

Caden stumbled back, shaking her head frantically. "You can't. You can't print that."

A sharp pain pierced through his gut. Before he even asked the question, he knew he wasn't going to like the answer. "Why not? She said I could."

Caden chewed on her fingernail, her gaze squinted and pained. "She didn't know what you were asking. She thought it was for a travel magazine. About the inn."

The truth washed over him like lava, searing him into place and stealing his breath. Caden hadn't told Marie that he wasn't the undercover reviewer. He'd broken a cardinal rule of journalism. He'd assumed.

Of course Caden had told Marie that he wasn't the travel writer. She had known the truth for almost two weeks. She'd certainly called Marie and filled her in on the situation.

Except she hadn't.

"Why didn't you tell her?" His words were sharper than he meant them to be, and she flinched as though they'd struck a physical blow.

Caden shook her head fiercely, defending herself even while her lip trembled. "There wasn't a good time. She was so focused on doing what she needed to in Boston. I didn't want to distract her with something she couldn't do anything about. And when she got back, she was so upset I couldn't just drop it on her."

His stomach churned, bile rising in the back of his throat. He'd thought she'd known what he was asking for. He'd gotten her on record.

Only it was the wrong record.

Pressing his fist to his forehead, he tried to release the pressure building there, but there was no relief. "I need her quote. It gives the whole article teeth."

"But her dad is suing her right now." She clapped her hands over her mouth.

"What?" His word was barely a breath, but it set off his pacing again. He stopped on the far side of the island and glowered at her. "Marie's dad is suing her?"

Slowly, surely, Caden cringed in affirmation. "Her mom left her a trust fund, and now her dad is fighting her for it."

It didn't even take him two seconds to put the pieces together. "A quote like this could be a blow to her legal case."

"Elliot Carrington is just what she said, and he'll spin it to the judge." Caden's chin quivered as she sucked in a tremored breath, clearly begging him to change his mind. "You can't run that article."

A slow breath seeped between his lips, a pathetic cover for the war zone inside him. He'd do anything not to hurt her. But he couldn't not save the church. "I don't have a choice. My job is on the line. And I owe it to Connor and his family. I can't not turn it in."

Her voice went hoarse. "Then we're ruined."

25

Caden wasn't surprised that Adam didn't show up for coffee the next morning. Or breakfast. She hadn't expected to see his crooked grin or shining eyes.

But she'd wanted to.

Instead she was left to stare at a quickly cooling cup of coffee on the counter — the one she'd poured out of habit, out of hope — as she dashed around the kitchen to get breakfast on the table on time. She was left to imagine him pacing his room, wrestling over the decision to submit his article.

She found herself dodging the spot where he usually stood blocking the sink. She took the longer route around the island because she'd had to all summer. Because he'd been there. He'd promised to be there.

His absence left a little hole in the kitchen, and one in her chest.

And Marie's frazzled arrival didn't do anything to help.

They locked eyes from across the room, and something about Marie's fluttering hands and incomplete smile made her chest ache.

Marie pointed to the tray of berry sorbet on the counter as though she was going to pick it up. Instead she sighed two small words. "Adam's gone."

Caden nearly dropped the freshly cut bread she was shuttling to the counter next to the griddle. She swallowed slowly and blinked three times, not wanting to believe the truth. "He left?"

"He got a cab this morning. He checked out as soon as I got to the office." Marie put her hands on her hips and tilted her face toward the ceiling. "He told me about the article he's been writing."

"Oh, Marie." Caden threw the bread on the counter and pulled her friend into a hug. "I didn't know about the quote until last night."

"I know. He told me that too."

"So you explained to him?" Caden pulled back so she could see Marie's face, tension still etched in every line. "You told him he couldn't use it?"

Marie shook her head, slow and firm.

"What do you mean? Why didn't you just tell him he couldn't use it? What if your dad sees it? What if it affects the lawsuit?"

"What I said was true." Marie's voice was so soft that Caden had to lean in to make out each syllable. And then she wished she'd missed them all.

"He offered to use my quote as a former employee of the company."

A fraction of the weight on her shoulders left. "Well, that's something."

"But my dad would just use his investigator to track down the source. And he'd probably start with me anyway." A flicker of a brave smile danced across Marie's lips, but it couldn't hang on under the truth of the situation. "I told Adam to use it. Not all of it. Not the part about my dad having no heart. But what I said about the church and the condo tenants. I told him it was on the record. I should have asked what he meant. I should have confirmed. I was in corporate marketing and communications. I know better than to flippantly agree when any writer asks me to be on the record. He did his job."

"What about the lawsuit?"

Marie lifted a shoulder like Adam's article didn't have the power to wreak havoc on their lives. "We'll face the fallout when it goes to print."

Maybe Marie said something more, but Caden couldn't hear anything except the violent rushing in her ears.

Adam had left without a word to her. He'd gone before she could try again to convince him to find another way. He'd told her the truth — he had to turn in the article. And he was going to do it.

No matter what it cost Marie and the inn. No matter what it cost Caden.

Because his job was on the line.

So was hers.

As Marie managed a shaky breath, Caden blurted out the only words she could find. "It's going to be okay." But she didn't know that it was. In fact, she had no idea what was going to happen. She just knew one thing. "You're not alone. We'll figure out how to get through this."

Marie barked a hoarse laugh. "So we're *not* going to be featured in the magazine, *and* my dad is going to have ammunition for his case."

"Something like that. But I have an idea that might help generate some extra income next summer."

Voices in the adjoining room drew their attention, and Marie pulled herself together. "I'd like to hear about it. Tell me after breakfast?"

Caden nodded, and Marie straightened her shirt and swiped her fingers under her eyes before scooping up the tray from the counter.

So long as they had a roof over their heads and guests in the dining room, breakfast had to be served.

The day after leaving the island, Adam sat on the last pew of St. Cassian's Chapel. The building was all but empty after the Sunday morning services, a moment of peace for his haggard soul. His fingers outlined the plaque on the end of the bench, but he'd had the words memorized since the first time he'd seen it.

In loving memory of Connor O'Dwyer.
The son, brother, and friend we loved.

"I let you down, friend," he whispered into the empty sanctuary. "I don't think I can do it. I can't ruin more lives. Not when nothing I do will ever bring you ba-ack." His voice cracked as he hung his head. "I'm sorry I couldn't do more. I'm sorry."

"Can I help you?" The voice that invaded his privacy was solid as a rock and vaguely familiar.

He turned to see an intimidating black woman, hands on her hips, standing by the large double doors at the back of the aisle. "Excuse me, ma'am." He stood and slipped out from between the benches, giving the plaque one more brush with his hand.

Her dark eyes didn't miss a movement, and she nodded at the bench. "You knew Connor?" She didn't wait for him to confirm. "You're the one who called, aren't you?"

That was where he knew her voice. "Yes, ma'am. You're Regina Holmes."

She harrumphed a nod. "I am."

Holding out his hand, he said, "I'm Adam Jacobs."

She slid her fingers into his grip like a princess. "Good to meet you." He wouldn't have guessed she was glad to make his acquaintance from her tone or posture, but he smiled thinking about this woman teaching Connor's Sunday school class and receiving his weekly wildflower offering.

She pursed her generous lips as her gaze surveyed him from head to toe. "So you found your way back?"

"Yes, ma'am."

"And did you find what you needed for your article?"

His heart staggered under the weight of her question, a weight she didn't even realize. "No. I don't think my article is going to run."

She shrugged, but it wasn't a careless toss of her shoulders. It was rigid with understanding. "I'm sure you tried."

"I did, but you see —" When she held up her hand, he slammed on the brakes.

"No need to explain." She motioned toward the old brick walls and beyond. "Our community is doing a fund-raiser. We might make enough." Her voice dropped. "If we had a bigger community."

"A bigger community?"

"More people. Who could afford to donate. But this isn't a wealthy neighborhood. Or a big one."

His gaze drifted to the David and Goliath stained glass window as a thought tumbled through his mind. It wasn't what he'd planned or how his experience said it should work. But maybe it would. "You just need more people."

"That's what I said." She waved a hand in front of his face. "You still with me, Adam?"

"Yes, and I think I might have an idea."

"What kind of idea?"

"Well . . ." He tried to put his thoughts together to make sense. "I'm a writer. I can write his story. We just have to find people to read it." He still wasn't making much sense, even to himself, his thoughts too jumbled.

But Regina surprised him when she asked not about his plan but about his motives.

"Why do you care so much about Connor and his bench?"

His tongue grew thick, and a bead of sweat trickled down the back of his neck. This wasn't the conversation he wanted to have. But if the church let him help them directly, they had to know it all. Half-truths wouldn't suffice.

"I didn't mean to, but I wrote an article that revealed the identity of Connor's translator. They were both killed in the bombing."

"Oh boy." She shook her head until her carefully curled hair bounced. "You've been carrying that around for a while, haven't you?"

He nodded but couldn't get anything else out around the lump in his throat.

"You can't spend your life thinking only of the ones you've lost. Not when the living need you too."

"Pardon?"

"Don't beg my pardon. Pay attention." She swatted at his arm. "What relationships should you be investing in right now? We all have a friendship or two that could use healing."

Dear God.

Two words. They hit him harder than a Humvee. And they were the sum of his only

452

hope for help in restoring the two relationships he'd abandoned because of his own shame, his self-condemnation.

A wild idea popped into his mind, an image of his brother and Caden and the island he'd grown to love. It made his heart beat a little harder, his pulse thrumming at his wrists as the idea grew and took shape.

Maybe — just maybe — if he let go of his regrets and worked on one relationship, he could fix the other.

"I think you might be right, Ms. Holmes."

"You're darn right I'm right. Now tell me about the plan you have to save this old building."

Caden wasn't sure which was worse — her rubbery quiche or her attitude.

She poked the leftover eggs in the pie pan, and they wiggled like Jell-O. She hated that she'd served the dish. Even though Jerome and Danielle had checked out, leaving Esther and Levi their only guests for the rest of the season. Neither had complained, but Caden knew.

She'd been struggling to put out a meal she was proud of because every morning in her kitchen was a reminder that it had become *their* kitchen. And she no longer had a *him* to share it with.

Three days without laughter and teasing and the touch of his hand had left her mood almost as dark as the coffee they no longer shared.

Leaning her elbows on the island, she covered her face with her hands and bit her trembling lip. It wasn't supposed to be this way. She'd known he was leaving. She hadn't expected him to stay forever.

But he hadn't even said good-bye.

He'd left without a word.

Left her to wonder if what they'd shared had meant anything at all to him, or if she'd just been a distraction. An easily dismissed diversion.

His career had clearly been more important to him. And rightfully so. He'd been a journalist a lot longer than he'd known her.

Recognizing that hadn't stopped her from hoping, from praying.

But all that was left was an aching wound deep in her heart, like a repeated stabbing, always in the same tender spot. As soon as it began to heal, another memory would surface, and it was ripped open again.

Yet none of that stopped her breath from catching when Marie called down the hall. "Caden, you have a call in the office."

Adam.

She tried to suppress the butterflies that

454

took off as she did, but they refused to settle down. Rounding the corner and flying down the hall, her feet slid on the hardwood, and she nearly slammed into the partially closed door.

Marie jumped at the commotion but didn't smile when she handed over the phone. "It's not Adam," she whispered.

"Oh." The hope that had crested inside her crashed like a stormy wave. Caden's shoulders drooped as she pressed the phone to her ear. "This is Caden."

"This is Jerome."

"Jerome?" She couldn't help the surprised lilt of her voice or the sudden uptick in her pulse.

Marie hopped up from her chair and pushed Caden into it. She gave a quick wave before closing the door behind her.

"Jerome Gale."

"Of course." She knew who he was, just not why he was calling her. "Did you forget something at the inn?"

His laugh was contagious, but hers came out as a nervous giggle, so she clamped her lips closed to keep from embarrassing herself further.

"No. I didn't leave anything behind." The smile was audible in his tone. "I have a proposition for you."

"For me?" Perfect. She sounded like a complete idiot. Taking a deep breath, she tried to make herself focus. "What did you — what kind of proposition?"

"I've been looking for a way to expand my brand."

Immediately her mind filled in what he was going to say. He wanted to take over the inn's kitchen. He wanted to start a line of B and B cookware. He wanted her to help him promote a new cookbook.

But none of those made much sense. The inn was small compared to the others on the island, and she wasn't a person of influence. Not even in her own community.

Thankfully, he was oblivious to her mental ramblings, and she was never more grateful than when he shut them down.

"I want to expand, but I also want to give back. To give low-income teenagers in Toronto a chance to learn a new skill. I want to show them what you taught your summer school students. So I'm going to start an after-school cooking program."

A blush of pride washed over her. Had she inspired the idea? "That's wonderful. I'm sure you'll be fantastic, and the kids will love it."

"Oh, I'm a terrible teacher."

She paused, pressing fingers against her

lips. "I don't understand."

His laughter returned, this time a little gentler than before. "I don't have the patience to encourage them when they don't get it or the time to dedicate to doing it right." His voice turned so serious that it made her hands tremble. "I want *you* to launch the program for me."

"I can't." The words popped out before she could form a single thought. But as her brain caught up, she knew it was right.

She couldn't possibly leave PEI or the Red Door. She'd spent a grand total of five nights in Toronto in her entire life. And she'd longed to be home every minute there.

She couldn't create and launch a program all by herself. She wasn't a trained chef. What if she gave the wrong instruction or the kids hated it?

"Oh, I'd never ask you to leave Rose's Red Door Inn," Jerome charged on. "My program would be only during the school year, so you'd still have summers free to work at the inn. Of course, we'd work together to set up the program — it'll have my name on it, after all — but then you'll be fairly autonomous."

"But . . . but . . ." There was a question on the tip of her tongue even though she couldn't find the words among the hundred other things racing through her mind.

This had to be a mistake. He'd clearly called the wrong person.

"But I didn't win the cook-off."

He grunted a note of displeasure that tied a band around her heart, squeezing with each passing second.

"You should have." He grunted again. "Your shepherd's pie was a delight of flavors and textures. It was a fresh take on an island classic, and I could have eaten the other judges' servings too."

She gasped. It couldn't be true. "You — you were the split vote?"

"You better believe it. You're an exceptionally talented chef, Caden. And I would like to work with you to create a program that gives teens a chance to learn something new. These are kids who would never have the opportunity for formal training otherwise."

"I . . . don't know what to say."

"Good. Think about it. I mean, really consider it. Then get back to me by the end of the week." He rattled off his phone number, and she scribbled it on a nearby pad.

She hung up after assuring him, "I will."

But she couldn't. She couldn't fathom living away from the island, making a life somewhere other than the one she'd always known. She couldn't start a program from scratch.

You already have.

Yes, but that didn't count. That was only five kids from her community. They were familiar faces who attended her old high school. She knew their parents and siblings. And not every class had gone as well as she'd hoped. And certainly Ford hadn't picked up all the skills.

You keep trying. That's the mark of a true hero.

Levi had called her a hero, but she wasn't.

Just because she'd kept teaching, kept entering the cook-off. That wasn't courageous. Brave was trying something new despite her fears. Brave was venturing out on her own. Brave was giving up the safety net of North Rustico.

Be brave.

The voice in her head stole her breath, and she pinched her eyes against the push and tug of the very idea. She wanted to be daring, to hear Adam tell her again how much he liked her fearlessness.

No, that wasn't right. He hadn't said she was fearless. Only that she didn't let her fear stop her.

She'd been afraid to accept the job at the

inn when it was first offered to her. And now she loved it.

She'd been scared to enter the cook-off again. And even though she'd lost, she'd received rave reviews from Jerome Gale.

She'd been terrified to spend her summer showing Adam around the island. And now she loved him.

The hole in her heart burned again, bright and excruciating. Oh, just to see Adam again, to have one more chance to convince him to stay.

"What will you do?"

She jumped at Marie's question. "Were you eavesdropping?"

Marie offered a guilty grin. "Only a little." She leaned a shoulder against the door frame. "What does he want you to do?"

Caden stared at the phone number she'd written down, not sure how much to share. Marie was her boss. But before that, she was her friend. "He wants me to teach a cooking class for kids." She sucked in a quick breath to make sure she could get the rest of the words out. "In Toronto."

Marie's jaw dropped open, but she forced it closed with what looked like considerable effort. She didn't blink for several long seconds, and the weight of her gaze grew heavier than the silence hanging between them.

"Aren't you going to say anything?"

Finally a blink, followed quickly by a furrowed brow. "Would you really go? Would you *like* to go?"

"I don't know." As she said it, she recognized the words weren't quite true. She would like to go if she weren't so scared.

But the very best things in her life came when she faced her fears.

"We could never replace you." A little tremble appeared in Marie's lower lip. "But don't stay because of us."

"You could hire Bethany Burke." She hadn't meant to mention Bethany, but the question had been lingering all summer. Would Marie rather have the best chef in town in the inn's kitchen?

Whatever doubts Caden had carried disappeared when Marie gasped a strangled laugh. "Bethany? No." She gave her head a forceful shake. "She asked Seth about a job earlier in the summer, and he told her in no uncertain terms that we're not interested."

"But why not? She's the best chef in town, and maybe on the island. Who else has had their own successful restaurant in Toronto?"

Marie's shock faded to a grin that tipped only one side of her mouth. "Obviously you

461

haven't heard from Aretha this weekend."

"Heard what?"

"Apparently a reporter who recently resided at Rose's Red Door did a little digging after he left town and sent some news to the ladies' auxiliary. So it stayed a secret for exactly three-quarters of a second."

Again Caden's heart betrayed her with a pained leap. "What did he find?"

"Bethany made quite a name for herself in Toronto . . ."

She'd heard that from Jerome at the lobster dinner, and her stomach clenched in a combination of dread and anticipation.

". . . for sending her customers to the ER with food poisoning."

"No!" Caden slapped a hand over her mouth, her stomach rolling in empathy.

"Yes. Almost two dozen cases in three months were linked to her restaurant, so she had to close."

A pang of sympathy speared her middle. Bethany had told the whole town that she'd come back to care for her parents, when she'd really been running from a failed business and a ruined reputation. Despite Bethany's constant barbs and prickles, Caden couldn't summon any joy at the news of the debacle. It must have been terrible to have to give up her dream.

But at least Bethany had tried.

And maybe some of those snide remarks were a result of her own regrets.

Caden didn't wish her ill. She also didn't want Bethany within a hundred feet of her kitchen.

"Even before we knew about Bethany's restaurant, we'd never have hired her."

Caden leaned forward, resting her arm on the messy desktop. "Why's that?"

"She's not our kind of people."

"Your kind of people?"

Pressing a hand to Caden's arm, Marie smiled. "She's not funny or quick or kind. She'd never give up her afternoons to teach a bunch of high school misfits."

Her eyes burned and a lump grew at the back of her throat until she couldn't even swallow it away.

"I know I've been a little distracted this summer, and I don't tell you enough." She paused long enough to catch Caden's gaze. "You are our kind of people, Caden Holt. Don't you forget that."

The sudden ache in her chest was new, different than the one she'd known since Adam left. This one was sweeter than icing and sharper than a paring knife. And all she could do was blink at the tears that rushed to her eyes.

"As long as our door is open, you have a job here if you want it."

26

On Monday afternoon, Adam was in his editor's office, sitting across from an unhappy man. The last time he'd been in this chair, he'd leaned all the way back, his arms crossed and chest tight. Now he sat straight, one ankle resting on the opposite knee, chin up. It was difficult to breathe again, but for an entirely different reason.

He met Garrett's probing gaze straight on.

"Where's my article, Jacobs?"

Adam pressed his palms against his legs and searched for the words to explain all that had happened in such a few short days. He'd been so sure, so certain, that he could complete his assignment.

Until Caden's lip had quivered and her eyes filled with tears and her tone begged him not to.

Nothing was more important to him than making amends. Except for maybe Caden.

Even now, he could see her wary eyes and hear the cry in her voice.

You can't run that article.

And for a long day he'd wrestled with it. Was still wrestling with it.

Connor's memory wasn't going to go away. But nothing Adam could do would bring him back. Levi had said the only way to deal with the regrets was with grace. In some way that meant forgiving himself for an accident. Caden had said it meant recognizing that he couldn't carry the weight of those regrets on his own.

"I don't have it."

Garrett popped a fist on the top of his immaculately organized desktop, his face turning red, angry. "What do you mean? I hand-fed you that story. I gave you all the pieces. You only had to put it on paper."

Adam had never seen him so upset, and the other side of the argument in his head voiced its opinion. Loudly.

He could turn the article in.

Maybe Marie's father wouldn't see it. Maybe it wouldn't affect her lawsuit. Maybe they'd find another way to keep the Red Door open. Maybe Caden wouldn't despise him for hurting her friend.

But that was too many maybes and too much potential pain — which he'd be responsible for.

That one realization ended every internal argument he'd had. Turning the article in would only injure more people that he cared about.

Turning it in would only trade one pain for another — Connor for Caden.

"I know you thought it would be an easy article, but there's more to it than you know."

Garrett had always played the part of an uncle — he'd been his father's best friend — but this minute he was wholly Adam's editor, his words low and firm. "It's simple, really. You owe me an article, and you have it. Not hard at all."

"I don't have a quote from Carrington's daughter."

"But you told me you did."

Adam pinched one eye closed and stabbed his fingers through his hair. "I did. I do. But I can't use it."

"Did you ask if you could quote her?"

"Yes."

"And what did she say?"

He licked his lips, praying he was doing the right thing. "She said I could quote her as long as I spelled her name right."

"Then we'll make sure you get it right."

With an uncertain breath, he shook his

head. "I'm not going to turn it in."

Garrett shoved his chair back, towering above Adam as he pressed his hands flat to the desk. "Let's be very clear here. I've always liked you and your brother. Your dad was a good friend of mine. I wanted to help you." His eyes narrowed and his shoulders twitched. "But your job is hanging in the balance right now. If you don't follow through, there will be no more contract offers from *America Today* or any other national paper."

Adam inhaled through his nose and exhaled in a long breath. When he closed his eyes, the orange fireball was gone, replaced by something infinitely sweeter. Caden's dimples on display.

"I understand."

"I'm afraid you don't. This isn't a vague threat. Gloria is going to blacklist you — today. No newspaper in town will pick you up when she's through with you, and the best job you'll be able to get is writing the local news in Buford, Wyoming."

Adam laughed. "I don't think I'll make it to Wyoming, and I think I'm done with the newsroom."

Straightening his tie, Garrett shook his head. "You're not the type to give up your pen."

Adam stood so that they were eye to eye. "I'm not planning on it."

Garrett's gray eyebrows met at the top of his nose.

"I wanted to thank you for that, by the way."

"For what?"

"For introducing me to your friend at *Leisure Vacations*. She wants me to write another article for them. And she gave me a tip on a piece for one of the airline magazines."

"Ha!" Garrett's laugh was dry, disbelieving. "You're not a travel writer."

Adam shrugged. "Turns out, maybe I am."

Garrett donned the uncle role again. "Where are you going to go?"

"Right now?" A swooping flutter of anticipation filled his chest. "To Nashville. I haven't seen my brother in eight years. I think it's past time for a visit."

Caden's morning Broadway music had grown more subdued since Adam had left almost a full week before. Gone were the disco-era tunes, replaced by the haunting melodies of *Phantom of the Opera*. Beautiful and melancholy, they didn't inspire any dancing, but the Phantom's broken heart seemed to echo her own.

She ran a sponge around the pan in her hand, dunking it in the sudsy dishwater for the fourth time. Or maybe the fifth.

She'd lost count just staring out the window, remembering the first time she'd seen Adam. She'd been looking out this same kitchen window, watching the waves, and he'd walked through the wildflowers.

It had been a lifetime ago.

And she'd give anything to go back to that moment. To not lose a single second with him.

His smile danced before her eyes, and she tried to conjure the whole picture, to hold on to a complete memory.

But she should be thinking about another man, a different future. She'd called Jerome that morning and told him that she'd come for the first year of his student program. They'd see how it went. She had only one nonnegotiable.

She had to be back to the inn by the first of May. After all, she'd be teaching guests how to prepare lobster and other local specialties only a week later.

He'd agreed, his delight evident even over the phone. More details would be arriving soon.

And she had to start packing. To start thinking about the new young faces that would soon fill her world, instead of Adam's — the one she wanted.

A knock on the back door returned her to reality, and she grabbed a towel to wipe her hands. She'd just grabbed at the string to loosen her apron and turned into the mudroom when she spied the visitor through the screen door.

She froze completely. No movement. No heartbeat. No breath.

"I don't have a reservation, but I heard this is the best B and B on the island."

Finally air seeped in, and she gasped and threw a hand to her mouth, blinking against the overflow of tears and too many emotions to name.

Through quivering lips, she sighed. "You came back."

Adam pulled the screen open and stopped with one foot on the top stop. His features were tight, a little wary. "I wasn't sure if I'd be welcome after I left without saying good-bye." He scratched at his freshly shaved cheek until one finger hooked over his chin. "I wasn't sure you'd be happy to see me."

"Happy?" The high-pitched reaction didn't begin to express the tumult inside.

Adam took another step inside, letting the door close behind him, and suddenly he was in her personal space. She couldn't back up, but neither could she look at him. She had to do something, so she wrestled her apron strings with fingers that had forgotten how to work. The knot at the front of her waist only got tighter, and she glared at it.

Without a word, Adam brushed her hands aside and easily undid the fastening and slid her apron off, the bright floral design out of place in his strong, tan hands.

He stared at it too.

"I left because I didn't think I could do it all. I didn't see how I could honor Connor's memory, keep my job, *and* not put the inn at risk. And I wasn't ready to make that decision. I knew if I saw you every morning I wouldn't be able to say no to you."

Her heart beat faster than a whisk, her fingers quaking. "Did you . . . did you figure out a way?"

His gray eyes shone as he shook his head.

Her stomach fell to the floor, and unrestricted fear crushed her chest. He was running the article. Marie was going to be ruined. The inn she loved was about to go under. The people she loved were going to be hurt.

With the tiniest uptick of his lips, Adam stopped her frantic thoughts.

"Turns out my job was the negotiable factor."

"You quit your job?"

"Eh." The apron in his hand danced with his so-so motion as his face contorted into the cutest expression. "Technically, yes. But I was going to be fired anyway."

Hope blossomed, pushing aside the strangling fear in her chest. "You're not going to run the article? You didn't quote Marie? Her dad isn't going to have any ammunition?" With each question, he gave a hard shake of his head until she threw her arms around his neck and squeezed until she couldn't breathe.

Apparently he couldn't either. A strangled laugh escaped him as he set her an arm's length away. But he never let go of her waist, even when the apron fell to the floor. Gasping a few breaths, he straightened his shoulders beneath his leather jacket.

He chuckled. "We'll get to that."

The promise made her insides line up for the conga.

"First, I have some good —"

"Danielle! It was Danielle!" Marie's voice probably reached to the fishing boats in the harbor as her feet pounded on the wooden floors in her race for the kitchen. "She loved the inn!" She slowed in the kitchen but descended on them in the mudroom in a flurry of bouncing hair and flapping arms.

"Oh! Adam." She slammed to a halt. "I didn't hear you come in." Her gaze traveled from his face to the point where he still held on to Caden, and it narrowed with concern.

Caden hurried to alleviate her concerns. "He's not going to run the article."

Marie frowned, her finger going back and forth between them. "You didn't say good-bye to her."

He frowned too. "I know. Stupid of me." Suddenly his eyes were only for Caden, and they set her simmering with hope and promise. "But if she'll give me another chance, I won't make the same mistake ever again."

There was no need for a second thought. She squeezed his hand with all the love she hoped he could read in her eyes.

Marie relaxed a fraction. "If Caden's happy . . ."

She nodded.

"I think you'll both be happy when I tell you that I think I can help you book at least a few rooms for a good chunk of next summer," Adam said.

Marie perked up.

"I went to talk to my brother —"

"But you haven't seen him in eight years,"

Caden said.

He nodded. "And it was about eight years too long. Turns out he's missed me too. We had a good talk and put the past behind us."

"You did?" Her heart swelled. There was too much joy with no place to go. It overflowed and kept pouring as she pictured Adam and his brother making up for lost time and beginning again. Fresh.

"He's getting married, and his fiancée is from the island. From North Rustico, actually."

"No one's from here except the people who live here."

"Natalie O'Ryan?"

Caden laughed. "Natalie and I went to school together. I haven't heard from her in years."

"Well, she and Russell are going to call you next week. They want to have their wedding on the island and stay here."

Marie's mouth hung open. "At the Red Door?"

"Yep." Adam's features turned boyish with delight. "Natalie and Russell will be here for several weeks. And they'll bring a bunch of guests from Nashville with them. You'll be bursting at the seams."

"I — I don't know what to say." Marie's

face glowed, and she pressed her hands to her cheeks. "Thank you."

"I'm glad I could help. This inn means a lot to me too, you know."

Caden looked up at him. "It does?"

"I fell in love here."

The bottom dropped out of her stomach, and her legs turned to pudding. He was in love. With her.

Like she was in love with him.

She nearly slid to the ground, but Adam was right there, his arm wrapping around her waist, keeping her upright.

Marie took a slow step back, her hand to her mouth. "On that note, I'll leave you to —"

"Wait. What did you say about Danielle?"

"Oh, I almost forgot." Her glow amped up to full wattage. "She was the reporter for *Rest & Retreats.*"

"No." Caden cringed. She'd been here when Marie and Seth were gone. What if Caden had done something wrong or gotten distracted by Adam? That had been known to happen once or twice.

"She loved it. She loved every minute of it! They're going to feature the inn in their spring issue. Maybe even on the cover."

News like this couldn't be celebrated from a distance, so Caden dropped Adam's hand

and squeezed Marie tight. "I'm so glad. No matter what your dad does, the inn is going to survive. Because of you."

"And you."

The recognition warmed her chest and almost brought up another bout of tears. "Thank you."

Marie let her go and took another two steps back. "Now I'm going to let you two . . . get back to whatever you were doing. And I'll keep Seth busy for a bit, so you shouldn't be interrupted." She disappeared in a snap, and Caden had never been so grateful to be assured of privacy.

Adam slipped behind her, wrapping his arm around her middle and nuzzling her neck. He took a deep breath, and she could feel his smile.

Until the door to the dining room swung open, and Levi poked his head into the kitchen. "I thought I heard something going on in here."

Esther followed her husband in, but stopped as soon as she spied the younger couple. Caden tried to step away from Adam, but he kept his arm firmly in place, holding her against his chest. It wasn't worth it to fight him. Not when she wanted to be near him too.

"Welcome back to the island, Adam," Levi

said. "How was your trip?"

Esther grabbed her husband's hand and tugged. "Come on. Can't you see they're in the middle of something?"

Caden's cheeks burned, but her smile couldn't be contained. It was nice to be in the middle of something with someone special.

Adam, always so much more collected, just grinned at his friend. "Good trip, but I'm glad to be back. I've missed PEI."

Caden craned her neck to see his face. "But you were only gone for a few days." As soon as the words popped out, she realized how they sounded. "I mean, I'm glad you're back too."

They all shared a laugh, and even Caden managed a self-deprecating chuckle before Adam replied, "I wasn't gone more than a minute before I knew I'd left something special behind." He squeezed her middle, sending a thousand butterflies to flight.

Levi nodded, a sage look in his eyes. "I thought you might be back. Think maybe you'd have time to look at my book? Just finished it."

With a swat to his arm, Esther glared at Levi. "I think he'll be busy." Her knowing gaze shifted between Adam and Caden.

Adam laughed again, and Caden leaned

into the low rumble. She didn't mind being teased, so long as Adam was at her side.

"I'd be honored," he said. "I have an opening in my schedule and some time at the beach on my calendar."

Levi grinned, hiding his age and experience beneath shining eyes. Reaching for Adam's hand, he nodded. "I'd appreciate it. I'll be in touch soon."

"We're leaving tomorrow." Esther sighed, a true sadness washing across her features. "There's something special about the island and this inn. We're going to miss it."

"And you'll be missed." Caden reached for the older woman, pulling her into a gentle hug. "Please come back to see us soon."

"Oh, you can count on that." Esther waved as she led her husband back into the dining room, leaving Caden once again alone with the man who set her heart racing.

"Did you mean what you said earlier? About spending more time on the beach — on the island?" She reached for his hands and held them tight.

"I've been thinking about moving to the island. Think you might want me around?"

She froze.

He must have felt the tension, and he

pulled her slowly toward him until only her arms were between them, her fists under her chin.

His eyebrows formed a concerned V. "Do you not want me around?"

"No. I mean, I do." It was barely a breath, the most she could manage when she could feel his heart thudding. He smelled like island air, like he belonged here. "It's just . . . I just agreed to take a job during the school year in Toronto."

His frown deepened, and she rushed to explain about Jerome's offer, the new program, and her summers at the inn. With every detail, his features eased until a lopsided grin fell into place.

"Toronto, huh? Toronto might be easier for me."

"Easier?"

"Bigger airport. I'll be traveling some for my new job."

As it tended to do when he was in the vicinity, her head spun. "What new job?"

His eyebrows leapt. "I'm a travel writer."

"No." She laughed until she couldn't hold her head up any longer, resting it against his shaking shoulder.

"What? Don't you think I'm suited for it?"

She slipped her arms around his waist. "I think you'll be wonderful. I think you are wonderful." But a nagging thought kept her from real and total bliss. "What about Connor and the church?"

A twinge of sadness flashed in his eyes, and it hurt her heart too. "People wanted to help St. Cassian's keep their doors open. They only needed to hear the story. Turns out I'm a pretty decent writer."

She shook her head, not understanding. He'd said he hadn't turned in the article.

"I helped them share the story on social media and create a crowdfunding page. At last count they were about six hundred dollars from paying off their mortgage. All of it."

"Oh, Adam. I'm so . . ." There weren't words, so she did the next best thing. On her tiptoes, she pulled his face down and looked him squarely in the eyes. "I'm going to kiss you now if that's okay?"

Apparently it was more than okay, as he didn't wait for her. Instead, he closed the distance between them, sweeping her off her feet and sending her heart into overdrive.

"I'm so in love with you," he whispered against her mouth.

"Me too."

"So, you think I can stay here tonight?"

She gave her best, her happiest, snort. "If we don't have a room, I'm sure we could roll out Taco Bed. If you think your back can handle it."

He laughed, and it was sweeter than any cinnamon roll in the world. When he cupped her cheeks with both hands, her stomach took off in flight, swooping on wings of joy and hope and courage.

"I'd gladly risk life and limb. Anything to be with you."

ACKNOWLEDGMENTS

Some books need a little help finding their way into the world. Some need a lot of help. The people mentioned below know which is true about this book. My enduring thanks to:

Michelle Lim and Kaye Dacus, whose incredible brainstorming and creativity astound me. They spent many hours helping me discover these characters and their story.

Trevor and Judy Pye, PEI innkeepers extraordinaire at the Shipwright Inn, who shared their love of the island — and afternoon desserts on the buffet — with my family and me on several visits.

My Canadian friends, especially Jennifer Major and Rachel McMillan, who answered numerous questions about growing up in the Canadian Maritimes. Any mistakes are entirely my own.

Katie Schroder, who regularly checked on me, cooked for me, and came up with the idea for Caden's entry for the lobster cook-off.

Michelle Ule and Amy Haddock, who read this book in its infancy and offered incredibly thoughtful suggestions.

Vicki Crumpton, Jessica English, Michele Misiak, Karen Steele, and the whole Revell team, who never cease to amaze me with their creativity, dedication, and overall brilliance.

Rachel Kent, agent, cheerleader, and friend, who kept me going during the most rigorous writing schedule of my life. I'm forever grateful for her encouragement.

Chris Essig, who has cheered me on my whole life, especially in my writing. I aspire to be half as good an aunt as she is.

Mom, Hannah, and Julia, who ventured back to the island with me while I was in the midst of writing this book. We made memories I'll never forget.

The rest of the Johnson/Whitson clan, who let me talk about fictional characters as though they're real and love me anyway. Being part of this family is my favorite.

And, of course, my heavenly Father, the

regret remover and grace giver, who created Prince Edward Island, my favorite place in the world, and invites me to create new stories with him every day. I'm so grateful for this adventure.

ABOUT THE AUTHOR

Liz Johnson fell in love with Prince Edward Island the first time she set foot on it. When she's not plotting her next trip to the island, she works as a full-time marketing manager. She finds time to write late at night and is the author of ten novels, a *New York Times* bestselling novella, and a handful of short stories. She makes her home in Nashville, Tennessee, where she enjoys listening to local music, exploring the area's history, and making frequent trips to Arizona to dote on her five nieces and nephews. She does not like lobster.